HANGMAN BLIND

November, 1382. The month of the dead. In the fifth year of King Richard's reign, a nun rides out for York and the Abbey of Meaux. As Hildegard travels alone through the densely wooded countryside, with only her two hounds for protection, she encounters a gibbet with five bloodied corpses, and in the next clearing the body of a young man, brutally butchered. The murder will touch Hildegard even more closely as she reaches her childhood home, for Castle Hutton is riven by treachery. She will need all her skills and bravery to counter the dark forces that are at work...

HANGMAN BLIND

HANGMAN BLIND

by

Cassandra Clark

Magna Large Print Books
Long Preston, North Yorkshire,
BD23 4ND, England.

British Library Cataloguing in Publication Data.

Clark, Cassandra
    Hangman blind.

    A catalogue record of this book is
    available from the British Library

    ISBN   978-0-7505-3087-3

ı\ı6

First published in Great Britain in 2008 by John Murray (Publishers)
An Hachette Livre UK company

Published in Large Print 2009 by arrangement with
John Murray (Publishers)

Magna Large Print is an imprint of Library Magna Books Ltd.

Printed and bound in Great Britain by
T.J. (International) Ltd., Cornwall, PL28 8RW

To my daughters

ENGLAND AND WALES IN 1382

Scotland

NORTH-UMBERLAND

CUMBERLAND

PALATINATE OF DURHAM

WEST-MORLAND

YORKSHIRE

York

PALATINE OF LANCASTER

LINCOLN

COUNTY PALATINE OF CHESTER

FLINT

DERBY

NOTTINGHAM

MERIONETH

STAFFORD

LEICESTER

ABBEY OF PETERBOROUGH

RUTLAND

NORFOLK

SEE OF ELY

SHROP-SHIRE

WARWICK

CAMBRIDGE

MARCHER EARLDOM

WORCESTER

NORTHAMPTON

HUNT-ING-DON

SUFFOLK

CARDIGAN

HEREFORD

BEDFORD

CARMARTHEN

GLOUCESTER

OXFORD

BUCKINGHAM

HERTFORD

ESSEX

BERKSHIRE

London

SURREY

SOMERSET

WILTSHIRE

HAMPSHIRE

KENT

SUSSEX

DEVON

DORSET

CORNWALL

ISLE OF WIGHT

N
W   E
S

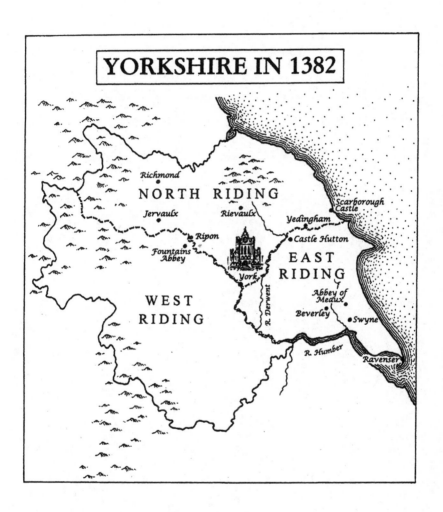

YORKSHIRE IN 1382

Richmond

NORTH RIDING

Jervaulx Rievaulx

Scarborough Castle

Yedingham

Ripon Castle Hutton

Fountains Abbey

EAST RIDING

York

Abbey of Meaux

R. Derwent

Beverley

WEST RIDING

Swyne

R. Humber

Ravenser

I

From the gates of the papal palace in Avignon issued a rider at a pace to make the sparks fly. With a leather bag strapped across his chest under the billowing folds of a cloak, he rode furiously northwards. Unencumbered by page or squire, he reached the court of the Duke of Burgundy in his castle at Dijon in less than a fortnight. When he arrived, the duke, uncle of the young king and controller of France, was preparing for war. Several meetings in the privacy of the ducal chambers took place before the rider set out again. This time he travelled in the company of the duke's own army, augmented by those of Berry and Bourbon and all the foremost lords of France with their seigneurs and squires. So great was the cavalcade that woodcutters had to be sent on ahead to fell trees in order to widen the line of march. Impervious to the sullen populace, who kept their shutters closed and refused supplies, the messenger accompanied the army as far as the River Lys at the border with Flanders. There, in the guise of a Flemish merchant, he left them en route to their bloody victory at Roosebeeke, and, taking a detour around the battle-front, made for the port of Damme.

Prologue

The novice slipped ahead like a shadow in the darkness, melting away only when Hildegard reached the great studded door and pushed it open. There she found the prioress in her private chapel, kneeling before a simple whitewashed altar lit by one tall tallow.

She turned at the sound of Hildegard's robes trailing the floor and rose to her feet. Voice low, she said, 'Thank you for coming so promptly, sister.' Her instructions were clear. 'Go to York at once. The time has come. God knows, we have waited long enough. Give this to His Grace.' She reached inside one of her sleeves and pulled out a parchment. Hildegard shivered as she glimpsed the papal seal by the light of the candle before thrusting the document into the secret folds of her own sleeve. She bowed her head. So she was right: it was horsemen she had heard riding on to the garth as night fell.

She listened carefully to the rest of her instructions which were detailed and succinct until the prioress said, 'And after York go to the abbey at Meaux but do not tell Hubert de Courcy you come from the archbishop.'

'To Meaux, mother?' She was startled.

She saw a brief light cross the old woman's powerful features. 'Yes, my dear. There you will have time to further your own personal wishes if you choose.'

'You mean–?'

'You may ask the abbot for permission to travel forth in search of a suitable grange for yourself and your chosen sisters. Tell him about your vision. He'll be persuaded by that. Before I die,' she went on, 'I want to see a daughter house issue from our conjunction with Meaux.' She chuckled softly in the shadows. 'With a priory to the south and one to the north this new abbot foisted on us by Avignon will be checked in a most satisfying manner.'

The prioress put out a hand and Hildegard felt the papery skin brush her own. 'Keep your eyes open, sister. I want to know what this new abbot is plotting. We know who sent him. Now we need to know why. Remember where the truth lies and who is best able to protect it. All blessings with you.' She added with a compassionate glance, 'We live in violent times. Go well armed.'

So it was, shortly before dawn, that Hildegard, dressed in the white habit of her order, with a cloak of burnet thrown over it, rode out from the safety of the priory at Swyne armed with a stave and two trained hounds, to set her horse towards York and the palace of the archbishop.

Chapter One

November. The month of the dead. The dry death of field and thicket had given way to unending rains. Close to the Feast of St Martin in the fifth year of King Richard's reign, the ditches were overflowing, the rivers in spate, the fields like vast lakes under a sullen sky.

Hildegard rode in darkness through lanes she knew well, picking her way across the marshes of Holderness, skirting gurgling dykes and the overflowing channels that divided the field strips until eventually she reached the quag that passed for the road to York and the limits of familiarity. Dawn came and a pale light drizzled over the landscape. Travellers hoping to enter the city as soon as the gates were opened were more frequent now and she joined the sombre flow.

It was mid-morning when she rode under the Monk Gate and encountered the tumult of the town, late afternoon by the time she left her horse and two hounds with the ostler and hired a boat, and it was evening, prematurely dark in the foul weather, by the time she shipped the dripping oars and lay unnoticed under some overhanging willows a little way upstream from the archbishop's palace. With the document from Rome hidden in the folds of her robe it was common sense to seek admittance via the watergate only under cover of darkness.

Night fell, with its swirling fogs and noxious airs. As soon as it was safe Hildegard entered secretly by the watergate and was admitted without delay into the presence of the archbishop. In his splendid robes he received her cordially, though with few words. When he held out his hand for the parchment, its seal dangling, she tried to gauge his allegiance by the glance he bestowed but he gave nothing away. Trembling a little at her own part in these weighty affairs, she was relieved to be shown to a guest chamber high up in the honeycomb of gilded luxury in which the prelate lived. A restless night on a pallet of soft wool followed. It was too unusual in its cloying ease to afford much sleep and next morning she was brought, pale and exhausted, to the second part of her errand.

It was shortly after prime and still dark by the time she slipped out through the watergate and sculled back downstream. The shock of the town when she returned to pick up her horse and hounds was overwhelming. Bellowing traders were advertising their wares from every corner of the marketplace, artisans displayed their stock in dozens of shops ranged cheek by jowl along the crowded streets, and the whole warren of the town was filled with musicians and conjurors, merchants and mountebanks, pardoners and herbalists, saddlers and friars mendicant, cloth merchants, wine and water carriers, sellers of meat, of bread, of cheese, and servants and pedlars of every conceivable kind. A hundred faces or more were grabbed by the light of flaring cressets then let slip back into the darkness. Animals added their own clamour, hens clucking, horses hobbled for purchase, beef bellowing on the hoof, goats, ducks, dogs and a dancing bear rattling its chain. And suddenly, as dawn broke, the rain began to fall. It sent awnings rattling over stalls and shopfronts as everyone rushed to avoid a drenching.

Such a mingling of sight and sound was almost too much to take in after seven years in a hermitage. Everybody, Hildegard realised, was here to buy and sell, including the girls hanging round the lighted ale-house in their low-cut gowns.

As she began to push her way through the crowd towards the stables she heard the beating of a kettledrum start up on the other side of the marketplace. The drummer banged out the brisk rhythm of a marching band but instead of the expected accompaniment of pipes and horns a cacophony of crashes and rattles took up the beat. It was a parody of music, rapid and violent, and as the players approached through the rain in the glimmering dawn Hildegard craned her neck like everyone else to see who they were.

Between the heads she saw four or five musicians carving an avenue through the crowd. They were beating pots and pans, the spasmodic jerks of their clubs accompanied by smiles of glee at the racket they were making. The bailiff and his men paraded straightfaced beside them with their staves at the ready. As the crowd opened to let them through she saw that the vanguard of this noisy procession was taken up by three young girls tied together round the waists by a length of stout rope. On their heads they wore striped bonnets, enough to announce their profession even if their ragged attempts at sexual allure had not done so. Some of the onlookers applauded as the girls passed by and shouted in support, others yelled insults and one stallholder, face contorted in disgust, hurled a small yellowing cabbage. It hit one of the girls in the middle of the back and she flashed round at once.

'Oh, it's you, is it, lover? See you at your usual time tonight, shall I?' The crowd near by roared with laughter and the stallholder, red faced, gave a snarl and turned away.

An old ale-woman had come out from a nearby inn to see what had brought her customers into the street. She stood with folded, beefy arms, and Hildegard heard her suck in her breath. 'Just listen to that!' she said to anyone who cared to pay heed. 'He'll be getting a walloping from his wife next and serve him right.'

'They're such very young girls,' Hildegard commented. 'But I suppose if men pay girls will play.'

The ale-wife turned to her. 'That mouthy one's seventeen. Been plying her trade some two years now. It's the little one I feel sorry for.'

The procession had drawn level and Hildegard could see the third girl dragging a little behind the two more brazen ones in front. She looked no more than thirteen. With a terrified expression she walked with her head down, allowing the two older ones to pull her along by the rope. 'You feel sorry for her because of her youth, I suppose?' asked Hildegard.

'And because of how she got into this predicament in the first place,' answered the ale-wife.

'And how was that?'

24

'Brought here from foreign parts by her so-called uncle. Big brute of a fellow. Set her to work straight away so he could sit on his backside and count her earnings.'

'Can't she get away from him?'

'He'd track her down. She's his little gold mine. He'd not let her get far.' The ale-wife shook her head in despair. 'Makes you think, though. She can't be any older than young King Richard. Not a day more than fifteen. But a very different destiny allotted by God Almighty in his wisdom.'

'I doubt whether even King Richard is content at present.'

'Aye, stuck with his uncles and their cunning. He's as bound by riches as that poor lass by poverty, and that's the truth. Those unless of his certainly see themselves fitted to rule more than a mere lad. Lucky for him he got the London mob on his side with his recklessness at Smithfield, don't you think?'

'I suspect it's made the council of dukes even more certain he's not the fabric a king should be patched from,' Hildegard replied somewhat guardedly.

'Ah, there's the stench of conspiracy everywhere you look.' The ale-wife cast a gloomy eye over the busy marketplace. 'We live in sad times. Where will it end?' She turned to attend to her customers, swarming back now the procession had moved off, and Hildegard, too, turned to go. It was true what the ale-wife said about the king. Although Richard had been perched on the throne of England for five years, ever since the death of his grandfather Edward III, his uncles, the royal guardians, were roused to a conspiracy of ambition, especially now, after the way he had supported Wat Tyler and his followers during their confrontation at Smithfield. The boy's sympathies had not endeared him either to his uncles, the dukes, or to the barons, who saw their vast estates threatened by the mob. The burgesses, too, were sent into a panic of fear at the prospect of losing their grasp on the monopoly of trade in the towns with further civil unrest. King Richard's apparent change of heart when he revoked his promises to Tyler and his followers, was said by some to have been forced on him by John of Gaunt under threat of losing his crown. Others saw it as an instance the boy-king's duplicity.

Making her way between the stalls towards the stables where her horse and hounds were waiting, Hildegard was frowning. It was not only the State which was in turmoil. The Church was fractured by dissent as well. Wyclif was stirring justifiable debate but had been silenced by the council at Blackfriars the previous year. Authority everywhere was being challenged. The rival popes, Urban in Rome and Clement in Avignon, had divided Europe and managed to bring the English and the French into opposition yet again. As the ale-wife said, these were sad times and there was no knowing where it would end.

The sound of the procession had almost faded and after a brief lull the marketeers started shouting their wares with renewed vigour. By now the girls would be approaching the stocks on the far side where they would endure further humiliations. Hildegard sighed. There was little justice to be had when the purchasers of such girls ran free and as often as not wore the chains of law and order on their chests.

Disturbed and saddened, her thoughts in disarray as she wondered what, if anything, she could do, she took charge of her palfrey, checked that the two dogs had been fed, then paid off the ostler and headed out towards the town gate.

Despite the dangers of travelling alone Hildegard felt only eagerness as she left the clamour and conflicts of York behind and rode out towards open country. She was prepared as well as she could be to face the bands of masterless men who roamed the forests nowadays. The many mercenaries on the loose since the apparent end to the French wars had developed an acquired taste for robbery with violence. They attacked whomsoever they pleased. She set her mouth in a firm line. The small cross she wore, hand carved out of hazelwood, was little protection in such dark days, but her stave was as thick as a bowman's wrist and her hunting knife had a long blade, recently honed. For extra assurance, she was accompanied by two hounds, a lymer for attack and a little kennet for the sharpness of its claws.

Two alert guardian spirits, they ran through the waving grasses beside the track within a whistle call.

The lymer went ahead. Answering to the dignified name of Duchess, she was a long-legged, rakish beast, with a heavy jowled head, floppy ears and an intelligent, melancholy expression. By contrast the kennet, Bermonda, was like a domestic table dog, shaggy, brindled and apparently docile. On closer scrutiny you could see a mouth full of sharp, close-set teeth and a complement of villainous-looking claws to match. Like Duchess, she had a good nose and could follow a track through anything, woodland or thick cover, and could mark a scent from any branch the quarry had brushed past, and, in fact, seemed able to pluck a scent from the very air itself.

The little animal would express her excitement as soon she found a scent to let everybody know. The lymer was different. Her purpose was to locate the secret hiding place of the quarry so that the huntsmen could bring up the hounds to flush it out, so she was trained to hunt in silence. Neither Duchess nor Bermonda would ever give up. Fear was something they might instil but was something they never seemed to feel. Although confident they would protect her, Hildegard decided to keep to the woods and avoid the highway.

She left the city under Walmgate Bar and took the road that led east over the Fosse river beside arable strips of manor land. After this the way to Meaux wended through the great forest of Galtres with its league upon league of oak and beech and then rose little by little to the chalk uplands of the wolds. The road was narrower there though still a well-worn track, and it would eventually lead to the distant town of Beverley with its great lantern tower lifted like a beacon over the flat fields. After that it was only a few leagues further to Meaux.

She soon left the white walls behind and rode

alongside strips of winter crops. The hayward's horn could be heard rousing the peasants to work, men, women and children pouring from their hovels at its command. Cursing the rain, the saints and the reeve himself, they stumbled along the lane, half blind with fatigue and hunger. She saw women walking barefoot through the mud, with sleeping children on their backs. A ragged man, bent double with some deformity, crept by on a stick. Another figure with head and shoulders covered by a sack against the rain muttered incoherently to an unseen persecutor and picked a stumbling path around the puddles.

After weeks of endless rains the field strips had been turned to mud. They were now nothing but stagnant corrugations, stretching into the grey distance, impossible to drive the oxen through. Even the strips on the higher ground were waterlogged; the heavy clay stuck to everything it touched. A girl, clearly pregnant, emerged from one of the hovels that clustered along the side of the road. She was carrying a mattock. Working such land must be a back-breaking task, Hildegard thought with compassion as she rode by. From behind the curtain of rain came the keening of a dog to give voice to the general wretchedness.

A better time will come, she thought. It must. It was imminent. Surely the signs were beginning to appear?

She left the fields and entered the wasteland. Here the sky seemed vast. Black clouds raced across it from the east, big bellied with more rain. Tucking the flapping edges of her cloak tightly into her belt she rode on, deeper still into the wilderness. She began to consider the task that lay ahead.

After the death of her husband in France was finally confirmed, Hildegard had emerged from seclusion in her hermitage at the Derwent Crossing determined to get on with life. She still longed for Hugh and had found no respite from her grief in prayer and meditation. There seemed little point in anything without him, but she knew she had to find a purpose. There was no excuse now. When the lawyers had finished picking through his estate, she had received a handsome fortune in rents and gold. It made her seek some use for such unexpected wealth. Then she had discovered what quickly became her life's purpose: she would set up her own house of nuns where she could teach the young and tend the sick. It seemed the best she could do in the confusion of the times when the poor were being ground underfoot by one faction after another. Her prioress had given her stout support. There was only one obstacle to her desire: the Abbot of Meaux.

In the short period of his abbacy Hubert de Courcy had established a reputation for austerity in keeping with the ideals of his order's founder. Discipline had been restored, harshness towards the novices became ingrained. Those who didn't like it left. The nuns at Swyne had soon discovered he was a man skilled in jurisprudence. He had several times represented the interests of his monks at the court of the King's Bench in London to the priory's detriment, had set up claims and counterclaims over land disputes all over the county. It was rumoured he was hoping to submit a plea to the French pope in Avignon as soon as he was summoned.

It was also true that he had revitalised the abbey's fortunes to something like their former health after the pestilence had carried away half the conversi and most of the monks a generation ago. And it seemed he could draw bequests to his order by the glitter of his silver tongue as easily as bees are drawn to the flower.

Even Hildegard's prioress had been moved to narrow her eyes and in acid tones let fall the observation that *fiscal restraint* was a phrase much heard at Meaux these days. 'It seems,' she said, 'this new abbot they've pushed in over the head of the old one – Hubert de Courcy as he's pleased to call himself – is something of a tough nut. But we shall see, no doubt of that.'

Pondering on the best way to approach him, Hildegard entered the dank and dripping woods.

She hadn't gone far when her thoughts were diverted.

From far off came a sound that started as a distant shrill of birds but gradually it began to fill the woods with a raucous screeching. A flock of crows, she guessed. She wondered what had disturbed them. Looking to left and right, she soon saw a living cloud rising and falling above the trees to one side. Turning the head of her palfrey, she deviated from the path and rode on into the thicket until the source of the disturbance came into sight.

Five bodies hung from a gibbet set among the trees. Little was left to show that the bloodied shapes hanging there had once been human beings. The crows had picked and fought so thoroughly to finish the job started by men that their entrails spilled to the ground like ribbons the crows clinging to them as they bit and fought to get the biggest share. Their beaks ripped without remorse at the hunks of flesh they had dragged into the grass while their companions at the feast gnawed at eye sockets and sucked them clean of jelly. Others cracked through the tender bones of fingers or gorged with bloodied beaks on the yielding parts of breast and groin.

Hildegard wanted to avert her eyes but was transfixed by the sight. Her skin broke out in a sweat of horror. The men would have been alive when their guts slithered out after the thrust of the butcher's knife. They would have been alive when they were swung into the air by their necks. But they would know nothing now of their life blood, leaking into the puddles on the scuffed earth beneath the gibbet where they must have struggled against their executioners.

Still unable to look away, she slid down off her horse out of respect and offered up a prayer. Her heart was thumping and her throat felt dry. There was nothing to be done for the victims now but pray. As she stepped forward she stumbled between two crows fighting over a piece of flesh. Their oiled wings lashed like weapons as they hooked their beaks over the same strip of human meat, until a blow from her stave broke up the fight. The reprieve lasted only moments, however. As soon as she remounted and began to push on through the undergrowth they started up again, as ferocious as before. She urged her horse onward, anxious to get away as quickly as possible from a scene of such bloody butchery.

But the horror was not yet ended. Riding on between the hawthorns that parted as her horse thrust forward, she emerged into a sudden clearing. It was like a secret room in the forest. Before she could get her bearings and return to the track she caught sight of something bright in the trampled grass. Her nostrils quivered with the stench of fox. Duchess came to attention by her side but remained silent. Bermonda whined.

A vixen, stunned by her abrupt appearance, quickly regained its senses and skidded back into the undergrowth. It too had been feasting and again the prey was human. On the ground was a man. That he was dead was obvious. His throat had been ripped out.

As she slid from her horse for a second time the clouds opened and the rain began to fall harder than ever. Suddenly the woods were bristling with the sound of falling water. Dragging her hood over her head, she waded through the wet grass.

He was young, she saw, no more than twenty, a squire for some local lord maybe, wearing no blazon nor any other sign to show to whom he belonged. He might be an apprentice from the town, she thought, seeing his leather jerkin and roughly woven shirt. He wore no spurs, nor did he carry arms, and he bore many wounds besides those of the fox, which must have discovered him only moments ago. Many attackers armed with steel, she realised, in order to overcome just one young man.

Looking off to the edge of the clearing she found it impossible to make out which way the gang had ridden off. The glade was deep in mud, the grasses ground up in the turmoil of the attack. Now the pelting rain was filling the deep grooves left by the horses' hooves. A rank smell of decomposing earth was released by the downpour.

Some masterless men must have done this, and only a short time ago, she surmised with a shudder. She had heard nothing above the raucous shrieking of the carrion, nor seen anything. A lone rider, she imagined, maybe on an errand for his master, the brigands seizing their chance? Or was it something to do with the hanged men at the town gibbet?

She knelt down and rested a hand on the youth's forehead. Already cold. And fair of face despite the bright neckerchief of blood at his throat. He was a youth with the ruddy cheeks of one used to the outdoors. No clerk, then, no journeyman working at his bench through all the hours of daylight. A wide mouth with full lips given to laughter. Blood bubbling and just beginning to clot at the corners of his mouth. The robbers had stolen their victim's dagger from his belt, she observed, leaving the sheath empty.

The rain was rattling through the branches, setting up a roar in more distant parts of the woods like an army on the march. It reduced everything, even the lifeless body at her feet. She gave him a closer look before she left. There seemed nothing else to note. A prayer for his departed soul fell from her lips. Her eyes glistened. About to ride on to seek help in getting him taken to burial, she hesitated.

There was something she had nearly missed. It was held tightly in his right hand. Tentatively she reached down. His body was not yet fixed in the rigour of death and she was able to prise his fingers apart one by one. Giving up what had been grasped so fiercely at the moment of death, his fingers softly opened.

He had been gripping a glass phial of some sort, no more than four inches high, with a wooden stopper sealed with red wax. The light was too bad to enable her to see what was inside the little bottle so she put it into the leather scrip on her belt together with her cures. It might be a clue to the young man's identity, or to his destination, or even to the thwarted purpose of his journey through the woods.

There was not much more she could do for him now. She dragged his body into the bushes and found a way of hiding it under some fallen branches to save him from the immediate notice of crows, then she stationed her lymer as a guard against ravening foxes until she could procure help from the monks. The abbey could be no more than two leagues away. With everything ordered as best she could, she took to the trail at once.

Shivering with cold, soaked to the skin, and with a heart filled with the horror of what she had seen, she was eventually conveyed over the wooden bridge that spanned the canal and rode on under the limestone archway into the sombre gatehouse of Meaux.

There was an air of excitement within the abbey.

35

Townsfolk, a good many of them women, were flocking around the open doors of the chapel. They held scarves over their heads and the rain seemed to make them skittish. Their frivolity struck a jarring note. Hildegard's thoughts were with the dead youth lying in the grass. From inside the chapel she could hear the sound of an organ growling out a flourish of arpeggios. A bell tolled briskly from the tower as if to hurry the already hurrying congregation. Catching a passing novice by the sleeve, Hildegard asked what was going on.

'The talking crucifix has been unveiled and the abbot is about to give a sermon. It's not to be missed!' He was full of enthusiasm. 'Who knows, sister, we may be in luck and the crucifix will speak today! You're fortunate to have arrived in the nick of time!'

Hildegard repressed any observation to the contrary. She watched the young man hurry away after pointing her in the direction of the office of the lay brothers, the conversi. By the time she had fulfilled her obligations to the murdered youth the sermon, together with any conversation involving crucifixes, would be over. But first she had to find the master of the conversi who ran the practical affairs of the abbey, and inform him about the body. Then she would have to guide his posse of men to the spot in the woods where she had hidden it, then, finally, in sorrow, bring it back to sanctuary.

She set about pushing a way through the crowd towards his office.

There were logs heaped on the fire, tapestries on the walls, and an obedient clerk in the corner taking notes. The heady scent of incense brought expensively from the east filled the air with a sense of luxury, as if to underline the fact that Abbot Hubert de Courcy had no need to make concessions to anyone. He had all the wealth and power of Avignon behind him.

Hildegard observed him without expression. In his late thirties, around her own age, in fact, and equally tall and vigorous in his manner, he was, of course, tonsured. No doubt if he had been a mere lay brother his hair would have been worn long, but it was clipped and dark and in its beauty matched his features. These were chiselled, even vulpine, helped by a Norman nose, cutting cheek-bones and a sensual curl to the upper lip that women seemed to find irresistible, judging by the congregation earlier. None of this did him any good now. Hildegard merely watched him with a glance as cool as the rain that fell in the garth. *I will not give in.*

He was a subtle and disputatious thinker, endlessly finding objections to her request.

In fact, after informing him of the body in the woods and hearing him tell his clerk to send someone to fetch the coroner from York, they had been politely fencing since tierce. He seemed to find her request regarding the small priory she wished to establish quite unfeasible.

He simply refused to yield.

Now she fingered the small wooden cross she wore and reordered her thoughts. She was still shaken by her journey here. First the hanged

37

men, the flock of carrion, then the youth and the fox. Nature itself seemed to be turning against man. The Church tried to explain it by saying it was because the Antichrist was approaching. Whatever the case, the murdered youth had been brought back to the abbey in the implacable rain and placed in a side chapel until the coroner arrived. Since then she had been forced to sit here countering endless objections from Hubert de Courcy. She was tired. She had scarcely had time to wash and change. There was mud in her nails and on her boots. The latter besmirched the abbot's polished tiles, as she was sure he had already noticed.

As she listened to him picking through his objections yet again she began to realise he must have misunderstood, for he was saying, 'This is a man's world, Sister. Alas for you, we don't have nuns throwing their weight around within the abbey precincts. *Absit invidia.*' He bowed his head a fraction, as if to take the sting out of his words. 'You can hardly expect me to flout the directives of St Bernard at your behest.'

'I thought you did what you liked, my lord abbot, within the Rule?'

'With two popes I suppose we could have a freer rein.' He paused as if struck by the novelty of the idea before mentally placing a colon and adding: 'Nevertheless, my dear sister, I administer the rules. If you want to be an abbess you'll have to go elsewhere.'

Hildegard frowned. Surely he didn't imagine she wanted to set up here? 'I don't seek to rival anyone, my lord. I simply want to establish my own small house in accordance with my vision.'

Hubert arched his fine, black brows.

'But I need your permission if I'm to fulfil its command. Meaux is our mother house,' she reminded him. 'I need your permission if I'm to go out and look at suitable property, and if you object only on grounds of proximity, that to have half a dozen nuns on the other side of the canal would be unsettling to you and your brothers, maybe we could discuss the matter of location instead?' She ignored the iciness of his glance. 'I have one or two granges in mind, my lord, ones at a distance to satisfy your need for solitude. And ours too,' she added. His brows rose again. 'I feel sure that when you see how hard working and sensible we are you won't regret giving us your support.'

His brow, she noticed, furrowed even more as it began to dawn on him she wasn't going to give in. His first objection on the grounds of danger had been countered. It was, she had agreed, dangerous for anyone, especially a woman, to travel the roads at these unsettled times. But she was prepared and able to defend herself. He had raised his eyebrows at that too. His next objection concerned the proximity of the new house. But she had made it absolutely clear she was as unwilling to set up on his doorstep as he was to have her do so. Now, she thought, any further objections would show he was simply being obstinate. If he persisted, it would soon become known, the prioress would make sure of that.

'The point is, my lord,' she felt constrained to go on, 'I don't intend to lay myself or my sisters open to harassment from Scots mercenaries, like those poor nuns up at Rosedale Abbey, not only having to herd sheep and live on berries, poor things, but at risk from any marauders that happen along. My suggestion is: allow me a tour of houses in the Riding, then I can assess which one will be safest for me and my sisters and will benefit us all with a new regimen. I thought, perhaps, I could begin with that little nunnery out at Yedingham–'

'Yedingham?' He visibly relaxed. It was quite far away. She saw the thought flit across his face. But he was obdurate. 'Unfortunately it's Benedictine, as I'm sure you know – although a quite charming little place,' he added cautiously.

'Yes. We sisters at Swyne think so too. Luckily for us the lord who endowed it is favourably disposed towards Cistercians.'

His glance sharpened. To him that would mean Avignon, not Rome, Charles of France, not Richard, King of England. It would also raise the question of how she knew the preference of this generous magnate.

'As well,' she continued, as if unaware of all this, 'it's on the north bank of the Derwent–'

'Ah,' he said. 'The Derwent.'

Regardless, she went on, '–and as the incumbents are getting on in years I gather they would welcome somebody with energy to run things for them – they even had a corrodian organising the dairy for them a few years ago, I understand – and of course we could take over the wharf there and see that it's maintained in a manner you would appreciate.'

He looked startled. 'That means taking charge of the wine imports?'

'Why, yes, if you insist. And apparently there are many hives–'

'Thriving honey trade, true.' He frowned.

'And plenty of swine, sheep and milch cows.' She thought she'd better get it all out straight away.

'Much cows,' he repeated, his tone suddenly heavy with foreboding.

'Oh, and all manner of interesting fish in the river as well as oysters and a good few orchards close at hand, so I believe, and–'

'And the passing trade to the coast for which you might offer your services as guides–?'

Was that sarcasm? She ignored it. 'And toll-keepers, yes. How clever of you to think of that!' She sat back. What would he say? There was a pause while she held her breath.

'And failing Yedingham?' he managed on a sigh, as he seemed to realise how well she had prepared her defence.

She leaned forward and gave him her warmest smile. 'If you really couldn't bear a group of capable nuns on the other side of the canal at Meaux – why, I suppose we could always look at Wilberfoss.'

His eyes flashed. 'The niece of the archbishop runs Wilberfoss.'

'Oh dear, so that's not possible. It will have to be some other place then. I'm sure we'll find somewhere.' Unable to resist a final thrust, she added, 'Of course, I hope your mind isn't entirely closed to the idea of a double house here at some

41

time in the future? Recall the success of the one at Watton, my lord abbot.'

'The Gilbertines are in there.' His tone was dismissive. But his expression was of a man finding himself inexplicably hog tied.

'Which demonstrates,' she continued smoothly, 'that we can all learn from each other. *Divisiones vero gratiarum sunt–*'

'There are diversities of gifts,' he agreed heavily, '*idem autem Spiritus* – but the same Spirit. Oh indeed, Sister, yes, how true.' Another deep sigh issued from his lips, as from a man setting out upon a rocky path instead of the easier one anticipated. 'And may I take this opportunity to tell you how delighted I am,' but no smile flitted across the marble features, 'that your husband, Sir Hugh, had the forethought,' he bowed his head and crossed himself, 'before his heroic demise in the wars with France, to make such ample provision for you. There can be nothing worse than being a woman lacking either a husband or a fortune. And now,' he bowed his head again, 'without the one, you have the other.'

'Yes,' Hildegard agreed. 'You can't imagine how restoring to the soul it is to have the power to endow a religious house and organise it exactly as one would wish.'

'No,' agreed the abbot, gloomily. His handsome features looked as if they would never break into a smile again. She rather pitied him, although not enough to forget they were still locked in battle.

'We religious,' she continued, still aware that he scarcely took her proposition seriously, 'are the bulwark against the rising tide of barbarity, allies

42

at the outposts of civilisation. Indeed, the grotesque forces of chaos are only held at bay by we monastics. We must all pull together, my lord abbot.'

'And with such a fair ally, Sister, who could be more certain of success?' He seemed to have come to a decision to concede a temporary defeat. It must be obvious she had run rings round him. Retrenchment was the sensible course. He would have realised she could be useful if he kept on her good side. Her priory, though small, ran a productive silk trade and somehow the prioress managed to attract regular bequests of land. It was a point he would be stupid to ignore when his abbey's need for grazing land was a pressing concern and they at Swyne had so much of it.

He spread his hands as if offering largesse. 'So there it is then.' It seemed as far as his pride would allow him to go.

'I have your permission, my lord?'

He gave a curt nod.

So he has a soft centre, she noted with delight, even if he is a sarcastic devil at heart.

His clerk had been assiduously copying down every single word they said. Now he was wiping his quill, well satisfied with himself. There would be many things I would change in the unlikely event I became abbess here, she thought as she prepared to take her leave. This clerk, for instance. He'd be better off working down at St Giles for a spell, with the lepers. That would teach him to be so sedulous in his note-taking. Hubert could not renege on having given his permission now it was written down in the abbey records.

There was a flurry for the quill and tablet again as the abbot, almost as an afterthought, said, 'Of course, sister, you could always talk to Lord Roger de Hutton. He's bound to have an empty property that would suit you.'

Hildegard levelled her glance. Lord Roger's lands were distant. Hubert de Courcy might just as well have told her to go hence to Uttermost Thule. But she kept this thought to herself and smiled instead. 'That's an excellent idea, my lord.' For a moment she toyed with her plain little cross until she noticed his glance, held as if hypnotised by the movement of her fingers. It made her wonder whether she had inadvertently led him to imagine unhasping it and letting it slither and... Not wanting to be damned for all eternity, she rose hurriedly to her feet.

'This has been most helpful, my lord abbot. I shall keep you informed of my progress.'

His morose smile followed her to the door, as if to say: I don't doubt it. What he in fact uttered was merely a reminder to attend the inquest when the coroner appeared.

The bell for vespers was already booming out across the garth, making the glass in the lancet rattle. The sound seemed to bring him back from a reverie and he became his customary brisk self. 'Before you leave, dear sister, will you join us at high table?'

Hildegard, thinking he would never ask, graciously accepted.

What the abbot said was true: Roger de Hutton had a finger in most pies, and if there was a suitable grange going begging he would probably own it. He owned almost everything that didn't belong to the monastery and, in the opinion of many, would be wise to allow a handful of devout and useful women to pray for his soul's ease.

Contrary to what the abbot might believe her heart was not entirely set on taking over Yedingham. It had been founded as a Benedictine nunnery but was so ill managed that Robert de Brus had been asked to take over. He was indifferent to the orders so long as they promised to offer prayers for him – politics were where his energy lay – and, with Lord Roger on her side, Hildegard was sure she could persuade him to let her take the lease to Yedingham. But it wasn't perfect. For one thing it was quite remote, at least two days on foot to York, the nearest large town. The advantage of Meaux, and the reason why, despite her words, she hadn't given up on the ambitious dream of having it turned into a double house, nuns on one side of the canal, monks on the other, was that it was only an hour's brisk walk from Beverley with its thriving market. By horse it was even less, of course. She thought it prudent to bear such facts in mind.

It was in a thoughtful mood that Hildegard prepared to set out the next morning. A messenger had arrived from York to tell them that the coroner was busy on important business and could not attend within four days at the earliest. The general opinion was that the feast in celebration of St Martin was the only important business that kept him in York, but she decided to take advantage of the delay, for now it gave her time to ride to Castle Hutton to seek Lord Roger's help.

As she had told Hubert de Courcy, she did not intend to bury herself and her sisters in some godforsaken wilderness where they had only each other for company. They'd go mad as well as being prey for brigands. *You can't be the Abbess of Meaux, sister. I'm the abbot*, he had said. Well, she didn't want to be at Meaux with him and his cronies breathing down her neck if that was his attitude. And Yedingham was good. Meaux was better. But there might be somewhere even better than both. She would take his advice then. She would consult Lord Roger.

Leaving Meaux shortly before dawn, she was pleased to find that the rain was holding off for the time being. She proceeded for the rest of the day through the forests of the high wolds in a haze of autumn gold. The air was sweet with the scents of the forest. Leaves lay in drifts underfoot, muffling the sound of hooves. Wrapped in her cloak, she travelled unworried, in the knowledge that there was little chance of coming across another gibbet in such a sparsely populated region. The few hamlets she came across were small, without even the benefit of stocks, and for the most part the only habitations were simple assarts, wooden shacks set in the midst of new clearings where the foresters and their families could live close to their work. If she had a fear it was of wolves. Packs of them scoured the wolds at this time of year. At least there is plenty of game, she observed, and I'll have to trust that their attentions won't turn to human flesh. The worst predators will be men, she decided. She sent the lymer on ahead to scout the trail for signs of outlaws. Then, close to nightfall, she took shelter in an abandoned barn, dined on rabbit brought down by the running dog, Bermonda, endured a fitful night's sleep wrapped in her cloak with the two hounds pressing close for warmth on either side, then set out again at first light.

Soon a familiar landscape came into view. It brought a tender gleam to her eyes. It had been seven years since she had set foot in the old place. It was another life, one she had lost for ever. She had no regrets, however. With her husband dead and her two children now old enough to make their own way in life, what better occupation could she have than the one she had chosen? But it would be heart-warming to revisit her old haunts once more.

The November mist that lay along the bottom of the dale began to thin as she travelled higher, and soon a fine rain began to penetrate her clothing and set beads of pearl in her horse's mane. With her hounds ranging wide through the undergrowth, she was on the point of emerging from the trees above the main track when she reined in with a sudden low whistle to bring Bermonda and Duchess to heel.

At the bottom of the dale a well-trodden path wound through a grove of oaks. Owing to the rain it was churned to a river of mud. It was empty now. But the drumming of hooves could be heard in the distance and soon a stream of

Saxon oaths, followed by the faint jingling of harness, came to her ears. Then she heard the distinct sound of a woman's laugh. Hildegard and the hounds withdrew behind a hawthorn brake and waited.

Their attention was rewarded when a band of horsemen burst into view. They came roaring out of the trees, lathered in mud and sweat, and at their head, resplendent in shining mail, a knight. His horse had socks of mud to its withers and its caparison of silver and green was besmirched most foully but this did not in any way detract from the glamour of the knight's appearance. He was followed by the laughing woman astride a spirited little mare. It, too, was caked in mud. At a word from her the whole crowd skidded to an untidy halt in the clearing.

Visitors to Hutton, Hildegard surmised, dazzled by the sight. The idea of visitors was pleasing. It might turn out to be a perfect time to ask a favour: Roger, the genial host, lavish with his hospitality, replete with manorial holdings – and generous to the requests of nuns.

Intending to go down to greet them, she saw the woman on the muddy little palfrey push back her hood with a gloved hand to reveal dark hair plaited in the Norman style. Then her voice floated clearly through the trees. It was light and amused. 'This is where I'd better get into the litter, sweeting. Out of sight of prying eyes.'

Hildegard hesitated. She saw the woman slip down from the mare into the arms of an eager servant with scarlet tippets on his sleeves and, with little cries of disgust, squelch back along the muddy track to a litter piled with furs hitched between two ponies. Adjusting her cloak, she flung herself on to it and, burrowing beneath the furs, commanded the troop to continue. More slowly now, they moved off.

Hildegard watched them go. 'Whose prying eyes?' she wondered aloud. Without answering, the two hounds followed her down the bank to join the trail on the final leg to Hutton.

It was dark when she arrived. Rain had been falling heavily for the last two hours. But even the weather could not destroy the impact of her first sight of the castle again.

It stood at the head of the dale and rose up gleaming white like the side of a chalk cliff from amid the tall forest beeches, its four towers alight with flaring cressets in every sconce. On the battlements she noticed the glint of arms and heard the commands of the serjeant as the watch patrolled. The drawbridge was down but guards were posted on both sides of the moat to check who went in and who came out. She was allowed across with no difficulty when they saw she was a harmless nun. A lad hurried forward to take her horse.

When she reached the gatehouse, however, the porter barred her way with a stick, hefting a torch so he could look into her face.

'I wish to have audience with Lord Roger,' she told him, momentarily dazzled by the light.

'I ain't got no instructions as such,' he replied with a scowl.

'That's because he doesn't know I want to see

him,' she explained.

'I don't know neither.' He looked undecided when she refused to budge. Then he called over his shoulder to one of the sub-porters. 'Here, go and ask yon steward if I'm to let her in.' He jerked his thumb at Hildegard.

She was impatient now. Her boots were pinching and her cloak seemed to draw rain rather than repel it. Besides, Bermonda was whining for food and warmth and her little whimpers broke her heart.

'Look, you can see I'm a harmless Cistercian,' she tried again. 'What's the objection?'

'I'm only doing my job, Sister, just as you do yours.'

Over his shoulder she could see straight into the bailey. There was a great confusion of serfs going back and forth. It looked busier than anticipated. She was desperate to get inside, take her wet clothes off and don dry ones. But the porter, it seemed, was not to be hurried.

'What's all this about?' she asked conversationally while they waited in the flickering light for the sub-porter to fight his way to where the steward was bawling orders at a line of servants.

'It's Martinmas,' he told her. Apparently relishing a chance to display his knowledge, he leant forward in a miasma of raw onion and garlic. 'Security's tight just now, Sister. My lord has his family and guests to protect. Everybody's on the road at this time of year, with the hiring fairs and that. And down in the village they're celebrating their own saint, Willibrod, and electing a mock mayor. *And*, if that's not enough, we've got some

Lombardy prince and his four henchman come all the way from abroad to talk loans!' He leaned back as if to say: so what do you think to that?

'It's certainly a hive of activity,' Hildegard remarked, 'and you at the centre of it all.' She was rewarded by a toothy smile. 'I can quite understand why you have to be so strict about anyone entering the castle but,' she lowered her voice, 'it must be a hefty loan Lord Roger's after to bring the Lombards all this way up north. I thought he was doing quite well. Why does he want a loan, do you think?'

'They're not just here on my lord's account. They're doing the rounds of the abbeys.' The porter gestured northwards, then tapped the side of his nose. 'Staple,' he mouthed.

Hildegard widened her eyes. This was news. 'Is the pope still after a bigger cut?'

'He wants the lot this time round. To get the better of Clement!'

'The monks won't be pleased. They rather favour the French pope, I understand.'

The porter chortled with delight at the prospect of a massacre to come, symbolic though it would be. He probably thinks mutual excommunications have been the best of it so far, she thought, each pope, Urban in Rome and Clement in Avignon, trying to outmagic the other. In her opinion there was worse to come. She turned to matters closer to hand. 'I can't stand here till Lauds. Let me through. I'll put you right with the Lord Steward. He knows me of old.'

'I can't do that,' began the porter, but Hildegard had already sidestepped his stave, slipped

51

through the snickel gate and, her hounds with bared teeth in close order about her, had entered the seething crowd.

The steward was easy to spot. He was six foot three at least, clad smartly in ermine and pers with a chain of office visible round his neck. 'Ulf!' she called as soon as she was within earshot. 'It's me!' Rain was pounding down in a fury now, sending people running for shelter, but when he turned she pushed back her hood to reveal her face framed by its gleaming hair.

He stopped in mid-shout and came wading towards her with arms outstretched.

'My sainted sister!'

Impervious to the bucketing rain, he swept her into his arms in a crushing embrace. 'When they said there was a nun at the gate I didn't suspect it was you! I can't believe my eyes! Are you real? Have they turned you out of Swyne? Is every-thing all right?' He gave her a close look.

'Everything's fine. Apart from something that happened on the way over. I'll tell you about that later.' Hildegard glanced at the crowd scurrying about the bailey. 'I was hoping for a quiet word with Lord Roger,' she said, 'but it looks as if he's going to have no time if your porter's to be believed.'

'Fear not, sweetheart. He'll see you any time.'

She gave him a sharp glance. 'Wife number five permitting?' News of Roger's recent marriage had reached the priory almost before it was planned.

'Don't worry about Lady Melisen,' Ulf said. 'She's Norman through and through. Knows the price of everything. A pleasure to do business with. She won't consider it worth her while to get in your way. What do you want with Lord Roger?'

'It's a long story. Let me get out of these wet clothes. But what's all the fuss about?' She gestured towards the melee of porters, sumpter ponies, kitchen staff and serfs. They were now augmented by what must surely be the five Lombardy men sauntering elegantly across the garth towards the refectory beneath a canopy held over their heads by a couple of soaked and grimacing servants.

Following her glance, Ulf grinned. 'Loan men,' he confirmed. 'Smart, aren't they?'

The black-clad Lombards were looking on the Saxon scrum with some amusement. They were close enough for her to hear them say something to each other in a kind of base Latin. Then they all laughed. Stepping over a trio of roiling villeins locked in combat on the puddled ground, they continued into the Great Hall with a flourish of cloaks. The bearers hoisted the canopy above their own heads and trudged off.

'You've arrived at just the right time,' Ulf said. 'The Lady Sibilla's due any minute and I reckon they're going to need all the help they can get.'

'Sibilla?'

'Lord Roger's sister-in-law. Sir Ralph's wife. After your time. You won't have met her.'

'I wonder if that's the party I saw on the way over? If so, Sir Ralph was astride a rather mettle-some stallion. Most impressively caparisoned–'

'That'd be Sir Ralph all right.'

'And his lady? Hair black as ebony, and wearing a blue velvet cloak?'

'And that'd be the Lady Sibilla. And what a size she is! 'Struth!' Ulf held his hands in front of an imaginary beer gut. Despite his height and job he was as thin as a lath.

'She didn't look particularly big to me,' said Hildegard. 'Rather slight, I thought. Anyway, the party I saw must have arrived ages ago, the pace they were going.'

'They did,' said Ulf.

'But I thought you just said she was due?' Hildegard was puzzled.

'Due. Yes.' He blushed. Auburn-blond, he blushed easily and his skin was now nearly the same shade as his beard. He cupped his hands round an imaginary stomach and Hildegard suddenly understood.

'But she was riding astride!' she exclaimed, rain on her lashes making her blink. 'And,' she added in surprise, 'she must be all of forty.'

'That's why Roger's going to be pleased to see you.' He tapped the scrip at her belt which he guessed was full of cures. 'Many hands make light work.'

'Too many cooks spoil the broth,' she replied automatically.

Ulf bent his head close to her ear. Rain dripped off his brow on to her shoulder. 'On to more important matters, sister. I've got a nice keg of Guienne in my pantry.' He squeezed her elbow. 'How about coming in later to give me your opinion?'

'Let me see how it goes with Lord Roger,' she told him. 'I'm not here for rollicking. I have business in mind.'

Ignoring his raised eyebrows, she left him. With the intention of getting out of her wet garments as soon as possible, she followed one of the servants through a maze of corridors to one of the guest chambers. She was relieved the journey was behind her. Now she could focus on her mission. But she couldn't help wondering whether it had been a mistake to come out here after all. What with Martinmas, Lombardy bankers and now a pregnant sister-in-law, would Lord Roger be able to give her the time and attention her project deserved?

Chapter Two

The great hall, just like the bailey, was seething with folk. As well as a host of relatives, friends, hangers-on, castle officials and a couple of mendicant friars, all with their own attendants, there were six tumblers, ten musicians tuning their instruments, and more fancily dressed squires, pages and servants than could surely be needed by one family. And yet, apart from the guests, there was no sign of anyone idling. The staff were run off their feet. Keeping close to the walls, well out of the ale-sodden straw, Hildegard picked her way towards the dais.

Four people were lounging up there just now, three men and a young woman, all very finely attired. They were surrounded by a crowd of liveried servants and sitting in front of a crimson cloth of honour stitched with the de Hutton coat of arms, a device, she noted, that involved what some might regard as an excess of gold thread. In the hearth was a blazing forest of logs.

Central to all, and apparelled with the magnificence of a doge – though sweating somewhat in a new style houpelande of scarlet velvet – was Lord Roger de Hutton himself. He was gloriously red-bearded.

When he saw a nun approaching he sprang guiltily to his feet. Then he recognised her. 'Hildegard! Is it you? I don't believe it! Am I seeing things? Did they let you out after all?' He reached towards her.

'I hardly had to be let out, my lord: I was never kept in. As such.'

'It seems to me you've been incarcerated for all eternity. But here, most happy greetings, my dear, dear girl!' He extended both hands and pulled her up beside him. She felt herself smile somewhat demurely when he grasped her round the wrists with such crushing force. 'You haven't changed a jot,' he murmured. 'I was worried you'd be all wizened and white haired after seven years at that blessed priory. But you're just as fair and fine as ever. More so,' he growled, tightening his grip.

'You haven't changed much either, you old rogue.' He was bigger, more physical, that was what was different. He seemed to take up all the space around her. She disengaged herself from his grip. It had been ages since a man had touched her and now two of them had done so in quick succession, bringing all kinds of memories that would only entail a trouble of confession and penance if

56

admitted. She simply hadn't the time for it.

'So what's this thing?' he was asking jovially, reaching out.

'It's a wimple, as you know full well, and I'm not sure I like you tweaking it.'

Suddenly aware of how her changed status cut her off from the usual ribbing that went on in his presence, he said with an embarrassed flourish, 'But look here, you haven't met my brother-in-law, Sir William of Holderness.' He indicated a bad-tempered-looking stranger with a broken nose and clipped beard. His chaperon matched his black expression and he seemed to imagine he owned the place, judging from the way he stuck his boots out to cause maximum inconvenience to the servants.

'Lady Avice's husband?' So this was he of ill repute. Hildegard bowed her head in greeting just enough not to antagonise him. She'd heard such stories it was difficult to believe he didn't sit in a pit of flames.

'You know Avice, then?' he drawled in a dark voice, lowering his brows even further and making her acquaintance with his wife sound like a crime.

'We shared a tutor here at the castle as young girls,' she replied, 'Roger's uncle was my guardian.' She gave him a glance as if she were already the Abbess of Meaux. He shifted uncomfortably, no doubt aware of his many sins which she had clearly discerned at a glance. Avoiding her eye, he threw a chunk of raw meat to a fierce-looking mastiff chained to his wrist as if he'd said enough.

'And here's little Philippa.' Roger smiled complacently in the direction of the young woman.

Hildegard remembered Roger's only daughter as a rather solemn child of ten with long flaxen plaits and a book forever in her hands. Now she was a self-possessed young person with a face of austere beauty. She bestowed a derisory glance on her father at this introduction but said nothing. A girl grown wise as well as beautiful, judged Hildegard with interest.

'And of course Sir Ralph you know already.' Roger made an offhand gesture to the third figure lolling on the dais.

Like Philippa, Ralph had changed in seven years. In the old days he had been just a youth, always running to keep up with his elder brother. Pale and lanky, he had been no match for Roger in the rough and tumble of boyhood. She had not recognised him as the perfect knight astride the horse. Now, out of armour, in silk and velvet, he was again unimpressive beside his brother. With his hair cut straight round like a poet's, he looked so frail he seemed to be woven from gossamer. When Hildegard acknowledged him he merely raised a limp hand in greeting before returning to the study of a small, ivory chessboard. For some reason there was a fur tippet lying across his lap. It's hardly cold in here with that heap of logs spitting and roaring in a hearth big enough to house a small army, she thought, moving closer into its radiance and stretching out her hands.

Roger took her by the elbow. 'Let's get away from this rabble. I want to have a word in private.'

'Exactly my own desire.' Pleased that she might get a chance to ask for his help so soon, she followed him up the gallery stairs towards the solar.

On the way he said, 'You'll never believe this, she's got me eating separate from the lads in the hall! She even wants me to employ a fool like the one Philippa of Hainault used to have. Can you beat it?' He was laughing jovially at the folly of, presumably, his new wife, and Hildegard was just about to make a polite enquiry when there was a shriek and a gaggle of women came fluttering along the corridor in the wake of a bejewelled young woman who looked like nothing more than a child in dressing-up clothes.

'Ah, here she is now,' said Roger, coming to a stop. He started to coo like a ringed dove. 'Melisen, my sweet–'

She ignored him.

To say she was pretty would be churlish, thought Hildegard. From her chaplet of filigree gold to the embroidered basquinets on her feet she was a vision from a *chanson d'amour*. She glittered. She sparkled. And she wore a single blood-hued gem as large as a duck egg nestling in her décolleté. *La belle dame sans merci*. What had Ulf said? The woman who knows the price of everything.

Roger was clearly besotted. Even though Melisen was stamping and screaming like a Calais fishwife, he smiled fondly through it all. Apparently she wanted her entire staff of Saxons thrown out on their thieving ears and a reputable bunch of Kentish maids sent up from her father's estates near Deal because of a lost brooch filched from off her very gown.

Roger's face blanched when he understood. He imagined, no doubt, the spies his father-in-law would smuggle in with such a wholesale incursion from Kent and began to chuckle in a hearty fashion that could not have concealed even from a deaf man, his utter desperation.

'Now, now, my pretty martlet,' he repeated several times, 'I'm sure we can sort it out without getting rid of them all.'

The screaming stopped briefly for want of breath and, quickly noticing his wife's expression and without an iota of guile evident, he said, 'On the other hand, my sweetkin, maybe you're right, you always are, you're so clever, so yes, let's get rid of them first thing tomorrow, why don't we? Then you can choose every one of your maids yourself.' A tentative smile flickered for a moment before he added, smoothly, 'Why on earth didn't I think of that?' He put a hand round her tiny waist. 'And now, gentle sweeting,' laying it on, judged Hildegard, who was observing the whole scene with interest, 'we must down to dine.'

So saying, he began to guide her towards the stairs. But wife number five was not to be so easily placated. She snatched at his sleeve and opened her mouth to start again. Luckily for Roger, before she could launch forth, a maid came pell-mell along the corridor with, in the palm of her hand, the lost brooch, glittering.

'Here it is after all, my lady!' said the maid, white faced but triumphant. Melisen picked up the brooch and stared at it as if convinced it was a trick of the light, but before she could demand to know where it was found and by whom, Roger, smooth as silk, took it from between her fingers and pinned it to her bodice. 'There now,' he murmured. 'It was worth all that just to see you look so lovely.'

'*Lovely?* Is that all you can say about me? You may as well be talking about the weather! I do believe you've forgotten how to admire me!' she snapped. Then she turned and caught sight of Hildegard standing in the shadows.

'And who on earth's *that?* Am I living in a nunnery or what?'

'This is the herb woman requested for Sibilla's confinement,' he lied without a blink. 'But come, sweet, to dine! Our guests are impatient to see you.'

While his lady and her retinue made their way with a kerfuffle of trumpets down the stairs to the Great Hall, Roger took the opportunity to lag behind. 'In here,' he ordered, backing Hildegard through a door behind the arras into an empty chamber. 'I need to ask a boon.'

'Ask.'

'As you heard, Sibilla is miraculously with child. I wish her a safe delivery as I intend to make the babe my heir if it's a boy. No!' He put up a hand. 'No time to discuss matters now. All I ask is you keep an eye on the midwife. I don't want any mishaps. Ulf has never stopped reminding me how skilled you are in the physick arts.'

'Of course I'll help. That's my job. I'd be delighted to do what I can.'

'That aside,' he smoothed his belly, 'look what you're missing, woman. All this could've been yours. What in God's name made you take the veil?'

Hildegard regarded him solemnly for a

moment then dropped her lids without speaking.

'Still brooding over Hugh?' he growled. 'Can't you forget him?'

When she lifted her glance he was twirling the ends of his beard and eyeing her with a speculative expression.

'Not brooding, Roger,' she reproved, 'but grieving. And the mystery of his death still puzzles me. I would like to know what really happened in France.'

'But he left you well off!' he exclaimed. 'With that sort of dowry you could have had your pick of us Norman lords. One of us would've been honoured.'

'I chose a higher lord, Roger.'

'Who? Oh...' He frowned when he realised what she meant. 'It's beyond me, all that. Anyway, come in to dine when you've had a look at Sibilla. It's been an age. I can do with some fresh gossip and you nuns seem to get to know everything first. Hildegard, you've been sorely missed.'

And as they came out of the little chamber he said, 'That white habit, you know, it really does something–' Then he collected himself and said, 'Let's talk later. We're living in dangerous times. It's not just your gossip I want to hear, it's your opinion too.'

And when she met his eyes he said, 'You probably don't realise it, tucked away as you are, but we're at the front line here. And I don't intend to finish up as mincemeat, ground between the French, the Scots and the bishops.' Then he looked sheepish and surprised her by saying, 'I know what you're thinking. I know she's a silly, vain little creature but when you get to know her you'll be as charmed as we all are.'

Without offering any opinion on the matter Hildegard allowed him to lead her towards the stairs. Roger explained, 'Her father's a staunch supporter of the king. There's only one thing I have to watch,' he told her, 'and that's my manners. Observe the valour of our efforts but,' he put his lips to her ear, 'make no comment!' So saying, and chuckling with his usual good humour, he called for one of his pages to show her to the place where Sibilla was lying.

The birthing chamber was set at the farthest possible distance from Lord Roger's private apartments. The castle had been greatly extended since her own day and she was soon lost in the labyrinth of new corridors and extra storeys that had been built on, but eventually the page showed her to a door on a separate landing in the new wing. From the other side came the unmistakable sound of a woman in labour. Holding aloft the lighted stump of a candle, Hildegard dismissed the page then hesitated with her hand on the door as a wretchedly hoarse voice rained down curses inside. Poor creature, she thought, remembering exactly what it was like. Blowing out the candle to save the wax, as had become her custom, she pushed open the door and entered.

Events were farther on than she expected after seeing Sibilla riding earlier that day. The midwife was definitely about to earn her fee. A high bed stood in the middle of the room with a birthing chair, at present unused, beside it. The rush light, illuminating the bed and its occupant, flickered as if a sudden draught had caught it, and the tapestries along the opposite wall shivered, casting grotesque shadows over the room. There was the faintest scent of jasmine on the air, as if someone so scented had just gone out.

There was no time to consider the matter for on the bed beneath a striped and padded coverlet Sibilla was raging with the sort of vocabulary usually confined to the stable lads. The two maids in attendance giggled and smirked but the midwife was undaunted. Shouting words of encouragement, she managed to keep track of every scream until, suddenly, her tone changed. It softened. She began to murmur and to coax. Hildegard held her breath.

'Gently now,' she heard the midwife murmur. 'Come on, girl, gently now.' And almost straight away she said, 'Steady now, here he comes.'

Sibilla gave one final howl as she pushed with all her force and then the baby came slithering into the world and the maids were rushing forward with cloths and hot water. The miracle brought tears to Hildegard's eyes. Without thinking, she dropped to her knees and by the time she rose to her feet the baby was making its first sounds as the cord was cut and it was rapidly swaddled in a clean cloth. The midwife handed it to one of the servants then turned back to the mother.

'You've never had so much attention, my lamb,' she said as she briskly attended Sibilla beneath the striped coverlet. 'You make sure you wring it for all it's worth. You'll never get a better chance.' Then she turned to the howling baby. 'And you, my young bratling, heir to all, so how fare you?'

'Is it a boy?' asked the maid who held the bundle, starting to loosen its cloth.

'Leave that!' said the midwife, sharply. 'Of course it is.'

'That's a piece of luck!' chipped the second servant.

'You'll be lucky as well if you keep your mouth laced,' snapped the midwife.

'Ooh, threats!' replied the maid saucily, twirling a lock of hair. It was red and lustrous and fell over one shoulder in a long plait.

Just then Hildegard stepped forward into the pool of light shed by two wall cressets. At the sound the women turned.

'Who in God's name–?' The midwife's mouth dropped open.

'I didn't mean to startle you.'

'I thought I told you to lock that door!' She looked daggers at the red-haired maid then, recognising the authority of the nun, she beetled across the floor, crossing herself obsequiously, her gnarled face distorted in a dishonest smile. 'An easy birth, sister, despite the usual cursing.' Showing she could speak smoothly when she wanted to, she was oil on silk. 'It was enough to split the eardrums,' she went on. 'I hope you didn't find it offensive. High and low curse in the same tongue, I fear.'

'No offence. Lord Roger asked me to offer my services but I see you have managed well without me.'

'Managed? I've been delivering babies for forty years. These gentl'men, what do they know? Do they think I'm a wet girl without a thought in her head? You tell them everything is as it should be.'

'And the baby?' Hildegard moved over to where the girl with the red hair was leaning over it, making cooing noises.

'A fine son and heir for Sir Ralph. You may tell him so without delay.'

Now the drama was over, Sibilla lay inert beneath a mound of covers, emitting small sighs of exhaustion, and showed scant interest in the son brought so noisily into the world. A ring, large and costly, gleamed on the finger of a somewhat roughened hand that lay outside the cover.

'Let her be,' said the midwife, following Hildegard's glance. 'She'll sleep now after all that. Then she'll not be parted from the little fellow. When she's herself again she may receive visitors. Her lord, of course, may attend her when he will.'

After Sibilla's delivery, Hildegard managed to find her way back towards the Great Hall with only a couple of wrong turns. The place was bursting with new arrivals, and she sent a servant into the thick of it to find Sir Ralph. While she waited she leaned against a pillar and watched the tumblers. Five of them had formed a human tower by standing on each other's shoulders, the one on top, his head almost touching the rafters, juggling with some coloured balls. When he finished he came somersaulting down into the straw with all the others amid hoots and cheers. The acrobats were the only ones not drinking. Everybody else was already looking the worse for wear, and things had only just started.

On the far side of the hall Ralph was dancing with a few others in a circle and concentrating fiercely on his steps. She saw him push his hair from his brow with both hands and spin from the group when a servant tugged at his sleeve. Roger noticed this too and, accompanied by the visitor from Lombardy, managed to reach her side first.

He planted himself in front of her. 'You have news. I can tell by your face.'

She beamed. 'Lady Sibilla has a son.'

Roger's expression was one of relief 'So, the succession is safe!' He raised a triumphant fist. In the hubbub of cheers from those nearest, Hildegard stared at him in astonishment. 'But what about your own son?' she blurted under cover of the cheering voices. 'Surely Edwin will succeed to your title and domains? In the distant future, of course. Or failing him,' she hesitated, 'you wouldn't let the law obstruct Philippa's claim?'

She noticed the Lombardy merchant, standing within earshot, narrow his eyes.

'The law is the law,' grunted Roger. 'I've no reason to kick against it. Philippa can either make a marriage or choose a nunnery. As for Edwin...' He scowled. 'I have no son called Edwin.'

Hildegard suppressed a reply. Puzzled, she watched him force his way into the midst of the rabble and hold up both hands.

'Cease your romping, friends!' At once everybody fell silent except for a lone lutenist who stopped playing only when he got a cuff on the ear from his master. Roger smiled expansively at his audience. 'We are, dear friends, blessed with an heir!' There were cheers. 'And,' he held up a hand, 'it's all thanks to my dear brother Ralph.'

'Sibilla had a part surely?' reproved Philippa from the sidelines.

'I thank her as well,' he huffed. 'It takes two. I know that.' He strode over to his brother and clapped him on the shoulder. Ralph, blinking in confusion, found himself smothered in a fraternal embrace.

Coming up for air, he asked, 'You did say a son?'

'Yes, you dolt!' Roger laughed.

'Have you seen him? Who says it's a son—?'

'Hildegard has seen him. Just now! This very minute past!' Roger was clearly elated at the news.

Ralph clasped his hands together and closed his eyes. 'Thank the Lord, the Blessed Virgin and all the heavenly host!'

Everyone cheered again.

'I must go to him.' He turned to the company and stretched out his arms to include them all. 'Kindred, dearest friends, honoured guests. Allow me a few moments alone with my wife and babe – if they allow a sinner such as me near so precious a being – and then you may come and admire!' With a bow to acknowledge everyone, including the merchant-prince, Ralph fled the chamber.

William could not resist a jibe. 'I doubt he'll be so enamoured of the brat when it shits and pukes over his best cloak,' he grunted. There was violence in his eyes. He might well rage for some time, thought Hildegard, now that in one fell swoop his own two sons were pushed back down the line of inheritance.

And what of Melisen all this while? she wondered, turning her head. She was standing to one side without uttering a word. As Roger received congratulations, as if it had been all his own doing, she stood twisting the brooch on her bodice. Only when her husband happened to catch her eye did she go over and slip into the shelter of his arms.

'We are happy for Sir Ralph and Lady Sibilla,' she announced to the company at large. 'May the babe be a blessing to one and all.' Standing close by, Hildegard could not help hearing her add in a quiet voice meant for Roger alone, 'But we too shall soon have cause for celebration, husband dear, shall we not? How could it not be so?'

Roger cupped her chin and looked deep into her eyes. 'Soon? You say soon?' He kissed her possessively. 'For your sake, my lady, I hope soon is the *mot juste.*'

Hildegard saw the girl's colour fade.

'I meant what I said about that wine,' said Ulf in her ear a few minutes later.

The noise of the revellers had reached a deafening pitch now there was yet another cause for celebration. Toast after toast was made. The wine and ale flowed without cease. Melisen was dancing in a provocative fashion in the middle of a circle of admiring guests while Roger huffed and puffed, torn between pride in the youth and beauty of his fifth wife and jealousy at the lascivious looks she was arousing among his men. Pride won. Hildegard raised her eyebrows at Ulf as they watched Roger step into the circle to take

69

his wife by the hand.

With the cheers and ribald comments of the guests ringing in her ears as Roger was put through his paces, she followed the steward into his little room off the Great Hall.

'So this is where you do your plotting!' she joked as she glanced round at the neatly ordered shelves containing what looked like documents relating to the many manorial holdings he administered on Roger's behalf. When she shot Ulf a glance, though, he wasn't smiling.

'Is something the matter?'

'Sit down, do.' He pulled a bench forward and threw a fur over it. There was a fire blazing in the new grate. She put her feet up on a log of wood, wriggled her toes in her scarpollini, the cork-soled shoes covered in cloth that made no sound on the stone alleyway of the cloisters, and gave a sigh. It was quiet in here with the door closed, the only sound the spitting of the logs in the grate.

'Peace at last,' she sighed with a sudden heart-felt feeling of relief. 'I had the most frightening journey over to Meaux. I'll tell you about it in a moment when you sit down.'

With a goblet of what turned out to be as excellent a Guienne as one could wish, she asked Ulf again what was troubling him.

'You can guess. It's Edwin,' he said, and stopped as if uncertain how to go on.

'Where is he?'

Ulf frowned. 'Dead for all I know.' He chewed his beard then came to sit beside her. 'Sorry. That's not very funny. He took off after an almighty row with Roger a couple of months ago: Roger swearing he was disinherited, Edwin vowing never to return. Since then, nothing. I would have expected a word by now. A sighting at least. I have contacts all over. But no, not a bloody thing. I'm fond of the lad and I don't know what to do.'

'What about Philippa? Doesn't she know anything?'

'She's worried sick. She thinks he's gone to France.'

'As a mercenary, you mean?'

'What else?' He gave her a sharp glance.

She ignored it. 'And what do you think?'

'She may be right. It's the sort of damned stupid thing he would do, just to show everybody. He'll probably come swanning back laden with booty.'

'Roger seems very hard on his children.' She thought of a ring she had seen. 'I was wondering about Philippa and whether she's betrothed?'

'You noticed her ring?'

'I saw *a* ring. She keeps it well hidden in the folds of her gown while that Lombardy fellow's around.'

Ulf sucked in air through his teeth.

She said, 'I didn't expect Roger to cut Philippa out of the succession. What on earth's that about?'

'He's Norman all right when it suits him,' muttered Ulf. 'Why he's following Norman law now of all times beats me. Old King Edward refused allegiance to France and young Richard seems to show the same spirit. So why is Roger coming out on the wrong–?' He broke off and, as

71

if to conceal his indiscretion on the subject of Roger's allegiance, made a show of wrestling one foot out of its boot, fiddling with the lining, then shoving his foot back inside with a scowl. He retied the drawstring. 'It's common knowledge folks on the coast down south are being overrun by French pirates but nobody does a blessed thing to protect them. Imagine, unable to sleep in your bed at night for fear of having your throat slit?'

'The French aren't everywhere,' she reminded him in an attempt to cheer him up. 'At least the courts are using English now.'

''Bout time too. But let's talk about you.'

She explained how unhappy she had been, living at the hermitage with no more useful purpose in life than to ferry people across the river and pray and think of Hugh. And then had come that night when she had the vision, or the dream, call it what you want, and it had all become brilliantly clear, and she had the funds, and she had permission from the abbot and the support of her own prioress, and she was going to set up her own small house where she could cure the sick and teach the children of the villeins to read so they would have a proper start in life. And it was more than she had ever hoped for in the horrible dark days of her solitude.

'But isn't it a dangerous thing to do these days? Teaching reading? There's plenty in power want to keep the labourers in the bliss of ignorance.'

'I doubt whether the poor think it's bliss not to be able to read the laws that bind them,' said Hildegarde. 'And if they learn to read Wyclif's

Bible for themselves that's surely to the good too.' She had gone farther than she had meant to in mentioning Wyclif, but Ulf was an old friend, even if there had been a gap of seven years.

He said nothing. She took his silence for agreement. As she hoped, when she went on to tell him about her need for a suitable place, he suggested a grange or two that might be available. Then she told him about the murdered youth she had found on her way to Meaux.

'It was a horrible discovery. He was no more than a boy. He reminded me of my own son, he looked little older than Bertrand–'

'I hear your young 'un's trying to earn his spurs with the army of the Bishop of Norwich?'

Hildegard nodded. 'He could so easily end up the same way as–' She faltered.

'As your gallant Hugh?'

'I was going to say as that poor youth – stabbed and left to bleed alone in some forest clearing. His mother living in ignorance of his death.' She gave Ulf a tremulous smile as fears crowded her mind. 'At least I persuaded some of de Courcy's men to carry his body back to Meaux. He lies in the chapel there, waiting for the coroner. My part in the whole sorry event is almost over.'

'And yet?'

'Am I so transparent?'

'I've known you long enough to read your face. You haven't changed all that much in seven years.'

She smiled at the recollection of a shared childhood, Ulf at five riding his woodsman father pick-a-back round the bailey, learning to handle his first bow, training his first hawk. The memories made her glance soften for a moment. Then, looking into the fire, she furrowed her brow. 'I can't help asking myself if I stumbled on something deeper than a random attack.'

'What do you mean?' Ulf leaned forward.

Instead of answering she asked, 'Can you tell me where the Beverley gibbet lies?'

'On the West Common, of course.' His eyes didn't leave hers.

'I thought so too. But after turning off the north lane to go on to the abbey I saw five men hanging there on a gibbet.'

If Ulf already knew about them he gave no sign.

She went on, 'I was surprised at how far from the town the gibbet was but took it as an official hanging place and assumed that the men there had been punished for some crime, tried and proven in the court.' Ulf was still watching her with a look on his face she had never seen before. It was coldly assessing, as if what she said were being rapidly balanced against other information he had. 'It was only afterwards,' she continued, 'when I was describing the place where I found the body, that I realised I was wrong. The abbot's sacristan is a local man and knows the woods like the back of his hand. When I said it was near the gibbet I thought he was being particularly obtuse in not understanding me. It was only later that I realised the gibbet I saw was nothing to do with the town.'

'And that means–?'

'Ulf, it was an execution! The mercenaries don't waste time building gibbets. They rob lone travellers and kill them if they resist and move on. Or they kidnap anybody worth a ransom. But they don't execute their victims. Certainly not by hanging–'

'And quartering–?'

'They hadn't reached that stage. It was left to the crows to finish. Possibly somebody disturbed them. You see, if it had been a band of masterless men they would have taken off the heads of their enemies and paraded them about on poles to demonstrate what they see as power. But this was different. It was an execution,' she repeated, wondering why he didn't react, 'it was the sort of punishment meted out to traitors, a most horrible death to inflict on anyone. And it was done secretly in the depths of the forest. Who would do that? And who do they judge as traitors?'

'What did the abbot say?'

She glanced down at her fingers and studied them. 'It's outside his jurisdiction. It didn't happen on abbey lands so he can't do anything. I had to bully his men to get them to bring the boy back before he got to know of it. I lied a little when he questioned me,' she admitted. 'I thought it was justified.'

'Lied?'

'About its exact location.'

When she looked up Ulf was still watching her.

'I wonder if he's to be trusted?' she managed, her thoughts running on. 'The Cistercians are bound to France, to Citeaux, to Clement, their so-called pope at Avignon. He appoints the abbots in the monasteries. De Courcy himself was put in over the head of the old abbot at Meaux by

75

Clement. They said the pope had to step in because of some irregularity in the election. But we, I mean the prioress and most of the sisters at Swyne, believe there's another reason. No one can deny that the Church forms a separate state within the state. And the war continues despite the treaty–'

'And you fear we have enemies in our midst?' His lips compressed, he seemed like a stranger, his expression revealing a harshness that had not been there in the old days. 'Of course,' he said softly, 'Rome is a foreign power too.'

There was a long silence while she took in this fact. He seemed to be staring at her monastic robes. The conversation had started amiably enough but it was now strangely weighted.

She considered what he might intend to convey of his own loyalties. Many people rejected both popes, wanting an end to the power the Church held and supporting Wyclif in his dispute with the authorities. They wanted Church lands to be given back to the people. They saw all clerics as the enemy.

It was politics and trade which made the king and his archbishop throw in their lot with Rome against Avignon. Maybe Richard's ministers even hoped that when he came of age he would acquire the crown of the Holy Roman Empire himself. His new, young wife was the emperor's daughter. But the choice of pope had turned into one more reason to quarrel with the French. It rendered more bitter the long war between the two nations that had already spanned several decades. The schism in the Church was doing nothing to bring the war to an end.

Except for the warlords and their mercenaries, people were sick of the whole business. They believed all popes, present and future, should be barred from interfering in English affairs and the rapacious taxes they imposed should be rejected. The Commons had petitioned against papal taxation many times until they were driven to the folly of trying to impose another rise in the poll tax in order to pay. That time the people had risen up in protest. Now it seemed as if Ulf was saying what many said: a curse on both your houses.

Hildegard gazed into the fire. Sedition and dissent are cousins, she decided, and it was best to keep quiet until she saw what new alliances had been formed since she was last out in the world. But she realised that she was in danger of being misunderstood.

Before she could explain Ulf said, 'To reject the clerics is one thing. It doesn't imply rejection of King Richard.' He frowned. 'We know what Master Tyler and his friends wanted. They wanted the king to rule and the clerics thrown out with just one archbishop in charge. It was agreed by the king at Smithfield then later revoked by his council in his name.'

His glance travelled over her white habit again and she could sense the questions he wanted to ask. But his eyes were of that dangerous blue that can be both as clear as glass and as concealing as the ocean. It made him difficult to read, and she was wary of uttering a careless remark that might acquire a more dangerous meaning if circumstances changed.

Trusting to their shared childhood, she decided to risk a small admission. 'I do believe we women are different to many of the men who join the orders. We take the veil for reasons that are often more secular than not. I believe we feel a greater need to do good in the world. Many men seem only interested in conquest and killing. I believe women bleed more easily for the poor, the sick and the dispossessed. It seems to me that only by joining forces with other like-minded women in our own houses can we garner the power to change anything. Even then, of course,' she gave a rueful smile, 'our efforts are like leaves in the wind against so much misery.'

She was on the point of adding: our allegiance is to humankind, not to some man sitting on a throne somewhere. But fear of going too far and appearing to speak against both king and pope made her hold her tongue.

'You say change,' he pointed out with a dry smile, 'but that can mean all things to all men. It can be a desire to turn everything upside down, to rip out corruption, root and branch, or it can suggest something more like a gardener retraining the branches, snipping off a bud here and there, digging out a few weeds. Both are kinds of change.' He watched her closely.

'That's true,' she agreed, without giving anything away.

The small chamber seemed to prickle with darker meanings. Neither could speak frankly. Trust was something that in these terrible times no one could risk. They were both aware of the penalty for dissent – France and Germany were aflame with the bodies of heretics. Thankfully that hadn't happened here. But the punishment for plotting against the king was equally violent. The heads on spikes at every town gate testified to it. It was as well to remember that power is as shifting as the wind, and an untimely confession of loyalties today could turn to betrayal tomorrow.

As the months unfolded after the riots in London it became clear that the king's strongest support came from the dissenters. That fact, or hope as some would see it, could lure the incautious to their doom. If Ulf looked askance at her Cistercian habit then she too had to remember that he was Lord Roger's right-hand man. And where, she wondered, did Roger's allegiance lie? I don't want to be mincemeat, he had told her.

Longing to speak freely, she watched Ulf reach out for the flagon and refill their goblets. Remember Wyclif, she warned herself. His writings while Edward was on the throne were radically different now his grandson reigned. It wasn't the king who had wrought the change but the logic of Wyclif's own reasoning which had led him to throw out his earlier beliefs. She had read his works. She understood their logic.

'Now then, what about Hubert de Courcy?' said Ulf breaking into her thoughts. His expression had acquired a gleam, inviting confession.

'He seems popular with the fine folk of Beverley,' she replied, matching his lighter tone.

'Especially the female side, I hear.'

'Quite so.'

'Is that all?'

Avoiding the probing of his glance she said, 'In

many ways his views are surely ones most of us find acceptable – the values of his order, I mean, such as poverty, humility, lack of prideful show of wealth–' She broke off when Ulf began to chuckle. 'What?'

'And this is the Hubert de Courcy you know?'

'I wouldn't say I know him at all!'

They both laughed in unison then but Hildegard doubted whether it was for the same reason. At least it enabled her to move the conversation on to the topic of Roger and his new wife. 'I expect he's drinking as much as ever he did?'

'He's not changed in that respect.'

'What about Melisen? Doesn't she mind?'

'She takes steps.' He gave a grimace and when Hildegard raised her brows he added, 'You probably haven't noticed her eyes? I reckon she's as out of it as he is by the time they tumble into bed. And him wanting another son? That's not the way to go about it to my way of thinking. It's been three months now and still no sign of a little one. That's why Sir Ralph's been able to step in.'

'Her eyes, you say?'

'That stuff she uses. You should know, with your electuaries and your weird cures.'

'Oh, you mean the belladonna? Well, I assume she knows how to handle it. It's common practice in France and Italy, I understand. For beauty's sake, they say. Of course, it might draw Roger to her bed but it's not going to make her pregnant. If that's what she wants she's going to have to change her apothecary.'

As she left Ulf to go to the privacy of her chamber Hildegard wondered why she had not mentioned the little glass phial she had found in the dead man's hand. Did she really not trust Ulf any longer, or was it simply a question of wanting to have a proper look at it herself before offering it to anyone else for interpretation?

With the door firmly closed she took it from her scrip and raised it to the light. The possibility of what she held made her shudder. She had been right to be cautious. The phial was intended as a reliquary. But she guessed it would be no saint's knuckle bone she would find inside. She hesitated before scraping away the wax and unscrewing the stopper. There was a sort of holiness implied by the care with which the contents were protected. But she had to be sure.

Inside she found a tightly furled scrap of linen. As she opened it out she knew her suspicions were confirmed. It was a piece torn from a banner. Roughly hand stitched, it bore a sign of some kind, a motif that could have signified an animal of which only the edge of one leg still remained. There was also a stain. Dark and somewhat stiff to the touch, it could only be blood. Rumours had brought news of this new type of holy relic. Certainly it was not for trade by any pardoner.

When Wat Tyler and his supporters, the men of Kent and Essex, had their demands met so swiftly by the king at Smithfield they later dispersed, taking with them the charters agreeing to their terms, complete with a royal seal and the banner from their own manor or vill. They had borne these proudly home as proof of the king's bond. But the hopes of the protesters had been dashed when the king reneged.

Some loyally said it was because Richard had forced him to withdraw promises not to the liking of them or the council of magnates and bishops. They said they had even threatened to take away his crown.

Others said King Richard had never intended to keep his word but had given it wildly out of fear of the power of the peasant armies that held London in their grip for three days.

Overnight the charters which the labourers hadn't been taught to read became worthless, the banners symbols of defeat. But meanings, like power, can change. Now it was said that the banners dipped in Tyler's blood were more sacred to the rebels than any relic of the saints.

After the labourers from Kent and Essex were butchered by the king's men the shock waves were felt throughout the country. Afterwards, the repression, so swift, so violent, was worse because it took place in secret. Known sympathisers simply disappeared. It didn't need rumour to blow it up into the stuff of nightmares. It was easy to fob off a grieving wife or mother, an inquisitive neighbour or concerned kinsman with an excuse for a sudden absence. She herself understood the grief of these vanishings.

But this relic, now.

When Tyler had been slaughtered by one of Mayor Walworth's men at Smithfield he had been taken to St Bartholomew's where he had lain dying for some hours, his followers, it is said, dipping their banners in his blood and vowing to fight on. Pieces of the banners were said to circulate as symbols of the continuing rebellion which was now forced underground. It was said that when the pieces were brought together it would be the signal for a second and more organised revolt.

Her fingers trembled. There was only one conclusion to be drawn from the relic she held in her hand.

The rebellion was moving north.

Chapter Three

The hounds had been kennelled in the yard beside the servants' kitchens. Now, when she returned, a scullion was feeding them scraps in the shelter of a thatched lean-to. A skinny little urchin not more than nine or ten years old, dressed in a grubby tunic of fustian and barefoot despite the time of year, the boy was settled on his haunches, oblivious to the rain pelting down outside his den, and conversing in a language known only to himself and his charges.

Hildegard contemplated the scene for a moment. No doubt the child would be bedding down beside the hounds this night and thinking himself lucky to have found a dry corner of the yard and two warm creatures to nestle beside him. He looked less well cared for than the hounds. Her heart melted. Just then he must have caught sight of the tip of her robe out of the corner of his eye because he uttered a little cry and scrambled to his feet. She waved him back down. 'They like you, elfling. You must have a way with animals.'

'She's a good 'un, this titch,' he tickled Bermonda behind the ears, 'but I'm a bit wary of the big 'un.' Indeed, the lymer's muzzle was almost on a level with his little face and Duchess could have bitten it off in one bite had she been so minded. Instead she nuzzled at his tunic and seemed quite enamoured.

'So what's your name, sir?'

Blushing to his carrot-top at being expected to speak to a woman in a nun's habit, he muttered, 'Burthred, my lady.'

'You may, Burthred, if you will, see to the care of these creatures for the whole time I'm a guest here. Provided they have not harmed either themselves or anyone else I'll make sure you're well rewarded. What do you say?' Of course he couldn't refuse. He was a serf. But she thought it fair to ask. His urchin smile gave her the clearest proof of delight she could desire.

She informed the kitchener in charge and it was agreed that the boy should be released from his other duties for a time. 'I expect to be away first thing tomorrow morning,' she told them.

A scene of such sweet harmony had brought a smile to Hildegard's face as she set off across the bailey, and she felt so well pleased that even the piercing rain could not dampen her spirits. She merely tightened the linen kerchief she had on over her snood and pulled up the hood of her cloak until only her eyes were visible, then, hitching her hem out of the mud, she fixed it in place with a couple of turns on her leather belt until she could get back indoors.

Such was her inattention to her surroundings as she did all this that when she reached the door she thought would lead to a passage into the Great Hall she found herself in a part of the castle she had never seen before.

A stone-flagged corridor ran straight and empty for a few yards then descended by six short steps to a further door studded with brass nails. Rather than turn round and go back into the rain again she decided to press on, and soon she was at the door and grasping the large ring-handle to let herself through. Believing it to be a short cut to her destination, she was surprised when she found herself in what could only be the undercroft.

A labyrinth of stone pillars rose before her out of the darkness. They were made visible only by a faint glow that came from the far side of the cavern. The muffled sound of men's voices bellowing some ale-house chant floated from the same direction. Assuming it was the sound of revellers in the Great Hall, she stretched both hands in front of her to counter sudden obstacles, and set off into the void, one step followed by another, gingerly, carefully, aware of the danger of an uncovered well or a sudden drop to an even deeper level of the cellar, but confident that she had found the short cut she was looking for. From all sides came the scent of spices and the stored fruits of summer: apples, pears, quinces and dried fruits, too, apricots and lemons, and a sweetness like oils from a warmer climate, all packed and bottled and trussed in the shadowy arcades between the pillars.

Eventually, unscathed, she reached the light that outlined the door into the hall and pushed it open with a feeling of relief. For a moment she was blinded by a blaze of light. It came, however, not from the many cressets and candles that lit the hall but from a single brazier, wild with flames, set in the middle of a small yard. Stone walls rose up on four sides, without a chink, to the height of the battlements. Acrid smoke was drifting through the rain and filled every nook.

Sprawled around the fire, faces crimson in its lurid light, were four men-at-arms. They were bristling with weapons and – hardened to the weather – ignored the rain that was now drilling spikes into the ground from a slit of sky high above. Instead, they gripped flagons of foaming ale in their fists with evident satisfaction. When Hildegard burst in on them they were in the middle of some raucous chant, mouths open to reveal blackened teeth, eyes small with drink. The blazons on the surcoats of the three nearest were not the red and gold worn by Roger's men but the blue marsh dragon of Sir William. The fourth man wore no blazon at all.

This one, dark haired like the others, was sitting facing the door astride the keg from which they all drew their ale, and had the attitude of being the man in charge. He was the first to see her and the instant she appeared his mouth froze, half open in surprise at what must have looked like an apparition. Her dark cloak and concealing hood may have alarmed him but he was not too drunk to forget his training. He responded with alarming speed.

Dragging a short, wicked-looking blade from the scabbard at his side, he leaped to his feet at once. The others, noticing something amiss, broke off in mid-chant and followed his gaze. There was a hiss of steel as they too drew their weapons but, unlike their leader, they did not bother to rise to their feet but lolled where they were on the muddy ground, waiting to see what would happen next.

After a brief pause the first man started to cackle with apparent delight. He had noticed Hildegard's cork-soled scarpollini under the tucked-up hem of her cloak and pointed at them with the tip of his dagger.

'Look, lads! I do believe St Martin has brought us the gift of a wench!' Pushing between the sprawling legs of his comrades as he resheathed his knife, he stepped round the brazier and lurched towards her. Before Hildegard could work out what his intention was he was looming over her with a leer on his face which his short, tufty beard could not conceal.

He shot out a hand and felt for her breasts. 'It's a wench, all right. Tonight's your lucky night, woman!'

'Take your hands off me! How dare you—'

'Come on, don't be like that!' As she turned to move away he reached out to grip her by the wrist and pulled her hard up against his chest.

'Stop this! I—'

'Shut up, whore!' He cuffed her on the side of

the head. 'God's looking after you. He's about to grant you four times the pleasure.' Taking both arms and forcing them behind her back so that she was trapped, he threw a glance over one shoulder. 'What do you say, lads? Who's first?' His companions started to shout drunkenly and bang their flagons on the ground, and one of them even managed to struggle to his feet to stake his claim.

Hildegard didn't wait to hear what they would propose next. Taking her captor by surprise, she wrenched herself from his grip, swivelled and plunged back the way she had come, straight into the black pit of the undercroft, but this time with no guiding light to aid her. Weaving blindly between the columns with the outraged curses of her pursuer echoing around the vault, she had gone only a little way when she felt him grasp her cloak to bring her tumbling back against his leather body-armour in a violent embrace. She screamed and began to struggle.

'When I say come back, I mean come back!' he snarled. She felt his fingers bite into her jaw as he jerked her face up. Then, before she could protest, he began to grind his mouth against her own, and no matter how much she struggled, her strength was no match for his. Only when she felt him fumbling in the folds of her cloak did her anger force her to kick him as hard as she could, knowing even as she did so that her cork-soled shoes were useless against the cured leather greaves he wore, but at that moment she was unable to think of any better way to defend herself.

'Bitch!' he ground out. 'You'll have to do better than that if you want to please me.' He drove his mouth against her own again in a stink of ale and bad teeth.

Over his shoulder she was aware of the blazing fire and the silhouettes of his companions as they jostled to get through the door first, but her captor turned his head and grunted, 'Get away, you bastards. You can have her when I've finished.' But just as he turned back to tear at the tightly belted folds of her cloak, she brought her right knee hard into his groin. It met the edge of his leather tunic and this second feeble attempt to thwart him only made him laugh with malign satisfaction.

'Come on,' he grunted, 'fight me! I like a whore with spirit! It makes winning all the sweeter.' He hit her on the side of the head. 'Show me, bitch! You want to fight? Come on, then, fight!'

As he was taunting her he was backing her feverishly into the darkness of the undercroft. His breath rasped with a feral urgency as his lust increased, and she knew that if she didn't do something quickly it would be too late. Her only hope was the knife in her belt but he held her in so tight a grip she could not get her fingers round it without revealing what she was trying to do.

To distract him she dug her nails into his face with all her force. His response was to shake his head to dislodge her grasp and laugh all the more. It was a grating sound that lacked any sign of joy, and in retaliation he ground his teeth into her neck, tearing at her cloak and all the while cursing the inconvenience it was causing him.

Discovering the leather belt that held it in place, he grappled at the buckle but could not open it. Angered, he slammed her against one of the pillars, and as she fell back her head cracked against it. She would have slumped to the ground with the shock but for the fact that he still held her round the waist. As he pressed his body against hers the rank smell of old sweat swept over her and the staleness of his unwashed garments made her want to vomit.

With an effort she forced her fingers into the notch of her belt and found the knife, but although she managed to get a grip on it she couldn't manage to turn the blade. Instead she had to bring it hilt upwards. She rammed it hard under his jaw. 'You devil! Let me go!'

The action took him by surprise. He obviously hadn't realised she was armed. His head jerked back but, professional fighter that he was, he recovered instantly and, enraged at being struck by a woman, grabbed her round the neck with both hands and began to shake her like a doll, grunting, 'I'll teach you, you bloody whore!'

His eyes locked on hers and she saw the madness of evil in them. There was no doubt about the end he had in mind. It was obvious he would relish the chance to gloat over her dead body after he had done with her what he willed. It would be ill-doing for its own sake. She had to loosen his grip.

While he was still fumbling under her cloak she brought her free hand up and jabbed two fingers hard into his right eye and rammed the hilt of her knife into his throat and, while his head jerked back and a cry of pain was torn from his lips, she twisted free. With a sob of fear she fled crazily back into the darkness and on, deeper into the labyrinth of pillars.

I must find the door, she thought in desperation. *But where is it?* Already her attacker had recovered and she could hear his feet pounding the stone flags as he came after her. His steel-tipped boots echoed like the sound of a dozen men. She ran first one way then another. His breathing seemed to fill the entire chamber.

With a gasp she saw a glimmer of light that seemed to indicate an exit and, with an extra spurt, she flung herself towards it. At her touch a door swung open and, sobbing with relief, she fell through to the other side.

Her relief turned to horror the instant she realised it did not lead to safety as she had hoped but was instead the entrance to a small, lightless cell. With the swiftness of thought that comes from fear she ran her hands over the walls, frantically searching for a way out, but found only stone beneath her palms.

Her pursuer was still rifling among the arcades crammed with provisions destined for the castle kitchens but she could hear the echo of his footsteps as he approached. There was a clatter of steel followed by a curse as he realised he had lost the trail and his sword came up against the wall. Her reprieve was short lived. There was a short pause, then his footsteps rang out again as, like a hound quartering on the prey, he regained the scent and resumed the pursuit. Stealthily she pushed the door shut, playing for time while she tried to find a way out. He was coming closer. At any moment he would find the door and all would be lost.

Then her heart leaped. By a sliver of light filtering through an upper window she could just make out a shape against the opposite wall. With her pursuer closing in, she fled over to it.

It turned out to be a spiral stair. She looked up and saw it climbing into darkness. In desperation she started up it then, hearing him come to a stop outside the door, realised it would be useless. He was almost within the chamber. She would be caught before she got to the top. He would drag her down, step by step, and then there would only be the blade of her knife as protection. She would be no match for a trained fighter twice her weight and enraged to superhuman strength by drink and lust.

Quickened by fear, she flung herself into the cavity under the first turn of the stair and crouched there in a wedge of shadow, her heart beating like a drum.

Across the chamber she was just able to make out the ring-handle of the door, visible as the frailest glint of light.

It began to turn.

A subtle shift in the darkness showed the door beginning to open. A draught of air from the undercroft followed. Then fingers appeared along its edge. He was coming in.

She held her breath until it hurt.

He became visible as a blurred shape in the doorway. Her fear made him twice his actual size. She watched as, instead of coming straight into the chamber, he remained on the threshold, every inch of him attentive to the wisp of sound that would give her away.

There was a nerve-racking silence.

She could not even hear him breathe.

When she was beginning to feel she couldn't stand the tension any longer he took one cautious step forward and then stopped.

A glint of steel leaped out of the darkness and vanished. With the stealth of a hunter he began to move slowly on into the chamber.

She watched the shifting in the layers of shadow that revealed his progress. He was creeping straight towards her. Now he was so close she could smell him. For a moment she thought he must be able to see in the dark. He was reaching out. Her fingers ached on the haft of her knife as she prepared to defend herself.

Then, when he was almost touching her and she was ready to cry out, to her complete astonishment, instead of reaching down to haul her from her hiding place, he was putting a foot on the first tread of the stair right beside her, then he was climbing two at a time to the top. A door banged open above her head and he vanished from view.

Unable to believe her eyes, Hildegard slid from her hiding place and ran breathlessly back into the undercroft. Never had such darkness seemed more welcome. She opened her arms to it, gasping with relief. But there was no time to delay. Retracing her steps by means of the distant glow from the brazier and the chanting of the men-at-arms in the yard, she found the door where she had first entered and fled back the way she had come.

The bailey was full of people going to the feast. Carrying torches, they paid no heed to yet another guest, and she went unnoticed into the crowd.

Rain was still falling. It fell on her upturned face.

Never had it seemed so wonderfully normal, never felt so sweet.

When Lord Roger threw a banquet he expected it to be as splendid as his cooks could devise. On all sides Hildegard's senses were assailed by the opulence of the occasion. Heat swelled over her in a tang of roast meats, baked pies, fish, oysters, honey, herbs and exotic spices from the East, all of it summoning a life far removed from the horror of the last hour and as different as could be from the one she had led since Hugh's death, in the austerity of her hermitage. To bewitch the senses even more, all the guests were attired in their most sumptuous apparel: silks and velvets dyed in colours she had not lately seen outside the stained glass of the priory chapel windows, bordered with ermine and miniver, decorated with trinkets of flashing gold, precious stones, lapis lazuli and silver.

It was as unlike the frugal mealtimes at the priory as could be imagined in the most voluptuous dream. Hildegard forced herself to walk between the loaded trestles without fainting. Still numbed by her ordeal, she could only fix a smile to her face to deflect attention. Her fingers fumbled her garments into place in the secrecy of the throng that pressed on all sides.

By some chance her kerchief was still wrapped tightly over her snood and, thinking it might be stained in some way, she pulled it off. It seemed to stink of the sweat of her attacker. She dropped it into the straw, then hid herself behind a pillar and tried to bring some order to her thoughts, wondering whether her persecutors would put in an appearance in the hall, and why they were drinking secretly like plotters in a remote yard, and why some instinct had made her stop short at telling that vile beast she was a nun. Somehow she knew this would be exactly the sort of thing to inflame him to further violence.

Roger's favourite hawk was sitting behind him on the dais. It occupied a perch covered by a scarlet cloth. Over its head was a cleverly fashioned leather hood, and the gold bells attached to the chain that held it to its leather jesses chimed as it shuffled in this imposed darkness. The delicate sound of the bells could not disguise the fact that the bird was trained for slaughter. Its very presence, brooding over the ephemeral scene of merrymaking below its perch, brought shudders up and down her spine.

For some reason she could not take her eyes off it. She could not stop trembling. That man, that fiend without the blazon, with his hidden identity, had the same function as the hawk, trained to kill without compunction. She had no doubt that he would have taken advantage of the secrecy of the little chamber in the undercroft to murder her after he had used her. But who was he? she asked herself again with a shudder. And to whose household did he belong?

From behind the pillar she searched the faces of the guests. Men and women were coming and going through the great doors all the time. Some wore the livery of the de Huttons, others the triple band argent on a ground vert of Ralph and Sibilla, yet others, fewer in number, wore Sir William's dragon badge. No sign of anyone who might be her assailant. There were other guests, burgesses from the towns, decked, like their wives, in all their gaudy show, jovial and ready to celebrate long into the night, accompanied by their own retinues of servants. It didn't seem likely he belonged to any of these groups. And yet, the spiral stair must have taken him somewhere. Into whose apartment did it lead?

Just then a larded boar was piped in with a boisterous fanfare. Skewered on a basting rod thrust through its mouth to its anus, it was decorated with great artifice to make it look festive even in death. The guests cheered. Platters were held up as the carver flourished his knife. Hildegard turned away. She felt sick. Her legs seemed incapable of carrying her. She sat down for a moment on the edge of a bench. Nobody glanced her way. She inspected the guests jostling by to get a piece of meat or help themselves to more liquor, but he was not there.

In the middle of all the commotion Melisen was being helped by her squire back on to the dais. It was evident she was hoping to conduct a game of Hoodman Blind as she held a black hood in her hand and spoke in a loud and admonishing voice above the melee.

The rules of the game were simple enough. All the hangman had to do was creep up, grab someone and say, 'Yield to me! I am the hangman and you are dead!' Then he had to guess the identity of the victim in his clutches before being allowed to remove his blind. The cleverness came in the skill by which a false identity could be created to lead the hangman astray and make one's escape.

It was no surprise to see Sir Ralph appointed as first hangman.

With a look of resignation he allowed Melisen to cover his eyes and tie a knot at the back of his head with the loose ends, then, trapped in darkness, arms flailing, he set off in pursuit of his first victim. It was then that the taunting began. Feet came out to trip him, pinches landed on his neck. He was buffeted from all sides. Groups of girls ran screaming in mock terror before him.

In no mood to be involved, Hildegard got up and stood to one side. Her hands would not stop shaking. She thrust them inside her sleeves and tried to say a calming prayer, and felt that but for the shrieks that accompanied the game and rekindled her own real terror she would quickly have got the better of her feelings.

She decided to help matters by going farther off. There was a silent group at the far end of the hall out of earshot of Melisen and her game. They were clustered round one of the tumblers, who was performing a balancing act on a tight-rope tied to two pillars. It required a lot of concentration. The audience played their part, waiting in silence for the fall.

As she made her way through the press towards this group she saw Melisen waft a scented kerchief in front of Ralph's nose as he gripped her squire by the trailing point of one of his sleeves. The boy was not happy at having his immaculate finery manhandled in such a way but Ralph held on, shouting, 'Now you're dead, Melisen!' until he heard her mocking laughter from across the hall. The squire pulled himself free with a crow of triumph. Ralph swore through his teeth. 'I'll get you yet, you bastards.' He moved his head from side to side, mouth set in an expression of cold persistence.

This is too close to reality, she thought, pushing more urgently through the crowd.

For some reason an image of the murdered youth in the woods near Meaux came back. The man who killed him would have been trained to kill, just like her assailant. Another man without mercy. It was a quality much praised but practised less. In these days of heartfelt spiritual and civil disagreements men trained in that way were never out of work. She did not realise that Ralph, still wearing the blindfold, had followed her. Now her heart leaped into her mouth as someone shouted a warning and she swung round to see him almost on top of her. He clutched a lump of dripping meat in one hand and reached out blindly with the other.

'I smell incense,' he hissed. 'I've got you now, Sister!' Nose twitching, he clearly believed he had a victim at last, and he made a lunge to where he imagined she was standing. With a gasp she managed to flick out of his reach in the nick of time. But then something happened. Maybe it was fear but suddenly everything went black and she was falling and she thought she was in a deep well going down until, abruptly, everything swam back as noisy and vivid as ever. She found herself gripped in an embrace.

Her eyes snapped open. Then her lips trembled. 'It's you! Master Schockwynde!' She wanted to hug him with gratitude but she pulled away in confusion. 'Oh dear, I think I was about to faint until you saved me.'

'My dear sister, your cheeks are like alabaster!' He laughed genially and helped her straighten her clothes. 'It's only a game, you know! No need to take it seriously! But come, let me whisk you out of harm's way.'

Meanwhile everybody was teasing Ralph and smugly feasting.

Dressed tastefully in tones of silver grey with a short cloak to hide his portly figure, a crimson liripipe flung theatrically over his left shoulder, Master Sueno de Schockwynde was the height of fashion. Small gold chains, much like the ones attached to the legs of Roger's favourite hawk, held the long points of his shoes in place so he didn't trip.

He was an architect involved in the latest bout of church building in Beverley. Now and then he came over to Swyne in the hope of persuading the prioress to fund yet another building or two after the raging success of his quire there. Hildegard had met him several times and had previously had to keep a straight face in front of his frequent pomposities, but now he was a figure of such engaging normality she was delighted to see him.

He was still peering anxiously into her face. 'You're looking most shaken, dear sister. Are these boisterous Saxons a little too much for you? I must say they lend a rather earthy vigour to Lord Roger's festivities.' He wafted a kerchief underneath his nose and cast a critical eye over the many signs of drunkenness in the hall before bestowing a benign smile on them. 'But what would we do without them, eh? They're our servants and they labour for us in all weathers, thank the saints.' Courteous and urbane – an ancestor on his mother's side was said to be Roman – he procured a goblet of wine from a passing servant and insisted she take a sip to steady her nerves.

'So,' she said as soon as she felt restored and could summon some steadiness to her voice, 'how good to see you at Castle Hutton, master. And how is your tower at St John's?'

To show he could take a joke against himself he boomed in a jovial manner, 'By God's will it still stands!' It was an oblique reference to one that had recently fallen, killing several apprentices in the process. 'As a matter of fact,' he went on confidentially, 'I've just come from the minster via Meaux, where I had a most interesting discussion with your lord abbot.'

Her ears pricked up. 'I gather he's hoping for some plans from you?'

'He seems set on an extension to the dorter.'

'So I believe.'

'It would, of course, seriously interfere with the integrity of the space between the frater and the main cloister.' He looked serious.

'And did you tell him so?'

'I had to. And I put forward a better suggestion.'

This was news. There had been endless discussion already. The prioress was highly amused by the whole business. 'Master Schockwynde will test de Courcy's mettle if anybody can,' she had opined.

Oblivious to this, Schockwynde beamed. 'I have the perfect solution. But there is one small problem. It means knocking down the nave. We've done with that old style.' He shuddered in mock horror. 'We can build higher than that, you know. The recent collapse taught us so. Height really is the thing these days.'

Hildegard was stunned. 'Does the abbot agree?'

Master Schockwynde gave an airy wave of his hand. 'He's no architect, although I suppose he's learned enough in his own field. He's bound to need a little persuasion.'

'My prayers go with you.' And with de Courcy, she thought. The recent build had been the pet project of the previous abbot and was still referred to as 'the new church'. And now Sueno wanted to pull it down! On top of that he seemed to disregard the fact that the order abhorred showiness. Soaring pinnacles were anathema to them. But perhaps he knew something about the new abbot's taste that she did not?

Feeling better for being able to converse about such practical matters for a moment, she was about to take her place on the dais before he could tell her more about the dorter extension – and the burden of the building regulations that forever limited the genius of his creativity, all of which she had heard before – when she thought of something.

'As you've just arrived from Beverley, master, I wonder if you've heard about the men who were slaughtered in the woods yesterday?'

Schockwynde frowned. 'Everybody's heard. Nasty business. Said to be five assassins plotting against the king. Deserved all they got, if that's the case.'

'Is that the story that's going around?'

'The whole town's seething with it. Rumours abounding.' He whispered, 'Although some are claiming they were Tyler's men. I tell you, Sister, I wouldn't like to be in the shoes of anybody the rabble brands a traitor.' He mimed slitting his throat. 'But which side will Beverley support should Gaunt insist on pushing matters farther? That's the question.'

'We've always been grateful in the Riding for the many endowments King Richard's father has made over the years.'

'We have indeed.' He nodded thoughtfully. 'He's given us some magnificent buildings. Alas, it won't be buildings to decide the issue, Sister. It'll be brute force of arms as always.'

Schockwynde was claimed by the master of the castle works and Hildegard left them both to talk shop.

To say she was surprised by what Schockwynde had told her was an understatement. He was wrong. He had to be. Why were those men rumoured to be assassins? She thought of Tyler's reliquary secreted in her chamber. Now it burned in her mind and she could almost see her room bursting into flames because of its presence. She should have left it as evidence for the coroner, but she had picked it up without a thought.

There was something else she had left behind. It had scarcely registered at the time. It was a little badge made of pewter like the ones the pilgrims wore. But this was no saint's badge. It was King Richard's sign, stamped from a die in the shape of a white hart, and had been adopted as a sign by those who gave support to the rebellion. Now she realised that by leaving it she had betrayed the unknown youth. He would be branded a rebel and as with his unfortunate companions on the gibbet his life's purpose would be misunderstood. But perhaps there was hope that the coroner would overlook it too and the boy would get his Christian burial after all.

The usher made a place for her at the table next to Sir William. He threw her a dark glance. Clearly he was put out by having a nun seated next to him. He happened to be gnawing on a bone that looked too human for comfort, and the grease made his clipped beard shine so that he looked most satanic. She remembered the blue marsh dragons on the surcoats of his men-at-arms. Was her attacker one of his men, too? If so, why was he not attired like the others?

William reached out and stripped off a length of venison from an enormous platter and threw it to her. 'Your Rule permits flesh?' He raised his black brows.

'On certain days,' she replied, staring askance at the hunk of animal meat but not touching it. 'Fish is our usual fare.' She roused herself enough to attempt a little light conversation as politeness required and heard herself say, 'Roger's yield from his ponds is, I understand, most impressive. And they tell me you yourself rely for your revenues on fish? Tell me,' she continued, 'how big is your annual catch?'

He gave her an eloquent look then growled something like, 'Big enough for Avice,' before turning away at a tug on his sleeve from his wife.

Hildegard glanced along the table to where Lady Avice was sitting. As Roger's sister, she was as unlike him in a physical sense as it was possible to be. Her dead white features were perfectly composed but her eyes held a dazed look as if her mind existed on another, more rarefied level of reality. She and Hildegard had shared a tutor in the distant past but now she didn't even acknowledge the nun's existence. Her gaze, in fact, was fixed exclusively on her husband. Such adoration was astonishing, considering the years they had been married. She looks besotted by the man, thought Hildegard, and she couldn't help wondering what William's secret was. It must surely come down to more than the size of his fisheries. She hastily crossed herself.

Her speculations were interrupted by Melisen, who had descended from the dais, helped most solicitously by her young squire, and now rejoined the diners in a great flurry and glitter of jewels. Roger reached out for her and pulled her on to his lap. 'You were bullying poor Ralph just now,' he murmured, nuzzling her ear. 'You're a wicked child.'

'Well, he deserves it. He isn't quick enough to catch anybody. Still, let's forget about him. I want to know what we're going to do next!' She glanced round. 'Has anybody got any ideas?'

When there was an inconclusive murmuring from those nearest she said, as if she had just thought of it, 'I know! Let's all talk Norman French like they do at court!' But this idea was knocked on the head by Roger straight away.

Roaring with laughter, he said, 'You'll have us all sitting like mutes then, and that wouldn't do!' He looked round at everybody and announced proudly, 'She even has the Yeoman of the Pantry and his assistants coming to blows over who's to place the salt!'

'Such things have to be done properly, and you're such a rough, tough, Northern prince,' said Melisen, bringing a smile to her face, and she pressed her little bosom against his shoulder to take the edge off her tone. 'But if they squabble over the placing of the salt, my darling lord, it simply means one thing – we need another yeoman to do the separate work.'

William gave a smirk. 'She's snared you there, Roger.'

But Roger was undaunted. 'I'll tell you something else. She has them leave our presence with three little bows as if I'm King Richard and she's Anne of Bohemia! Just watch this, everybody!'

He hollered for the third yeoman and, when he appeared, bowing gracefully, Roger looked past him and said vaguely, 'Oh, you here again? No, I don't think I need you.' And he waved him away. As predicted, the yeoman backed out, bowing with elegant little flourishes of his hands, to roars of noble laughter.

'That's very unkind of you,' said Melisen, in a tiny, affected voice amid the general merriment, but clearly a little nastiness made Roger rise in her estimation and she snuggled closer. 'My father's fief in Kent is less far from the court in Bohemia than this remote domain of yours, my cruel cuckoo, and he would never dream of playing such tricks on his servants.' She suddenly lifted his mazer in both hands and held it to his lips. 'Drink to me,' she commanded. 'And I will drink to thee.'

When she replaced the mazer on the board he lifted her girlish hands to his lips and planted a lingering kiss on them, like a promise of greater intimacy to follow.

Hildegard sighed. She saw no chance of getting him on one side and broaching the question of a grange for her nuns. All I want is a few moments, she thought. A vision of her little nunnery and its orchards went floating rapidly away on a tide of food, drink and mindless festivity.

If that weren't enough her muscles were beginning to ache from the attack and she felt a swelling on the back of her head where he had banged her head against the pillar. When she touched it, it felt puffy and sore. I need some cure, she thought, maybe arnica, some knitbone. They were all in her leather scrip in her chamber.

The thought of walking back alone through the empty corridors filled her with alarm. What if she came face to face with him again, would he recognise her? She was sure she would know him. And yet it had been almost dark. His face had been in shadow. It was his eyes, small and full of malice, which she remembered most. That and the smell of him. It seemed to cling to her and she had an overwhelming desire to wash.

Rising suddenly to her feet, Hildegard sat down again just as suddenly. Her knees were like jelly. Give it a minute or two, she told herself. You'll have to get over your fear if you're ever going to be of any use again. She recalled the long nights alone in her hermitage when she had never felt any fear at all. I'm being ridiculous, she thought. I'll go up in a moment.

She allowed a servant to pour her another goblet of wine. The chances were she would never come across her attacker again. The castle was teeming with people. He wouldn't even be looking for a nun. He might not be looking for anybody. In the sort of life he led, women must come and go all the time. What was one that happened to get away?

Hildegard decided to go up as soon as she had collected her thoughts. It was important to settle the matter of a grange here with Roger, but he was talking in a most intimate manner with Melisen and was clearly not in the mood for discussing leases. She would catch him tomorrow, though she knew he would rise late and she would be lucky if she managed to speak to him before noon.

She was gnawing her lip.

The musicians, at an order from the steward, began to swarm down from their gallery and, augmented by a couple of singers who had arrived from Beverley in Master Schockwynde's contingent, struck up at once. It was the signal for most of the assembled to rise to their feet. Hildegard watched the floor fill up. William stayed behind, brooding darkly beside his wife.

Hildegard decided to ask Ulf to find a servant to conduct her to her chamber. Such a request would not give rise to questions. She would wait until the dance ended, and then she would–

She stifled a scream.

From behind the fire-screen someone had pounced. But it was not her they grabbed but William. 'Got you!' cried Ralph, sweeping off the hood and blinking down in triumph at his captive.

'Don't be a buffoon,' growled William, refusing to budge. 'I'm eating. I can't believe you're still persisting in that ridiculous game. Go and catch a Lombard. They're sitting ducks.'

The Lombardy men, in fact, were in a group watching the dancing while lounging randomly round one of the serving tables. Now and then one of them would hold up a dish, they would examine its contents with professional curiosity and then a lengthy discussion would follow. Philippa, dancing close by, observed all this just as carefully as their leader was observing her.

Still shaken by Ralph's sudden eruption from nowhere, Hildegard reached for the aquifer and poured a little well-water on to the edge of her sleeve then surreptitiously wiped her face. Then she crumpled the damp fabric between her palms and scrubbed them vigorously under the table, as if by doing so she could erase all vestige of the stranger's touch. Ralph wandered off, trailing the hangman's blind and muttering about fair play.

Philippa, she noticed, was accepting an invitation from the Lombardy merchant and, with much meshing of glances, they took to the floor. Clad from head to foot in black velvet, with a thrusting nose and foreign eyes, he would be a romantic figure to a young girl, she thought. No wonder the poor child seemed to be in a daze. She heard Ludovico begin a conversation in Latin that closed the door on anyone else and, scarcely moving from the spot, they danced with locked glances, in their own private world.

Beside her William jerked to his feet. Without saying anything he swept a nearby serving woman on to the floor. His wife looked on.

If only Philippa knew it, Hildegard thought, striving to keep her mind off what had taken place in the undercroft, she's the spitting image of her mother. Alfreda had been the daughter of a Cumbrian earl who supplied arms at different times, and sometimes at the same time, to both the Scots and the English, with an impressive augmentation of his wealth and a commensurate diminution of trust from his allies.

Roger made full use of his father-in-law's connections but when Alfreda died during a resurgence of the plague – Philippa was only two at the time – Roger had been beside himself with grief. He had flung himself headlong into marriage with the younger sister of one of his knights but it failed and the unfortunate bride had been packed off with a satisfactory sum to a distant manor and disappeared from the tongue

109

of rumour.

He married again, this time to a Norman of high blood, and their issue, Edwin, became heir to the de Hutton line. This wife died too and Roger returned for some years to a state of scandalous bachelorhood.

In some sense, she thought, watching him dance with the wife little older than his daughter, it still continued.

Meanwhile, Philippa, it seemed, had been found a suitor. Hildegard tried to get another glimpse of the betrothal ring she had noticed earlier but it was hidden in the girl's gown. She frowned. I do hope everything's all right, she thought. No word had filtered through concerning a wedding. Speculation would have been rife among the sisters if a whisper had reached them, but it hadn't, which suggested it was probably recent. And judging by the way she keeps the ring hidden, Hildegard deduced, not welcome. The Lombardy prince, of course, had noticed the ring and she saw him make some comment, holding the girl's fingers against his lips before covering the ring with his hand and concealing it in Philippa's skirt as if he couldn't bear the sight of it. Clearly it was no gift from him.

Hildegard felt her heart contract in sympathy at the problems that might lie ahead but, before she could speculate on Roger's reasons for thrusting an unwelcome suitor on his daughter, her attention was distracted when Ulf pushed his way into the crowd and held up his steward's staff until he had everyone's attention. 'I beg you, friends and kinsfolk, recharge your goblets!' he called out. A horn player blew an intricate flourish.

Flagons were poured and the guests of honour thronged back to the dais while the rowdies down in the hall were shushed. Assuming it was going to be an invitation to view the baby, she watched Roger stride up to the dais with his mazer in his hand. When he turned to look at them his cheeks were flushed, his eyes glazed and she saw his chest heave as he raised his voice so that it carried to every corner of the hall.

'A toast!' he bellowed to her surprise. 'A toast to my dear friends gathered here!' Everyone cheered as he took a gulp of wine. 'And to my new born nephew, my beloved heir!' Another deep draught to rather more speculative applause. 'And also,' he announced, 'I wish to propose a toast to–'

Before he could finish he gave a gasp, clutched his left side, and then the high lord of the northern realm, master of the castle and warden of the King's Forest, Roger de Hutton, gave a roar that pitched him forward over the board, where he lay, felled, among the upturned dishes, his right hand still clutching his mazer, though the wine in it had spilled out and dripped, drop. by drop, on to the freshly laundered linen cloth, where it spread like a pool of blood.

William leaned forward. 'You old fraudster! Get up!' He poked Roger with the point of his dagger. Roger didn't move.

'Drunk again,' said Ralph, smugly.

'That's it, everybody! Another toast!' William got to his feet. 'To me! William of Holderness! Lord of the Ale!'

There were a few scattered cheers from around

111

the hall from men wearing the sign of the marsh dragon but mainly there was an anxious murmuring. Roger's face, it was plain to everybody, had turned an unhealthy shade of green. Beads of sweat stood out on his brow.

With a jangling of bracelets Melisen shook him by the shoulder. 'Roger? Are you drunk? Wake up! Stop frightening us!' As soon as she touched him his eyes rolled up. Her hands flew to her lips and she let out a horrified shriek, then fell back, right into the arms of her squire.

Hildegard reached over to place her hand on Roger's forehead. It felt like ice.

Ulf was beside her at once. 'What's the matter with him?'

'Too soon to tell. But it's not drink. Get him taken to a private chamber with all speed. Hurry!'

Chapter Four

Ulf threw everybody out except Hildegard then barred the door.

'So?' he said.

She had already opened her scrip and taken a potion from it and was now applying a liquid with a bitter scent to Roger's lips. Ulf watched as next, she ripped aside his shirt of English linen and began to palpate his chest in the region of the heart.

'Is there anything I can do?' He crouched down

112

beside her. 'I feel so helpless.'

Hildegard was flushed by her exertions but did not pause. 'Keep everyone out. This is a terrible thing. Who would want him dead?'

'Dead? You believe someone tried to poison him?'

'I do. Who could it be?'

'You want a list? The long one or the short one?'

'Later then. Let's try to make sure we don't finish up with a corpse on our hands. He's balanced between heaven and hell.'

Somehow, patience and skill were rewarded. First Roger's colour returned. Then his eyelids flickered open. And then he spoke.

'Where the hell am I?'

Clearly relieved, Ulf gave a delighted chuckle. 'Why do they always say that?'

'Just checking, no doubt,' she replied, beginning to smile.

'Do we look like devils?' Ulf asked, spinning round like a jongleur, clearly delighted at his lord's recovery.

'Not devils,' said Roger, his voice a mere wisp of what it usually was, 'angels!' He reached for Hildegard's hand. 'Don't think I don't know what happened. I remember every damned thing.'

'Tell me.' She leaned closer.

'I remember Ralph and that bloody ridiculous hood. And Melisen with her loose bodice. And the Italian signing our agree—' He stopped abruptly and his eyes darted up to see who else was present.

113

'It's only Ulf,' she said. 'You can say what you like in front of him.'

Roger reached for his hand. 'Good old Ulf,' he mumbled, tears in his eyes. 'Best steward I've ever had, you bloody Saxon.' He gripped his steward's hand and tried to kiss it.

'He's keeping everyone out for the present,' said Hildegard briskly. 'But tell me what you remember.'

'I remember lifting my mazer, then being pole-axed. Next, I turn up here–' A strange thought shot into Roger's mind, causing him to jerk up-right. He grabbed hold of Hildegard by the arm and dragged her close, then, breath rank from the herbs, searched her face. 'What in the name of Satan happened? I blacked out, didn't I?'

'Yes.'

'Why would *I* take a tumble? I'm not drunk. I can hold my liquor as well as any man!' He was turning scarlet. 'What happened? Your opinion, Hildegard. Was it a seizure?'

'I suspect not.'

'Of course not! I'm as fit as a flivver. So why did I fall?'

'I really can't be sure at this point.' She didn't want to anger him needlessly. He looked as if he was already being swept by one of his famous rages.

'Come on,' he gripped her arm harder still, 'it can only mean one thing!'

She knew it was useless to try to put him off the scent but she wanted his unbiased view. 'What do you think it means?'

'I think it means there's somebody I can't trust.'

He eyed her narrowly.

'From your symptoms–'

'Say it straight out, Sister.'

'It could have been, yes, something put into your food or drink to make you fall like that.'

'But we all ate from the same dish. Has anybody else passed out?'

'No.'

'Then it must have been something in the wine.'

'You think so?'

He ground his teeth. 'Who in God's name would do a thing like that?'

'Your enemies are best known to yourself.'

Roger reached for Ulf and raised himself into a more commanding position. 'Steward, you know as well as me I'm beset by enemies! Saxons! Danes! Celts! Lombards maybe? Scots for sure! And Frenchmen, popes and anti-popes, clerics and laymen. Even a few Normans, maybe, ones gone to the bad. And now, beyond all reason, one of these has dared to attack my person in this underhand way! Poison!' As soon as the word was out he looked puzzled. 'Poisoned? Me? Who would dare?'

Hildegard shook her head.

Roger fell back, his face ashen. Instead of being enraged he seemed saddened. Sweat trickled into his russet beard. After a moment's reflection he spoke in an ominously calm voice. 'Ulf,' he began, 'if you owe me anything, repay me now.'

'Anything, my lord.'

Roger took hold of his steward by the hand. His voice was hoarse. 'Root out this poisoner. Show no mercy. I want to see his entrails in a pot! I want his head on a pike! I want his beating heart in my hand! Meanwhile,' he added, still softly, 'I shall be taken in a catafalque to the abbey at Meaux. Full mourning shall be observed, the catafalque to be pulled by six black horses.' His eyes narrowed. 'Lulled into false triumph, rotting in his midden of deceit, the poisoner will reveal himself. Let it be done!'

He fell back, exhausted.

Ulf was thrown into a turmoil of planning and he counted the points off on his fingers. His astonishment was audible in his voice. 'You want me to tell them you're dead? Then you want to be carried all the way to Meaux on a catafalque with six black horses?'

'Plumed,' said Roger.

'You'll suffocate and do the poisoner's job for him, plumed horses or not,' objected Ulf. 'In a box? I've never heard anything like it.'

'Dolt. I shan't be *in* the box. I shall be safely borne away to the abbey by other means, there to remain until the plotter can be discovered.'

'I see,' said Ulf, not moving.

Hildegard interrupted. 'If you're really bent on this course of action, Roger, the services of a couple of trusted yeomen might better expedite the matter. And if I may suggest a dray covered in black velvet? A catafalque,' she explained, 'though impressive, would properly have to be open. I think we are best to avoid the catafalque.'

'Dray, catafalque, whatever, this is no time for pedantry, Hildegard.' Even sapped by poison, Roger was tetchy.

She gave him a long look. 'I do see a further

difficulty, my lord.'

'Only one?' Ulf ran both hands through his hair. 'Speak!'

'The matter of Melisen, your wife.'

'What about her?'

'She will wish to view your–'

'Some contagion can be the supposed cause of death,' Roger told her. 'Hence the need to keep the body first in a sealed room then in its sealed coffin. Nobody will want to touch and breathe the pestilential air of a dead man, least of all her.' Suffused with a strange energy, he was clearly ahead of them both in terms of plotting.

'She may wish to kiss you in farewell,' Ulf suggested.

'Then you prevent it. What do I pay you for?'

Ulf said, 'And about this empty coffin.'

'Fill it with stones, man, what else?'

'A moment!' Hildegard stepped back. Roger, suddenly whiter than wax, threw up all over his own hose. 'That improves things,' she said when he'd finished. 'Better to expel these matters. But there will be more. I think the idea of riding alone to Meaux a bad idea. I suggest another way be found of conveying you there.'

Roger wiped his beard with both hands then wiped his hands on his capuchon.

'I'll get my two trusties to take him out in a logging cart,' said Ulf. 'Have him ready as soon as you can.' Eyes alight, he was already at the door. 'There's a host of things to do! And,' he added, 'lies to be told and later untold. By St George,' he continued, 'this is the sort of action I thrive on! Come on, Hildegard, pinch that candle out so nobody can see him. My lord, hold your retching for a trice and lie dead. I shall fling wide the door to announce your demise. Now we'll see who your real friends are!'

So saying, and waiting only for Hildegard to snuff out all but one long tallow, Ulf unlocked the door. Then he stepped through into the Great Hall and a deep silence fell as he began to speak. Lord Roger lay as still as the corpse he had so nearly been.

'Only the poisoner will know we're lying about my having the pestilence,' said Roger in between spasms of retching and violent shuddering when the door was safely closed again. 'Who can guess what the terror of imminent discovery will make him do?'

'He'll lie low for a while, I should think,' replied Hildegard. She had mopped up most of the contents of Roger's stomach with a cloth and a pail of water that was thrust into the room by one of the lowest-ranking serfs, for even they had a hierarchy which they fiercely maintained. The ruse of putting it about that the Black Death had invaded the castle ensured that no one would enter the chamber.

When Ulf returned two menservants were carrying a coffin, which must have had a prospective occupant standing by or one rudely thrust out. It was decided to smuggle Roger inside it into the chapel. Once there he could escape unobserved through the vestry door to a waiting cart in the lane outside. The timber trade between Hutton Ambo and Meaux was thriving; nobody would look twice as the cart rolled by.

Protesting somewhat, due to a fear of suffocation, Roger was coaxed into the coffin and had the lid closed over him. The two brawny servants Ulf had chosen for the job hoisted it with some difficulty on to their shoulders and staggered towards the door. Let into the secret that their lord was still alive, they kept their smiles off their faces and carried their burden out into the hall towards the bailey, with a show of solemnity that had everybody fooled. The guests fell to their knees and crossed themselves as they passed. With Ulf leading the way and Hildegard taking up the rear, they made slow but steady progress towards the chapel. Once inside, with the doors firmly shut, the two bearers lowered the coffin and Ulf lifted the lid.

Lying in fresh vomit, Roger emerged with as much alacrity as he could muster. Half crawling, dry retches shuddering through him, he made his way towards the vestry door. As soon as they had him safely hidden in a nest between the timbers on the logging cart, the men climbed up behind the horses, gave Ulf the thumb to show they were ready and began to roll away on the track to Meaux. It was almost morning now, and mist, behind which anything might be concealed, lay in gleaming folds across the dale and the moonlight threw shadows between the trees as if phantoms walked abroad. But no mere phantom was as frightening as a poisoner on the loose.

Seeing his liege lord safely into the dawn, Ulf returned with Hildegard to where the guests still lingered in little groups. 'One of these,' he muttered to her through clenched teeth as he cast his glance over them, 'one of these. But which one?'

'It's mad, Ulf. How long does he expect to keep it up?'

The steward shrugged. 'I don't ask questions. I do as I'm ordered. That's how I keep my job. And my neck,' he added as an afterthought.

Hildegard accompanied him when he went to rouse Roger's chaplain from his bed and inform him of the night's events. He ordered him to say a requiem mass straight away. As the dazed cleric scurried to make the announcement, Ulf said, 'The advantage of herding them briskly together gives us the chance to get a look at the face of the devil who did this. He'll be discomposed even yet. There'll surely be some telltale sign of guilt to mark him out if he's human.'

Hildegard nodded in agreement but was secretly doubtful. Anyone tricky enough to poison Roger could surely dissemble in other ways. She did not expect to see signs of guilt on the face of the man who had attacked her either, although a black eye might be proof of his identity.

Standing beside Ulf in the arched doorway of the chapel, she watched carefully as the mourners filed inside.

What Melisen might call the *poraille* came first, crossing themselves and weeping copiously out of innate dread of the hereafter. Then came the personal servants, sobbing quietly; next, the guests, elegantly grief stricken, and finally, with the composure befitting their status, came the family.

Roger's wife was the only one missing.

'She's lying down but will be along shortly,' whispered Ulf when Hildegard remarked on Melisen's absence.

The place filled up until there was standing room only. The coffin, loaded with pieces of limestone and two chunks of damaged Purbeck marble Ulf had somehow got hold of from the new building works at Beverley, was placed on a trestle in front of the altar where it received many sad-eyed glances. It was covered by a black silk stole embroidered with the de Hutton arms in gold thread. No pile of stones had ever been more grandly returned to its maker. An avenue of tall candles cast a flickering light over church treasures: jewel-encrusted rood, censer, chalice, urceole, pyx, pax and monstrance. Adding lustre to the shimmering splendour was a melange of gold, gilt, ebony and bronze ornament. Roger de Hutton was being buried in style. Hildegard was amazed at the extravagance after her years of austerity in the hermitage.

The only thing lacking, she judged, was a choir. The family had not been so pious as to run to such display, but the whispering from the highest to the lowest gathered there speculating on the reasons for the sudden demise of their lord almost amounted to a chorus. His death had plainly thrown the inhabitants of Castle Hutton into confusion. Some knelt, stunned into prayer, others whispered fearfully to their neighbours and looked for signs of the plague. The communal grief was expressed by the one Beverley chorister still standing after a night of drinking and singing with Roger's minstrels. Heroically ignoring any suggestion of hangover, the purity of his voice was enough to set tears in the eyes of everyone who listened.

'I feel close to tears myself,' Hildegard whispered to Ulf.

'Roger should have stayed half an hour to see all this. He'd have been mighty pleased.'

'Except for the fact that his murderer is one of these doleful mourners,' she reminded him. The back of the nave was filled by men-at-arms. Their weapons lay in a heap in the porch. There was no sign of anyone with a freshly blacked eye.

The priest, a quiet fellow who usually kept himself to himself, was unable to resist the lure of power when he had his church bursting at its seams, and no doubt he considered a little penitential praying would do the assembled some good.

After an hour, when he still showed no signs of desisting, Hildegard whispered to Ulf that she had an idea she wanted to follow up. Before she could leave, however, Melisen made an appearance. Accompanied by half a dozen maids and her squire in a smart tunic of black velvet, she was attired from top to toe in a mourning veil so fine that the paleness of her skin and the beauty of her haunted glance seemed to be artlessly accentuated. To most of those here, thought Hildegard, she must be a figure to soften a heart hewn from the same Purbeck marble that now fills the coffin. In one hand she clutched a beribboned kerchief with which she dabbed her cheeks beneath the veil and in the other she gripped a cross studded with pearls.

Hildegard watched as the young widow made her way down the nave towards the bier. The congregation fell back respectfully, making an avenue through which, eventually, sobbing and halting, she reached the rail in front of the altar. Pulling two maids down with her, she crumpled to the floor in a cloud of black silk.

She certainly knows we're all watching, thought Hildegard. The widow crossed herself, then, with a few sobs, allowed her maids to help her to her feet. But then she turned, and with a loud cry staggered over to the coffin and flung herself across it with a sob that must have wrung every heart in the place.

Well, well, said Hildegard under her breath as she slipped outside. In the porch she hesitated, trying to remind herself that compassion was a virtue. But another voice told her that stupidity was not.

She set off towards the Great Hall. It would be empty now, she was thinking. Most people were still inside the chapel. Could Roger have as many enemies as he suggested? Their grief seemed genuine. A look at the scene where he was poisoned might help narrow down the search for the culprit. There might be clues to be found.

Before she could get halfway across the yard, a rabble of five or six men-at-arms, wearing Sir Ralph's silver-and-green blazon, came roaring round the corner from the direction of the stables. They were in high spirits, massacring some song from the previous night. At the same moment, one of the congregation chanced to come out of the church. She had noticed him a few moments ago, standing in the side chapel with a companion, both men cowled like friars, muttering prayers.

Now, she saw him stop in his tracks. With his face still covered as if the air was too much for him, he uttered a sharp comment about showing respect for the dead. The gang, drunk as a sack of frogs, decided that an unarmed friar was easy prey so they surrounded him, loudly demanding by what right a thieving mendicant could lecture them on how to behave. They were free men one and all, they said. There were cheers.

Undismayed, the friar replied in a direct manner. He said, 'By what right?' He seemed astonished. 'Why, by the right of my right fist of course!' He jabbed the ringleader so soundly in the face that he fell back, scattering his companions like skittles. The friar folded his fist back into his sleeve and sauntered away across the yard.

His companion had just come out of church in time to see this rout and he gave a chuckle of satisfaction. Ignoring the men, who were picking themselves up from the ground and grumbling about their muddied cottes, he came over to Hildegard and said, 'Sister, I have a puzzle. Can you tell me who my host is now Lord Roger is dead?'

'The lord steward, I imagine.'

'But after that?'

'Some think Sir Edwin is the rightful heir.'

'But he is banished?'

'So I'm told.'

'And how might his claim be viewed by the generality?'

'As just, I would imagine.'

Thanking her, he walked off with a noticeable military swagger.

At a slower pace and deep in thought, Hildegard followed.

The doors to the Great Hall groaned as she pushed them open. Inside, a scene of devastation greeted her: straw soaked with the night's beer and piss, tankards upended, half-chewed bones thrown down, lost garments draped at random, dogs jumping up on the tables to finish what their masters had started, and a few blear-eyed drunks still lying about in various states of consciousness.

The kitchen staff, however, looked daisy fresh and were sitting around the table in front of the fire-screen, working their way through the leftovers, and speculating about their future employment. When they noticed Hildegard, they sprang to their feet and pretended to be busy.

'Be at rest after last night's labours,' she said. 'I'm not here to chivvy you.'

'Can I get you anything, Sister?' asked one who took it upon himself to take charge.

'A small beer would be pleasant,' she replied. She sat down close to where Roger and the family had been sitting earlier. Nothing had been cleared away and trenchers and earthen platters lay scattered where they'd been dropped in the confusion of Roger's fall. His two-handled mazer, intricately wrought, and for that reason unmistakable, lay on its side, the contents drained. Her glance sharpened.

A greenish stain surrounded the vessel. Over the intervening hours it had dried into the cloth covering the table. She looked at it more closely. Surely the wine they had been drinking would have stained the cloth red?

Further down the board the two friars, their features in shadow beneath their hoods, were sedulously tearing strips off a jugged hare and murmuring secretively to each other. Some of the servants were beginning to clear up around them but they took no notice. For the moment no one was looking in her direction. With nostrils dilating, she bent her head to the cloth and sniffed it. There was a faint and lingering scent, barely discernible. Not quite trusting her senses, she sniffed again. Was she imagining it?

Her beer was brought. For a moment she eyed it with misgivings before telling herself she was a fool. She drank thoughtfully. Her instinct to give Roger an antidote, made up of poor man's weather glass and various other cures she always carried in her scrip, had been fortunate. His symptoms clearly suggested poison: the abruptness of the attack, his frightful colour, the vomit. It was lucky he had expelled it before it was able to do its work. But how could anyone have poisoned him with so many people watching?

Belladonna, she surmised. Something like that could have been mixed with his wine. She thought of Melisen and recalled her dilated pupils. Certainly she was close enough to Roger's mazer to be able to slip something into it. And yet everyone had their eyes on her all night.

She recalled how meticulously Melisen had insisted on having the wastel bread assayed during the feast. Why would she make such a fuss about that? Was it to deflect suspicion from the wine? All the dishes brought to the board were tested by the clerk in the kitchens. It was true that traditionally the wastel was tested with a certain amount of ceremony and Melisen was a stickler for having things done properly, so Roger claimed, and it would have been nigh on impossible to poison the food without bringing down the whole household. Ergo: it had to be the wine. But how? Surely that would have been just as difficult? It had been poured from a common pitcher. She remembered how Melisen had even raised the two-handled mazer to Roger's lips herself. Then she drank from the same place.

'Drink to me,' she had said, 'and I will drink to thee.'

Roger's thirst had seemed insatiable. Was the sharing of the goblet deliberately intended to deceive? But how could she possibly have poisoned the goblet with all eyes upon her? Perhaps more puzzling still, what on earth could Melisen gain from Roger's death?

Chapter Five

Hildegard couldn't sleep. Her bruises ached whichever way she arranged herself on the horsehair mattress. It wasn't only discomfort which kept her awake. It was the thump of drumming from outside the castle walls. In theory this was the big autumn festival in honour of St Martin, but in reality the villagers were paying homage to their own St Willibrod, the Saxon saint, a celebration in defiance of their Norman masters. The feast also coincided with Samhain, a far more ancient cult, and, truth to say, poor St Martin scarcely got a look in.

Now the tenants were preparing to slaughter all the surplus animals so that, instead of teetering on the brink of starvation through the winter, they would have salted meat to see them through the cold, dark months. The shriek of pigs having their throats slit was audible above the raucous sound of horns and whistles, and along with the noise came the non-stop chanting of the men in their drinking bouts. It was hardly safe to walk abroad at this time of year. To make it worse the Lammas lands, she knew from experience, would be covered in smoke from a multitude of open fires. There would be races involving dangerous-looking tar barrels spouting flames, which had to be carried unlikely distances by the reeling contestants, and all in all, it would be mayhem. Now was just the beginning.

By contrast, inside the castle, silence lay like a pall. With everybody up most of the night and with the further excuse that it was supposed to be a time of rest from daily labour, those who could had taken the opportunity to stay in their beds. Unable to sleep, however, Hildegard eventually got up, threw on a cloak and made her way along the empty corridors with the idea that Ulf might still be about. She badly wanted to ask him more about the enemies Roger thought he had. She couldn't believe they had both gone along with his ruse to make everybody think he was dead. As a plan for drawing out the poisoner it had failed miserably. They were no nearer finding out who had tried to poison him than at the moment he fell. In the meantime, the poisoner was free to try again, maybe with someone else for all they knew.

In a niche below the kitchen stair she found Burthred curled up under a threadbare cloak with the two hounds beside him. About to wake him, she thought better of it. He looked as if he needed a rest, poor mite. There were dark circles under his eyes and one skinny wrist lay protectively over the hounds' backs. She smiled softly, gave Duchess and Bermonda a pat when they looked at her with expectant eyes, and went on into the hall where the offices for the castle officials were to be found.

Ulf's door was open and, as she had guessed, he was still up. He smiled when she appeared and pushed some papers to one side. 'Can't you sleep? Nor can I.'

'I'm exhausted after that ride yesterday, then being up all night and–' She broke off. She couldn't tell him she had found it painful lying in her bed just now, covered in bruises. There were more important things to discuss.

'That blessed drumming,' he said, unaware of her thoughts. 'It's keeping me awake as well. Still, it's only for a night or two. They need to let off steam now and then, poor devils.'

'These enemies of Roger's,' she began, 'are there as many as he seems to think?'

'My fire's gone out.' Ulf gestured towards the ash in the grate. 'Let's turf the chamberlain out of his little den and sit in there so we can talk. He's always got a blaze going.' He led the way to the chamber next to his own. On the way he whispered, 'He's what you healer women call melancholic. Hardly ever leaves his rooms. It'll do him good to take a brisk turn round the bailey.'

They found the chamberlain in a stifling hot chamber surrounded by towers of castle parchments. They gave off a smell of tanned leather. He was meek when Ulf told him to go for a walk.

'There's no point in sitting uselessly here in the warmth when I can be out and about. The cold will probably do my rheumatics some good.' His voice was barely audible. 'You know what's best, steward, as always.' The chamberlain's pale face made him look ill. 'Your need is obviously greater than mine. I expect you have really important matters to discuss with the sister. Things I know nothing about. What do I know?' He turned to Hildegard. 'I can't imagine why Lord Roger puts up with me.'

'Well, he won't have to now, so you needn't worry about that.' Hildegard was brisk. She hadn't time to dole out false sympathy.

The chamberlain dragged on a lush fur that fell to his ankles and, putting on a brave face, went out.

Ulf was chuckling. 'That'll blow a few cobwebs away,' he said as he gestured towards a comfortable-looking chair by the fire then sat on a bench opposite. Throwing an extra log on the fire until it roared up the back of the chimney, he frowned into the flames. 'Enemies,' he murmured. 'It's as good an approach as any: name them then whittle them down, one by one, until he falls into our hands like a rotten apple from a tree.'

'He?' Hildegard interrupted.

Ulf's head jerked up. 'Who have you got in mind?'

'No one in particular. I simply think we shouldn't limit our search at this stage.'

'I thought you meant Melisen for a minute.' Ulf seemed to find it difficult to go on, but then he said in an undertone, 'I don't meant to be disloyal to Roger but he can be his own worst enemy. I mean, how would you feel if your husband kept joking that you'd be out on your ear if you didn't produce an heir?'

'You think she might have tried to ensure her future by acting first?'

'Well, as the chamberlain just said, "What do we know?"' Ulf shrugged.

'Would Melisen automatically inherit Roger's fortune if he died?'

'Unless he's secretly made some other provision, yes, I think she would have a good case.'

'Motive enough, then?'

Ulf frowned. 'It seems scarcely credible. She's just a silly young girl. And I believe she does care for Roger in her way.'

'She certainly flirts with him. But it's not the same thing as love.'

Ulf reached for a flagon of the chamberlain's wine and poured them both a beakerful. Hildegard looked at him over the rim. 'There's the problem of opportunity,' she said. 'His eyes never left her all night. How could she have put anything in his mazer?'

Just then there was a knock on the door and a servant poked his head round. 'My lord, the guest-master would like a word.' Ulf nodded and rose to his feet. 'Let me deal with this while you sit here, Hildegard, and keep warm. I'll be back in a trice.'

He had no sooner gone than there was another knock. This time it was Sir William. He looked surprised to see the nun sitting in the chamberlain's chair.

'So what's going on?' he demanded.

'What do you think's going on?' she riposted.

'How the devil would I know? You're the one who listens to everybody's secrets. All I know is Roger's dead. Did I bring the Black Death in? No, but I would say that, wouldn't I? So who the devil brought it in? Nobody else's dead, are they?'

'Not that I know of.'

'So why isn't the chamberlain sitting in his chair?'

'He's gone for a walk.'

Sir William snorted. 'If I were Roger I'd've sacked him long ago.'

'If you were Roger you'd be lying in a coffin in the chapel,' Hildegard reminded him, quickly fingering her beads.

'Quite right, sister,' said Sir William. 'Forgive me.' He did not look contrite. Flinging himself on to the bench on the other side of the fire, he stretched out his long legs and gave her a baleful look. 'Go on, then, question me.'

'I really have no intention of questioning you. I'm sure you're not in the mood for questions so soon after your brother-in-law's–' Hildegard coughed, to avoid another lie but her mind was beginning to race.

Why had William come inside when he saw that the chamberlain wasn't here? Did it mean he had something to tell her? He was looking surprisingly sober after last night's roistering, but now he was glaring into the fire as if there was something serious on his mind. She stretched out her own legs in their leather buskins to re-establish a little space.

'Is there anything you would like to tell me?' Hildegard asked in a soft tone when he didn't speak. She waited the normal length of the confessional pause but William seemed to have lost the use of his tongue. His lips worked but no words came forth. He looked so murderous she had to brace herself to speak again.

'I'm aware of your closeness to your brother-in-law,' she prompted gently.

Still nothing.

She eyed the jug of wine.

Before she could offer him a drink to loosen his tongue he suddenly jumped to his feet and strode from the chamber. Ulf was just coming in.

He watched him go. 'What the devil did you say to him?'

'Nothing.'

'He's flying along the corridor as if the bats of hell are after 'im.'

'I can't imagine William being afraid of bats.' Hildegard looked thoughtful. 'I wonder if he

133

knows I'm not supposed to take confession?'

'Aren't you?'

'I have a feeling that's what he was building up to until his courage failed him. What on earth could be on his mind?'

They both looked at each other in silence.

Ulf spoke first. 'It would never do him any good. There's no legal way he could get his hands on Roger's lands.' He shook his head.

'Not even through Avice? She is Roger's sister, after all.'

She gave a start. 'What about Edwin? He must be the legal heir. I mean, he would be if Roger really were dead.'

'But he's banished. So it's up for grabs.'

'I can't believe Roger would banish his own son.'

'Nor can we. But there it is. Roger's word is law.'

'When he knows his father's dead – should the deception continue – surely he'll come back to claim what's legally his?'

'Ah, but possession is nine-tenths of the law. He'd realise he'd have to bring an army and take it back by force.'

She gave a sigh. 'This is speculation, isn't it? We can count Edwin out as he wasn't here. We can count William out because, although he had the opportunity to tamper with Roger's drink, he doesn't stand to gain anything. And we can count Melisen out because, although she could gain, she couldn't possibly have had the opportunity. So where does that leave us?'

'Having another beaker of the chamberlain's

wine,' Ulf said, upending the flagon. 'I wouldn't count any of them out just yet. Certainly not William. That was the exit of a guilty man just now – or I'm sitting in Avignon with a crown on my head calling myself pope.' He gave a hollow laugh.

'And then there's–' began Hildegard, but there was a knock at the door.

Ulf scowled. 'For God's sake, it's like Beverley market in here. How does the chamberlain ever get any work done? No wonder he's so miserable.' He called, 'Come in, then.'

When the door opened Master Sueno de Schockwynde was standing there. He looked most apologetic. 'I heard the sister was here, steward, and actually I'd rather like a private word with her.' He fiddled unhappily with the end of his liripipe.

'Be my guest.' Ulf gestured him inside and, with a covert glance at Hildegard, took himself out.

Master Sueno was a bundle of nerves and quite unlike his urbane self of the previous evening.

'Please, master, do take a seat,' she invited. 'A cup of wine for you?'

He shook his head. 'I don't know where to begin.' He wouldn't look at her and once on the bench he stood up again and paced about the room in a fret. 'It's this,' he began at last, but haltingly, his back turned, as if what he had to confess were so shameful he couldn't be viewed while he said it. 'I was invited to Castle Hutton...' He paused again. 'Oh well, I may as well be blunt. I was invited here to discuss an unlicensed crenellation.'

He went to perch on the edge of the bench. 'To be honest,' he blurted, 'I thought we'd get away with it. But some swine reported us. Now we've got the king's men on our backs. I came to see Lord Roger in order to discuss our strategy. It looks well.' He brightened. 'Quite the best crenellation I've done. A pattern for many years to come. But will the king's council see it that way?' He sat back in a gloom. 'They're barbarians to a man, and most have never stepped foot in a viable building in their lives.'

'Westminster men, are they?'

'All right, I give you Westminster.' He snorted. 'I've seen the plans. But what is all that timber about? Sixty-seven feet of it! With hammer beams! Please! God forfend they ever build it. Our little crenellated manor, on the other hand, is a gem of contemporary design in local York stone. It lies in a sequestered position, perfectly adapted to the vernacular. Yet they object! Just what is their objection based on, exactly?'

'Roger's death is most inopportune, then?'

'It'll be the ruination of me if we're hauled before the powers. Who's going to trust me again? I'm a dead man.'

'Metaphorically speaking. As compared to Roger.'

'Yes, yes,' he replied irritably, but then, realising his gaffe, corrected himself. 'Don't imagine I'm not upset about him. He was as uninformed as most people about the art and science of building but he knew his limitations and left me with a free rein. He was a joy to work for. Now what am I to do?'

'Perhaps in the circumstances the king's men will wait until a new owner is able to discuss matters?'

Master Sueno perked up at once. 'I hadn't thought of that. If there's nobody for them to talk to they won't be able to talk. If they can't talk then the building stands.'

'For the time being.'

'That's enough for me. We're so far off the beaten track they'll probably forget we're here at all.'

'I'm sure someone could persuade them to forget.'

He began to beam. 'Sister, you understand the ways of the world so well. You've been most supportive.' He got up. 'I shall come down to Meaux with the cortège and then make my way to Swyne. You may be sure I shall satisfy my obligations to your prioress most generously.'

'She will no doubt receive you with her customary warmth.'

With a little bow he left.

'Well, well!' Hildegard exclaimed when Ulf immediately poked his head round the door. 'Did you hear all that?'

'Obviously.' He chuckled. 'Builders! Masons! What a bunch! Gold solves everything!'

She frowned. 'Back to business. We haven't mentioned Ralph in all this. Surely with Edwin out of the way he has the best claim of anybody?'

'Yes, but you're forgetting one thing. Roger has just made Ralph's son his heir, so why go to the trouble of poisoning him and suffering an eternity of hellfire?'

137

'So Ralph and Sibilla will be guardians until their son comes of age?' Hildegard gave him a look. 'I think I'll go and see them.' She got up.

'They're all emerging from their cots with hangovers. I'll talk to you later. Do you know the way to Sibilla's apartment?' he asked.

Biting her lip, Hildegard nodded. 'I'll find it.' And get over my fear of coming face to face with that fiend from the undercroft, she told herself. As she went out she said, 'Tell your cook to make a syrup with the juice of a red cabbage. Two spoons of that should cure their heads!'

Hildegard had much to preoccupy her as she made her way out into the now busy yard. Yawning and pale faced, the survivors of the previous night's revelries were beginning to emerge. The doors of the Great Hall stood open but she ventured only as far as the entrance, where there was a stairway leading to the upper floors. Coming down the stairs was Philippa. Her eyes were red, her cheeks pale, and she was dressed in unbroken black. Grief for her father had clearly brought her low. Hildegard felt a pang of guilt. Did Roger realise how cruel his trick was on those who loved him? She felt an urge to tell her the truth. She waited until she drew level. To her surprise the girl gripped her by the hand as soon as she came close enough. 'Please, Sister, a word in private.'

'By all means.' Hildegard followed her into a small antechamber off the stairwell.

The girl took a deep breath. 'I'm told the Lombards have already left. Were they not asked to stay for the funeral?'

'I heard they had a meeting at Rievaulx but intend to ride on afterwards to Meaux.'

'Why was I not told they had left?' she exclaimed.

'I understand you were in church and they were forced to leave at once in order to catch the abbot before he went out on a visitation.'

Philippa dabbed her eyes. 'This is a legal question, Sister.'

'I'm really not—'

'Oh, I know you're not a clerk or anything but you have so much more experience than I have and it occurred to me that with my poor father dead there's no one to hold me to a betrothal. After all, it was his idea, not mine. That's right, isn't it?' She seemed to fight the tears back as she waited for Hildegard to reply.

The answer was obvious but clearly needed saying. 'The betrothed might consider holding you to it perhaps?'

Philippa's reply was swift and unequivocal. 'He'll do as he's told. He was simply bullied by father into saying yes. He doesn't give a damn about marriage. He'd rather be off fighting somewhere and picking up a wench as the fancy takes him.'

'So that leaves you free, you believe?'

'I most fervently hope so.'

'And?'

'And it's not fair. Ever since I was twelve Father's paraded a string of suitors in front of me, but they were all such a miserable bunch I'd have been better off in a nunnery than marrying any of them. Recently, though, he began to insist.

139

The usual raging. "My patience is at an end!" And there was this one fellow he preferred and there seemed no way out but then, quite un- expectedly–' Biting her lip, she broke off. 'It was dreadful. He would not listen to reason. Oh, I know you all think he's a good fellow, but he's not your father! He can be totally unreasonable. And he starts to shout. And that makes me shout. And then we both say things we regret. Things get thrown. And now, after all that, he's … he's…' Her face crumpled and with a wild look she wailed, 'I don't know what to do next, sister! I'm at my wits' end!'

'You were saying: "but then, quite unex- pectedly". Do you mean something happened?' asked Hildegard in a soothing tone.

Philippa nodded. 'It made me change my mind about the idea of marriage. Though not,' she added fiercely, 'about the specimen Father lined up for me.'

'Are you suggesting there's someone you prefer?'

Philippa was young enough to blush at the thought. 'He really is special, sister. Not like any of the louts you find round here. He's a man of real style, well travelled, a scholar, but witty too and a brilliant swordsman and quite the most handsome man I've ever set eyes–'

'Sometimes,' Hildegard broke into this eulogy, 'it's usual for a young woman to seek a period of contemplation before embarking on the duties of married life. Especially in the present unfortun- ate circumstances. I understand,' she continued artlessly, 'that the Abbey of Jervaulx is a perfect place for just such a retreat.'

Philippa was very quick. 'Jervaulx?' she countered, blinking away her tears. 'But what about Fountains or Rievaulx?'

'You mean the abbeys the Lombards are visiting?'

She was unable to stop herself from blushing.

Hildegard weighed up several words that would inhibit Philippa's headlong escape from her father until the exaggeration of his death could be revealed. 'I feel,' she said, 'it might be considered rather undignified to appear to be in pursuit of a man, no matter how desirable he is.'

For a moment the girl was thoughtful. She fiddled with a ring on her right hand. It had a little jewelled boss she could open and close. 'I suppose you're right,' she said at last, snapping the ring shut. 'Jervaulx, then. It involves a special journey, being quite hidden in the wilds. That will prove something about the intentions of anyone who chooses to visit, I should think.' Then she smiled. 'And of course, they're expected at Meaux, so maybe I won't need to go on retreat at all!'

She turned to go, but not before bursting into tears again as if abruptly remembering she was supposed to be grieving. 'Oh, my poor dear father,' she wailed. 'Why was he always so unfair?'

That gives us almost all the family, Hildegard murmured to herself as she continued up to Sibilla's apartment: Melisen, William and Avice, and now Philippa. If anybody had a solid reason for wanting Roger out of the way, it was her. But

141

the idea was inconceivable.

As for the others, there were obstacles there too. William, for instance. Although he must be furious at Ralph's baby being preferred above his own sons his prospects wouldn't be changed by getting rid of Roger, as Ulf had pointed out. There were too many other claimants to the de Hutton title and lands. Besides, to poison somebody needed planning. Roger hadn't announced his intention to name Ralph's son until shortly before he drank the poison. Even Melisen had looked stunned by the news. That seems to put William out of the running. It was an act that had required forethought.

Well, at least Ralph was off the list of suspects owing to his good fortune in having sired the heir. She could easily envisage him patiently playing the role of regent. It was what he had always done, played second fiddle to his elder brother. But Sibilla? She didn't know the woman at all.

As Hildegard made her way towards the sound of a crying baby she considered others who had been present the previous night. There were the visitors, Ludovico and his men, plus Master Schockwynde, of course. Not much change from a penny there. Who else? There was a throng of guests below the salt, burgesses from York as well as Beverley, some wool dealers and their wives, and she had a vague memory of the two friars way down at the far end. Then there were the servants. In and out. Now here, now there. All the yeomen of the board, present in abundance, had had open access to the top table, where Roger sat with his family.

Lady Sibilla was looking remarkably crisp in a lace nightgown. Her hair with its white blaze was swept back, making her look rather regal. The baby had fallen asleep in her arms. She smiled warmly when she saw Hildegard come in. 'I've just got him off,' she warned. Closing the door quietly, the nun tiptoed over to have a look. The baby's small face was framed in a bonnet of fresh cotton and lace. His eyelids were like tiny rose petals.

Ulf had told her with a grin that he took after Ralph in looks. 'A chip off the old block,' he said. But she was not so sure. She watched Sibilla tease a little sigh from him with her long, white fingers and, noticing the high neck of Sibilla's gown, she asked, 'Aren't you nursing him yourself?'

'Certainly not! I've got a wet-nurse. She should be here any minute.'

They regarded the baby in silence. He lay there sleeping peacefully and Hildegard wondered how he would turn out when he was fully grown. She asked about the name.

Sibilla frowned and dabbed her eyes with a corner of the baby's gown. Her rings flashed. She wore many more than the one garnet Hildegard had noticed during her labour. But there it was, as dark as blood on her finger. 'We had,' she said with a sigh, 'intended to ask Roger if we might name him after him. But now, oh, what now? Poor, poor Roger. Why did it happen now of all times? And how? He seemed so fit. He was such a *man*.'

'I'm sure Roger will be proud to give his name,' said Hildegard, momentarily careless with her tenses.

Sibilla, unnoticing, brightened. 'If you think so then I suppose it would be all right to make the announcement? We are not too precipitate?'

'What does Sir Ralph think?'

'Ralph will follow me.'

Sibilla seemed confident of that, Hildegard thought. It was no surprise. Ralph had the air of a man for whom decisions were what other people made. Head in the clouds, just as in the old days. And yet he was astute in many ways, no ignoramus, whatever he might pretend to the contrary, and, she recalled, even at the age of ten he had been outstanding chess player. There was a board over on a table by the casement with a few pieces set out, offering an intriguing challenge to the white queen.

Hildegard said, 'I'm so glad we've met at last, Sibilla. I knew Sir Ralph when he was a boy. Of course, he's ten years younger than me.' Than us, she thought, thinking of Hugh.

'So he told me. He said you were a sharp one.'

'He did?'

Sibilla laughed. 'He said, "Nothing gets past Hildegard." I admire you, not remarrying. I suppose you're free to do pretty well as you like nowadays?'

'Except for the Rule,' Hildegard reminded her.

Ralph entered. He was carrying a cat.

'Do you want to say hello to Master Jacques?' he asked.

'Oh, you found him. Clever you!' cried Sibilla. 'Where was he?'

'Up the new chimney. He's still puzzled by them.' Ralph stroked the cat sensuously from head to tail, and Hildegard realised that what she had taken to be a fur tippet was Master Jacques the cat. 'Sweet creature.' He kissed him on the nose. Then he glanced up. 'Hildegard, it was good of you to look in on Sibilla last night. The midwife told me how you went up to help. How are you these days?'

'She's a nun, Ralph,' said Sibilla.

'I suppose you're using your Latin all the time now, are you?'

'Some of the time.'

'Getting a bit rusty myself.' Ralph kissed the cat again. *'Gatto angeli est.* Or is it *angelo?* Is it even *gatto?'*

'I'm sure Hildegard doesn't want to talk Latin to you, sweeting,' said Sibilla. 'Would you if you were visiting someone?'

'It would depend why I was visiting them. Why are you here?' he asked. Sibilla and Ralph both turned to look at her.

Hildegard felt a sudden tension in the air.

'Why are any of us here?' she replied.

'I suppose your answer is: to do God's will,' said Ralph.

'Indeed. I'm also here to ask Roger if he can help me out with a spare grange or out-of-the-way manor house if there's one going begging.'

'You are?'

Hildegard didn't elaborate on the Vision, merely saying, 'I thought I might use Hugh's money to set up a house of my own with a few like-minded women.' It seemed an age since she'd been able to give her purpose for coming to Hutton any thought at all.

'Shrewd idea!' said Ralph. He turned to his wife. 'I told you she was a sharp one.'

'Better than remarrying and letting your fortune fall into the hands of some penniless knight.' Sibilla sounded waspish, but her glance trailed past Ralph.

They discussed Hildegard's project for a while, Sibilla now and then cooing over the baby, Ralph stroking the cat, but neither with anything practical to suggest. The conversation soon petered out.

Hildegard got up to go when the wet-nurse arrived. Ralph's an odd one, she thought as she left. He paid more attention to his cat than to his own flesh and blood. And *'gatto'*? It wasn't Latin at all. How did it come about that he was picking up dialect from the Lombards?

Still pondering, she came across Ulf, in his mourning apparel of black velvet, although he still wore his wide belt hung with keys to all the locks in the castle. He teasingly put his stick of office across the door when she tried to enter the Great Hall. 'Satisfied yourself it's not Ralph?' he asked.

'I suppose so. He and Sibilla seem very settled. I left when the wet-nurse arrived. Who is she, do you know?'

'Somebody they brought with them,' he said. 'Haven't seen her.' Then his eyes gleamed. 'You're homing in on someone, I can tell from your face.'

'That's nonsense and you know it.' Then she met his glance. 'There's only one person so far who seems to gain anything by Roger's death but you won't want to hear it.'

'Try me.'

She gave him a level stare. 'Philippa.'

He gave an exclamation of disbelief. 'Philippa? Are you mad?'

'I knew you'd protest. But with her father out of the way, she can marry Ludovico.'

'I don't know what's come over you.' He stared down at her for an age, shaking his head and muttering, 'Philippa? Of all people!' Then, ''Struth, Hildegard, tighten the reins, do.'

They went in to break their fast. Considering the events of the previous night, the place was surprisingly busy. There was a buzz of conversation that lessened momentarily as Ulf proceeded between the trestles, but resumed with equal fervour when he was out of earshot.

'They're making a meal of all this. Looking at each other for signs of the plague. I'm surprised they've come down to mingle.'

The kitchen staff hurried in and out with pies and ingeniously reconstituted leftovers and Hildegard picked at something set down in front of her with a thoughtful expression. 'I've had another idea,' she said, gazing after the servant who had just placed an enormous platter of something not immediately identifiable in front of Roger's empty space.

'Your yeomen of the board. Have you realised they're the only ones who could have poisoned Roger without anybody looking twice?'

'Come on, not my lads,' Ulf scoffed.

'None of them bear a grudge?'

147

He shook his head. 'Happy as crows.'

She shivered at his choice of words, recalling the cloud of carrion feasting on the entrails of the hanged men in the woods near Meaux. But when she glanced up Ulf was frowning too.

'What is it?'

'Nothing.' He pulled at his beard.

'Tell me.'

'It's just the revolt last year. It unsettled them.'

'I would have thought what happened to Wat Tyler and John Ball would have settled them right back again.'

'Even so.'

'Are you trying to tell me they're disloyal to Roger?' Hildegard asked in an undertone.

Ulf didn't reply.

'The way people are feeling, what with the disappearances and the repression of any preachings the archbishops don't like, it's not going to take much to stir things into outright revolt again. All they want is a sign.' She kept her voice low. How much did Ulf know? she wondered, watching him.

His eyes narrowed. 'I'm aware of the unrest. But Lord Roger treats his bondmen fairly. We've never had trouble up here in the shire. It was down south, with the Essex men, Kentish freemen, Londoners.'

'So why are you worried?'

He stabbed at the remains of the pie in front of him. 'The village does have a kind of unofficial moot.'

'What sort of moot?'

'A society of like-minded folk, rather like the

burgesses with their guilds. I turn a blind eye.'

'But the burgesses are in town. They organise themselves for trade purposes, to keep up standards and, to be honest, to keep everybody else out. Your men have a monopoly. What do they talk about?'

'The usual matters, I expect. They're beginning to feel they should negotiate their wages rather than having a figure thrust upon them by Roger, take it or leave it. Something to be said for it. They're in a strong position. There's demand for labour these days.'

'And?'

'As I said, it's nothing. They talk, that's all. I agree, they're restive, but they'd never support an insurrection.' Despite his words, Ulf looked uncomfortable.

An image of the pewter badge she had glimpsed when she found the body of the youth – plus the relic in his hand – seemed to burn in Hildegard's mind. She felt as if her complicity were branded on her face. But she could not betray a dead man. She wondered whether she could trust Ulf enough to tell him what she had found. He might not oppose the aims of the Company of the White Hart so long as they acted peacefully. He had always been keen for justice in the old days. But now? She glanced at him. In his velvet and miniver, with the keys of the castle on his belt, he might conceivably find it more convenient to be pragmatic. Deciding it was too risky to confess her own feelings at present, she said as lightly as she could, 'Your villagers – they're not like the ones who wrecked the Savoy down in London, then?'

Instead of smiling, he looked shocked. John of Gaunt's palace on the Strand had been thoroughly destroyed during the people's rising, the previous summer. Fortunately for Gaunt himself, he'd been on campaign in Scotland at the time. Archbishop Sudbury had been less fortunate.

Ulf muttered, 'I'll never believe they nailed the archbishop's mitre to his head when they killed him.' He looked around. 'Come on, let's get outside if you've finished here. I've something I want to say to you in private.' He jerked to his feet.

Together they went out into the damp air of the courtyard, shrugging their winter cloaks round themselves and pulling up their hoods. Ulf walked beside her for a moment, kicking a stone ahead of him. Eventually he stopped.

'That's what the villagers call themselves, *the Savoy Boys,*' he said. 'It's just their little joke,' he defended, jutting out his lower lip. 'It's probably more to do with the fact that it rhymes. They're not the sort to do anything wild.'

'Hm.' But we can't count them out, she thought to herself, feeling a chasm of uncertainty opening up all around her.

Ulf paced ahead, nibbling the corners of his beard, but after awhile he slowed to look back at her. 'They're good lads, Hildegard, believe me. Sudbury was a politician first and foremost. He was chancellor as well as archbishop. He supported Gaunt's incessant taxation. He had no heart. His treatment of the poor was a scandal. We felt the burden in every corner of the kingdom. There's only so much folk can bear before they break. But that's nothing to do with Roger, is it?

150

What would the Hutton lads have against him? He's always tried to be fair.'

'We have to suspect everyone,' she told him unhappily. 'Servants, family, guests. Even Philippa, for heaven's sake. Don't you think it breaks my heart to say this? So far she's the only one with a motive and the opportunity. It's well to believe in people's goodness. It's your great virtue, Ulf. Heaven will open its arms to you when the time comes. Even so, there's a line between loving your fellow man and being a gullible fool. I'm afraid we're on the wrong side of the line. Someone made that treacherous attempt on Roger's life and it's only by God's grace that he survived.' She took the plunge and lowered her voice. 'I'm not saying the villeins don't have a case. It's just that I believe in right and wrong. And violence is wrong.'

'Do you think they're planning another rebellion?' He gave her a searching glance, as if to find out how much she knew, and she realised she couldn't see into him at all. The sensation of blindness passed, leaving only an uncomfortable residue of disquiet.

'We'll soon find out if it's going to go that way,' she managed. 'Meanwhile we can only wait and see.'

Feeling a sudden chill deep within her, she pulled her cloak more tightly round her shoulders and followed him. Ulf was her old friend, but the times in which they lived had made him a stranger to her. Rain was beginning to fall. The day had turned sour.

Before they parted she said, 'I came here to

ascertain whether Roger could help me find a suitable home for my nuns.'

'I know that.'

'And now I'm caught up in other people's problems. My task is to find six good women to join me. It's not easy, setting up a nunnery. Especially when somebody with the power of the lord abbot is praying for our failure. I can't stay here indefinitely.'

'Don't leave, we've got to find this poisoner. He might strike again.' He added quietly. 'There's no one else I can trust.'

Surprised that he should be the one to voice the issue of trust after her own doubts, Hildegard turned to look directly into his eyes. 'You must know where my loyalties lie.'

He took her by the arm. 'Then stay. I beg you. For Roger's sake. For everybody's sake.' Releasing his grip, he turned abruptly and made his way to his office.

Chapter Six

Hildegard went back to her chamber and stretched out, the better to think. As the porter had mentioned when she had arrived at Hutton, the village would choose a mock mayor today to be burned in effigy. Then they would elect a Saxon port-reeve in his place, just as they did in the old days before the Conquest. The sounds of drumming that accompanied this were reaching

152

a frenzied pitch already. Everything seemed to be turning into a riot. Often on these occasions there were random killings and mutilations. Scores were settled. New quarrels invented. Feuds continued. If Roger's 'death' might be expected to put a damper on events there was no sign of it, judging from the noise outside.

The question was: who hated him so much they would want to kill him? Was it somebody inside the castle, avid for wealth and power, or someone outside, down in the villages, fighting poverty and injustice and yearning for a better life for all? And why poison, when these days a knifing in some dark corner would do? It suggested someone without physical strength or courage. A woman.

She thought of the family: Philippa. Sibilla. She pondered the question of Melisen.

Her thoughts tossed and turned and she recalled a surreptitiously clenched fist and a murmured 'Long live Wat!' when she was standing unnoticed within the bailey the previous day, watching the servants unload the packhorses. She had taken it as high spirits, a sort of ironic humour. But now, as she recalled one of the fellows involved trying to clamp a hand over the mouth of his companion, the incident leaped out like a warning sign of the trouble that lay just under the normality of everyday events. The two villeins had noticed her watching them and sloped off pretty quickly. This made her think of the two men Ulf had sent off with Roger in the logging cart. They had seemed jovial enough, but what was that raised fist? She shuddered at what they might do – might, indeed, have already done

153

– once they got Roger alone in the woods. It seemed that everywhere her thoughts turned, they saw only betrayal.

It's this constant drumming, she told herself, trying to be sensible. It's driving me mad. She got up and went outside with the intention of seeing her hounds.

The smoke from the field fires was beginning to seep inside the castle. A thin haze lay across the bailey. It was more than just an autumn mist, it was blue woodsmoke giving off a tang of beech and hawthorn. People were beginning to cough. If it's not the rain it's smoke and fog, Hildegard thought. How uncomfortable life is at this time of year. More uncomfortable for Roger, however, lying, sick, on his bed of logs. She would be on hot nails until the two escorts rode back into the yard with the news that he was safely ensconced at Meaux. Better still, Roger would perhaps send a message telling Ulf to call off this ridiculous charade and they would all be able to talk openly once again. Even at a fast clip, however, an impossible feat with that load on board, they wouldn't reach Meaux before nightfall. And if they started back at first light tomorrow it would be after noon before they appeared again at Castle Hutton. By then the cortège might have set out for Meaux. She hated the thought of processing with a stone-filled coffin all the way back through the forest to her starting point. But so far it looked as if she had little choice.

She decided to ask Ulf to let her meet the self-styled Savoy Boys before the cortège set out. It might be useful to ask them a few questions. Her prioress would be interested in how far north the rebellion had crept. The monastics, whatever their views, would be first to come under attack should the worst come to the worst. Swyne was a peaceful part of the Riding, but once the rebels' blood was up there would be no reasoning with them.

But first things first, she decided. We must winkle out the poisoner. Only then can we turn our thoughts to protecting ourselves.

Just as Hildegard made her way back from the kennels across the muddy slats of wood lining the kitchen yard, she was distracted by the screeching of a frightened bird.

When she went up to the yard gate she saw a couple of men on the other side. They were pitching stones at one of the hens that were running loose. The creature was already down on one side and struggling valiantly to remain on its feet in a confusion of mud and brown feathers. Every time it managed to scramble up, however, one of the men would pitch another stone at it and roar with delight when it went down again.

In a flash she was into the yard and standing between the men and their victim. 'Stop it at once! If the creature's destined for the pot put it out of its misery and stop taunting the poor thing!'

She glared at the two men.

One of them, a scruffy individual, wore a grubby, bloodstained tunic with, faintly visible, the blue marsh dragon of Sir William on it. The other man bore no such device and, indeed, was

155

surprisingly well attired in a jacket of rich stuff with dancing scarlet tippets running down both sleeves. She had seen that decoration before somewhere.

He scowled and muttered something to his companion, then took two long strides to where the hen was floundering in a pool of blood, picked it up and, his eyes never leaving Hildegard's, stretched its neck until it cracked. The hen gave a squawk and flapped its wings.

When it was dead he asked, 'Does that satisfy you, Sister?'

She gave him a bleak look and began to retrace her steps, pausing only when she heard William's man snigger, 'I'll wager that's the only satisfaction she'll ever get, poor sow.'

And the reply she was surely intended to hear: 'I'll give her satisfaction any time, make it her lucky day!' Their guffaws followed her, as, seething, she carried on towards the gate.

The words echoed those grunted in the darkness of the undercroft and the memory made her turn her head. A black look was following her. It did not swerve when it met her own.

Despite the lateness of the hour, Melisen was lying down in her solar when Hildegard went in. In contrast to the mud and brutality of the kitchen yard here there were fresh rushes laced with dried flowers on the floor, giving off the heady scent of summer meadows. It seemed exotic at this time of year, making it a place apart. Thick tapestries on the walls kept out the cold, and there was a gauzy canopy over the bed through which Melisen's recumbent form was visible. A fluttering of maids was in attendance about the chamber. As Hildegard was being ushered in one of them was bending over the bed, urging, '–for your own good, madam, please, I beg of you.' The scent of roses mingled with the bitter aroma of a herbal tisane.

When Hildegard made her presence known by a little clearing of the throat the girls stopped what they were doing and turned like startled sheep. The one holding the tisane dropped it.

One of the other maids had already poked her head inside the veils and whispered something, and now Melisen flung one arm out across the pillows while the other, glittering with bangles, lay limply on her brow in the very image of despair. When Hildegard accepted the stool one of the maids offered and drew up her robes to sit, Melisen murmured in a reedy voice, 'So good of you to come, Sister. So, so good.'

Eventually the arm was withdrawn to reveal two tear-stained eyes. 'What am I to do?' she whispered. 'What am I to do without my darling Roger?'

'Are you going to be up to the journey to Meaux for the funeral?' asked Hildegard in a soft voice.

'I must. Whatever happens I must attend. How could I not?' She gave a grief-stricken sigh and closed her eyes.

Aware that she and Ulf could only bow to Roger's wishes until they heard from him, Hildegard looked on the girl with compassion. Roger had ordered that nobody should be told the truth, but it seemed heartless to let Melisen suffer like this. Her grief seemed genuine: this child could not be guilty. Hildegard recalled the joy on her face the previous night as she held the mazer to her husband's lips.

There was a sound at the door and Melisen's young squire came bowling in. He came to an abrupt stop when he saw the visitor. Melisen, hearing his exclamation of surprise, quickly opened her eyes and sat up, running a hand over her face and pushing back her hair. Although she gave him only the briefest glance, it was enough to suggest something covert. Hildegard's skin prickled and she turned her head to get a better look.

He was young and handsome and wearing a richly figured black velvet tunic that set off his poetic features. He could not be much older than Melisen herself. Hildegard remembered how Melisen had fallen back into his arms in a swoon as soon as she appeared to realise Roger was sick. Wouldn't it be natural for them both to see her elderly husband as someone to be duped, an encumbrance to be got out of the way in the only manner the impetuous immorality of youth might suggest? Hildegard shivered and touched her cross.

But Melisen was lying back in a swanlike pose among her pillows again, and her voice when it came was wispy with something that sounded convincingly like grief. 'When, dear sister, do they expect the cortège to set out?'

'Tomorrow perhaps, or as soon as you're ready to travel with it, my lady.'

'Then I must rouse myself and not allow my weakness to betray the memory of my beloved lord,' she whispered. 'Tell the steward to prepare the household for departure. We will leave as soon as everything is ready.' She glanced across at the young squire, who was standing by the door as if waiting for his orders. 'Isn't that the best thing, Charles?' She pronounced his name in the Norman way. It sounded unexpectedly sensual. 'We should leave for Meaux at once, don't you think?'

He came swiftly across the chamber in response. 'If my lady so commands.' He bowed his head, pale, solemn and, thought Hildegard, quite unbelievable in his perfection, an immaculate youth, as fresh as the month of May. Now he was begging to be allowed to do something for his lady, anything, he was murmuring, anything at all.

She took her leave.

Often what the troubadours called *jouissance* was what the Church called lust. It didn't bother Hildegard that Melisen delighted in twisting men round her little finger. What she got up to was not her concern. But what Hildegard did care about was the happiness and health of her old friend Roger. She began to long for the ordered calm of the cloister.

'Clear thinking, that's the thing,' she said to Ulf, throwing off her cloak and shaking her head free of its snood when they met up again in his private chamber off the Great Hall. It was late morning by now. The smell of baking bread from the nearby kitchens filled the air.

'We've looked at motives,' Hildegard went on.

'I trust your superior knowledge on that score. Now let's look at opportunity and consider in detail what happened after Roger came down to drink the baby's health.'

'Is that what he was doing? It seemed like business as usual to me,' said Ulf.

'Let's clarify the picture,' urged Hildegard. 'First, do you remember who was sitting next to him when he fell?'

'No, *first*,' said Ulf, 'where was he sitting?'

'He was sitting in his usual place on the dais in front of the firescreen.'

'Some of the time, yes. But when the minstrels piped in the boar, *then* what?'

'Then what?'

'He got up.'

'Where did he go?'

'He gave a turn or two in the dance with Melisen.'

'So?' She couldn't fathom where this was leading.

'Who was attending the food on his platter and the drink in his goblet when he was dancing?'

Knowing his opinion, she replied cautiously, 'Your yeomen of the board?'

He let that go. 'No, the problem is that nobody and everybody was attending him. He himself was up and down all evening. Dancing. Getting up to try his strength with the merchants. Flirting with the maids. He even had a quick game of thrayles. Anybody could have put something in his drink at any of those times.'

'And Melisen certainly made sure he kept on drinking.'

160

'I noticed that.'

'Why was he so thirsty? He seemed insatiable.'

'Always complaining of thirst these days is Lord Roger.' Ulf laughed in an indulgent way at the capacity of his lord for drink.

'But Melisen shared his cup. That's what I can't understand. They drank from the same cup. It has to have been poisoned *after* she took a drink from it.'

'How long does that stuff take to work?'

'A few minutes. She was sharing his cup all the time.'

'Between the bringing in of the lombard leche and the scoffing of it,' Ulf mused to himself, as if trying to summon up a picture of the whole scene.

'Was that the last course your people brought in before he fell?'

'It was.' Lombard leche was adored by everyone. A cream of almonds and honey, only the foreign cooks knew how to bring it to perfection.

'And what was going on while it was being carried in? Didn't everybody get up to do the branle? It must have been then that somebody physicked his wine. But how?'

Ulf was frowning. 'Was it the branle, though, everybody dancing together, or was it an estampie? If the former we've no way of knowing who wasn't up, but if–'

'Actually, when the leche came out it was the estampie,' said Hildegard.

'Are you sure? So everybody had a partner.'

Hildegard closed her eyes the better to summon the image forth. 'Roger and Melisen

161

together. Yes, I remember that. And then there was–'

'Philippa and Ludovico,' Ulf broke in, a look of relief on his face. 'Yes, I remember now how they danced – you know...' He blushed. 'Sorry, a wild fancy–'

'What?'

He mumbled, 'As if, they were tied together with invisible love knots. The look on her little face. She's growing up into such a beauty.' The somewhat dreamy look left his face. 'Let's hope that bastard treats her well. Anyway, to go on, there must've been William and Avice. William loves to show off his fancy steps–'

'Wait, that's not right,' Hildegard interrupted. 'I definitely remember William was dancing with the red-haired maid, the one who I saw assisting the midwife.'

'That's strange. Sir William and a maid. Not like him to be so open about it. So where was Lady Avice?'

'I believe,' said Hildegard slowly, 'she was talking to Master Sueno. They were certainly sitting at the table together. But for how long? Can't you remember, Ulf? I wasn't watching all that carefully.' Indeed, she remembered, her thoughts had been dwelling somewhat on her recent experience in the undercroft. She shuddered. Forcing herself to continue she asked, 'Are we sure it was during the estampie? Everything hinges on that.'

'If Sir William had noticed a mere mason sitting with Lady Avice he would have broken his neck.'

'The way I remember it,' said Hildegard drily, 'his attention was totally engaged by his partner.'

Ulf pursed his lips. 'So, we can account for Melisen, with Roger all evening, and William in the thick of the dancing, Philippa and the Lombard likewise, and the only ones at the table: Sueno and Avice. Could either of them have slipped something into his drink?'

'Getting rid of Roger would be the last thing Sueno wanted.'

'Or so he hinted.'

They were both silent.

At length Hildegard gave a heavy sigh. 'Anyway, they would have had to be in league because one couldn't have doctored the wine without the other one noticing.'

'It's ridiculous.'

'What is?'

'The idea of those two forming a conspiracy.'

Feeling she was clutching at straws she said, 'Of course, we're forgetting the other guests. I wasn't watching them, were you?'

'It's always the same at these events. Everybody's up and down, back and forth–'

'Just like the servants, in fact.'

'The last thing they'd want is Roger dead. You've got quite the wrong idea about them. It's because of the Saxon lads, isn't it?'

'Mostly. There are other reasons.' She pictured the little phial, the reliquary, at present hidden in her scrip. 'The crux of the matter is, Ulf, we don't have anything to go on. This is all guesswork.'

'Let's go and sit out in the hall ourselves,' he suggested. 'I know it's rowdy but we might pick up a few clues if we have another look at where it happened.'

'I had a look round when everybody was in chapel,' she told him as she got up, 'that's when I noticed the wine stain. Truly, Ulf, if we don't get a lead soon I'm going to have to go back to Swyne and continue my search for a grange. I don't have permission to stay away for ever.'

They made their way over to the Great Hall, crossing the bailey on the cordings. They were slippery with mud but at least they kept people's feet dry. It was raining even now. The entire yard was like a quagmire.

Indoors, the servants had made an effort to clear up after the previous night. Ulf looked round with a critical eye but could find nothing much to complain about. He called for somebody to bring them a sample of a new brew that had just arrived from the lowlands, and they stood next to one of the wooden pillars to watch the servants coming in and out from behind the screens.

They were laying the board for the day's eating, first a spoon, then a goblet, next a spoon, then another goblet. The napkins were brought out by the third yeoman, the one Roger had called forth only to send away again in order to see him go out backwards. He looked as morose now as he did then as he placed the folded napkins then went back and stuck spoons in them all. He had the air of a man who thought he was capable of better things.

After he had finished the two yeomen of the salt processed in. Judging by their expressions it had taken a fair amount of ambitious jostling to get the job, and they seemed mighty pleased with themselves. Together they hoisted the salt cellar on to the table. It was a massive object of solid silver, skilfully fashioned in the shape of a high-sided cog under sail.

'That's a fine piece,' observed Hildegard. 'It must have cost something.'

Ulf chuckled. 'It impressed Melisen no end when she first saw it. Roger had it modelled on one of his wine ships that come into Ravenser.'

They watched as it was heaved into a precise position according to some rigid rule known only to the yeomen and their mistress. Then the most senior man produced a small key and with great ceremony unlocked a lid on the deck and inspected the contents by dipping a finger inside and licking. Screwing up his face, he pronounced himself satisfied and, bowing to the salt, he and his assistant backed out.

'The points on their poulaines are ridiculous,' Hildegard remarked. 'Do they have to follow court fashions so slavishly?'

Ulf snorted. 'They're daft, aren't they? It's a wonder they don't trip over themselves. They shouldn't be longer than two inches. That fellow's are at least four. I'll have a word.'

'I didn't remark on them to get him into trouble.'

As she spoke she observed that no guest places were laid below the salt. Everyone seemed to have fled, even Schockwynde, usually not one to miss an invitation to dine with his betters. She assumed he'd gone to eat in his chamber away from the *poraille* and the risk of the pestilence. Ralph's place wasn't set.

'That baby still hasn't been brought down, has he?' Hildegard asked. 'Maybe Sibilla thinks it'd be tactless with Roger gone.'

'Nobody knows whether to celebrate a birth or mourn a death,' Ulf said gloomily. 'They're all at sixes and sevens. I feel tempted to tell them the truth. I'm having to bite my tongue.'

'But we'd better abide by Roger's decision for the moment until we know what he's planning.'

'You think there's more to it?' Ulf asked.

Hildegard didn't answer but instead went over to look at the table again. Ulf followed and they sat down. The table had been cleaned and a fresh cloth put out. There was one goblet for William, one for Avice and one for Melisen. The latter was a delicate silver affair studded, of course, with gems. Roger's goblet, a big, practical piece, was inverted.

It looked poignant like that, even though she knew Roger was probably faring well enough with Hubert de Courcy in the comfort of the abbey. 'I wonder how the old devil is?' she remarked. 'I hope he's taking that medicine I gave him.' It was more than his health which worried her. The two escorts were never out of her mind. She was just thinking, 'there's no remedy for a slit throat,' when there was a commotion outside.

The main doors flew open to let in a rabble of excited castle servants. Seeing Ulf, they headed straight for him. He was already on his feet by the time they reached the dais, and Hildegard saw his hand stray to his dagger. She gripped her cross but remained seated.

'Sir, sir, it's bloody murder, that's what it is!

166

And here, within the bailey! Look, sir! Come and look!' There was a clamour of voices nearly drowning out his words, confirming what he said.

Ulf gripped the man by the hood and hauled him on to the dais. 'What?'

'Murder, sire! Come and see for yourself!'

'Who's been murdered?' He shook the messenger until, nearly choking, he managed to splutter, 'One of the maids of the bedchamber, sir!'

Ulf released him and the messenger dropped to the floor, coughing and rubbing his neck. The other servants fell back as Ulf sprang from the dais with one long stride.

'Show me!' he commanded, grabbing the messenger and hauling him along by his cotte as he made for the doors.

Hildegard lifted the hem of her robe and followed him at a run.

II

In the tavern where he sat out the hours before embarking for England, the papal envoy smiled to think that the Count of Flanders, Louis de Mael would be as interested as himself in the conversation taking place at the next table. A vociferous group of Flemish weavers were boasting of the numbers willing to bear arms against the count and his ally Duke Philip the Bold of Burgundy. They could not know of the overwhelming numbers who rallied to the duke's cause. They could not know that their leader, Van Artevelde, would be dead within the month. They could not know of the thousands to be drowned in the mud of Flanders fields in the coming slaughter. Their optimism at the prospect of battle brought a further smile to the envoy's lips. He pulled the hood of his black cloak over his face and leaned closer to hear more.

Chapter Seven

They ran at the head of the mob out of the hall, across the muddy cordings, through the kitchen yard, past the workshops, and out again to the stores. Hildegard was carried along by an army of excited servants. Everybody was shouting; two men came to blows. Ulf dealt them a clip round the ears. The head man came to a breathless halt in front of one of the grain stores, where two pike-bearers stood guard.

'It's not a pretty sight, sir. Maybe the sister would like to stay back?'

'I'm sure I've seen worse,' said Hildegard. 'I haven't lived in a cloister all my life.'

'As you wish.' Still breathing heavily, he pushed open the door and stepped aside to allow them through. Ulf went first. Hildegard heard him swear. She followed quickly into the grain-scented darkness. The indescribable stench of blood rose up to mingle with the sweetness of barley and rye.

'Poor child,' she murmured crossing herself. It was indeed one of the maids. Despite her disfigurement, Hildegard recognised her as the girl with red hair who had attended the birth of Sibilla's baby and had later danced so provocatively with Sir William during the feast.

The first thing to notice was the blood. There was more of it than could be imagined to come from one young girl. It pooled copiously round the body. The second thing was her belly, hacked open, her guts revealed like coiled snakes in a pit. Worse was what had been done to her mouth. Someone had stitched her lips with twine.

Ulf went to the door and growled at everybody to get back. Some were craning their necks to have a look. He used his stave on the most forward ones. 'You, Sigbert, did you find her?' He turned to address the man who had led them here.

'No, sir. It was a scullion sent to get a shovel of barley. Fair sent him out of his wits, it did.'

A quick glance showed no barefoot scullion among the onlookers. 'Where is he?'

'Back turning his spit handle if he knows what's good for him.'

'Have him brought to me now,' Ulf ordered.

The man was gone in an instant to do the job himself.

Ulf closed the door, shutting out the jabber of the mindless jostlers outside, and stood beside Hildegard without speaking. A trickle of light seeped down from a high window. It was usually enough to enable the servants to carry out their business in the store without need for tapers. It enabled them to see a scuffle of footprints in the doorway. Closer to the body, however, there were three distinct patterns, those belonging to the maid with her small heels, those they knew to be their own, and a third set.

'We must look at those,' Hildegard said, pointing to them. She turned her attention back to the body. The girl's hair was caked with blood where it escaped its linen cap. It spread in shades of varied red and gold over the chill stones. 'She

174

still wears her coif.'

Ulf gave Hildegard a glance. She knew the colour must have drained from her face, for he placed a hand on her shoulder. 'You needn't stay, you know,' his voice was gentle. 'It's clear how she died. No poison here to be found and examined. It must have been a drunken fiend with a knife last night.'

'This is more than a man driven by lust,' Hildegard replied.

Looking again at the stitches sewing the girl's lips together, she was transfixed by a memory. It was of simple words, spoken casually, half in jest, but now they aroused her revulsion by what they truly meant.

'We must go to Sibilla's chamber,' she whispered in alarm. 'The midwife. We must speak to her.'

'Midwife?'

'Before she hears we have found the body. I'll go alone. You stay and do what you have to. The footprints. The weapon.' Hildegard turned, leaving Ulf gaping after her as she pushed the door and shouldered her way through a crowd that stood in silence as she passed.

The late morning air seemed sweet outside the confines of the store and she took a deep breath to steady herself. Then, scarcely daring to allow her thoughts to direct her, she set off towards the bailey. Only when she was approached by one of the servants who had followed her across the grain yard could she summon the words to ask him to conduct her with all haste to the chamber of the Lady Sibilla. He obeyed without hesitation.

'Sibilla, where is your midwife?'

Lounging on the bed amid her furs when Hildegard came in unannounced, Sibilla sat up abruptly. She was clearly shocked by the sudden entrance of the nun. 'Midwife? Why? Is one of the maids in need?'

'Where is she?'

'Gone, I expect. How should I know? Her services were paid for, no doubt.' Her tone was sharp.

'Sibilla, I must know where she is. It's urgent.'

She pretended to yawn. 'Oh, ask Ralph. He deals with day-to-day matters. Do you think I can be bothered with all that?'

'And where is Sir Ralph?'

'Who knows? Hunting? Playing with his cat? I can't be expected to know where he is.' Sibilla gazed at Hildegard as if weighing up the likely moves of an adversary. 'I'd like to know what's happened to your famous humility. You seem remarkably peremptory for a nun.'

'A maid is dead,' she replied.

Sibilla seemed not so much shocked now as hostile. 'A maid? What maid?'

'One of those attending your delivery.'

'*What–?*'

Hildegard observed her change of colour with curiosity. 'Yes, one of those maids, Sibilla. The one with red hair. Surely you remember her?'

'Why on earth should I?'

Her glance not straying from Sibilla's face, Hildegard replied, 'Considering she's been murdered you might care to give the matter a little thought.'

'Murdered?' Sibilla laughed and picked at one

176

of her furs. When Hildegard merely waited with an air of unruffled patience she said, 'This is ridiculous. You burst in here talking wildly of murder as if it's anything to do with me! How should I know anything about her? These maids cannot be controlled. And anyway, I don't have a red-haired maid. She must have come in with the midwife.'

'And you say the midwife has left?'

'I expect so. How should I know? I've told you, ask Ralph. He'll have paid her off by now.'

'And where is he, did you say?'

'I didn't.' Sibilla glanced away. When she looked back Hildegard was still watching her with a level glance. It was close run as to who would make the better card player, but with her training in meditation and prayer, Hildegard had the edge on self-control. Grudgingly Sibilla conceded that Ralph was out hunting with William. 'But don't ask me where. And now, if you don't mind, I'd rather like to sleep. I've had a trying time.'

With that she plumped her pillows, pulled a cover to her chin and closed her eyes. Almost at once she opened them. 'I'm sorry about the girl. But they come and they go. I can't be expected to know them all.'

Outside in the corridor Hildegard found the servant who had brought her here. She grasped him by the sleeve. 'Your name, sir?'

'Edberg,' he told her promptly.

'Edberg, I want to find Sir Ralph. Do you know where he is?'

'I can find out for you, Sister. Follow me.'

He led the way down some nearby stairs. To her surprise they emerged in the passage separating the kitchen from the Great Hall. The ease with which anyone from anywhere in the castle could have approached the dais and done their work with the poison astonished her. The whole place was like a honeycomb, every cell leading on to the next. Edberg accosted one of the scurrying menials and rapped something out in Anglo-Saxon in a dialect that went over Hildegard's head. When he turned he said, 'He's just been through here. Getting fish for his cat. If we hurry we'll be in time to stop him before he rides out.'

Robes flying, Hildegard tore across the yard after him and they burst into the stables just as Ralph was being hoisted aloft a tall bay. His own horse, the black destrier she had seen his squire leading in the forest yesterday, hung its head over the door and snickered in its eagerness to come out.

'Ralph! A moment!'

With a final hoist by his grooms he was in the saddle. He looked down at her. 'Can't it wait? I'm going hunting and I'm already late.' He clearly had no intention of dismounting. She went to stand in front of him. His horse poked its nose into her sleeve and she fondled it as she asked him whether he had any news of the midwife, as a woman in the village was in need of her services.

Ralph frowned. 'I have no idea,' he said. 'I paid her off, lavishly I might add. Why should I know where she is?'

'Do you know where she came from perhaps?'

'No idea. Don't midwives travel around?'

He made as if to urge the horse on but Hilde-

178

gard stood her ground. Being handled so delicately appealed to the horse and he lowered his head and breathed warmly into her hands. Ralph brought up his whip but put it aside when he saw her expression. 'Look, if this is urgent, I'm sure the maids know more about her than I do. Why not ask one of them?'

'Which one do you suggest?'

'How would I know? They all look the same to me.' He lifted his whip again.

'Even the one with the red hair?'

'Ah, I see which way this is going.' He hesitated for a moment, then threw one leg over and slid down. 'So it's William, is it?'

'William?'

'In the old days it wouldn't have escaped your eagle glance, Hildegard, but now you're so holy maybe you don't see what's going on under your nose.'

'Maybe so,' she said. 'What should I have seen?' She deliberately widened her eyes.

'William and that maid you've just mentioned?'

'Really?'

'Indeed.' Ralph's glance narrowed. Turning to his groom he barked, 'Too late to go out now. Unsaddle the brute.' He clapped the horse on the flanks then, gripping Hildegard by one elbow as if she were a captive, he marched her out of the stable and into the yard. 'Come with me, Sister. We need to talk.'

Aware that Edberg was following at a discreet pace or two she allowed Ralph to lead her back towards the main building. Once inside he hustled her up the side stairs and into his own chambers.

'So,' Sir Ralph closed the door, 'What's William done this time?'

'I don't understand you,' said Hildegard.

'Oh, of course, he married into the family after you left. And as you're cloistered out of the daily stream of the world,' Ralph raised his glance to the ceiling, 'you'll know nothing about him, but everybody is aware of his depravity.' His glance flew to hers, suddenly sharp, and then, almost in an instant, veiled and as vague as always.

'You'll have to explain, Ralph,' said Hildegard. 'It's true. I do lead a secluded life. When I was anchoress I never saw a soul from one month to the next.'

'I was astonished when they said you'd taken the veil,' Ralph admitted, easing himself into a chair and crossing his boots at the ankle. 'But what a change of fortune, eh? Hugh dead on some godforsaken battlefield. You a nun.'

It rankled that Ralph should embrace Hugh's death in the phrase 'change of fortune'. But all Hildegard said was, 'You're right. There have been changes.'

He put up a hand. 'Excuse me a moment.' He hollered for one of the servants. A man appeared, carrying Master Jacques on a cushion.

'There he is,' said Ralph, taking up the lolling creature and giving him a stroke. To his servant he said, 'Bring us some ale, there's a good fellow,' and after the man had gone he said, 'William has a foul temper. You know about that business with those thieves down at the docks in Ravenser? He strung all fourteen of them up, guilty and innocent alike. That shocked a lot of people in

180

the Riding.'

'I didn't know,' said Hildegard quietly.

'The other thing is wenches,' Ralph went on. 'I don't know how Avice puts up with it. Sibilla wouldn't stand for it.'

'You sound envious,' Hildegard suggested.

'The difference between William and me that is I'm happy with my wife,' said Ralph. 'In fact, I'm a happy sort of fellow altogether if you want to know the truth. As long as I've got my lands and Master Jacques here, what more could a man want?'

He wore his usual affable smile. His eyes were like pale blue glass and as guileless as those of a child of five, but it seemed to Hildegard his smile was like a mummer's mask. She wondered why he had not included the birth of his son in his inventory of good fortune? And what did he mean by *his* lands? Everything he had came courtesy of someone else. His rents from Roger, the rest from Sibilla. Of course he looked every inch the perfect knight. Like his brother in grandeur. Only with Roger it had substance and the force of law to back it up.

'What are you trying to tell me about William?' Hildegard asked. 'And why did my mention of that particular maid cause you to forgo your hunting?'

He laughed softly. 'In the old days you'd never have posed a question like that. You must have seen them dancing. And I'd lay bets he didn't finish up in his wife's bed last night.' He raised his brows.

'But Avice?' she asked. 'What about her? She

181

must be sorely distressed at the thought of William's philandering?'

'Avice? She has a heart of ice. Even as a child, don't you remember? It's the only way that marriage can last. Except for fear, of course,' he added appraisingly, 'she wouldn't dare leave him for fear of retribution. Only way she'll get out of it is if he throws her out. But why would he do that when she's so compliant? And why would she not comply? She's got no better protection against slings and arrows than William.' He began to chuckle. 'No, my dear stepsister doesn't care about maids.' He gave a bark of laughter.

'Perhaps I ought to tell you something,' said Hildegard.

'What's that?' Ralph kissed Master Jacques behind the ears and began to stroke him slowly from nose-tip to tail.

Hildegard hesitated. 'The red-haired maid has just been found dead.'

Ralph's hand froze over the cat. 'What did you say?'

'Her body was found within the hour in one of the stores.'

'Dead?' He turned to her, eyes like stones. 'But how can she be?'

'She is, and how she came to be so is another question.' Hildegard watched him carefully.

'This changes things.' He gave a narrowed glance. 'Of course, you would not entertain the idea that William would be involved?'

'William?'

'Not in anything like that, not here.'

'Like what exactly?'

182

He looked confused. 'Dead, you say? By her own hand, presumably? You really can't blame William,' he said half-heartedly.

'Why should I blame him?' Hildegard replied.

'Quite. We agree. But the death of a servant in the castle bounds? People search for someone to accuse. It's only natural.' Ralph gave a heavy sigh. 'So young. What a tragedy. Maybe she died from a similar cause to the one that afflicted Roger?'

'I think not.' Hildegard was relieved to be so emphatically truthful for once.

'No?'

'Foul play. No doubt of it.'

Ralph frowned, as if considering the matter. Hildegard could not put her finger on what made her uneasy. His attack on his brother-in-law and then his haste to contradict himself? It didn't ring true.

Now he said, 'Much drunkenness and wantonness go on in Roger's castle. He employs too many Saxons. I'm not surprised something like this has happened. It was only a question of time. We can't trust them. He used to bewail the fact that he was surrounded by enemies. But what did he expect? They hate us. Always have. Always will. We took their lands from them. They don't like that. Who would? I told him a thousand times. Set spies among them.'

Ralph crooked Master Jacques in one arm and paced back and forth, as if unsure what to do next. 'You must be looking forward to getting out of here,' he suggested. 'First Roger, felled by fate, then a young maid, cut down by an unknown hand. You'll come to Meaux with Roger's cortège, I assume, before going back to your priory?'

Hildegard nodded. 'But the maid? Do you have any views on her?'

'Probably got what she was asking for,' he said with an abrupt callousness which, even if he did not know the details of her death, took Hildegard's breath away.

Edberg was waiting outside Ralph's chamber when Hildegard came out. William had gone out hunting, he reported. 'Won't be back till nightfall,' he explained. 'Allus makes a day of it, does Sir William.'

'Nightfall comes early at this time of year,' Hildegard mused. 'We'll curb our impatience.'

'Back to Ulf in the barley store, then, sister?'

'What do you know about all this?' she asked Edberg as he accompanied her across the courtyard once more.

'She was a smart girl till this one mistake,' he said. 'It's a terrible business. We're all set on catching him that did it.' Then he added, 'We're loyal to Ulf. When he sneezes, we catch cold.'

'How unfortunate for you.' Hildegard gave him a glance.

He nodded but didn't elaborate as they were already at the grain store and both of them were conscious of the sad and gruesome spectacle that lay within. Hildegard asked him in a lowered voice to wait, then tapped on the door for Ulf.

He opened it and quickly ushered her inside. His face was haggard. 'You took your time. Did you find anything out?'

'The midwife has left, or so they claim. All else I heard was Ralph's opinion of his brother-in-law.'

'I could have told you that for nothing.'

'What was she called?'

'Ada. She's been with Sibilla since she was eight.'

'That's interesting. Sibilla pretended she couldn't remember who was at the birth of her son. And denied any knowledge of a red-haired maid, one, I would imagine, who rather stood out from all the rest. How old was she – sixteen, seventeen?'

'Sixteen.'

'Ralph may have pretended not to know what has happened but I wasn't convinced. There was something in his manner. He knows something, I'm sure of it. If the midwife has been allowed to leave by your reliable porter, your men should be able to catch up with her quite easily. By the way,' she added, 'one of your men has accompanied me ever since I left this scene.'

'Edberg.'

'I thought you would know him.'

'You'll trust 'em when you know 'em better.'

'I have an entirely open mind on the subject. Did the scullion have anything useful to say?'

'No, he's half out of his wits with shock.'

'May I take another look?'

Ulf, who had been attempting to shield the body of the dead girl from view while they talked, stepped to one side.

Without touching anything, Hildegard inspected everything that might give a clue to the attacker's identity. Blood, congealed and sticky, had flowed over the stone floor and mixed with the layer of dust from the grain sacks lined against the walls. It made an unpleasant mulch in which several footprints were mixed along with mud from the yard.

There were the smudged shapes of her own soft leather buskins, and beside those the large and well-defined outlines of Ulf's round-toed working boots. At the door, but no nearer, were the barefoot scullion's prints. Near the body was the clear shape of a pair of wooden pattens, and next to them she noticed a soft, elongated shape, narrow and, for that reason, possibly made by a woman: the prints of the murderer.

She straightened up. 'If only we could identify them.'

Ulf followed her glance and nodded. 'You can trample on them as much as you like. I took their measure while you were gone.'

'That was quick.'

After she had looked around, noticing the one door in and out and the walls and racks filled with sacks of grain, most new and unopened, she took her courage in both hands and prepared to examine the body more thoroughly.

'What do you make of it?' she asked Ulf in an unsteady voice as she kilted her skirts and knelt down.

'William in a fit of lust?'

'That was certainly what Ralph was hinting. Lust or rage.'

'There have been stories, as I'm sure he told you. It looks as if he can get away with anything, tucked away down there in Holderness. Then there are the women. Nothing proven, of course. And no one can touch him, being who he is. And the women being who they are and often so

186

much down in the dirt of life, half the time they keep quiet, knowing there'll be more punishment if they speak out.'

Hildegard ignored the sudden bitterness in his tone until she could give it her full attention later on. 'There are many reasons why women keep quiet about such matters,' she told Ulf, biting her lip. 'But these stitches,' she said, changing the subject. 'They're well made. I don't have William down as a seamstress.'

'You really believe this was done by the midwife?' he asked, his voice rising a notch.

'Only because of something she said about keeping the girl's lips laced. Whoever it was, they're able to sew a fair seam. Look for yourself.'

'We do have men whose livelihood depends on sewing boots and harness.'

'I do realise it could have been an unfortunate coincidence of words on her part.'

Hildegard had to keep talking otherwise her stomach, clenched in revulsion, would have released its contents all over the floor. This had been a girl of genuine beauty. That she was also lively and something of a wit Hildegard herself could testify. Maybe somewhere there was a lover, a youth who might walk to the ends of the earth for her. There would be a family. A mother perhaps, brothers and sisters, cousins. People for whom her absence would be a source of unending grief.

'How would she come to be here in the store?' she forced herself to ask. 'Is there any legitimate reason for her being here?'

'None that I know of.'

'There must be other ways to persuade a girl to keep quiet,' she murmured. The girl's features were distorted by the macabre lacing but, gently, with forefinger and thumb, Hildegard prised forth a short black hair that had somehow become trapped under the stitches. It was so fine as to bend to every breath when she lifted it close enough to examine. 'Not coarse like beard hair, nor curly, like William's black locks, but short and straight.' She held it up so Ulf could see it.

'Could be anyone's,' he surmised, peering at it. 'It's not Saxon, at any rate.' He seemed relieved about that.

Carefully Hildegard placed it in a fold of cloth taken from her scrip for closer inspection and possible matching later on. Now she had two objects taken from two young people, both brutally murdered, the boy in the woods and now a maid. 'There is no knife here,' she observed. 'Didn't you find one?'

'No, but it looks like they used an ordinary hunting knife. The sort any man carries. One broad enough to gut a hog or a hind.'

'So I thought. With a single edge. Notice the shape of the incisions.' She rose to her feet. 'Ulf, do you have a rough plan of the castle?'

'I'll draw you a plan myself. I know every stone of this place.'

'Perhaps this poor child can be taken to the mortuary,' Hildegard suggested. 'Then, when the formalities are over, she can be carried into the church, where her soul may gain some repose at last.'

Chapter Eight

They were sitting on opposite sides of a table in the kitchen clerk's office when Ulf placed a slate between them. Hildegard took a good look at a chalked sketch then said, 'If this is a plan of the castle it wants for detail.'

'It's the shape of a footprint. But whose I don't know.'

Staring at it she said, 'I heard a story once, long ago, told to me by my husband, which he must have got from his grandfather who himself must have got it from a Saracen during the Crusades. It concerned a maiden who left a gilded slipper behind after a great feast. And the prince, finding it, and having become ensnared by the maiden, searched the length and breadth of the kingdom in order to find the one the slipper would fit.' She raised her glance. 'Let's hope we don't have to travel so far to find the owner of this one.'

'It will be no maiden,' judged Ulf, 'seamstress or not.'

'But are we agreed it's a woman's print?'

'I can't say. It's certainly narrow enough. But it's long. She must have had big feet. The other prints can be matched with the shoes of folk who had a reason to visit the store. Look at this one.' He indicated one of the sketches on the slate. 'These are the kitchen clerk's wooden pattens. Next are the clogs worn by the baker. This is the

189

only one I can't match.'

Hildegard repeated her uneasiness about the midwife and her threat.

'But you can't believe a woman with so sacred a calling would commit murder?' Ulf objected.

'Belief isn't required. Only facts will suffice. Do you happen to know the woman?'

'No. I thought Ralph brought her in with his retinue.'

'If that were the case I would have noticed her when they stopped in the forest.'

'When was that?'

She reminded him how, on her journey here, she had seen Ralph's party on the way. Then she told him how she had watched as Sibilla had been helped down from her horse and went to recline among the furs on the sled with that strange remark about prying eyes. 'The midwife must have arrived separately,' she suggested.

'I'll see if I can discover more about her. Somebody must know who she is and where she's from.'

'So you agree, it's important to find her?'

Ulf picked up the slate with the chalk drawing of the unidentified print on it. 'I suppose so.'

As she turned to leave a thought struck Hildegard with sudden force. It sent a flood of ice down the length of her body. *The scarlet tippets.* She had noticed them twice. Once in the woods on the way here ... and again in the kitchen yard this morning. No time to work out what it meant. She put out a hand to steady herself.

Ulf had quizzed his staff. It emerged that the midwife had been engaged by Lady Sibilla her-

190

self some time ago and had arrived alone, riding on a pony, the previous afternoon. She had supped privately in the chamber set aside for the birth, done her work and left without anyone taking much notice. The blacksmith's lad mentioned something about the pony but couldn't say for sure when it was there and when it wasn't. She could have set off at any time after the birth – and in any direction.

'That means we have the whole county to scour.'

'By hook or by crook,' Ulf vowed, 'we will find her whose foot this slipper fits.'

They went back to his office and had the servants parade their footwear and once more ruled them out. Hildegard judged the girl to have been stabbed only two to three hours before she was found. The clerk of the kitchen ran a tight ship and prided himself on knowing everybody's whereabouts at all times of day and night. 'Not one of my folk,' he told her. 'Impossible. I had my eye on 'em all till break of day.'

Hildegard realised that they only had this one set of footprints to go on, that they were unaccounted for was a mystery they had to solve. Too narrow to belong to any of the men and too long for a boy's print, they had to belong to a woman, but none of the women servants had been near the grain store for days, apart, that is, from Ada and the wearer of the shoe. The print suggested soles of unpatterned leather. They had picked up the surface dust and chaff of the storeroom floor, leaving a clear trail. Whoever had been wearing such shoes had walked over to the sacks where Ada must have been standing. A skirmish had taken place at some point. That was all they knew.

'What business had Ada in the storeroom?' Hildegard asked Ulf.

'None that I can see.'

'Unless she had an assignation with her killer.'

'You're thinking of Sir William.'

'Could he have arranged to meet her there? It fits with what Ralph was hinting about them spending the night together.'

Hildegard inspected the drawing of the footprints again. The footsteps of the kitchen servants in their wooden pattens had ridged soles to keep them dry above the stinking mesh of the hall and could be tracked in and out of the grain store and even, if they had wished, across the bailey until they merged with others on the trampled cordings. But these? Hildegard stared at Ulf's sketch and tried to work out what they reminded her of. Who would wear such footwear?

'They must have had very long, narrow feet.' She frowned, remembering how the midwife had beetled across the floor in that obsequious bobbing motion. It was the gait of someone with small, probably painful feet. They had reached stalemate.

One of the ladies of the bedchamber appeared and, looking nervous, stood in the doorway of Ulf's office with one hand protecting her throat. 'You were asking about that midwife,' she began. It was strange none of them knew her name. 'Well, I do know something. Not that it's much. It's just that she wanted some barley grain to

192

make a posset and,' she lowered her eyes, 'I directed her to the store myself.' Her glance flew to Ulf. 'I hope I didn't do wrong, my lord?'

When questioned further the maid could not say whether the midwife had found what she was looking for.

'Why would she need barley for a posset?' asked Hildegard after she had left. 'That sounds most unorthodox. I wonder if it could have been an excuse to get in somewhere she shouldn't have been?'

'Helping herself to grain, no doubt. These itinerant servants are the very devil with their light fingers.'

Hildegard went to ask Sibilla whether she had been given barley cup after the birth. She was vague and insisted that she remembered little of the entire event.

'Convenient,' grumbled Ulf, when Hildegard returned. When she questioned him more closely about what he meant, he didn't know. He furrowed his brow and tapped his skull. 'But there's something trying to surface.'

'You know the workings of your own mind best,' suggested Hildegard with a patient smile. 'If it's a nudge, explore it, but, nudge or no nudge, we need to talk to the midwife.'

Owing to a private understanding between Ulf and one of Melisen's ladies of the bedchamber, vague gossip about the midwife's possible destination eventually filtered through. His informant was called Celota. 'I want you to hear what she told me,' Ulf said to Hildegard.

They found her in the wash-house amid the steam from a dozen tubs of boiling water, where laundresses with red arms were pounding the garments for the entire household. Celota was there to keep an eye on three delicate silk chemises belonging to Melisen.

When asked about the midwife she confirmed that she saw her arrive by herself on the same afternoon as Ralph's party. 'She'd come from another birth,' Celota said. 'I've become friendly with some of Sibilla's maids on their visits here so I was looking forward to seeing them again. They're a gossipy bunch and always spice things up. But they were all of a dither about the birth, though not pleased at being told to keep out of it. Then right from the moment the baby popped into the world they started saying there was something wrong with it. I mean, you can understand it, for why else wouldn't it be presented for everybody to see? But no! It was kept in Lady Sibilla's private chamber, with only the midwife, the wet-nurse, Ada and another maid permitted entry. Even the family were only allowed in for a few minutes, though that might be put down to the death of Lord Roger,' she added as an afterthought.

'And did you get to speak to the midwife herself?' Hildegard asked.

Celota shook her head. 'I only know what Ada told me, that she was a tough old bird and didn't suffer fools.'

'I suppose you knew Ada well?' asked Hildegard as gently as she could.

'Everybody knew her. She was good company.

We'll all miss her.' Celota wiped a tear from her face. 'She didn't hold with all the secrecy around the new baby, though, and, being her, she said as much. "It's all my arse and Uncle Toby" – that's the way she talked, sister,' Celota apologised. 'She said, "Don't they think you're good enough? What's the game? I'll get you in to see him," and she did her best, poor love, but they kept the door of the birth-room locked.'

'Did anybody know why there was this secrecy?'

'Rumours fly as they will. They said there was summat wrong with him. Said he'd been born with the head of a cat. That he had five fingers on his left hand. Or that he got up in the night and roamed the castle accompanied by the Devil and six hellhounds. We thought that last one a bit far fetched. Probably the poor little thing has nothing more than a crooked back.'

'Poor mite,' said Hildegard. 'And what about the midwife? Did Ada tell you what she thought?'

'Well, yes, and it added fuel. She declared she'd never known anything like it.' She leaned closer. 'They do say she was afeared to be brought to account and that's why she left in such a hurry.'

'She must have been annoyed with Ada trying to get you all in to see the baby?' suggested Hildegard.

Celota sketched a brief, sad smile. 'Said she'd rue the day if she didn't keep her trap shut. But nobody could be mad at Ada for long.'

'You mean there was no real falling out between them?'

'No! Not with Ada! You could never hold a

195

grudge against her.'

'Celota, do you have you any idea where the midwife went after she left Hutton?'

'Not really. Everybody assumed she'd be going on to another birth. As I told the lord steward, a place twelve miles distant was mentioned, where she had kin.'

'Twelve miles. Well, that's not far. We'll soon find her.' Despite his words Ulf did not look confident.

'Is Celota reliable?' she asked him as they made their way out of the laundry.

'I think so. Why?'

'The head of a cat, indeed!'

The baby had seemed to be a sweet little thing and looked most perfectly formed. It was odd, though, that, so long waited for, it should be kept apart. If the pestilence was thought to be about, together with the state of mourning that prevailed throughout the castle, then maybe it was understandable. Now things looked somewhat different, however, for it seemed that Ada may have known more than she had admitted to Celota, and the midwife hadn't been happy about it. But what could make somebody want to get her out of the way in such a brutal fashion?

'I'm wondering,' said Ulf, 'whether any of this is connected to what happened to Lord Roger?'

'In what way?'

He shook his head in mystification. 'I don't know.'

'Well,' said Hildegard, 'one thing's clear: this midwife must know something. Why else leave in such a hurry?'

'Twelve miles,' mused Ulf. 'But in which direction?'

Celota had not been able to name the midwife's destination but the second clue was provided later that day by a lad who worked for the ostler. He came forward nervously, helped by the ostler's grip on the scruff of his neck, to admit that he had helped saddle up the midwife's pony before she left. When he saw he wasn't going to get into trouble he admitted that she had set the pony's head towards the east.

'Towards the Driffield road, then.' Ulf frowned. 'But that's well over twelve miles away.'

'Maybe she's heading for somewhere along the road?'

'It's thick woodland. There's nowt there apart from an assart or two. And the water mill.'

Hildegard refused to be daunted. 'For that reason,' she said, 'she should be easier to find.'

The drivers of the timber dray had not yet returned from Meaux and Ulf was determined to be on hand to hear the news from Roger when they appeared.

'Leave it to me,' said Hildegard. 'I'll track her down. Loan me a good horse and a man I can trust. I'll try to get back before the cortège moves off.'

And so it was she set out late that afternoon with Edberg, her hounds and the boy Burthred in the direction of the manor of Driffield.

Chapter Nine

Burthred had scarcely set foot outside the castle walls since the day he was born and, being ignorant of the purpose of their journey, was as delighted as a sprite to be taken along to keep an eye on the hounds. Hildegard thought they would relish the exercise and perhaps afford some protection against robbers. She let the boy dance on ahead with Bermonda and Duchess while she and Edberg rode side by side on two horses Ulf had had saddled up for them.

After casting about in the groves of winter woodland that lay beyond the edge of the demesne, they found the hoof prints of a pony separating from the rest of the busy traffic of horses and carts that had churned up the mud along the road between Hutton and York. Edberg at once hoisted the child on to the pommel in front of him and they struck out across the wastes in pursuit. He said he knew of an assart deep in the forest and guessed the midwife must be making for that. They proceeded briskly on beyond Hutton lands into the valley known as Heldale.

It was a narrow defile that cut between chalk hills and was thickly wooded, a haven for outlaws. Hildegard imagined the midwife setting out alone through such terrain and wondered about her thoughts in such an isolated place. She also considered the knife she might be carrying and her skill in its use.

As if drawing attention to the loneliness, somewhere through the blanket of trees they could hear the waters of a beck gathering in volume as they rode along. After the deluge of the last two days the streams and ditches were brimming with flood water. The horses were constantly splashing up to their girths through the puddles that lay across the path. At worst they were forced to scramble to higher ground in order to pass at all. The riders bent low under the densely growing trees, their hoods constantly tugged off by low branches, cloaks ripped by the thorns of trailing bramble and eglantine. Lower down, the surface of the beck carried a scum of yellow foam. To Hildegard the branches being dragged downstream looked like the raised arms of children caught in the flood. It made her cast a glance at Burthred, but he was holding on to the mane of Edberg's mount with a look of rapt joy at being out in the wild. The swirling waters crept inch by inch up the bank sides as they rode along.

'We'll follow yon stream as far as the assart. Hopefully we'll be lucky there. If not, the track leads on to the mill,' said Edberg when they paused for a moment to take their bearings at the top of a muddy slope. 'Then it's down towards Driffield across disputed country.'

'Disputed? How so?'

'The old lord of the manor died childless in his bed a year since, and his wife long dead. What's left of his kin can't settle things between them. With nobody to hold the whip, folk are running wild.'

'By that I suppose you mean we should beware of other travellers?'

Edberg made no reply but kept his face set towards their destination and his eyes keen.

The branches of oak and ash and beech were leafless now, spreading skeletal arms overhead, but the rowan and the evergreen holly were covered in scarlet berries. The only sign of the track was the occasional paler underside of broken leaves. From the right came a constant roar of the unseen river forced between the banks.

After half an hour they came to a clearing. They could make out the shape of a slant-roof dwelling on the other side. Woodsmoke drifted its incense their way, reminding them of stoked fires and hot pottage.

'Can we depend on the help of the folk in there, I wonder?'

'You read my mind, sister,' said Edberg. 'These are folk I know nothing of, being beyond the bounds of Lord Roger's demesne. It's many years since I've been this way. But who can turn away those in search of a midwife?'

They approached the building. A roughly thatched roof sloped low to the ground. A cur tied to a stake in its shadow set up a racket to announce them but almost at once, scenting strangers, gave a whine and tried to flatten itself into nothing against the wall. Bermonda growled, but not with animosity, rather as a speculative greeting, but Hildegard told Burthred to get down and take charge, just to be on the safe side. No point in antagonising the inhabitants before they'd even opened the door.

Edberg slid out of the saddle and strode over.

'Who's there?' called a cracked voice from within before he'd even raised his hand to the latch.

'Edberg of Hutton. Open up.'

Grumbling accompanied the sounds of somebody shuffling through straw. The door was inched open a crack and a grey head thrust itself into the space, followed by the blade of an efficient-looking knife. 'What?'

'Trust us, we mean well. We seek a midwife and were told she came this way.'

'Midwife, is it?' The door was opened a further inch and an old man peered out. Hildegard got down from her horse and, noticing the nun's habit under her riding cloak, the man shook his head, obviously imagining some foolish girl bringing the two of them out on the road like this. He chuckled. 'The same old dance, but you're doubly out of luck, sister.' The knife disappeared and he opened the door a little wider. He was leaning on a stick. Behind him was an unlit rush lamp on a hook and behind that the sense of an empty barn.

Hildegard asked, 'Why are we out of luck, then, sir? Is she not here?'

'She's been. She's gone,' he told her. And more helpfully, 'Gone down Driffield way.'

'What was she doing here?' she asked, prompted by curiosity. 'It'll be a miracle for the abbey records if it's been you in need of her services.'

He wasn't offended. 'Kin, me,' he told her. 'Sees me whenever she's in the district. She's a good girl.'

'Girl?' asked Edberg. He turned to Hildegard. 'I thought she was–?'

'The midwife we want is the one who's been in the job for forty years, or so she claims.'

'That's my Bertha. How old you reckon I am?' Judging them harmless, he suddenly seemed set for a spell of conversation.

But Edberg clapped him on the shoulder. 'Not a day over twenty-one, sir. But as you know, time waits for no man and we must be off. Shut that door firmly and stay safe.'

'And you take a care not to freeze your bollocks off, my master. There's snow on the way, you mark my words. Good luck to you. And I can tell you,' he called out as they turned away, 'she left just before midday on that little pony that never troubles itself to more than a trot. You'll catch her easy.'

Again they set out, but this time with more optimism, for their horses could easily outpace a pony. The tantalising aroma of cooking was left behind, and to take their minds off it Hildegard broke pieces of bread and cheese into lumps and handed them round as they rode along. Burthred was nodding with sleep, despite his excitement at being out in the wilds with his hounds and on a real horse with one of the most powerful masters in his small world, and Edberg wrapped his cloak round the child and rode ahead as if bearing a talisman against danger.

'It's strange she hasn't tried to cover her traces,' remarked Hildegard after they had gone some way along the track. 'Is the woman not afraid?'

Edberg grunted as if everything was strange and nothing existed that was not a cause for perplexity. They rode without further comment, the only sound the roaring of the flood as the beck filled and widened behind the net of trees.

Hildegard sank deep into her own thoughts. It was true there were outlaws and herds of wild boar and wolves and all other manner of perils in the wildwood, but she was aware that she had been more afraid at the castle, expecting at any moment to come face to face with her attacker. For one thing, I am not alone here, she thought. Edberg was one of Ulf's trusted men and would be staunch in a fight should they chance on outlaws. There were also, to be hoped, the saints and the Blessed Virgin, who would surely aid them in their quest and bring the perpetrator of this horrible crime to light.

What troubled her most was the fact that the midwife had taken so little care to conceal her flight. Surely she would have warned her father not to be so forthcoming about her movements if she had had something to hide? The thought struck Hildegard that she had lost her belief in the midwife as a murderess. She had made such a poor attempt to cover her tracks. It didn't suggest guilt. All the time they were out looking for her the real killer was at large. Fear spidered up and down her spine.

Edberg's silence encouraged the dark shiftings of her thoughts. He hardly opened his mouth, even when the track broadened sufficiently for them to be able to ride side by side. He seemed content to keep his own counsel and for her to keep hers. As her escort through the forest he could not be faulted, but so enigmatic was he, it prompted her to wonder whether he was guardian or guard.

It was late afternoon. After a few miles they began to notice a change in the air. Spurring their horses down the track, they began to scent something like burning timber. Curious, they increased their pace to a gallop. Smoke began to catch at their throats. They started to cough. They had to pull the corners of their cloaks over their mouths and take muffled breaths. The horses tossed their heads and began to roll their eyes. Even before they burst through the trees on to the riverbank, the crackle and roar of a fire could be heard. Then heat hit them like a blast from a furnace.

Edberg pulled his horse to a rearing halt and pointed. The massive shape of the wooden building on the bank of the river was ablaze. The great wheel flamed in the heart of the fire like the wheel of St Catherine herself.

Clinging to the mane of her plunging horse, Hildegard's thoughts flew at once to the fate of the miller and his household. She shouted above the roar of falling timbers, 'Can you see anyone, Edberg?'

He tried to urge his horse forward but like her own mount it was rearing and flattening its ears and, with eyes rolling, refused to go anywhere near the flames.

'We'll never get inside!' he shouted hoarsely. 'There's nothing we can do!'

'We have to do something!' The thatch crackled

as she spoke and then the planked walls bulged outwards from the pressure of the heat inside and, with a soft boom, burst asunder as they watched. A stray gust of wind fanned the flames, sending sparks glittering up into the trees, lighting everything in the glade with an unearthly glow.

'Them flames are higher than the oaks!' exclaimed Burthred, dazzled out of his silence. 'No hope for any folks inside that!'

Hildegard's prayers flew to the miller and his household, but before she could do more she gave a shout of alarm as Edberg jumped from his saddle and ran desperately towards the burning mill, as if to find a way inside. 'Edberg! No!' she shouted.

The heat of the flames beat him back again and again until at last he was forced to retreat. He came to stand beside her, his clothes reeking of smoke. 'Poor devils,' he panted. 'What a way to die. Pray God the saints have mercy on them.'

'Maybe they got out in time.'

'Aye, maybe.' He looked unconvinced. 'But where are they, then? I don't see 'em.' His smoke-blackened face was grim. She felt Burthred slip his hand into her own. Under the sound of the roaring flames and the thundering of water through the sluice there was an uncanny absence. And certainly no sign of a midwife.

'We should get on to Driffield and tell the folk there what's happened,' she suggested. Edberg nodded in agreement but before he could get back on his horse a sound in the undergrowth made them turn.

Edberg pointed to a movement in the bushes.

'There's an animal of some sort.'

'It'll be a wild boar,' piped Burthred, drawing back.

The sound came again. The shrubs were turned to tumult as a creature lurched into view, fighting as if to free itself from some bond.

It was a pony, bristle-maned, pied.

Hildegard slipped down and went over to it and Burthred, jostling at her heels, followed eagerly, reaching out with an air of professional confidence to run his small hands down the pony's neck. By the time Edberg came up, it was snuffling for treats in the boy's tunic.

'Look, sir, the old woodsman told us the midwife was riding a pony and now here he is, and all alone, the poor little brute.' Burthred rubbed the pony's muzzle and it snickered with pleasure.

Hildegard turned to Edberg. 'The child's right. So it looks as if she made it as far as this.'

'Aye, but now where might she be? Surely she'd show herself if she could?' He cast a glance towards the mill. The fire scorched all the grass around and sent burnt leaves spiralling to earth.

'Assuming it's her pony,' Hildegard replied cautiously, 'she must have been inside visiting the miller and his wife when the fire broke out. But,' Hildegard continued the thought, 'why would she tether her pony under the trees, out of sight?'

'Why not stable it with the other horses?' Edberg agreed.

'Unless, of course, she was on some secret woman's errand, to one of the servants.'

'That's a possibility.' He smiled thinly. 'In which case she's got short change for her efforts.'

206

The boy tugged at Hildegard's cloak. He had the pony's head-rope held tightly in one hand as if he would never let it go. 'May I ask a question, my lady?'

'You may.'

'If the poor woman is gone to heaven in those hell flames, Mary preserve us, might I care for her creature here until we get to our destination? And,' he added, before she could reply, 'it would not be stealing to my way of thinking, merely borrowing.'

This was the longest speech Hildegard had ever heard from him. She was surprised by the sharpness of his reasoning. After a moment she said, 'I see nothing to prevent you riding him to safety. It would be a service to its owner, and if she has perished in the flames then it makes no difference who rides her pony.' She hesitated. 'My only doubt is that she's in hiding somewhere and hoping to ride on when she feels it safe to do so.'

'In hiding?' Edberg turned to her. 'Why would she be in hiding unless she'd fired the mill herself?' His words trailed away.

Hildegard frowned. 'That's a wild supposition. Maybe she came on the scene as unwittingly as we did?' She sighed. 'But that doesn't make sense either because from what her father told us, she would have reached the mill some time before the blaze erupted, so in that case why didn't she ride on to get help at once?'

'We can't ignore the fact that it might have started accidentally while the miller and his family were absent.' Even as he spoke Edberg looked sceptical. 'Anything is possible, Sister, speculate

207

as we will.'

'My suggestion is, we observe what happens from the shelter of the trees to see if anyone returns to claim the pony. Our arrival may have scared them off. What do you say?'

He nodded. 'One course seems as good as another. And our time is our own.'

'We'd better take the pony with us to give ourselves the advantage. His apparent theft might flush out the owner.'

'Can you keep quiet, boy?' Edberg looked down into Burthred's little face.

'As a mouse, sir.'

'Do that, then. Meanwhile bring the pony along with you.'

They moved off as if continuing up the road but after a while turned off into the undergrowth. There they tethered all three animals and made their way back with soft footfalls to a convenient vantage point with a view over the remains of the mill.

The flames were still licking up what they could and the great wooden wheel lay hissing half in and half out of the race. There was no sign of the miller, his household or, indeed, of the midwife or anybody else who might lay claim to the pony, but they settled to wait. Burthred seemed transfixed by the roaring flames, even though they were beginning to burn themselves out now that the roof had caved in. There was just a groaning roar at the heart of the inferno and the black waters streaming past taking bits of burning debris with them.

An hour or so later, the mill was nothing more than a pile of glowing timbers. No one had come to claim the pony. 'If the midwife's still alive, poor soul, she might have continued on foot. Though why she would walk and not ride I can't imagine. I confess I fear for her.' Hildegard felt close to tears at the thought of the victims trapped inside the mill.

Sobered, all three made their way back to where the horses were tethered and, with Burthred astride the pony, set off towards the distant manor.

'We'll have to inform the reeve as soon as we can,' Edberg pointed out.

'Assuming he's blind and hasn't noticed,' Burthred said, hushing himself but unable to refrain from adding, 'I do hope the villeins round here won't be without bread for long. It's a bad thing to starve to death.'

Edberg caught Hildegard's eye at the child's insight. But she could see he was as grim in his heart as she was herself. He gave a harsh laugh. 'Mebbe nobody's noticed. Their drinking's likely taken their minds off things. But they've got their Samhain fires now, by George.'

It was possible, thought Hildegard, whistling up her hounds, that the fire had started accidentally, but the destruction was so complete it looked deliberate. The midwife, dead or alive, seemed to leave nothing but devastation in her wake.

They had gone no more than a mile along a narrow defile between a bluff at the head of the dale when the thunder of approaching hooves alerted them. Drawing to a halt in a stand of pines by the side of the track, they waited to see who would appear. They saw the outlines of a dozen horses approaching through the trees.

'Let's declare ourselves,' Hildegard suggested. 'If they're looters they won't want to be bothered with us.'

Indeed, they had little choice as the defile held no hiding place, so when the horsemen came within hailing distance Edberg rode forward with his hand raised. 'Hold!' he called.

The man in the lead pulled his horse to a halt. He was accompanied by a band of rough-clad riders, faces hidden under fustian hoods. 'Declare yourself!' he demanded in an accent marking him out as a stranger to the locality.

'Declare yourself, sir!' retorted Edberg stoutly, refusing to budge.

The rider said something in a dialect to his men. He must have noted the one man against many, the child on the pony and Hildegard, her nun's habit visible beneath her riding cloak, accompanied by two elderly hounds. The sight evidently struck him as comical because he threw his head back with a roar of delight, his own hood falling off to reveal a straggle of straw-coloured hair. He pulled his hood back with an easy gesture and asked, 'So what's this? The Church already sifting through the remains? There'll be no bones for you to pick here, sister. The wealth of the mill must be ash by now.'

She felt Edberg bristle.

'We were on our way to inform you of its destruction,' she said with no sign of rancour, 'if you come from the manor at Driffield.'

'And if we do not?'

As I know you do not, she thought, still trying to place his accent. 'Then what has happened is as much our business as yours,' she said.

The man frowned. 'You're on the road late, sister. And with only a man and a child for protection. Have you no care for your safety?'

'I trust in God. Besides, why should anyone wish to harm us? We are on a mission of mercy.'

There were sidelong glances around the group which now encircled them. Those who were not carrying broadswords carried cudgels. Hardly the sort of implement to help put out a fire, Hildegard judged.

The leader circled them insolently, aware he held their fate in his hands. In the watery light something glinted on his cloak. It was a small pewter badge. But it wasn't a pilgrim badge. Hildegard's eyes fixed on it. It was the sign of the hart. The ruffian held his horse still enough so he could lean down and ask, 'And what mission of mercy might that be, Sister? Enlighten us, if you will.'

Avoiding a direct answer she replied, 'I see you knew about the fire. We ourselves came across it by chance while seeking a midwife we were told was attending someone here.'

There were guffaws at this. 'You nuns,' said the leader, shaking his head in mock admonishment, 'so you need a midwife, do you?' He said something to his men in their own language and they roared with laughter. It was a coastal dialect, with something Danish in it, if she was not mistaken.

211

It was a long time since she had heard it spoken, and she blushed with anger when she realised what he had said.

She held her tongue, however. Despite their amusement, the appearance of three travellers on the road at this hour seemed to have thrown the men into confusion and they milled about, unsure whether to offer threat or safe passage. Several options were suggested, none offering much to improve the health of either Edberg, herself or the boy, but before any of these ideas could be put into practice, she noticed Edberg's hand shifting towards the knife beneath his cloak and she heard him say, tight lipped, 'I should think you'd show the sister more respect than this. Move aside and let her through.'

The leader drove his horse forward so his spurs scraped Edberg's boots and, leaning down, said into his face, 'And if I won't, my little man?'

Hildegard interrupted, one hand resting discreetly on Edberg's wrist. 'Let me describe this woman we seek, good sir. Maybe you've seen her on the road and can help us. She's short of stature, somewhat advanced in years, and will no doubt be carrying a bag containing the instruments of her calling. It's most important we find her.'

'And the miller is a red-faced scoundrel, his wife a termagant, the brats are brattish, his serving wenches comely. And we have found *them*. That makes us the victors in finding. We did not, however, find a midwife, nor anyone of that description. So?'

'So, sadly, you can be of no help to us. Praise be that the miller and his family are safe.' She made as if to turn the head of her horse to ride back the way they had come and then stopped, as if a sudden thought had entered her head. 'I wonder, sir, as your knowledge of the miller is more complete than ours, what information you have on how the fire started? No doubt he divulged the cause?'

'Nothing to worry your head about,' the spokesman replied. 'He and his wife and his six brats came straggling up the track a short while since. The walk will have done him a power of good though it did little for his temper. I reckon these millers, like your churchmen, do well to get off their fat arses now and then. What do you think?'

'I bow to your superior knowledge, sir,' she replied. 'But I wonder, were there any fatalities?'

'What's it to you?' he asked bluntly.

'Every soul is something to me,' she replied.

'Well, rest assured, the miller's as safe as he ever will be. I won't vouch for anyone else.'

The conversation ended there with some abruptness but the men did not move to let them go. Instead, the leader urged his horse closer. 'And now, as it's home time, my weary travellers, we shall escort you as far as the mill then watch you ride back the way you came.' And the men, forming a tight group, began to carry them along in the press like captives.

Hildegard leaned towards Edberg and whispered, 'Best keep our tempers. I don't doubt your courage, but it would be stupid to provoke them.' Even Duchess and Bermonda would be no help in a predicament like this, although they

213

crouched on the edge of the group, eyes alert, poised to obey her slightest command.

She could see Edberg was furious at the way they were being treated, but it was equally clear they could do nothing and they allowed themselves to be taken back as far as the mill.

The fire still sputtered and glowed and the scent of burning rye grass from the thatch that had once roofed the building filled the air. If the strangers had been seeking booty they must have been disappointed. They circled in the uncanny glow as if in the light of a million candles lit by day.

Hildegard rode alongside the leader. 'Our quest has been futile. We'll ride back to Hutton at once if you permit.'

At the name Hutton his manner changed. He gave her a long, slow look. Yet all he said was, 'Safe journey, then, and to your escort and the lad.' He suddenly reached down and grabbed the pony's bridle. 'Or would the little serf like to ride with us? What do you say to making your fortune with your Saxon brothers?'

'I'm happy where I am, sir.' Burthred glanced hurriedly at Hildegard as if he expected her to shoo him away into the keeping of the strangers, but she smiled reassuringly and he wheeled the borrowed pony, digging his heels hard into its flanks as if to be sure not to be turned into an outlaw, and Hildegard swept up the ends of her cloak, knotted them on top of the saddle and set off after him. Edberg, in silent fury, followed. The hounds came on like shadows through the trees.

When they were at a safe distance and could

slow to a trot Hildegard said, 'I'm surprised they let us go so easily. Who do you think they were?'

Edberg wore a murderous look. 'If I'm not mistaken they're a notorious band of villeins who fled their manor over Barmston way last Lady Day. They've plagued the lands round here ever since. Nobody's sent a big enough force to give them their just desserts. Lord Roger deemed it not his concern–' He broke off as if having said too much. They rode on while Hildegard pondered his words.

It was, she decided, in Roger's interest to have his neighbour's lands in disarray as they could then be nibbled at without restraint. It was a fertile, grain-growing region, the mill itself an important part of the wealth accruing to the lord of the manor in whose title it was held. If, as Edberg had already told her, the old lord had died a year ago and his lands were disputed, it was obvious that rogues and villains would range the country and take what they wanted without hindrance. There was that badge too. Did Roger know it was the Company of the White Hart who ran here?

All the way to Castle Hutton Edberg raged. It was a poison, he said, that affected those required by law to work the land. Their resentment was a blight, he said. Somebody had to work, he said, or their hatred would bring down the whole country in a bloody conflagration that would make the burning of the corn mill a mere spark, mighty though the flames seemed as they watched the roof fall and the timbers flare.

'We haven't seen the end of it,' he went on. 'No

215

one is safe in their beds. Hutton can fall as easily as anywhere now that Lord Roger is dead and Sir Edwin banished. Who is strong enough to hold his lands? No one. The rebels will turn them to waste. Doom will overtake us, bringing back famine and the Death.'

Chapter Ten

Mist lay in wreaths over the fields and cottages of Low Hutton as they arrived back later that afternoon. Black pennants fluttered on top of the battlements. Hildegard was astonished to see above the keep Roger's personal banner raised halfway up its staff as a sign of mourning.

They emerged from the trees on to the lane through the village. Here and there smouldering tar barrels littered the walkways as evidence of the previous night's excesses but otherwise the place seemed quiet except for a hardy group singing lustily round one of the fires. Hildegard recognised the song. Translated from the Saxon, it went something like: 'This is the rebel's riot feast, humanity will be king, there is no lord but the one true prince...', and then a line or two about the King of Stamford, followed by three sharp cheers.

After that they sang it all over again.

It was a song from the old days when King Harald fought his great battle not far away at Stamford Bridge, defeating the traitor Tostig and the Norwegian king, then marching his wounded and weary army down the entire length of England in only three days to face Norman invaders from across the Channel. It was the second battle, the defeat by William at Hastings, that changed for ever the fortunes of the English.

Desperate days, she thought, now long gone. The battle lost. Nobody knew what life would have been like had the Saxons continued in their peaceful farming communities instead of being overrun by the Normans and forced to submit to their hierarchy, their laws, their taxes.

In this part of the country it was still remembered that all three Ridings with their hundreds of farming villages had been laid waste by the Conqueror's Harrowing of the North. Entire communities had been wiped out. Houses and farms were burned to the ground. Crops destroyed. Women, children and the old were slaughtered without mercy or left to die from starvation. The few survivors were forced into serfdom, their lives riven by the ambitions of their Norman overlords. Since then the country had been dragged unwillingly into endless wars against the kings of Scotland and of France in order to bolster the power of the Norman usurpers. It was no surprise the village folk still sang the old songs, still dreamed the dream of freedom.

They reached the foregate and proceeded alongside the moat in the shadow of the walls. Edberg hailed the lookout in the tower. The drawbridge was lowered and the portcullis raised. Hildegard was overcome with relief as they clipped across the bridge into the bailey. Her fear of the outlaws had been checked with an effort. She knew her nun's habit was regarded with hostility. Only caution seemed to have held the men from violence.

As the portcullis crashed shut she slipped from the saddle. Safe at last, she thought. Then she saw a group of men with the sign of the blue marsh dragon on their tunics.

She turned away.

Edberg took hold of her horse's bridle. 'We'll see to the horses and your hounds, sister. You'll want to speak to the steward.'

I certainly will, she thought, as she stamped her feet to bring some life back. Her cloak smelled strongly of smoke as she went to find Ulf.

In the bailey, they were already preparing the wagons for the cortège. Several carts were draped in black. One of them, a char, was more elaborate than the rest. The sides were made of decorated wood panels. Black dyed canvas was stretched over wooden hoops fixed across the vehicle itself. At the head of the cortège, covered by a cloth of scarlet and gold, was the coffin containing its secret cargo of stones.

This is madness, Hildegard thought as she began to make her way through the crowd of servants loading the sumpter carts. Why on earth was Ulf allowing the funeral to go ahead? She found the steward on the steps of the hall overseeing everything with a frown of concentration. When he saw her he said, 'So you didn't find her?'

'No, but we found her pony, a burning mill and a band of looters.' She briefly explained.

'Let's talk more fully later. I want you to come

218

and meet the moot-folk in the village. Then that's one line of enquiry we can put to rest at least. Do you mind coming with me now?'

The self-styled Savoy Boys met in the village that lay close to the castle's outer defences. When it wasn't in the throes of St. Willibrod's feast it was a thriving community of serfs and freemen called Low Hutton. The reeve's house was a convenient meeting place for those who worked inside the castle and for those who worked the fields.

The village itself was a higgledy-piggledy group of something like fifty wattle-and-daub dwellings thatched with rye grass and linked by a meandering network of narrow lanes and what the locals called laups. Surrounding these one-storey habitations were the strips for beans, peas, turnips and grain and then the Lammas lands and the orchards. Enclosing all of it was the Royal Forest. Apart from scutage, sending men-at-arms to serve the king, Lord Roger's main responsibility to the Crown was his stewardship of this vast tract of country and the preservation of game for the king's own table. There was a lodge in the forest for the use of hunting parties, halfway between the castle and York.

As they made their way into the village the moss-covered roofs and slanting lintels were half hidden under a fog of lung-wrenching smoke that lay like a pall above the ground. Usually well ordered, today hooded villeins loomed out of this roke as they prepared for the feast that would begin when night fell. Meanwhile the lanes were filled with screaming swine and the pungent stench of fresh blood. In the poor light the fires burned out of the November fret as if through breaches in the walls of hell, while soot-faced stokers turned from their task to watch as Ulf and Hildegard walked by. The stench of death was everywhere.

The reeve's dwelling was a little bigger than the rest, as befitted his status. The hurdles set round it to keep in the pig and poultry were made with skill.

They stooped under the lintel, a chorus of gruff voices rising and falling in the heat of argument, but when the steward followed by a nun came in, a chilling silence descended. Hildegard peered into the gloom. By the sound of it there must be at least half a dozen villagers already present, she guessed, cottars, bordars, villeins and the like. She could just make out a few shapes hidden behind the smoke from an open fire that sputtered in the middle of the floor. The only other light was a rush lamp on a pole by the door. Hildegard's nostrils twitched at the rank smell of damp wool, fresh manure and sweat that pervaded the place. The smoke from the fire pit was sucked up by the draught towards a hole in the roof but owing to the direction of the wind it continually spiralled back again into the cottage. Everybody, it seemed, was taking turns to cough. Before long, Hildegard found herself joining in.

A spokesman distinguished himself from the group, introducing himself as the reeve. 'I'm Dagobert, son of Dagobart.'

A Saxon then, of course. Hildegard gave him a straight look. 'Honoured to be here.'

He was a big man, with a dignified manner, and he peered at Hildegard with a certain genial curiosity. 'You're the first Cistercian we've had visiting down this way,' he told her. 'You're welcome.'

'There was that pardoner last week,' a voice corrected from the gloom.

'Different kettle of fish, Caedwin,' replied the reeve without turning his head. 'He was a Fleming, trying to fob us off with fake relics, and his assailant was a sot-wit southerner in the same game. I think we can tell the difference between a Cistercian and a pardoner.' He returned Hildegard's straight look. 'The lord steward tells me you've been frettin' about where we stand on certain matters – given the unrest at the present time?'

Her reply was direct. 'I can see you have a strong case for wanting change. You seem to feel the Normans are bleeding you dry and the Church is doing likewise?'

'That's the long and short of it,' he replied. 'What we want is an end to all these taxes so what we earn by the sweat of our labours we keep to enjoy. Instead of as now, when all our profit goes to fuel the wars or keep the pope in idle luxury. It's not right.'

'I worked it out t'other day,' a voice behind the smoke broke in. 'I get fifteen days a quarter to tend my own crops, and the rest of the time I have to work for the lord of the manor for nowt. What can I do in fifteen days? We want to be hired labour, not bonded labour like slaves. Are we not men?'

'And women,' said a different voice.

'*When Adam delved and Eve span*,' said another, and the rest chimed in with, '*who was then the gentleman?*'

'I see,' said Hildegard, 'but I was wondering what you felt about Master Tyler's other demands?'

There was some uncomfortable shuffling behind the haze. From outside, the squeal of a stuck pig came loud and clear. It sounded strangely human. Dagobert began to bluster. 'I don't think any of us want to go that far, sister.'

Inside the cottage there was an ominous silence.

Hildegard was glad Ulf was standing beside her. She glanced at each of the shapes as best she could through the smoke and said, 'As I understand it, Master Tyler wanted an end to punishment by outlawry? That seems just. It is often used as an excuse by the courts to seize a man's lands and increase those of his accuser.' The silence continued. 'He also wanted an end to all nobility but the King?' Nobody interrupted. 'And to all clergy but the Archbishop of Canterbury?'

'Too late for Sudbury now!' A nervous laugh was quickly stifled.

A voice she hadn't heard before began to intone from behind the smoke. 'The great lords of the realm have stolen our land! The Roman Church has stolen our liberty! The usurpers have taken our grain, our herds, our homes! What's left to the poor but blood and bones? The spirit of the people cries for vengeance while we sit by and

222

watch. Misery on us! Misery on all who sit by!'

Dagobert cut through this and the rising murmurs of agreement it aroused. 'The sister doesn't want all that. What she wants to know is what we're asking for. And it's this.' He linked his thumbs in the front of his tunic, looking set for a speech, but it was short. He said, 'What we want is no tax more than one fifteenth of movable wealth. Flat.'

There were cheers.

'The question is, sister, why should we have to pay one tenth of our crops to the Church?'

'Birth, marriage and death. They tax the lot. Soon it'll be the air we breathe,' a voice added.

Dagobert interrupted again. 'I believe we've put our case clearly enough, Sister. At least it's a country where we're still free to speak our minds. But we could sit on our backsides all night arguing. I'm to my bed. It's well past eight o' the clock.' He began to urge his visitors towards the door with a sudden, determined haste.

There was a scramble to get out once it was clear the meeting was over. Ulf thrust out his mace to make a passageway for Hildegard but she drew back and waited in humility until the last villager had left. The reeve loomed over her. 'Don't take it to heart, Sister,' he apologised. 'It's not personal. Your people do good work down at Swyne.'

When she and Ulf got outside she turned to him. 'I wonder if the Archbishop of Canterbury felt it wasn't personal when they stuck his head on a pike and put it on London Bridge?'

They set off up the muddy, ill-lit tunnel

between the cottages. They hadn't gone far when they heard the voice of two men raised in argument on the path ahead.

'What did you expect him to say, you stupid bastard?' one of them was demanding fiercely.

'Keep your festering gob shut then!' came the reply. There was the sound of a scuffle and a woman's voice cut in, 'Oh, leave him, John, he's not worth it. He's only a fuller.'

'Aye, get back to your vat, you stinking idiot!' There was a thump. When Hildegard and Ulf turned a corner they found two villeins squaring up to each other. The men didn't hear them approach and it was only when Ulf was almost on top of them that they realised they were observed and fell back in confusion. Ulf merely carved his way between them without a word. Hildegard was impressed when they backed off – they were thick-set fellows and there were two of them – but by the time she reached them they were doffing their caps and trying to lose themselves in the shadows.

She caught up with Ulf and they had reached the end of the lane when a voice came floating after them. 'You're Saxon like the rest of us, steward. When the day of reckoning comes, don't you forget it!'

Hildegard gave Ulf a glance. His face was set in stone.

It was in a darker frame of mind that they returned to the castle. The raucous shouts of drunks and their constant drumming down by the bonfires on the green, together with the list of injustices experienced by the villagers, underlined

224

the rage that was still brewing in the land. The whole world seemed to teeter on the brink of chaos just as Edberg had claimed on the way back from the mill. How long, she wondered, before the people rose up again and butchered their oppressors? It wasn't only in England. Look at the *Jacqueries* in France a few years ago, she thought. They had rampaged round Paris slaughtering the landlords and burning their houses and castles without restraint. Even the Dauphin had retreated behind his walls, like a prisoner in his own kingdom. Now the Companies of Routiers had more power than anyone else but the peasants themselves had been reduced to even worse poverty by the devastation of their farms. There was the rising in Flanders as well. It could happen here on the same scale. Civil war. Rebels exterminated. Famine the result. She believed in the justice of the people's cause but the violence of an armed revolt filled her with horror.

Ulf looked grimmer than ever. Before parting he took her by the arm and muttered, 'if this goes on, everybody's going to have to take sides. Blood will flow.' With this warning, he flung abruptly away.

Hildegard walked slowly over to the tower staircase leading up to her chamber. She was wondering what would happen if it became known what she had in her scrip: a relic that symbolised the sacred covenant of Wat Tyler with those of his fellow-countrymen who dreamed of justice.

As Hildegard was passing the guest-master's chamber on the floor below her own, the guest-master himself came to the door with a couple of gloomy-looking jongleurs. '–so there'll be no more work here, lads, not for the time being at any rate,' he was telling them. 'Best get on over to York in my view, until this place is back to normal.' They parted and after watching them go Hildegard approached the guest-master. He was a pot-bellied, rosy-cheeked old fellow with a clipped white beard and was dressed convincingly in parti-coloured hose and the ubiquitous poulaines. The points were at least four inches long and she wondered fleetingly how he managed to get about.

She smiled. 'Greetings, master. I was wondering whether you would do me the favour of answering a question about a couple of guests?'

'Most certainly, Sister. Come inside and ask away.' He settled her comfortably in a chair and when he was seated himself beside his pile of ledgers he leaned forward. 'Well?'

'I've been wondering about the two friars who are staying over for St. Martin's week.'

'Good fellows,' he said, sitting back. 'No trouble whatsoever. Kept themselves to themselves. Pity they've gone–'

'Gone?'

'Left at dawn when the Lombards rode out. Be back in Beverley by now I should think. But they weren't friars.' He chuckled. 'One of them had got himself a nice little post as corrodian, though he didn't say what service he rendered the brothers in return for his keep. The other fellow was a companion from his youth and they'd decided to take a short break together over Martinmas. I reckon they had more entertainment than they

226

bargained for.'

'It was put about that they were friars–' she insisted.

'I don't know how that rumour started. We haven't had a friar in here for the last year. Not even to take Lord Roger's confession, save his soul.'

All she wanted was to go up to her chamber and catch up on her sleep, but instead Hildegard went to find Ulf. He was overseeing the guests who remained in the hall.

It was a sombre occasion. Sir Ralph was the only man at the top table. Avice and Sibilla were present. Philippa was just leaving. The servants went back and forth without a smile. There was no singing.

Ulf turned as she approached and she said, 'I'm not here to eat and drink. I just thought you might like to know that those two so-called friars have already left.'

'So-called?'

She nodded. 'One of them was a corrodian at the friary in Beverley. The other was just a companion. Neither of them were friars as it turns out.'

'Let's not drag those two into it,' advised Ulf in a harassed tone. 'There are more important things to consider. You remember you asked me right at the start who would want to poison Roger and I said–'

'Did I want the long list or the short one? Yes, I remember. And have you a list?'

'Let's go somewhere quiet. I want your views.' He cast a glance round the Great Hall. There was nothing that needed his attention just now. He led the way to his office.

'I didn't want to set too many hares running,' he said as soon as they were seated. 'I hoped somebody would have given me a useful whisper by now and we'd have caught this poisonous devil. But there's been no hint of a name.' He poured them both a drink of Rhenish. 'So now I'm going to give rein to my blackest thoughts, the saints forgive me. But don't forget, I've lived cheek-by-jowl with the family all my life, I know their ways, and I'm forced to it.' With a grim expression he began. 'We have to look at motives. And we need to start with the folk closest to Roger.'

'The family, you mean?'

He nodded. 'Clearly young Edwin's not involved as he's banished and probably in France. So, who do we have who would gain from Roger's death? First, there's Melisen. She knows full well that if she doesn't produce an heir soon Roger will have no compunction in throwing her out. You know what he's like. However,' he frowned, 'I've had a look at the marriage settlement since we last discussed matters. With Roger dead, heir or not, she'll inherit a fortune.'

Hildegard was stunned to hear him talk so cynically. It was unlike him. Putting that thought to one side she asked, 'What about Sir Ralph's baby son?'

'His claim could be set aside. It was only proclaimed in the hall during a drunken riot. There's nothing written down. And of course,' he added with a crooked smile, 'should Melisen happen to find herself with child now, that would strengthen her claim.'

'How could she, with Roger dead?'

'With the help of a virile young squire, perhaps?'

Slowly she asked, 'Are you suggesting they might have plotted together to get him out of the way?' She remembered the immaculate youth escorting Melisen into the church for the requiem mass. With that image in mind the idea suddenly seemed less far fetched.

But Ulf continued. 'As well as that, as a widow, at her age, with or without a child, but with the sort of wealth she would inherit, she could remarry whomever she liked, royalty included.' He added, 'I don't think she's without ambition despite her whims. Then,' he went on before Hildegard could do no more than open her mouth, 'There's Sir William. It's well known he's jealous of his brother-in-law. He owns barren lands near the Borders, a place you'd only go to if you wanted to see your guts served on a platter. Lady Avice came to him with a tract in Holderness but it's nothing but marsh. The best she offers is portage in and out of Ravenser and a tax or two from Wyke now it's called Kingstown on the Hull. Otherwise it's fish, fish, fish, import, export, and continual fights with the burgesses over who should pay what, and all revenues finishing up in King Richard's coffers after Lord Roger's had a dip. You can imagine how William feels about that.'

'So what difference does it make to William if Roger is dead? He can't get his hands on Hutton lands—'

'He could put a strong case for being the only one capable of running the estate. He's hardly stretched at present.'

'But there's Sir Ralph–'

'Do you seriously imagine Ralph has the will to organise a candle stall?'

She reserved her opinion and instead asked, 'So by default–'

'William would take the reins as guardian–'

'But the others wouldn't stand for it. I mean, despite what you say, Sir Ralph would object most strongly and–'

'And Sir William would take up arms to force his case.'

They contemplated the blood-shed that would ensue should it come to that.

Ulf hadn't reached the end of his list, however. He said, 'And then, of course, there's Lady Sibilla. If Sir William has a rival, it's his sister-in-law. This birth, convenient of course, but do you imagine she's going to sit and wait until the child comes of age before reaping the benefit? Not on your life. She'd be perfectly capable of running things herself on the child's behalf. She has a good case.'

'I understand she has lands to the east along the coast?'

'She has. To an ambitious woman, Hutton could be a gem beyond compare. She would own a swathe from the sea to the gates of York itself, and it won't have escaped her notice that she could compete with the Nevilles if she got her hands on all this.' He waved an arm.

'She struck me as being pretty shrewd. And it's lucky to have borne a son–' She furrowed her brow. 'In that connection–'

'Let me go on.'

'There's more?'

'You want the full list of those who could benefit, don't you?' Ulf gave a heavy sigh and reached for his goblet. He drank deeply then wiped dry the gold hairs of his beard. His frown deepened. 'As you so rightly observed, sister, there's Philippa.' His tone was heavy. Clearly he didn't like the suspicions that were apparently teeming through his mind. 'With her father out of the way, Philippa could marry where she chooses. You said she told you as much.' He looked so troubled Hildegard's heart went out to him. She could see he was having difficulty going on. 'Not only could she many anyone she liked,' he admitted, 'she could apply to have the law set aside and prove inheritance on her own behalf. She's the eldest. She's of age. All that stops her inheriting every stick and stone is her father's adherence to Norman law. Which brings us,' he paused, 'to the Lombards.'

'Ah.'

'You must have noticed how intimate she and Ludovico are?'

'Is this the first time they've met?'

'I suspect he turned up in Kent after Melisen and Roger's wedding. Philippa stayed down there for a couple of months. And these Lombardy men get everywhere.'

'But what would Ludovico have to do with it?' she asked cautiously.

Ulf looked unhappy. 'I don't believe Philippa would think up something like this by herself.' He gave her a wild look. 'But Ludovico must have realised when they first met he could be worth a pope's ransom if he controlled both ends of the wool trade, production here in Yorkshire, the finishing and making up in Italy.'

'You're seriously suggesting he could have put her up to poisoning her own father?'

'Sometimes a black-hearted devil can persuade a soft, gullible girl to do anything he likes so long as it's in the name of love.'

Hildegard gave him a sceptical glance. 'Do we know he's black-hearted?' She ignored the question of the gullible girl.

'We can't know he's not.'

'You said there'd be a lot of hares set running, Ulf. What you're saying, in brief, is that every member of the family benefits from Roger's death.'

Hildegard went up to her room. It was late by now. She couldn't stop yawning. There had been no sleep since the ride out to the mill and back. She flung her cloak on its hook, removed her boots and lay down on the straw pallet in a corner of the chamber. Ulf had made it clear who would gain from poisoning Roger – practically everyone – but he hadn't answered the real question which was: who would *want* to poison him? It might have a somewhat different answer.

A cock crowing shortly around dawn drew her from the depths of sleep. She stretched. She sat up. A pall of silence seemed to lie over the entire castle. She rose from the pallet, went to the window, and looked down into the bailey.

The carts were still lined up against the walls,

232

augmented by one or two more since yesterday. A steady downpour puddled in the ruts their wheels had made. Melisen's char with its black awning seemed to have been filled with green branches. When she peered closer she realised it was yew. Appropriate for a funeral. She couldn't help wondering why Roger hadn't sent instructions to Ulf to stop the charade. His 'death' hadn't flushed out the poisoner as he had hoped. Eventually people would have to be told the truth. She wouldn't like to be in his shoes when he made a clean breast of things. She wondered how he would try to wriggle out of it. He wouldn't be able to put the blame on his steward because she was a witness to his orders. And if he tried to blame her – the idea was unthinkable.

Pulling on her cloak and ramming her feet back inside her boots she went out in the hope of finding something to eat in the Great Hall.

There were plenty of people about, she noticed, when she pushed open the doors. The servants, as ever, were run off their feet, keeping everybody fed and watered, and an army of others were hauling packs of food from the kitchens to load on to the rest of the sumpter wagons. She stood to one side to let them through. There was a strange atmosphere about the place. She couldn't name it. But you could cut it with a knife. Then Melisen, weeping, came out.

She was already dressed for the journey in a long black cloak with a sweeping hood and was escorted by a retinue of servants. Her squire lent his strong shoulder while she dabbed feebly at her eyes and drooped against him. They stepped outside into the rain. The squire raised a stole above her head and they hurried towards the char. They were followed by Philippa. She wore a grim expression and acknowledged Hildegard with a distracted bob of her head. After her came her personal maid, carrying a large object covered by a cloth.

Glancing across the bailey Hildegard saw that Sibilla and the baby were already sitting in the second char on a mound of furs with Sir Ralph in attendance. A hooded shape sat behind her which Hildegard took to be Avice.

Overhead the sky was weeping on one and all. It was a dreadful day to have to set out. She went indoors.

Ulf, wearing a black surcoat with his riding cloak thrown over his shoulders, was pacing back and forth in front of the dais. When she approached he glanced up with a start. 'Didn't you hear all that last night?'

'The singing in the Hall? I thought it rather subdued–'

'No, I don't mean that. You've no idea what's happened, have you?' He gave a stricken shake of his head. 'This place must have a curse on it.'

'What do you mean?'

His lips tightened. 'Sir William killed a man.'

'Sir William?'

He nodded.

'Who–?'

'Godric, the third yeoman.'

'You mean the one who serves Roger at table?'

He nodded again. Behind him a row of kitchen staff were hauling out the last of the provisions with their heads lowered.

'But why? What happened?'

'He came barging in half way through supper, ranting something about yeomen, and when Godric stepped forth William drew his knife and slashed out at him. It was witnessed by the entire household. He put Godric's eye out. The man was dead within seconds.'

'What did you do?'

He glanced away and his lips tightened again. 'I wasn't here. I had some business to attend to. They had to come and fetch me.' He didn't elaborate.

'So how has William accounted for himself?'

Ulf looked even more enraged. 'He hasn't. He fled. Half a dozen of his men went with him. They rode away before anybody could stop them.' Ulf was furious and glared round the hall. 'I won't blame them. It's not their fault. They were unarmed.' He gave Hildegard a fierce look. 'If you're ready, we're leaving at once.'

'Hold on, I've got to get my bag.'

She ran up to her room and began to gather her things. William. They knew he had an ungovernable temper. But to kill an unarmed servant was shocking. Just then there was a noise outside in the corridor. With her mind in turmoil she would have ignored it but it was accompanied by the sound of running feet. An irritable voice shouted something. The voice came again, this time high and wheedling. A crash followed as of an object being thrown. Strong language followed. Then she heard pounding feet and another crash.

With her bag half packed Hildegard poked her head out in time to see one of Ralph's men picking himself up off the floor.

'What's going on?' she asked.

He gave her a scowl. It was the man she had outfaced earlier in the kitchen yard over his cruelty to the hen. She felt a shiver go through her.

'It's Sir Ralph's cat. It won't leave. It doesn't like rain.' He straightened his clothes and began to make for a chamber at the far end of the corridor into which the cat was just disappearing with a flick of its tail.

Thinking she might be of some help in cornering the animal, as well as making sure it went unharmed, Hildegard followed. At that point Sueno de Schockwynde came up from the yard.

'They're all waiting, sister,' he boomed, 'And Sir Ralph will not leave without his little cat. Where is the naughty fellow?'

'Come and help,' called Hildegard over her shoulder and as she turned into one of the rooms after the servant she added, 'He's in here.'

Master Jacques was crouching on a bench, fur erect, tail lashing, angry hissing issuing from between his pretty jaws. Ralph's man was inching towards him without a sound. Suddenly he hurled himself on the cat but at that precise moment Sueno reached the doorway and exclaimed in his usual voice, 'I say! What a wicked little devil!'

It was enough to distract the servant, and Master Jacques, seizing his opportunity, hared off towards the chimney and, with a flying leap, sprang for safety inside. His escape was brief. He was at once sent back down in a shower of soot, to land in a yowling heap on the hearth.

The servant threw himself on top of the confused animal and secured him by the scruff of his neck. 'Got you, you little bastard!' he muttered between clenched teeth.

'Well caught, sir!' exclaimed Sueno, sauntering on into the room with a beaming smile.

The cat was all teeth and claws but once trapped, he was not going to escape. The servant, grimacing and with fresh scratches to add to the ones already visible on his face bore the protesting Master Jacques towards the door. He had to pass close to where Hildegard was standing and as he drew level he swivelled his head with something like surprise. Where before his expression had been merely hostile, now a look of confusion came over his face. His glance swept her from head to toe then travelled back to her face. Without a word he took the cat outside.

'Only at Hutton, eh?' Sueno smiled up at Hildegard. He was unaware of any undercurrent. 'Sir Ralph really is incorrigible. But now I suppose we can move off. May I accompany you to Meaux, sister?'

'Thank you, Master Sueno, but would you give me a moment?' She looked down the corridor to see the servant hurrying towards the stairs with the cat held at arm's length, claws well out of range of his face. He started the descent to the yard at a rapid clip. She put him out of her mind. There was something else to consider. It was Master Jacques. He had been ejected with startling force from inside the chimney.

While Sueno ambled over to inspect recent work on the window embrasure Hildegard went to the chimney and, resting one hand on the ledge, peered up to see what had prevented the cat's escape. Sure enough there was a blockage. Reaching up she tugged at a piece of cloth that was jammed inside. It was velvet, she realised as soon as her fingers touched it. She dragged it down and shook it free of soot.

When she unfolded it she found it was a chaperon of triple-died velvet, a little singed at the back. Wrapped inside was a pair of poulaines with double latchets and the sort of long points that had prompted Ulf to mention a statutory fine for the wearer of similar footwear earlier. Of course, no fine would be payable if they were the property of the owner of the chaperon. She rubbed it between finger and thumb. It was the best quality fabric and only somebody with the status of a knight would be allowed the privilege of wearing such an expensive dye. The shoes themselves were made of soft leather and had a pattern of incised cross-hatching. More significantly, they were stained with several dark blotches, the colour of dried blood.

By the time she returned to the yard accompanied by Sueno de Schockwynde, who had noticed nothing of the find she had hidden under her cloak, the cortège was about to move off. All sounds were muffled even though the place was seething with people. The swift feet, soft shod, the lowered voices of the noisiest Saxon serving man, and even the muffled rattle of the horses' bridles, confirmed that the castle was in deep mourning. There was an additional atmosphere of stunned fear at the enormity of what Sir William had done to one of their own.

Ulf had a face like thunder. When Hildegard approached, he growled, 'Just because we're still going to Meaux they imagine he's going to get off.' He gave a grimace. 'Not if I have anything to do with it.' Bestowing on her a look of anguish, he walked away with long, hurried strides that took him to the head of the convoy.

The de Hutton contingent set off first, followed by Sir Ralph's family, his household taking up several wagons. As she walked over to take her place at the end of the line she spotted Ralph's man-servant sitting with Master Jacques and some of the other personal attendants. She drew level. He lifted his head to watch her and his black glance held hers in a prolonged stare until the wagon carried him away out of the yard.

His rich attire showed he was one of the favourites. Apart from an untidily clipped beard and a bloodshot right eye, he would have looked convincing enough in the role of upper servant. There was something at odds, however, between his manner and his garments. He wore them awkwardly. And it was that red eye, she thought. As she had looked into his face she had been unable to miss it. A shudder of revulsion drove through her. There was no doubt who he was. It was barely conceivable that one of Sir Ralph's own attendants should behave as he had done. He was more than a mere man-at-arms like those other louts he had been drinking with. He was one of the upper servants with privileges and responsibilities. Now, by the malice of his glance, she guessed he knew who she was too.

Master Sueno was a welcome distraction as he fussed around to help Hildegard climb into the space he had saved for her by his side. They occupied the last wagon to leave. Her two hounds had been reluctantly released by Burthred, the little kitchen serf, but, to his great excitement, he now travelled with Roger's kitcheners so that he could watch over the hounds when they reached Meaux. Duchess and Bermonda loped along beside the cavalcade, as attentive as guardian spirits.

As the wagons rattled on down the lane into the forest Hildegard pondered over the bundle she had found in the chimney and wondered if the poulaines would match the prints beside the body of the murdered girl. She would wager a large sum that they would and her heart was heavy to think what this might imply for Ralph's part in the terrible and mystifying events that had swept them all into their coils.

Chapter Eleven

It was a full day's ride down to Meaux. Apparently there had been some discussion about whether it would be advisable, owing to the shortness of the days, to break the journey and spend the night in one of Roger's hunting lodges. Sibilla was keen to stop for the baby's sake and Ralph agreed. But Melisen had to be consulted. Sueno explained all this to Hildegard.

'And, sweet girl,' he went on, 'she was in floods of tears at the thought of Lord Roger's body being shaken to bits in its coffin on the rutted track so she pleaded strongly that we should travel directly as she could not bear the thought of it all continuing "endlessly, endlessly, end-lessly–" her very words and intonation,' he pointed out, looking pleased with his perform-ance. Hildegard said she did not doubt it.

His expression changed. 'But it's a bad busi-ness, Sir William behaving in that way. What on earth got into him? It was all so sudden.'

'Were you present, master?'

He shook his head and gave a shudder. 'I'd gone to my bed long before but I heard all about it this morning. They say–' he leaned forward confidentially, 'that it was jealousy.' He sniffed. 'Sir William fighting over a woman – a *servant!* Whatever next!'

The carts creaked alarmingly as they trundled over the track after the hearse. Their pace was slow because of the mud that kept clogging the wheels. Every few minutes a cry would go up from the carters, 'Dun's in t'mire!' and the whole train would have to halt for a while to let the servants dig them out where they were stuck. Spare wheels were carried among the baggage, she noted, Ulf's foresight against breakages.

She longed for an opportunity to show him the velvet chaperon and the fashionable shoes and see what he made of them, as well as to hear what else he had to say about William. But he was far up the trail, riding beside the driver of the six plumed horses.

The twists and turns of the track together with the failing light as the day drew on made the leading wagons difficult to see, and as they entered the thickest part of the forest even Melisen's foliage-bedecked wagon was lost in the gloom. Soon they were guided only by the scent of crushed yew, the occasional commands of the servants, the jingle of harness and the light of flares carried by the lamp-men, visible as a chain of fire between the trees.

There were more shouts from in front and the train came to another halt. The two horses pulling the wagon Master Sueno had requisitioned were backed up by the cart in front and by the time the grooms had placated the skittering animals the shouting from up the track had increased.

It was augmented by a sound like the clash of steel. Hildegard stood up in the cart and tried to make out what was happening.

'Somebody else stuck in the quag,' suggested Sueno affably.

'I think not. This is something else.'

Hildegard stepped down, lifting her hem above the mud, and took a few paces towards the front, but before she could go further there was the sound of horses crashing through the under-growth and she was just in time to make out three shadowy riders, cloaks flying, riding their horses off into the night. She began to run. Her hounds followed. Slipping and panting, she reached the lead wagon to find Ulf crouching on the ground, one hand clutched to his left shoulder.

'I'm all right,' he managed to gasp as she knelt beside him. 'Nothing but a flesh wound. It's Melisen.'

'What?'

'They've taken her.'

There was a commotion in the undergrowth as half a dozen men on foot came panting back. 'We lost them almost at once, sir. They vanished like wraiths. It's too dark to follow. They must know these woods like the back of their hands.'

'I'll show you the back of my hand,' gasped Ulf, evidently in pain, 'if you don't get on your horses after them.'

Arguing among themselves about who was to blame for giving up so quickly, and why the horses hadn't been unstrung at once, and how there were no such things as ghosts, the men peeled off in separate directions while Ulf raised himself to his feet. He leaned heavily against the side of the wagon in which Melisen had been travelling and Hildegard could see blood darkening the cloth of his surcoat.

'Let me look,' she said tersely. The swamping scent of funeral lilies filled the air.

With a small exhalation she saw that it was, as he had guessed, only a flesh wound. But it was bad enough. She staunched it and cleaned it as best she could, then bandaged it while he told her what had happened.

'I'd gone on ahead with three or four men to inspect the trail. The others were at their ease coming on foot to rest the horses. Then we heard a commotion behind us. When we rode back we saw Sir William with Lady Melisen across his saddle and one of his guards holding a knife to Sir Ralph's throat. I judged Ralph well able to take care of himself so I threw myself after William, only to be cut at by some fellow who sprang at me from behind a tree. They had obviously planned the whole thing with care. The knife-wielding fellow fled before Sir Ralph could scramble from the wagon and grab his sword. He'd put aside his weapons in order to ride for a while with the baby.'

Ralph was standing in the middle of the track with his sword raised against the long-departed attackers, bellowing with rage. 'I can't leave Sibilla. Nor dare I leave little Roger,' he was saying as Hildegard walked up. He turned to her. 'He must have taken leave of his senses. What can he want with Melisen, for heaven's sakes? It defies all reason.' He glared at Ulf. 'You must have your ear to the ground, steward. What the devil's he up to?'

'Haven't an inkling, sire. Yesterday was bad enough but this – it beats all imagining!' He turned to Hildegard and spread one arm. 'What's his game?'

'I don't know Sir William,' said Hildegard carefully. 'Has he taken her with malicious intent, do you think, or is there some other, more subtle reason?'

Sir Ralph waved his sword. 'No time for speculation. Drive on, steward! We must get my lady and the babe to safety with all haste. Let's keep them from harm at least.'

Reluctantly Ulf climbed into the saddle. He

244

was scowling. 'If they value their necks, the trackers will find their quarry and bring him to us at Meaux.'

The remaining men, scattered in some disarray, were gazing helplessly off into the trees with their swords drawn. He ordered them to their horses. The few who wore Sir William's blue dragon badge stood in a disconsolate group, clearly not knowing whether they were to be put in shackles as punishment for Lady Melisen's abduction or have their throats swiftly cut, but Ulf gestured for them to follow under escort.

He turned to Hildegard. 'Have a care. Don't loiter at the end of the train. Ride with me. Who knows what further evil that fiend has in mind.'

'I'll ride with Master Sueno,' she said. 'He'll be glad of the company. And besides, I think it's only Lady Melisen William requires in this particular game.'

Despite his pleas to the contrary, she waited by the side of the track with her hounds close about her while the wagons of the de Hutton household, followed by those of Ralph and Sibilla, passed. The manservant, still in charge of Master Jacques, had drawn a broadsword and was glancing from side to side as the wagon made its way through the trees. He noticed her because she saw his black eyes flicker over her as he went by.

When the last wagon hove into view Hildegard climbed aboard. The horses were whipped to as brisk a pace as possible through the mud. With her mind busy with the possible reasons for William's latest eruption into violence, she described to Sueno what had taken place, pausing only when she noticed how his hand was gripping the hilt of his sword. The thought of Sir William, armed, rampaging through the forest with the intention of abducting whomsoever he pleased, was enough to frighten anyone and it made the master builder's eyes stare in shock and his tongue, for once, fall silent. In fact it was not only Master Sueno who started in fear at every sound coming out of the dark wood. The servants huddled together like sheep waiting for the onslaught of a pack of wolves and the men-at-arms, those left to protect the cavalcade, rode all the way with their swords at the ready and their eyes pricked for further attack.

And so it was, some time later, when the moon hung suspended like a great lantern in the void and shed its sinister glow over the forest, that they finally arrived at the Abbey of Meaux.

Chapter Twelve

'What the devil are you doing here?' Roger spoke between gritted teeth in a voice so low that only Hildegard and Ulf could catch his words. 'God's nails!' he rasped. 'Have you taken leave of your senses? And is that supposed to be me in there?' He gestured towards the coffin. 'What the hell am I supposed to tell Hubert? He'll think I'm stark staring mad.' He surveyed the cortège from beneath his borrowed cowl with disbelief.

The moon gleamed down, covering the bustling scene in the courtyard with sheet silver. A light mist ghosted about in the nooks and crannies. To an observer the hand on Ulf's arm was merely to detain him long enough to indicate where the household was to be lodged.

'I thank you, Father Prior,' said Ulf in a loud voice as Ralph escorted Sibilla and the baby across the garth to the guest lodge. As soon as they were out of earshot he demanded, 'What do you mean, have I taken leave of my senses? I'm following orders.'

'I only meant if – *if* – you didn't find the culprit straight off, to tempt him out by ... oh, I don't know! I wasn't thinking straight, for heaven's sake. Would you think straight if somebody tried to poison you? I never dreamed you'd take it to these lengths. Plumes for God's shite! Sorry, Hildegard.' He broke off. 'It's just a shock. I was delirious, couldn't you tell? Anyway, you'd better both come inside. Thank heavens Hubert's praying again.'

As Ulf and Hildegard were swept along in his wake Ulf said, 'Am I mad or is it him? He distinctly said–'

'He's unhinged by everything that's happened,' Hildegard assured him. 'He doesn't know who to trust, which way to turn. Be patient. It's now he needs you most.'

'Wait until I tell him about Melisen.' Ulf looked as if he were about to be hanged.

Hildegard paused outside the chamber in which Roger had been so comfortably lodged – while they had been embroiled in the hellish events at Castle Hutton – and asked a lurking novice to bring hot water.

Ulf overheard her request. 'You're not thinking of adding water to the lord abbot's wine, are you? I warn you against such desecration.'

'I have herbs with me. Mixed with hot water they should rebalance Roger's humours and make him more amenable to reason,' Hildegard explained. 'Don't tell him anything until after we've supped.'

'I'm not supping herbs right now. That's the last thing I want,' grumbled Ulf.

'You won't have to. This is for Roger only. We'll have the wine you mentioned.'

For the first time since they had emerged from the forest into the courtyard at Meaux Ulf's spirits seemed to rise and a small gleam of hope entered his eyes at the thought of Hildegard with a plan. He went inside to find Roger lolling on a couch heaped with sheep-skins. Underneath the threadbare habit, he wore an ankle-length garment of stitched skins with the wool turned inwards for extra warmth.

'Well, steward,' he snapped, 'why haven't you discovered this poisoner? What's the matter with you? Can't your spies come up with a name?'

'There are several problems, my lord,' Ulf began. Catching Hildegard's eye, he slowed his speech and appeared to be sorting his words in order to give Roger the facts as clearly as possible – but in fact to give Hildegard time to mix her potion.

Luckily at that moment the door opened and the novice brought in a pitcher of wine and the flagon of hot water she needed.

248

As choleric as always, however, Roger was jumping with impatience. 'Come on, man, spit it out! A name is what I want! What do you think I pay you for?'

'Then you've had no news from Hutton since you arrived here?' Ulf stalled.

'Not a whisper.'

'A lot has happened,' he stalled again.

By now Hildegard had mixed some of the water with the herbal concoction. 'A moment, Roger. I've made you a balancing draught against the poison you drank.' She handed it to him with a warm smile.

'Always get your own way, you, don't you? I remember how you used to–' Her steady gaze stopped him in mid-sentence and he cleared his throat. 'I still can't get my head around your changed life. Anyway, *ge vu!*' He threw the potion back then smacked his lips and held out the beaker for more.

'That will suffice for now,' said Hildegard. 'You don't want to overdo it.'

'I am entirely in your hands,' replied Roger, settling back on the couch and putting up his feet in their kidskin night boots. He began to yawn and Hildegard caught Ulf's eye and gave him a slight nod.

'Well, sire,' began the steward in a slow soothing tone.

Roger yawned again. 'Where's Melisen? I didn't notice her in the garth.'

'She still believes you dead, sire,' Ulf began in a reproachful tone.

Roger chuckled. 'You really did take me at my

word, didn't you? It was the poison speaking. I would have thought you'd realise that, you sot-wit! So how is the silly goose taking my demise? Plenty of tears?'

Ulf looked shocked. 'She's inconsolable if you want the truth.' He leaned forward to emphasise what he was saying. 'You ordered me to tell everybody you were dead. You said it would flush out the poisoner. You said, "He'll be revealed in his midden of deceit." I did as you ordered.' His voice cracked. 'As a result some terrible things have happened. I can hardly bring myself to speak of them.'

'Go on.'

Ulf braced himself then seemed to decide to give it to Roger straight. Even so his tone roughened when he said, 'Ada, one of Ralph's serving women, was murdered the night before last.'

'What?'

Sparing him nothing, Ulf described the murder scene. As he went into detail Roger stroked his beard and when he finished he said, 'I can't believe it. As soon as my back's turned all hell breaks out. There must be some madman running loose.'

'We might be able to name him,' said Ulf.

Roger raised his eyebrows.

'I told you some terrible things had happened? Well, Sir William stabbed one of your yeomen in full view of everybody. And next–' His hand, noticed Hildegard, strayed to his dagger. Not to attack, she knew, but to defend himself.

Roger was watching his steward closely. 'And next–?'

There was a pause.

Roger's thoughts must have raced like demons to their conclusion because the colour drained from his face and he asked, 'It's Melisen, isn't it?' His voice became hoarse. 'No! I won't believe it! Is she dead too? My pretty martlet, *dead?*'

Ulf shook his head at once. 'Not that I know of, my lord,' and he added quickly, 'merely abducted by Sir William and a brace of cronies.'

'*Merely?*' Roger's tone was dangerous. '*Abducted?* What the devil do you mean?'

'He fought valiantly to prevent it,' Hildegard interrupted, 'but was himself pierced by a sword–'

'You have a wound?' asked Roger, voice cold with disbelief.

'It's just my shoulder,' said Ulf.

'Let's see this wound.'

Reluctantly Ulf pulled aside the neck of his hauberk to reveal the dressing that Hildegard had applied. It was blood-stained.

Roger nodded and with an abstracted frown gestured to Ulf to cover himself. 'What happened?'

'It was Sir William with his henchmen. They swooped down without warning on the cortège as we were approaching Brocklebank Dip, snatched Lady Melisen from the funeral wagon and made off with her. I sent men in pursuit. They should be here with news before long.'

'With more than news. Hopefully with the lady herself,' snarled Roger. 'Did she struggle?'

'Like a wildcat, my lord.'

Roger put his head in his hands. When he eventually looked up his expression was bleak. 'Anything else?'

Hildegard said, 'Ulf's told you everything that happened. There's nothing we can do now until your men return from their pursuit of Sir William.' She hesitated. 'Meanwhile perhaps you might consider these.'

She picked up her bag from where it rested beside her chair. 'I found these objects hidden in a chimney shortly before we left.' So saying she opened the bag and drew forth the velvet chaperon and the stained poulaines.

They all looked at them in silence. Rain dripped on to the floor of the room above.

Eventually Roger reached for the chaperon and shook it out. 'Who does this belong to?' he asked.

'Possibly Ada's killer,' Hildegard suggested.

Roger held it up. 'William would never wear a thing like this. We can count him out! Look at it! And whose ridiculous footwear is that?'

'As yet we don't know.' Hildegard turned to Ulf. 'If you look closely you'll see that the pattern is similar to the drawing you made of some of the prints beside Ada's body.'

Ulf fingered the soft leather and gave a grimace. 'I know who these belong to. We have found our princess of the lost slipper.' He glanced from Roger to Hildegard and back. 'They belonged to Godric, the third yeoman. I warned him about a fine if he persisted in wearing them.'

'So the footprint in the barley dust might be his?' asked Hildegard.

'Looks like it,' he replied.

'The inference being: he murdered Ada?' she raised her brows.

Moving close to Roger, Hildegard took him by

the arm. 'So far, my lord, I haven't told you where I found these things but you need to know everything. I found them stuffed inside the chimney in the solar where Ralph and Sibilla were lodged.'

'Ralph? But he's my brother! Are you trying to say he's this murdering madman?' For a moment Roger looked as if he'd been felled by a physical blow.

Hildegard said quickly, 'We must be careful not to jump to conclusions.'

Roger rose to his feet. 'Either Ralph did it or if not it must have been this bloody yeoman who hid them there.'

'No chance. Someone would have noticed him. It's out of his territory,' replied Ulf at once.

Roger fumbled for his sword propped against a nearby chair. 'Where is Ralph? I'll rip the truth from the bastard's throat myself.'

Ulf moved swiftly, crowding Roger so he couldn't leave. 'We must decide whether it's advisable to reveal all our best cards in one fell swoop, my lord. Remember, he thinks you dead. And he may not have put these things up there at all, so by accusing him you might forearm the real culprit.'

Roger shouldered his steward aside, all effects of Hildegard's potion apparently worn off. 'To hell with talk! I'll deal with Ralph when I get back. While we sit here chatting, Melisen's a prisoner. I must ride out after her. Knowing William he'll have taken her to his stronghold down in Holderness, damn his eyes. If he touches her, I'll not be responsible! Come on, man, rouse the forces! Let's go!'

Given that they had been riding since early the previous day and it was now just after midnight and the rain was still falling like steel rods, Roger's men turned to with remarkably little grumbling when they heard what they were being ordered to do. The prospect of a good scrap with Sir William's Holderness forces seemed to raise their spirits at once. The handful of William's men who had ridden over from Hutton with the cortège offered to change coats at once and bear arms on Roger's behalf but they were regarded with scepticism, and put for safe-keeping in the abbey prison. Sir Ralph's men, of course, were lodged at close quarters to their lord and lady in the guest house, and knew nothing of this night-time exodus from Meaux.

After a short announcement by Ulf, there in the stable-yard where most of the Hutton men had been about to bed down in whatever dry corners they could find, they were astonished when a monkish figure strode into their midst and, pausing only for a moment, threw back his cowl to reveal Lord Roger himself.

There was a collective intake of breath. A voice cried, 'A ghost! Save us!' This was quickly followed by a rousing cheer and cries of 'God-a-mercy!' and 'A miracle!' and a sudden spontaneous hymn of thanksgiving when it became obvious that the man before them was no apparition but flesh and blood and spoiling for a fight. A host of hands patted him on the back and their enthusiasm brought a flush to Roger's cheeks. He muttered something about preparing for what lay ahead and they set about getting

254

armoured up with alacrity.

The abbot, having returned from his prayers, was alerted by his servants, apprised of the situation, and magnanimously allowed the use of fresh horses from his own string, as well as requisitioning a couple more from some merchants who were passing through. These two were not best pleased at this but, roused in the middle of the night by the prior and two hooded monks, thickset fellows with fists thrust menacingly into their sleeves, they chose not to demur. Soon the small army was ready to set out.

It was still raining. By now the drops were as big as pebbles and chimed off the helms of the men, hit the ground then bounced up again and struck their greaves, sending spatters of mud everywhere. The din made speech impossible, but the men were undeterred.

Ulf – shoulder freshly trussed – was astride a sparky bay belonging to the precentor, and his face gleamed with pleasure at the prospect of the fight ahead. 'It's marshland down that way,' he told Hildegard, as if she didn't know, 'not what we're used to! It'll be a real challenge picking our way through the waterways to that devil's lair. But then we'll see what's what.'

'Remember, don't use your left arm for anything,' warned Hildegard as she walked along beside him towards the gatehouse. 'Despite the weather I wish I was coming with you to keep an eye on things.' She crinkled her eyes hopefully.

'It might turn nasty,' he told her with relish. 'You're best keeping yourself safe and dry here within the abbey.' He paused and added awk-

255

wardly, 'And don't forget to pray for us.'

'I'll do that,' she called as they clattered under the arch out of the garth. They set off straight away at a roaring gallop, making their pennants fly, and the hens and ducks sleeping in the newly formed puddles on the foregate scattered, squawking, from beneath their iron hooves.

An unnatural silence seemed to fall after they swept from view. I will pray for you, thought Hildegard, but there's much else to do besides. She turned towards the chapel where the bell was being rung for lauds then changed her mind and squelched towards the cloisters. There, with the gargoyles spitting jets of water from the roof, she paced with her head bowed and her fingers playing over the multicoloured beads she wore at her waist until she came to her starting point. And then she paced on for another half-dozen circuits. The rain was a continual background roar to her whirling thoughts.

William might be a despot, and a hothead, and a murderer of yeomen, and a rapist, and all those other things he was rumoured to be but it did not necessarily make him the murderer of Ada. Nor did it make him a failed poisoner. The chaperon and the poulaines seemed to prove it. After a closer look at the stains, they had decided they were blood, as Hildegard had first suspected. The wearer had trodden in it as he sewed the stitches. But, as Roger had said, William would never wear such things. There was a deeper secret hidden here, she realised.

Soon the monks started to come out of chapel after the last office, some walking in procession to the stairs that led up to the dorter, others finding an excuse to stand and listen to the rain. Tugging her cloak more tightly round herself, Hildegard left them to it and made her way back inside. Roger had been housed in private rooms reached by a spiral stair from the slype. It was secluded, a place where the abbot could entertain guests at his discretion, and she settled down there amid the sheepskins to think.

One small question kept rubbing away at her thoughts, like a grain of salt in a wound, and, in the midst of everything else that had happened, she could not banish the sense of unease it brought. It was Ralph's manservant, his bloodshot right eye, his look of confusion as he jerked to a halt in the doorway after recapturing the cat. Something had jogged his memory. His black look proved it. She shivered and tried to imagine what had given him the clue to her identity and then, feeling more uneasy than ever, she wondered what he might do now he knew who she was.

Despite what Ulf had remarked earlier it was scarcely safer here in the abbey than on the field of battle.

Prime came and went. Hildegard heard the bells. She heard the soft shuffling of the monks as they went down to the refectory for mixtum and came back again to read in the cloisters underneath her chamber, or, if they were novices, to go to their lessons, until eventually the time passed and the bell began tolling for Lady-mass.

Soon after that she heard a large group assemble below and begin to process round the cloister to the summons of the second bell. She pulled on her buskins and took her cloak from the hook.

Sibilla and her nurse would be unlikely to take the squalling baby into mass. Now would be a good time to pay a visit to the guest house across the garth. Aware that she might come face to face with Ralph's servant, she braced herself and set forth.

Set a distance from the main buildings with its own stables and servants' quarters, the guest house was a solid, four-square building with a pleasant aspect and the comfort of a manor house. Smoke billowed from its kitchen chimney. A few conversi, abbey servants, could be seen, bustling about on different errands. To add to the peaceful scene, from the nearby chapel floated the varied voices of the singing monks, an empyrean sound, drifting with unexpected harmonies and the ethereal treble of the boys. Hildegard's boots sank into the soggy grass as she cut across the garth. She sniffed the air for signs of snow. Maybe the marsh puddles and brimming ditches down in Holderness would be brittle with ice this morning. The horses' hooves would make a sound like breaking glass.

When she went inside, a fire was burning in the hall. Sibilla was sitting in a chair close to the hearth with the baby on her lap. The wet nurse was standing over her. As soon as Sibilla heard someone enter she lifted her head and, seeing who it was, gave a flustered greeting, wafting the maid aside as if in play.

'Go away, will you? You can have him later. Let me hold my own child.' The nurse gave a sullen curtsey and backed off. 'The silly girl imagines him hungry when he makes the slightest peep, sister. Does he look hungry to you?' Sibilla asked.

'Not at all.' Hildegard inspected the swaddled infant. He had sweet, small features and a tuft of fair hair sticking out of his bonnet. His cheeks were rosy with the warmth of the chamber and his tight swaddling bands. 'He looks most peaceful,' she remarked. 'Quite charming, indeed.'

The wet-nurse, buxom and high coloured in the Saxon way, had her eyes fixed on her charge. She was evidently ready to pounce as soon as Sibilla was off guard. There seemed nothing wrong with the baby at all. No cat's head or devil's scales. The little fingers on both hands were of the accepted number. Despite the bickering, he was sleeping peacefully with his eyes tight shut. All in all he seemed placid and content and perfect.

'Dear little Rogerkin,' observed Sibilla as soon as the nurse had left the chamber. 'No wonder the silly girl's so besotted by him. Who wouldn't be? He's such a darling.'

'Do you know what happened to her own child?' asked Hildegard.

'Died, I suppose,' Sibilla said carelessly. She poured a goblet of wine for them both with the baby crooked in one arm, then called for Ralph. He appeared at once carrying Master Jacques.

'There now,' he addressed the cat, 'you can come in freely again. How they banish you from the baby-chamber, my little angel! Don't they

259

know what a soft sweeting you are?' He smothered the cat in kisses.

'Oh, do stop fussing over that detestable animal,' said Sibilla. She turned to Hildegard, 'Why was there the sound of horsemen leaving the abbey in the middle of the night?'

'Horsemen?' Hildegard cleared her throat. Both Roger and Ulf had decided to keep Roger's resurrection secret for a little longer. All those who knew the truth, apart from the abbot and his serviciars, were now far away in the south of the county. She gave a vague smile. 'Did you say horsemen?'

Sibilla looked uncertain. 'Well, I thought that's what I heard.' She pursed her lips. 'Maybe it was just the drumming of the rain on the roof.'

Hildegard moved on. 'I was most distressed to hear what had happened at Hutton while I was away,' she began. 'Did you see the whole sorry incident yourselves?' She glanced from one to the other.

Ralph had gone over to the chessboard but now he raised his eyebrows and gave a mock shudder. 'I'd just sat down at high table, wondering where William was – we were all there,' he explained, 'Sibilla, Avice, Philippa, quite a little gaggle of women and me the only knight among them – when that poor fellow paraded in with the jugged hare. He was just setting the hare on the table when William burst into the hall. He came storming up to the dais, brandishing his sword, and yelling, "Which one of you carls is number three?" The yeoman arranged the hare very slowly on the dish then looked up into William's face. I'm not saying he was defiant, but he certainly wasn't cowering with respect. "I am he," he said, just like that. "I am he." He must have known what it was about. He stood there without blinking. And William, with one great leap, sprang on to the dais and went slash, so!'

He demonstrated with the hand that wasn't cradling the cat. 'And the poor devil fell back with both hands to his eyes. There was blood gushing everywhere. There was nothing we could do. All the women screamed and drew back and the man fell without a cry. He was quite silent. It was as if he was suffering something he knew he deserved but was not bowed by. I thought it very odd.'

'In what way odd?'

Ralph shrugged. 'Why did he not cry out? And William losing his temper like that and all over a serving wench. What on earth got into him? I don't know what Avice is going to do.'

'You mean he killed Godric because–?' Hildegard let her words trail away.

'Because he was jealous, I suppose. The fellow must have had a prior claim. But William's always been like that. Any wench is fair game. It's when he gets found out he loses his reason. Same old story.'

'And Godric? He didn't strike me as a man who would get involved with a serving wench.'

'No,' agreed Sibilla. 'He was quite the little gentleman. But it's not surprising he fell for her, she was stunningly pretty. She could turn anyone's head.' She glanced briefly at Ralph, caught his eye and smiled.

'But I remember you telling me you didn't

261

know her?' Hildegard reminded her.

'I just hadn't connected her with ... don't forget I'd just given birth,' Sibilla lifted her hand to her throat. 'I'm still a little tired now. That ride from Hutton! And Melisen! Do you think she and William planned it together?'

'Planned it?'

Sibilla shrugged. 'I can hardly think straight.'

'That's understandable.' Hildegard got up to go. 'It's been an eventful Martinmas so far.'

'And it's still not over.' Ralph came with her to the door. 'Roger's funeral will have to be delayed, of course. I'm going to have to rouse up a few men shortly and escort poor Avice to Watton. She wants to stay with the nuns for a while and who can blame her?'

'And when you return, Ralph?' Hildegard asked.

He looked confused.

'Someone has to take the reins at Castle Hutton,' she pointed out.

'Ah, yes, indeed.' Ralph threw a glance over his shoulder at Sibilla. 'The reins. I must say it does rather seem as if the Hangman has caught his victim after all.' He began to chuckle. 'Remember the other evening when I couldn't catch a single one of you? Now it looks as if I've got the whole pack!'

Chapter Thirteen

As Hildegard left the guest house, Ralph's disconcerting delight at getting the better of everyone prompted a somewhat macabre chant to float into her head. It was one they used to sing as children and went something like: *Who will hang the hangman blind? Who will snap his neck?* And the reply would come: *The hangman hangs the hangman blind, the hangman hangs...* And then everybody would shout the name of the next victim. It was a warning to flee for your life.

She shuddered. Heaven forfend there should be another victim.

Briskly crossing the garth after looking in on Burthred and the hounds, she noticed the abbot coming out of chapter. In the western alley a few novices were questioning a senior monk over the readings for the day as she walked past, but the next moment the abbot himself was hurrying towards her. He cut across the cloister court and quickened his pace, reaching the door just as she put her hand on the ring-handle of the door in the slype. She glanced up in surprise. 'Sister,' he said, 'I wonder if you can answer a few questions about the situation with Roger and events at Castle Hutton?'

'Of course. If I can. There are many puzzles.'

He gave a grim smile. 'Come to my chamber.'

'And the chaperon and shoes were hidden in Sir Ralph's quarters?' Abbot Hubert de Courcy frowned and made an empty steeple with his fingers, as if the answer would emerge between them. 'You rightly call it a puzzle, sister. A puzzle within a puzzle.' He paused. 'Within a further puzzle.'

Hildegard had explained in as orderly a fashion as she could the circumstances of the attempt on Roger's life, the murder of Ada and William's subsequent though not necessarily connected killing of the third yeoman, Godric.

Hubert was sitting in an impressive carved wooden chair with a high back to keep out the draughts. It also served to conceal the occupant from anyone entering. Hildegard sat on the other side of the fire on a comfortable sheepskin-covered bench with a goblet of Hubert's wine to hand.

'And Roger's steward recognised the poulaines as belonging to this same yeoman, you say?' Hubert frowned. 'The prints, you suggest, set deliberately in the barley dust beside the body in order to cast suspicion on him?'

'Or to turn suspicion away from someone else.' Hildegard took a sip of wine. 'That's one idea that's been mooted. Although of course we can prove nothing. And we're even further away from finding out why anyone would want the maid dead.'

'But this footwear.' Hubert frowned. 'Quite distinctive, and you say they were hidden in the vacated chamber of Sir Ralph and Lady Sibilla?'

'Yes. And but for Master Jacques they would no

264

doubt be there even now.'

'But clearly not put there by the yeoman himself, God bless his soul.' Hubert crossed himself. 'He would never have had the opportunity, as the steward, you say, pointed out.'

Hildegard was thoughtful. 'We have no real proof that the yeoman even entered the grain store. Only that his shoes did.'

'Are you suggesting they did so of their own volition?'

Hildegard smiled. Hubert's mind was obviously on less material matters, and it wasn't surprising. The Talking Crucifix for which the abbey was famous had, just last month, offered apparently sound advice to a local merchant, and a handsome endowment had been given in thanks. She returned to the matter in hand. 'I don't think we can assume Godric himself was wearing the poulaines. And if he wasn't, then someone else wielded the knife that killed Ada.'

'A knife so far unidentified?'

Hildegard nodded. 'Nor do we have any idea why Godric would wish her dead.'

'Nor why Sir William would wish him dead.'

Hildegard hesitated. She remembered Ralph's theory, and William coming into her makeshift confessional with something weighing heavily on his mind, followed by his hasty departure. But instead she said, 'It was unfortunate that the midwife's shoe-print was so similar to the one beside the body. Both long, both narrow, both blurred. That's what sent us off in fruitless pursuit.'

'Yet her presence in the store, corroborated by the clerk of the kitchen, is not in doubt, which therefore suggests that her observations may have been pertinent, so, but for her disappearance, it might not have been so fruitless after all.'

Her eyes kindled. 'Quite so. Thank you, my lord abbot, though I take little comfort from our failure to apprehend her.'

'Your first suspect disappears so you cannot question her and your second is killed so you cannot question him,' observed Hubert, in a musing tone of voice.

She nodded.

'That is a similarity of sorts but whether meaningful or meaningless I would not venture to guess. It seems that our suspicions are based on nothing more than an unfortunate coincidence of footwear.' He frowned. 'Could the midwife, perhaps, have worn the poulaines? But no,' he corrected himself, 'for how on earth would she have got hold of them? Perhaps we should turn our attention from the prints and ask ourselves why she disappeared from the scene? That in itself raises suspicion. Those who flee are usually guilty.'

'Again, there is only supposition. She had a genuine errand in the store. Whether she discovered Ada's body and, fearing to be implicated, fled, we can only guess at this stage. But in my opinion she fled as one not seriously troubled by fear or guilt.' She mentioned how freely the midwife's old father had told them how they could catch up with her. 'Maybe, her job done, she simply went off to offer her services elsewhere.'

'But again, is it coincidence that a fire should break out at exactly the time your suspect – as she was then – was about to be apprehended? I find the whole issue of the fire most disturbing,' Hubert rested his chin on his steepled fingers. 'I do fear, however, that it is more likely to have been an act of arson and has nothing to do with your enquiries. There is much unrest among the people in that region. Our granges are continually bothered by them.'

'I understand the freemen resent having to pay to have their corn ground at the lord's mill. They feel he takes advantage of his monopoly with resulting high charges.'

Hubert nodded. 'These manorial lords are often rapacious. They claim to fear more bad harvests, hence the need to stockpile their stores. But in fact they're bleeding the country dry. In the meantime many of them fail in their responsibilities towards their bondsmen. Smarting under a sense of injustice, the people run in confusion. They are lost souls. To counter their wretchedness they take refuge in drink and fornication...' He cleared his throat. 'But a county cannot thrive in turmoil. Justice must prevail to allow all souls salvation.' He seemed lost in thought for a moment, then with an effort roused himself. 'Still, to get back to our puzzle...'

'The fire,' Hildegard agreed. 'No matter how it started, the question is, was our midwife inside or outside the mill? Is she dead? Or is she alive? And is she the key to this mystery or not?'

'*Patientes vincunt.*'

'Patience is all very well but I fear for her safety. And cannot but believe that her flight has some secret reason connected to Ada's murder.'

'Time reveals all, Sister. Meanwhile I have to ask what inference you draw from the fact of the red chaperon?'

'At first I thought it was a mere wrapper for the shoes. But then, why wrap them simply to push them up inside a chimney? It didn't make sense. Then I realised that the garment itself must have some bearing on the matter, and on inspection saw that it was singed. Where are the fires that would singe a garment in this way, across the back as if the wearer had reason to stand close to a flame? In the kitchens there's such a fire. But there was also one in Lord Roger's Great Hall of course. On the night he was almost poisoned there was a huge blaze, the screens were put up, and a servant could easily have waited there for an opportunity to poison the wine.'

'Sounds plausible,' observed Hubert. 'Is there more?'

'I don't remember any particular person in this colour,' Hildegard continued. 'There are hundreds of servants at Hutton, all dressed gaudily, but there is one who might stand unnoticed so close to the fire.'

He narrowed his eyes. 'You mean this yeoman fellow?'

'He was the one to supervise Roger's wine. He was coming and going throughout the feast. All he had to do was stand behind the screen and wait until everyone was distracted, reach forward, slip a potion into the goblet, and—'

'And why could someone not have done this in the kitchen before it was served?'

'Because the wine was brought to table in a

flagon. And I assume it had to be administered to Roger only and that the yeoman did not wish to poison the entire household.'

Hubert blew gently through his nose. 'So then we have to address the question of motive.'

'Some hatred for Lord Roger?'

'He seems popular with his men.' A smile lightened Hubert's sombre features for a moment. 'I find him a most congenial guest, appreciative of our hospitality and knowledgeable on many topics of mutual concern.'

'That, my lord abbot, is what I don't understand, why a yeoman would want to kill Roger of all people. There seems nothing to gain from it. The popular view is that the yeoman also murdered Ada, but again, there seems no motive for it. They're saying it must have been from thwarted love and that he was driven to a frenzy of jealousy when he saw her dancing with Sir William at the feast the previous night. Then William killed him out of rage due to his naturally violent nature or as a form of retribution.'

'I see from your expression you regard this as mere guesswork?'

'Indeed.' She hesitated before deciding to voice a niggling disquiet, but the abbot's expression invited her to speak. 'This is no way a plausible reason for murder, but I did notice something, a small incident... It so happened this particular fellow was forced to submit to some ribaldry in front of the guests. I gather it was a regular joke.'

She remembered the expression on Godric's face when Roger called him in and then told him to go away again, just to amuse himself at the way he was forced to bow and walk out backwards. 'Of course he had to obey, but his eyes were full of fury at being mocked in front of everyone.'

'Pride,' observed Hubert. 'A grievous sin.' The light from the new window fell at such an angle that it highlighted the chiselled cheekbones of Hubert de Courcy as he spoke, giving him a handsome and saintly look. The effect could almost have been seen as collusion by abbot and architect to enhance the reputation of both, if they had been prideful enough.

Hildegard chased the idea from her mind. Hubert and the concept of pride were incompatible. He was rigorous in pursuit of the ideals of his Order.

The sacristan shuffling past seemed to distract Hubert. It would soon be time for the next office. 'So many more questions I might ask, sister,' he said to Hildegard. 'And then there is also the subject of that other sad matter of the body in the wood. The coroner has sent a message to say he is on his way. You will stay for the inquest?'

'If you will it.'

'We shall meet again before he arrives, perhaps at dinner?'

'I shall be honoured, my lord abbot.'

Hubert's saintly smile followed her to the door, where, with enough humility to match his own, she bowed her head and left.

None of it made sense. Every lead seemed to end in a blind alley. As if to echo her thoughts, Hildegard now found herself entering the alley where the monks played bowls. It was a rectangular enclosure lying in the shadow of the south tower. There was only one way in and one way out, through a wicket gate made of crucked elm. She pushed it open and, with her hounds at her heels, stepped inside.

Ahead lay a strip of immaculate turf blocked on three sides by the high walls of the dorter, the latrines and the outer defences. With the monks in church there were only two players just now, a couple of guests taking the opportunity to have a game and lay a few bets on the result. The pleasant sound of wood on wood echoed across the green. She stood by the gate and watched them play for a while until one of the men came over.

'Greetings, sister. Forgive us our idleness but our horses have been requisitioned at the abbot's request by some high-handed Saxon fellow.'

'High-handed, was he?' Hildegard smiled at the thought and saw no reason to tell him that would be the steward from Castle Hutton.

'More like a Norman than otherwise,' said the second fellow, coming up. 'You could tell which side of the fence he sits.' He had a jovial red face and didn't seem to mind Ulf's behaviour. 'We were speculating on the reason for wanting our old amblers,' he told her. 'Not another war, is there? Is it the Scots at it again?'

'Something more local, I believe.'

'So we'll get our horses back in good time, will we?'

'Quite soon, I would imagine.'

He bent to pat Bermonda on the head and she permitted this fondling with a dignified silence. 'Nobody seems to know a blessed thing,' the man said. 'You ask one of these monks and they pass you on to another and he passes you on to a third and on down the line till you're back where you started. Not that I'm complaining,' he added hastily, with a glance at her habit.

'I expect they're as much in the dark as you,' she replied. 'I understand the men had to be mustered in a hurry. I'm sure you'll get your horses soon. Where are you heading for?'

'We're wool merchants from Doncaster en route to Hutton. Or were, till now. We heard there were some Lombardy loan-men up there recently. We thought we might get a cut ourselves.'

She smiled. 'No hurry, then, as there's much disarray at Hutton and the Lombardy men have gone up to Fountains to do business and may be some time, unless they decide to come here on account of Lord Roger and his household.'

'In that case we'll wait and enjoy ourselves feasting on the good cheese and ale of Meaux,' the second merchant said cheerfully. He wore a Flemish beaver hat and lifted it before turning back to the game with a jaunty, 'Let's go!'

In the easy nature of their companionship they reminded her of someone she had forgotten in the confusion of recent events. Now it came back. It was the corrodian and his friend. They too had been travelling with a similar air of companionship and lack of haste.

It was the first meal of the day, the least meagre, when the monks broke their fast. Understandably it was eagerly awaited. When Hildegard made her way towards the frater there was

272

already a procession, freshly washed and carrying knives, approaching two by two along the north cloister. When they reached the doors they stood in silence waiting for somebody to open up. She could tell from the way they were looking at each other they were impatient to get inside, but she knew better than to try to get into conversation given the penalties they would incur, so she too stood in silence until at last the abbot made his appearance on the garth.

For the occasion Hubert had thrown a silk stole over his shoulders. It was a silvery colour and reflected the winter sunshine as he walked. Hildegard recognised it as a piece made by her sisters in the priory at Swyne. It certainly added glamour to his plain Cistercian robes of undyed burnet but, of course, she thought, pride being such a snare, he would be unaware of that. Her lips curved.

As the abbot approached the doors a servant on the other side flung them wide. With a sombre expression, Hubert made his way between the brothers and processed down the frater towards a dais set beneath the great Rood at the east end. Apart from Hubert and herself, the prior, the sub-prior and the precentor were also seated there. The run-of-the-mill brethren and the novices sat at tables ranged down both sides in the body of the hall, while the lay brothers, the conversi, hurried in and out with platters of food. Hubert, of course, had his own servants to perform this duty.

Hildegard watched the food come out and remembered some of the thin fare dished up at the priory. But at least the nuns could talk all they liked. Here, it seemed, Hubert insisted on the rule of silence. Except for one of the monks reading aloud from a text, those on the dais were the only ones who talked. 'The cellarer,' explained Hubert in an aside, 'is unfortunately on a visit to one of the granges.' He told her this in a tone suggesting it was a cause for regret.

While the first course of herrings in mustard sauce and a meat pudding were being eaten, talk ranged over everything but the rumours that were flying. They mentioned the weather and the state of the roads to and from Beverley, they mentioned the latest scandal among the burgesses, they discussed litigation over the lease on some fisheries down at Hornsea, they talked of falconry and how it had declined since the Norwegians started selling their best birds to the Flemings, and they talked of every blessed thing and did them all to death without once mentioning Roger de Hutton, his poisoning, the abduction of his wife and the murder of two servants within the precincts of his castle itself.

Hubert allowed his brother monks to talk without interruption. He had a brooding look and Hildegard could tell his mind was as active as his tongue was silent.

Eventually the second course was brought in and they helped themselves to a good selection of tarts and spiced vegetables, oysters, eggs and capon. The others down below were drinking the beer for which the abbey was famous, but the top table had a choice of imported wine from Burgundy and, remembering Ulf's approval, she gratefully accepted what Hubert offered. Then building plans were mentioned.

There was something of a flurry, she noticed, between the prior and the sub-prior as they turned to give Hubert a glance. He sighed. 'This is somewhat tedious, sister. We have yet to decide on the ideas Master Schockwynde and his fellow masons are keen to execute. Indeed, their very urgency sends alarm bells ringing.'

'Indeed,' agreed the prior, nodding. 'It's not their own money they'd be squandering.'

'I understand from Master Schockwynde that he inclines towards the demolition of the chapel?' said Hildegard cautiously.

'Imagine that!' sniffed the sub-prior. 'A place as imposing and powerful as Meaux! It's unthinkable!'

'I'm sure even Master Schockwynde wouldn't want to go that far, even though there are those who might,' she murmured somewhat provocatively.

'Oh, we all know about the attacks on our namesake at Meaux in France. But that's over there, where anything's permitted these days. There's no social control what with the dukes at each other's throats and their Dauphin a mere child.'

'Perhaps you'd care to see the plans yourself, sister, back in my chamber?' Hubert interrupted. 'A fresh view is often all that's needed.'

The prior and the sub-prior swapped glances again.

'The sister has some knowledge of these maters,' explained Hubert smoothly. 'She was instrumental in the plans for the new building at

275

Swyne. Master Schockwynde built a most pretty quire. It's a shame neither of you are allowed to see it.' There was a pause while everybody imagined under what circumstances their abbot had been allowed into the priory. Unruffled, he observed, 'It will stand for a thousand years. Believe me, it is most effective.'

Just then one of the servants came to the foot of the dais. 'My lord abbot, forgive the intrusion, but there's a woman outside wanting to speak to you. We tried ejecting her but she got back in along the river path and refuses to leave.'

'Why does she not send her petition in the usual way? If necessary it can be discussed in chapter,' suggested Hubert, mildly.

'She claims it's too urgent,' the servant bowed his head.

Hubert lifted a benevolent hand. 'Send her in. Let's have a look at her.'

The servant left and in a few moments returned with a strong-looking woman of about thirty. Contrary to what he had told them she was no peasant, as such, but wore townswoman's garb with a white kerchief on her head – and she was in a towering rage.

'My lord,' she began in a loud voice without any preamble. The monks in the hall turned to stone. The young lector fell silent. 'Your abbey through the mouthpiece of your sub-prior here is demanding heriot tax. Fair and fine. It's an unjust tax but it's the law. However,' she went on when Hubert opened his lips to say something, 'he is demanding I hand over my husband's horse, cow *and* pig. What will that leave me with?

276

Nothing. So? What do you suggest I do in order to feed myself? Wear a striped bonnet like a harlot and ply for trade in Beverley market?'

There was a gasp and the prior, a sugary fellow with silver hair and a skin like a York rose, began to fan himself with a corner of his sleeve. The sub-prior, more stalwart, got to his feet but Hubert restrained him. 'If what she says is true it does seem rather harsh.'

Feathers ruffled, the sub-prior said, 'But it's the law, my lord. Are we to break the law just because a woman with a loud voice requires us to?'

'And that's also a fair point,' observed Hubert, giving the woman a measuring glance.

'Fair to you, sitting up there in your luxury of fine eating! Not fair to me with my scraps and bones and even less when you take my means of subsistence from me! How fair is that? I'm a widow now, so what am I supposed to do? Curl up and die?' She seemed about to go on but stopped when she heard the gasps of horror from the novices sitting behind her. Hildegard felt herself warming to the woman. She certainly had courage.

'What happened to your husband?' Hubert asked in a gentle voice.

'Killed by falling limestone at the North Cave quarry,' replied the woman. She looked fiercer still, and Hildegard could see she was fighting tears.

'And the animals, you say, were his?'

'That's right. As was I and everything I possess according to the Norman law.'

Hildegard's heart went out to her. It must have

277

taken a lot of nerve to bring her to the source of the power that oppressed her and speak up so strongly against it. This was the sort of strength she was looking for in her recruits for the priory. She wondered how Hubert would resolve the matter. It would be instructive. It would also demonstrate what manner of man he really was underneath his smooth exterior and the glamorous silk stole.

He surprised her by addressing her directly, saying, 'Sister, we are only men. Maybe as woman to woman you can find a way of resolving the issue to the benefit of all? Why not talk to the supplicant in private?'

The prior and the sub-prior bristled. Thinking it diplomatic as well as true Hildegard replied, 'I understand the desire to uphold the law. On the other hand no one would wish to force a widow into either harlotry or starvation. Perhaps, as you suggest, there is a way to untangle this knot without undue loss on either side.'

So saying, she stepped down from the dais in the profound silence that followed this exchange and asked the woman to follow her into the cloister. This she did sullenly, with a backward glance at the men high up on the dais which made Hildegard feel that, if her mere glance could have brought them tumbling into the straw, all three would have been picking wisps out of their clothes for some time to come.

The cloister seemed too busy a place, too public, for a conversation of the sort Hildegard expected, so she led the way into the nearby slype, not caring whether this broke some abbey rule or not.

'Well then,' she said, when they were inside and the door was closed. 'Tell me about it.'

'I told you in front of the abbot and his henchmen. There's nothing more. They want my best cow. And how can I get milk without a cow and how without milk can I make cheese?'

'Is this your occupation?'

'I'm a regrator at Wednesday market, adding to what my husband got for hewing stone in the quarry. He was killed and I'm thrown into penury because of laws these men invent to suit themselves.'

'So if you kept the cow you could continue to market your cheese?'

'Of course. I've only me to keep now. My son's apprenticed since past Lady Day.'

'No doubt they expect you to remarry?'

'I don't want that.' She gave a small smile. 'Why should I remarry and become a house slave again? I know no man I want to set my cap at. He wasn't bad, him, but I'd rather keep my freedom now I've got it.'

'It's hard for women outside the conventional bounds,' Hildegard pointed out.

The woman gave her a derisory glance. 'Hard outside. Hard inside. That's life. Though you nuns seem to have it easy enough.'

Unruffled by this observation which, anyway, she had heard many times before, Hildegard said, 'Widows often live contentedly inside the priory walls. We have a power we wouldn't have, alone, on the outside.' She gave the woman a close look to judge how she took the hint.

She understood at once. 'What, me? You must be joking. With all the rejected heiresses and the old maids?' She gave a hoot of laughter. 'Go into lauds, have a bit of a sing, come out. Go into matins, have a bit of a sing, come out. And so forth ad infinitum? Oh, aye!' Her laughter was full of derision. 'Now there's a life and a half for a woman with spirit. My language alone would make their hair curl!'

Suddenly she threw her shawl over her head. 'Oh, mercy me! What have I gone and said now? And you here to listen to my side of it! Well, that's me finished, isn't it? No disrespect to you, sister, it's just my way. I'm sorry I've wasted your time. I'll manage somehow. I always have and I always will.' There were tears in her eyes. They appeared in a sudden welling that made them glitter in a way that might have been mistaken for rage.

She went to the door at once and put two hands to the ring to tug it open.

'Stop just there!' said Hildegard in a scolding voice. 'Are you off already to put on your striped bonnet? God help you if you're always so hasty.'

The woman looked at her in astonishment. 'What do you mean?'

'I'm not one of those fellows sitting up on a dais with pursed lips. I welcome frankness.'

A look of puzzlement crept over her face and her mouth fell open.

'First,' said Hildegard briskly, 'I'd like to put you straight on the matter of living in a nunnery. If you think it's a soft life you're wrong. It's definitely not all wine and roses when you've got the lord abbot as well as the chapter of the mother house to contend with. You've no idea how carefully we have to tiptoe around them. Which is why,' she found herself saying, 'I'm setting up my own house. Seven of us. Living off our own produce. Teaching the basics, healing the sick. So come back here and start talking sense, will you?'

The woman, having been defeated by the door-ring and intrigued by what Hildegard was saying, came back, still gaping in astonishment. 'You're not sending me packing, then?'

Ignoring that she asked, 'What's your name?'

'Agnetha, Sister.' She let her shawl slip from her head and settle humbly round her shoulders.

'Let's see if the prior will accept the loss of a cow. You will, of course, have to hand over the other beasts.'

'He'll never say yes.'

'He may not, but the abbot will.'

Telling Agnetha to stay where she was Hildegard went out just as the monks were leaving the frater and beginning to process into the cloister. Guessing that Hubert had already gone to his chambers, she made her way there at once. His servant, an elderly one-legged fellow, ushered her into an anteroom then left her to make her own way to the inner sanctum. The door was already open so she approached, soft footed, ready to announce herself.

To her astonishment, sitting with their feet up, were the whole crew, the abbot himself, his prior, the sub-prior, the precentor and an elderly strong-faced monk Hildegard had not seen before.

As if they had just come in from the fields,

their cowls were thrown back and they were lolling round a well-stoked fire. There were goblets of wine in their hands and the sub-prior even had his sandals off, feet on the rail, wriggling his toes with pleasure. As silver filigree as always, his companion the prior was holding forth in a delicate voice, and when Hildegard reached the doorway he was in mid-sentence. Whether she wanted to or not she could not help but overhear.

'–and then I saw it was that great lanky Saxon steward of Lord Roger's, you know the fellow – wild man, always goes armed, a real villain if ever I saw one–'

'Ulf,' interjected Hubert.

'That's the man. And on top of that,' he lowered his voice, 'I cannot help but notice how he speaks most freely with Sister Hildegard. Have any of you noticed that?' He glanced round the group and there were murmurs of agreement. She saw Hubert narrow his eyes.

The sub-prior chuckled. 'I, for one, wouldn't cross swords with the likes of him. Not for all the gold in Christendom. Would you, Gilbert?' At this they all roared with laughter at the incongruity of such an image and because of their uproar they did not hear Hildegard's voice when she tried to announce herself.

Before she could try again, more audibly, Hubert himself added in a tone of mock reproof, 'And I hope for your sake, Theobald, it will never come to swords!' At which they all roared again at the image of their fragile brother prior in a tussle with a hulking Saxon roughneck.

At this point Hubert caught sight of Hildegard standing in the doorway. As soon as he indicated to the others that they had a visitor they all scrambled to their feet. The prior smoothed a hand through his silvery strands and picked up a book. The older monk flipped his cowl back over his head to obscure his face. And the sub-prior thrust his feet back into his sandals and gave Hildegard an innocent smile. The precentor came forward. 'Please, sister, do come in.'

In their white habits they were most convincing as seraphim, she thought as she returned their glances. Beaming faces, twinkling eyes, serene and untouchable grace. But for holiness melting with compassion, Hubert, with his large, dark eyes, outdazzled them all. What cutting cheek-bones, she observed, as if for the first time. That haughty Norman nose did not detract from his look of piety one whit – in fact it seemed to add a dimension that was most singular.

Hildegard's observations faltered as he strode towards her in sandalled feet across the chamber. As he came closer he seemed to tower over her, which was nonsense as they were both of a height. It was the effect of the way he moved, suggesting rugged strength and a disconcerting physical power, she decided in confusion. She became aware of a honeyed scent with an undertone of mint that obliterated all other senses until she managed to regain control, but just then, as his lips moved, she noticed the edge of his linen undershirt. It was scarcely visible, nothing more than a hint of white at the opening of his habit, and the thought flowed through her mind that it was unusual to see him rumpled and that it did not detract from his look of holiness but enhanced it. Somehow it were suggested that he was as much a victim of human frailty as they all were. By contrast his spiritual strength seemed the more formidable.

As Hubert stood there before her, flooding her mind with these unexpected thoughts, it was a moment that seemed to go on for ever. Then she realised he was saying something. She inclined her head.

'Ah,' was in fact the total of what she heard, then he gazed at her for a time as if aware of the swamping of her feelings. She saw him brace himself. He seemed to pull his thoughts together one by one. And order was restored.

Gesturing towards a parchment spread out on a table beneath the window he said, 'You must be here to see the plans. But first, that question of heriot.' He was brisk now. He gave his fellow monks a hard stare but they were already beginning to leave in somewhat hasty disorder. After the last one had left he closed the door and turned to her. 'Would you like–' He paused, as if having lost the thread of his thoughts again, and instead merely gestured vaguely towards the vacant benches.

Hildegard's knees collapsed under her just as she managed to reach the nearest one. With an effort she gathered her wits. I must be strained by all that's happened recently, she thought, wondering why she was trembling as if with the ague. Pushing the matter to one side, she was determined to support Agnetha in her plea as strongly as she could, but she had no sooner begun when Hubert nodded his agreement.

'Our dairy herd is complete enough for our purposes,' he told her. 'It seems a most fair compromise to let her keep the cow.' He went to stand at the window and gaze out on to his garden. His shoulders were broad, his back straight, his dark hair looked due for its monthly cut and curled boyishly round his ears. After a moment's thought he swung round and she felt her colour rise under the piercing scrutiny of his glance.

'You say she's called Agnetha?' he asked. 'That's a down-to-earth sort of a name. A lay sister who can make a good cheese, handle the domestic animals and arrives with her own cow would be an asset in any priory, I should think.'

Hildegard looked at him in astonishment. 'Our thoughts shadow each other, my lord abbot.' At least in some respects, she acknowledged to herself. 'But there'll be work to do to persuade her to change her view of monastic life.'

He made her colour rise again when he said, 'I have the highest regard for your persuasive powers, sister.' He bowed his head. 'I'm sure our thoughts shadow each other in many respects.' She caught a complicit glimmer in his eyes that made her wonder what was coming next, but he merely added, 'not least on the question of Master Schockwynde?'

'Undoubtedly, my lord.' She could not restrain the gleam in her own eyes as she returned his glance. A man is judged by his actions. He had dealt fairly with Agnetha, now the least she could do was support him in his battle with the master

285

builder. Except for the matter of a linen under-shirt and a liquid glance, she would have felt the situation was firmly under control.

Chapter Fourteen

Hildegard left the abbot's chamber and went to find Agnetha. 'I don't know how to express my gratitude, Sister,' the woman said, tears in her eyes. Together they strolled towards the kennels, where Duchess and Bermonda were being treated like deities by Burthred, and, as they approached, one of the conversi came hurrying out of the lodge. He had a message. It was to inform Hildegard that the coroner had ridden in from York and the inquest on the body found in the woods was to be held in the mortuary as soon as he was ready. By now Burthred had been given an errand to run for the kitchener and her hounds, after sniffing in a friendly fashion at the hem of Agnetha's kirtle, had turned their attention to their mistress. She decided they might as well go with her.

'I have business in Beverley later today,' she told Agnetha. 'If you care to wait until after the inquest I can come in with you and you can share my horse.'

'I'd like that and I'm in no hurry,' she agreed. 'Take your time, Sister. I'll wait.'

Accompanied by her hounds, Hildegard crossed the garth. It was beginning to snow. Large flakes fell one by one but did not settle. The mortuary stood next to the chapel. When she stepped inside she was met by an icy chill. It was due to more than the weather. It was death freezing the soul. The body of the unknown youth was lying on a trestle under a slant of light. It had been surrounded by blocks of ice ever since the men brought it back to Meaux.

Already in attendance were the elderly infirmarer with an alert-looking novice in a threadbare habit of burnet whom she assumed to be his assistant, and the chaplain, his face sombre with the sorrow of his duty. Everyone looked cramped with cold.

The chaplain began to explain that the coroner was dining in the guest lodge and would be along any minute when the doors banged open and a man entered followed by the hunched figure of a clerk. The coroner himself was a tall, stooped man, and he paused in the doorway until all eyes were upon him, then, making the most of a long black cloak, he swept down the nave, boots stamping the flagstones as he tried to dislodge the mud on them. His beaked nose was red raw and his eyes seemed to blaze red too as they glared round the group. Hubert followed quietly and stationed himself off to one side so he could observe the proceedings.

For some reason Bermonda began to whine and flex her claws. The lymer, Duchess, eyes fixed on the coroner, bristled but maintained a well-trained silence. Hildegard glanced down in surprise. She could see no obvious reason for their hostility.

'So where is the corpse? Is this it?' With scant reverence the coroner pulled aside the linen shroud that preserved some privacy for the dead man and let it drop to the floor. Blood was frozen in black gouts on flesh that looked blue-white against the ice. 'Where was it found?' he snapped.

'In the forest between here and York,' said the chaplain, his face etched with distress at the indignity shown towards the corpse. But there was worse to come.

'You mean to tell me I've been dragged away from my lodging to this backwater to view nothing more than an outlaw with his throat cut?' He drew himself to his full six foot four inches and would perhaps have thundered abuse at the gentle, round-faced chaplain if Hubert de Courcy had not stepped from out of the shadow of one of the pillars and made him pause. In the face of such calm grace the coroner stopped short.

'We are required by law to report any suspicious death,' the abbot pointed out in a mild though firm manner. 'These days we have no jurisdiction to conduct matters such as this in our own court.'

Hildegard's glance moved from the abbot back to the coroner. The latter's face was a stone mask of rage but there was nothing he could say. Unpaid though he was, it was his duty to conduct all inquests on behalf of the king when foul play was suspected. He glanced down at the body with irritation. The youth's tunic had been ripped open, no doubt by the infirmarer during his first examination, and three stab wounds were visible in addition to the one that had slit his throat. The blood of all four wounds had clotted and turned black. The boy's face, drained of blood, gleamed like pearl in the shaft of light that fell from the north window above the trestle. The time passing seemed shaped by the reality of his final moments on earth. It held all the tragedy of a life abruptly ended before its full maturing. Hildegard was suddenly moved to tears which she had to blink away.

The coroner gave the body another cursory glance then ground out, 'Death by stabbing.' His tone indicated his belief that he was dealing with simpletons. 'No one found with a knife at the scene of the crime? No? Then my verdict is murder by persons unknown. Will that suit you?' Before anyone could say anything he asked, 'So who gets the bounty?'

There was a general movement of consternation.

'We have been unable to ascertain the identity of the youth,' observed the abbot. 'It may be premature to talk of bounty. We have no evidence he was living outside the law.'

'So what's your version, then?' the coroner peremptorily demanded.

'We were proceeding with our enquiries,' replied Hubert smoothly, 'until such time as you arrived to take over. However, if you would like us to continue—'

'I've given you my verdict,' snapped the coroner. 'And that's the end of the matter.' He pointed a finger at his clerk. 'Written that down?'

The clerk nodded, plainly too cowed by his master to speak at all.

Without bothering to pull the shroud back into

place, the coroner turned as if to go. The abbot glided forward to stand in his path. There was a smile on his face but his eyes were like steel. 'My own wishes are irrelevant here but as Abbot of Meaux I have a duty to satisfy the law of the Chief Justiciar. Sister Hildegard is first finder and her observations need to be recorded.'

Hildegard stepped forward but the coroner, turning, gave her a freezing glance. Despite this she was about to tell him where and how she had found the body, and also, though reluctantly, what she had found in his hand, when he forestalled her. 'I do not need a woman's evidence.' He jerked round, turning his back on her. Before he could take a step Bermonda gave a whine and, belly scraping the floor, claws outstretched, crept towards the coroner and growled at his feet.

He caught sight of her out of the corner of one eye. Then, to everyone's shock, his boot lashed out and he kicked the animal brutally on the muzzle. Bermonda yelped and, but for the leash by which she was held, would have thrown herself at her attacker and sunk her teeth into his thigh. At the same moment the lymer stiffened and Hildegard had to restrain both hounds.

When they were quiet she led them from the scene without a word.

The infirmarer's assistant hurried after her and they came to a halt in the porch. 'Is the poor fellow harmed?' he asked, bending to run an expert hand over the dog's back.

Still shaking with rage, Hildegard managed to say, 'The poor fellow is an old lady and has suffered worse from similar uncivilised brutes.'

'I'll warrant they're more her own size than that brute in there,' he replied.

She fondled the little kennet. 'No bones broken, I'm pleased to say.'

'She's a fine hound,' he observed. 'Where's her partner?'

'Killed by a too valiant attempt at a boar some years ago. Both belonged to my husband. They were already elderly when he left for France and I was given them so they could see out their days in comfort.'

Satisfied that the hound was unharmed, they both gazed out on to the garth as a sudden flurry of snow and sleet swept across. It was unforgiving weather.

'I expect they guard you well, sister, especially the lymer.' He looked warily at Duchess.

'I'm puzzled as to why they both showed their hostility in there. Unpleasant though the coroner was, there was no reason for them to behave like that. It's not like them.' They were both standing quietly enough now.

'They must have caught a scent of something,' said the assistant. 'Blood, no doubt. There's plenty on that man, I'd guess.'

With a kind smile, he turned and re-entered the chapel.

His concern had mollified Hildegard's rage somewhat at having her evidence dismissed in that arrogant manner and then having her hound kicked into the bargain. But she was still angry. The phial and its contents were inside her sleeve. There they'll remain, she decided, until someone shows concern about this boy's sad death.

There was also that other thing she had seen: her mind went back to the glade where she had found the body.

At the time she had noticed the small pewter badge he wore but had not given it much thought. Just now, when she had looked for it, there had been no sign of it. Someone had seen fit to unpin it from his tunic. Was it to protect the youth from a charge of outlawry, or to hide the fact that the Company had such a strong though secret presence in the neighbourhood?

While she was thinking it over the door of the chapel crashed open behind her. A curse followed. The coroner, hood pulled over his face with only his beaked nose protruding, stood in the portico for a moment with a look of hatred at the sleet that was now flying horizontally across the grass like the long lashes of a whip. He plunged into its teeth, followed by the scurrying figure of his clerk. Hildegard saw them disappear in a swirl of hail into the porter's lodge.

Then Hubert was by her side. 'That was a most unfortunate encounter, sister. I gather your little hound is unhurt, but maybe your own feelings are rather more deeply bruised?'

'Not at all. Many officials take their role to be so special it sets them above ordinary folk in everything but manners.'

Hubert revealed his teeth in a brief smile but he still maintained an expression of concern. His warmth surprised her. Many things about him surprised her. She said, 'If he had shown more patience I could have given him something that might have made him think. But he didn't give me a chance. It's something I found with the body and took for safe-keeping pending the inquest.'

'If that's the case, instead of standing here in this foul weather we might go back indoors where you can show me what it is.'

So saying he led the way with his head uncovered.

He was wearing sandals, she noticed. His feet were long and well formed but now they looked raw with cold. A cure for chilblains was her next thought. She decided that the pleasant young assistant to the infirmarer would be a channel by which she might alleviate Hubert's future discomfort.

Hildegard drew the phial from her sleeve and held it out. The abbot took it, looked at it for a moment then prised out the stopper and tipped the piece of linen on to his desk. Whether he knew what it was she could not tell because his expression did not change. One finger poked at the fabric.

'There's a sort of symbol drawn here but I can't quite make it out with this bloodstain.' He paused. 'Is it an animal? A hart perhaps?' His quick glance told her straight away that he knew exactly what he was suggesting and what the implications were. 'The sign of the Company of the White Hart,' he murmured to confirm it. He lifted his head. 'Is that what you suspect too?'

'It seems likely,' Hildegard agreed. 'But who was he, carrying a thing like that? What was he doing in the woods? And where did he come from? His appearance wasn't like someone living wild. His hands were smooth, only calloused by the constant use of some implement, and his nails were clean enough.'

'No blue-nail, that's for sure,' agreed the abbot, using the popular name for unskilled labourers. He indicated a bench beside the fire. 'Let me tell you something you may not have heard.' He sat down on the opposite side in his wooden chair. 'While you were away at Hutton news reached us that five apprentices from York had been hunted down by a rival gang and executed in woods outside the abbey lands. It was a terrible slaughter, most heinous. The point is it was close enough to suggest a link between this solitary murder and the others.' She felt he was watching her with extra concentration. He probably guesses I was deliberately vague about where I found the youth, Hildegard thought, biting her lip.

'I saw them on my way over here,' she admitted. 'Do you mean they've caught their butchers?'

Hubert frowned. 'Rumour can always supply an identity. Unfortunately there are enough influential sympathisers to silence it.'

'You mean the murderers are going to get away with it?'

'So events indicate.'

'That's appalling.'

'Without anyone willing to come forward to give evidence – and who would risk their life and perhaps the lives of their kin – then yes, they will escape punishment.' He gave a grim smile. 'If the inquest was conducted in a similar manner to the one just now, I can't see anyone ever being brought to court for it.'

'Does rumour also explain the quarrel?' Hildegard asked, wondering how it would be linked to the relic that now lay on Hubert's desk.

'The Guild of Corpus Christi is the most powerful in York. Their apprentices, assured of better prospects than most, were up in arms, quite literally, objecting because a group of less privileged journeymen and their apprentices in the leather trade were demanding rights the Corpus Christi men deemed to belong to themselves alone.'

'The right to work?'

'And several other associated privileges.' Hubert glanced at the relic. 'The hanged men were also rumoured to be more than leather workers. They were said to belong to a secret society. The Company of the White Hart. Of course, the Corpus Christi apprentices deny all knowledge of the murders, claiming they had a legal quarrel to be settled in the town court before the guild-masters and the mayor.'

'They would, wouldn't they?' Conscious that she had more information to divulge Hildegard said, 'I've heard of this company you mention but thought it was probably more dreamed of than real – like the tales of Robin the Outlaw,' she added. 'But the white hart is King Richard's badge.' She paused, then added hesitantly, 'It's commonly thought to be the sign of those who want an end to the present rule by Lancaster.'

The abbot's glance held hers. He said, 'The Corpus Christi men are temporarily for Lancaster. They don't bother to conceal their allegiance.'

There was a prolonged silence. Indeed, there

was little to say without toppling over into a morass of speculation wherein to admit their personal allegiance would become inevitable. Everything the abbot told her confirmed her suspicion that support for the young king was moving north. But it didn't give an answer to the question her prioress had posed before she left and now she was forced to probe a little further into the abbot's secret allegiance. It was as important as life and death to avoid misunderstanding.

'After Smithfield some said Richard had been forced to renege against his own inclinations by John of Gaunt. Others say it was his plan all the way along.'

'There is much confusion about the true beliefs of the king,' Hubert admitted without giving anything away.

She tried another line. 'Some believe the influence of the King's young wife, Anne, sways him towards the sort of freedoms Wyclif espouses.'

'The king's mother, Queen Joan, is said to favour Wyclif too.' His expression was as enigmatic as before.

'As did Gaunt to begin with,' she invited.

'What do they call Wyclif? The eagle flying in the midst of heaven?'

There was no irony in his tone. She was puzzled. Any personal hostility towards having the scriptures written in the language of the people, as Wyclif wanted, was not in evidence. Hubert's order of Cistercians had one fixed view about that, but what was to stop Hubert having another? Since his arrival the scriptorium here had begun to make its name as a centre for scholars from all branches of the Church. Many monastics were said to favour wider dissemination of the text on which their beliefs were founded. Wyclif's recent translation of the Bible from Latin into English was applauded by many and it was often discretion that made them keep their opinions to themselves.

'So if I understand you correctly,' she pursued, 'the coroner already suspected that the youth I found was involved with the Company of the White Hart? And perhaps this makes it expedient to brand him an outlaw to conceal the spread of the king's support?'

'Thus, in the cause of politics, the young fellow goes to an unmarked grave, if not a pauper's pit, while those who love him grieve in ignorance of his fate.'

Despite trying to assess the abbot's allegiance, she turned pale at these words. They mirrored the situation she faced regarding her husband, Sir Hugh.

'Sister?' Hubert peered at her through the eerie light caused by the billowing flakes of snow against the glass.

Hildegard told him quickly about her husband and how apparent confirmation of his death had brought her into the order. He sat for a moment considering her with a grave expression. Eventually he said, 'Unfortunately there's nothing I can do to find out what happened to your husband. But I shall send someone discreetly to York to ferret out the truth of this youth's identity. Rest assured this is one death which will be marked with all the prayers and rituals necessary to honour his brief life. We shall start with his name.'

So far Hildegard had omitted to tell him about the badge of the white hart she had seen attached to the youth's tunic. Nor had she mentioned its absence. Wondering whether he knew about it, she considered the possibility that the chaplain, like so many of the lower clergy, was the son of a craftsman and therefore likely to be in sympathy with the Wycliffites. He might have removed it to protect the youth from the coroner's expected disdain. If that was the case she would not be the one to betray him.

Chapter Fifteen

Hildegard was considering the question of poison. Not by accident was she approaching the apothecary's in Beverley. She had accompanied Agnetha to the toft where she kept her husband's old horse and a rather skinny pig that she would shortly have to hand over to the constables and as they parted, Agnetha had pointed out the direction she should take. 'You'll see his sign above the door,' she told her, then, before turning away, added, 'My views about living in a priory are beginning to change. Not all nuns are like you. If you need me you'll find me at my stall in Wednesday market.' She gripped Hildegard by the wrist. 'All blessings, sister, you saved my life.'

As well as accompanying Agnetha so that they could get the measure of each other on the way,

Hildegard wanted to follow up a few ideas about what had been sneaked into Roger's wine. It was when she was in the tranquil ward of the hospitium at Meaux that she had broached the question of poison to the infirmarer. He had listed the possibilities, adding, 'If you were serious you wouldn't want to trust to some homemade concoction of weeds from the wayside. Beverley's a good place to make the appropriate purchases, I would think, unless the poisoner went all the way over to York.'

After leaving Agnetha Hildegard pushed on down the street alone. The weather was so vile that her heart had softened at the prospect of her hounds being dragged out into the rain for no good reason, so she had left them in the kennels under Burthred's spoiling. Now the snow was turning to sludge and the rain was bitter, a knifing wind making it worse by forcing it in squalls between the packed buildings on both sides. Battered and soaked, Hildegard struggled between the houses until she came to a breathless stop under the sign of an enormous mandrake. An apothecary might have some useful suggestions to offer. Belladonna was not the only possibility. She rapped on the shutters with wet knuckles and waited for someone to open up.

There was a gleam of candlelight within the tenement but no sound of anybody approaching the door. She pulled her cloak more tightly round her and rapped again. Roger had fallen with that great oath, she remembered, arms outstretched, and then lain still. She recalled his colour, the palest hue, as in that stage of drunkenness they called swine-drunk, said to correspond to the humour of melancholy. Roger was hardly the melancholy type. But his lips had turned almost black, as if stained. After ingesting an antidote, he had quickly become himself again.

It was true that belladonna could kill, but, if taken in a limited dose, it led only to sleep. It had come into her mind first because it was obvious Melisen used it to add mystery to her eyes. The Lombards could provide it, she assumed. It was in common use in Italy and France. And no doubt they would not object to doing business with other than Melisen, a yeoman, for instance. After all, trade was trade, though what excuse a yeoman might have given for wanting belladonna was anybody's guess.

Of course, it could also be obtained locally if you knew where to look, but it was unlikely that Melisen would try to poison her husband with a bane so easily linked to herself. She would have to be very stupid and somehow, in spite of her obsession with her looks, she did not seem stupid in the least.

There were many other local plants that could kill: death was easily dealt by anybody who set their mind to it. Most plants had a dual nature and some wise folk thought that knowledge of their malign use was too easily available. On that account the wise women and the apothecaries were alike in holding their secrets close.

At last Hildegard heard someone struggle on the other side of the door and when, helped by the wind, it flew inwards, she entered the shop on a blast of air. She shook the rain from off her cloak, pushed back her hood and looked around. The wind, running down the street like a wild animal and trying to force its way inside, had set the bunches of herbs rustling where they hung from the roof beams to dry, so that for a few moments after she had forced the door shut she stood in a sea of sound. In all this she glimpsed a child scamper out of sight into an inner chamber.

Putting the latch on the sneck she peered through the gloom for the apothecary. A ginger fellow in his mid-thirties was standing at a trestle in the darkened back of the shop, pounding some root or other in a mortar.

'Good day,' she called.

He glanced up, observed her Cistercian habit, affected not to notice, then indicated the contents of the mortar he was working. 'Another case of the running tetters,' he announced.

'No doubt you've tried green mast?' She went over to have a look.

'Poultice or ointment?'

'Either will do. And also the water that collects there in the hollows of the decaying tree. I find that most efficacious.'

'Aye. As a wash or a poultice both. If this fails, which I doubt, I'll try that.'

'My best advice would be to tell him to lay off animal flesh and eat his greens.'

'But will the fellow listen? Now, sister,' he said, after this brief checking of credentials, 'what can I do for you?' He came round the trestle, wiping his hands on a cloth stuck in the front pocket of his leather apron.

She said, 'I have a query regarding resurrection.'

At his quick smile she recounted the symptoms, omitting only the identity of the patient. When she finished the apothecary scratched his head with stained fingers, thought for a moment and admitted, 'Your guess is as good as mine. But I do have one or two suggestions.'

He went over to his shelves and scanned the labelled flasks and bottles, muttering under his breath all the while. As she waited she breathed in the aroma of drying herbs hanging in bundles in every nook and cranny. The vapour that escaped from a retort simmering over a flame near by mingled the scents of lavender, sage, rosemary and thyme, and there was the perfume of spices too, cinnamon, cubebs, ginger, nutmeg. She felt a deep sense of familiarity, transported back in time to when a certain wise woman of her childhood had taught her a few simple remedies in an aromatic cell much like this one.

The apothecary returned with two containers. One, a glass phial, was a third full of a viscous liquid, tinged pink, which he swirled a couple of times before holding it up to show her what it looked like against the light. The other, a small pot with a peg stopper, held a blackish root, which he tipped out into the palm of one hand. 'You say you used a distillate of gentian as an antidote?'

She nodded. 'Mixed with one or two other things.'

'And the question is what might be purged by such?'

'As might hemlock, for instance, with the copious amounts of wine that had already been imbibed.'

He smiled faintly. 'Some say wine is our saving grace in this vale of tears.' He held out the root. 'If this is ground small and put into a distillate it will do its work in secret.' He pursed his lips and frowned. 'Or an opiate such as poppy would be easy to administer and by itself would not be fatal. I grow the white in my garden back there.' He gestured towards the rear of the building. 'It's useful in mithridate for fluxes and women's courses as well as for promoting sleep. Of course, if the seeds of the cornfield poppy had been used instead,' he frowned again, 'it would be a different story. Your gentian would not have been strong enough.'

He sighed. 'We have so many banes, growing naturally, bluebell and the like, and it's only folk's lack of curiosity that keeps their secrets safe. In my opinion the culprit might have been mistaken for what grows innocently around the kitchen garden – parsley, for instance, and hemlock can seem the same to the careless. Have you thought of that? Except that it's unlikely hemlock would have been growing there. But maybe you suspect there was no mistake involved?'

'Hemlock, hellebore or henbane, not to mention all the rest?' She smiled and shrugged her shoulders. What the apothecary said was true. There were several poisons that could have been put in Roger's drink, deliberately or accidentally, and gentian, plus the wine, would have purged them.

The apothecary swirled pink liquid in its glass bottle then handed it to her with a swift complicit smile. 'I'm told the pope at Avignon has a poison so potent the merest scratch will bring death in an instant.'

'I've heard that story too. Do you believe it?' Hildegard peered at the phial and its contents but did not remove the stopper. When he gave no answer she said, 'You're being most helpful, master. But I wonder if you can tell me whether you ever do business with servants from Castle Hutton?'

She watched him. His colour changed. For a moment alarm seemed to flash across his face. Glancing towards the door he turned and with a confidential gesture invited her to follow him into another room. She had to bend her head under the lintel. Inside, logs blazed in the fire-pit and the draught from an open vent sucked the smoke outside. A large pot was simmering on the hob, sending its sweet scent into the air. Through a small window covered by slats she could see a walled garden in the dull colours of winter. It was neat and orderly, canes, shaken by the wind, tied up in rows, the earth turned.

'I see you have setterwort out there.'

'Aye, black hellebore, as they call it. It won't bloom till Christmas and not then if this weather keeps up.'

She observed the rain-lashed leaves, the only green thing growing, then turned back into the warm room and raised her brows to show she had not forgotten her question.

He lowered his voice. 'I heard there'd been a bit of trouble up there.' He ducked his head. 'News travels. But I keep a list. You have to keep track of what works and what doesn't.' He bit his lip and the look of fright came over his face again.

'I'm after information only. You're in no trouble. No one but me knows you're the supplier.'

'I'm not saying I am.' He went to a shelf where some pages were weighted underneath a piece of rose quartz. Thumbing through them he suddenly stopped, extracted a page from all the rest and held it out to her. As soon as she took hold of it he went out of the chamber with some speed, calling from the front room, 'I haven't seen you do that.'

She read the rough letters he had inscribed in black ink and wondered who had taught him his letters and his trade. His list had a scrawl like a rough attempt at the de Hutton crest on the first page. She took it to stand in lieu of a name. Nothing if not discreet, this apothecary. Then she scanned what was written underneath:

to supply second day since St M's
decoction of tansy
decoction of henbane and ointment the same
syrup of white poppy one bottle bladder-sealed
distillate of wild poppy flowers

and, finally, an electuary, but of what, not stated. She replaced the page among those still under the block of quartz and went back into the shop. So someone from Hutton had come all the way to Beverley to obtain a potion. Any of these, she realised, given in the appropriate dose, could have caused Roger's symptoms. In the appropriate amount they could kill. When she went back into the other room the apothecary was back at his mortar and pestle and looked up anxiously.

'Master–' she began.

'Dickon,' he replied briefly, his glance never leaving her face.

'So, Master Dickon, do you remember who was sent on this errand and on whose behalf?'

'If they've taken an overdose it's not my fault,' he began. 'I was a bit wary about supplying the henbane but you have to trust folk to be responsible when they get their hands on stuff like this.' He spread his arms. 'And if anybody's taken more than they should–'

'Everything's under control. News of the patient's death was a little premature.'

'Oh aye? But they say the cortège is at Meaux already?'

'But not with Roger in it. This is between ourselves, of course.'

'Of course.'

She tried a shot in the dark. 'I imagine a servant is often sent on behalf of the Lady Melisen?'

The apothecary gave a lopsided smile. 'She's been sending to me regular for cures, ever since she come up to Yorkshire. Always the same fellow she sends.' He rubbed his fingers together and sniffed in absentminded pleasure at some perfume there, but his mind was busy as he thought back to the visitor from Hutton. 'It was always this thin stick, as I recall, melancholic type, togged up like an aristo with one of them capuchons twisted up on his head like a cockscomb and one sleeve – I ask you, one, just the one, right down to here.' He indicated his knees. 'Fashion down in London, I suppose, the silly sod. I could have prescribed something for him, all right. Balanced his humours properly for a change. But he was here on account of wanting something for promoting sleep and for women's problems, as you've seen from the list.'

He was clearly describing poor Godric. Hildegard smiled. 'I understand ointment of henbane is also useful against the French pox?'

He looked startled that a nun should know this, then gave a bark of merriment. 'Mebbe that was in his mind?' He added slyly, 'And tansy you'll know as well?'

'By reputation only.' Her eyes gleamed. It was used for promoting women's fluxes with the result that it could cause an abortion.

As if some barrier of suspicion had been breached he turned to a stoup of wine warming by the fire, gestured and, when her eyes brightened, he returned with two clay beakers. 'Nicely mulled,' he said, 'just the job on a day like this.'

They drank in companionable silence for a moment or two. Hildegard felt her body begin to tingle with warmth down to her toes. She could hear a woman singing and a child's occasional chatter behind an inner door, and she thought how pleasant it must be to be an apothecary in a warm house on a November day with your family cosily by in the next room. Cupping her hands round the beaker, she said, 'I'd welcome the recipe for this, if it's not your own secret, Dickon. But now, I wonder about this other prescription. There seems much to do with sleep?'

'A choleric lord. Who knows? Quieten him down? I don't question, not in a case like this when the servant was so clear about what he wanted.'

'He was?'

The apothecary described how the yeoman had rapped out his orders then lounged around, fingering everything while he waited for it to be produced. 'Damned nosy devil, he was, peering into everything, wanting to know what was what, as if I give away my secrets. I'm not doling my learning out to the likes of him.'

'Quite right,' agreed Hildegard peaceably.

'Anyway, I was always glad to see the back of him. Used to come up regular, pestering the life out of me. Over the last few months, that is, since Lord Roger came back from Kent.'

'With his new bride.'

Dickon nodded but kept his own council, only the gleam in his eyes betraying his assessment of the state of Roger's spring-and-autumn marriage, as it might be termed.

Before she left Hildegard asked a casual question regarding his opinion on the murders that had taken place in the woods and was unsurprised when he came up with another rumour: they were French mercenaries on their way to rouse the Scots. But then he gave a laugh. 'The less glamorous story is that it was a pitched battle between apprentice lads from York. I reckon that's the most likely tale. Sad, though. You'd think their masters could keep a better rein on their folly.'

There was no hint he knew about the secret company of dissenters. Either it wasn't yet common knowledge, or, despite his apparent warmth towards Hildegard, he was not yet ready to trust her with such knowledge.

She came away with the mulled wine recipe together with one or two ingredients, not easily obtainable, for her own scrip of medicines, and he finished by inviting her to call by any time she was in the locality.

Warmed both inside and out, she was still left with a puzzle. Clearly Melisen had sent the yeoman to procure remedies, but had Godric used the errand as a pretext for making an extra purchase on behalf of someone else? Or was that someone himself?

Tugging her cloak tightly round her shoulders, and with her hood pulled up against the rain, she set off through the empty streets towards the town stables to collect the horse loaned to her by Hubert.

Chapter Sixteen

Despite the brutal weather Hildegard decided to go back to the stables by way of the minster. It was only a slight detour and would give her chance to see how Master Schockwynde's men were getting on with the building works so that she could keep Hubert up to date. The wind cut into her as she rounded the corner of the building at the bottom of Trinity Lane. On the left was the Dominican friary and alongside it ran Walker Beck, overflowing with all the stench and foulness issuing from the tenements of the town. The wind blew this stench full in her face, and when it changed direction there was an equally strong smell from the tanneries where they were steeping the leather in urine acquired from the town privies.

It was such a contrast to the sweetness in the apothecary's little domain that she put her face in her sleeve and hurried on until she was almost running in order to get away from the stench. A couple of black-robed friars came out of the gate-house just as she was passing and the three of them at once became entangled in a whirl of flying cloaks as the wind snatched at anything it could grasp. One of the friars steadied her by the sleeve, shouting above the wind, 'Come with us, sister. We're on our way to St John's. We go by a more sheltered path than this.'

So saying, with robes flying out like rooks' wings, the two led the way down a narrow snicket between the buildings until eventually they came out on to East Gate where there was protection from the high walls of the buildings. She was grateful for their local knowledge and thanked them. 'I'm quite lost with all this new work going on.' It had been seven years since she had last visited the town. Extensions to the minster were continuing and St Mary's was a building site.

By the time the three reached the minster yard they were breathless and took shelter in the lee of the great tower, where they could shake out their cloaks. One of the friars produced a bunch of dried lavender to hold under his nose. He offered it to her. 'Our apologies, sister,' he said cheerfully. 'When the wind is in the wrong direction the beck stinks like the River Styx itself.'

'It certainly does. Can't they do anything about it?'

'We should welcome the odour,' said the second friar with a reproving glance at his companion. 'It reminds us of our vow of humility.'

'When the least shall be first,' agreed the first friar with a comfortable smile. 'And those with delicate noses rejoice. Tell that to the burgesses. Well, what brings you from out of your priory in this foul weather, sister?'

'Business,' she replied vaguely, falling into step with them as they left their shelter and turned towards the portico of the minster of St John of Beverley.

On every side hooded figures hurried to and fro, undeterred by the sleeting rain. Masons, surveyors and master carpenters issued instructions to separate groups of men from the shelter of the finished walls. The labourers wore sacks over their work tunics and one or two had leather aprons on, but all were getting a thorough soaking from the rain.

Four men were heaving stones off a cart. Hildegard and the two friars watched as they hauled them on to one of the creaking hoists. Another couple of men worked the windlass and slowly, with a lot of shouting, the blocks were lifted up the side of the tower on to a wooden platform above their heads. High on the scaffolding more men hefted the great, worked stones into place. Their shouts echoed off the half-built walls. Oaths, issued heedless of the fines accruing, and the piercing whistle of the foreman as he nursed the blocks into place from his vantage point above, added to the hubbub.

Everybody looked frozen to death, even the master mason in his fur-lined hood and the surveyor with hands stuffed inside his sleeves. The workers' faces were chapped and raw, their hands roughened by their labours and some dripping blood on to the stones.

Hildegard watched as two of the team swung down from the swaying ropes to land in the mud and squelch across the puddled waste to one of the stone carts. Their cheap leather boots are no protection against the wet, she noticed. She couldn't help but pity the hardness of their labours and the dangerous work they had to do as they began to heft another block up the ramp to the hoist.

The first friar, with the lavender under his nose, was a talkative type and began to tell Hildegard about their own building works which were now under way. 'Our friary lads have a bit of a wager with the minster lads as to who'll get most done in each seven-day. Then they come and confess their iniquity for betting on the Lord's work,' he added with an indulgent smile.

Hildegard could imagine the winners losing everything they had gained to the Dominicans before they even opened their mouths. As they chatted for a moment in the shelter of the west door she happened to mention the two guests up at Hutton. Her description of the corrodians brought blanks looks from both men.

'We have only three corrodians, an aged

retainer from the royal house, foisted on us to our great expense, and a couple of elderly churchmen too decrepit to get out of their fireside chairs,' said the first.

'Nobody you'd describe as in the first flush,' added his companion. At her look of puzzlement he asked, 'Are you sure they weren't staying with the Franciscans?'

'Maybe,' she replied. She took her leave.

On the way back to the stables she decided to make a further detour.

The Franciscans had a friary situated just outside the town walls near Westwood Green. Despite the weather it was too good an opportunity to miss. She left the town through Keldgate Bar and within minutes found herself at the gatehouse of the white friars. A brief description of the two corrodians, as they had called themselves, provoked only a shake of the head from the porter.

'None of that type here, sister.' He pondered for a moment then asked, 'Have you tried the Dominicans?'

She thanked him for the kindness that had prompted this suggestion, then braced herself for the walk back to the stables. As she made her way in through the town gate she was frowning. This is most peculiar, she thought. How is it nobody appears to know those two? The answer seemed obvious. They had been lying.

Qui bono? she asked herself. That was the key to the whole mystery.

Even though the day was an hour short of curfew

313

the traders in the corn market had given up and gone home or escaped to the nearest ale-house. No one could blame them. The market square was scoured by the wind and sleet flew in rapid dagger-like squalls across the cobbles so that everything that wasn't weighted down flew before it. The stables were near North Bar and not as busy as they would have been in better weather.

'This is no day to be out on the road,' grunted the ostler sympathetically as he saddled up the borrowed mare.

'I have little choice, master,' she replied.

He waved away her offer of a stabling fee with the words, 'You look after us. We look after you.'

The light was fading as she left the town. The gates were being hauled shut behind her and she was the last one to ride out as curfew fell. Her detour to the two friaries had taken up longer than she had anticipated. Now it threw up all kinds of dire suspicions. If the two alleged corrodians had broken through the security surrounding Castle Hutton and spent some nights there, making use of Roger's hospitality, they must have had a purpose.

She feared there could be only one answer. They were involved in the attempt on Roger's life. It occurred to her that they might have been foreign spies. She shuddered. Confusion filled her mind.

Compline had been and gone by the time Hildegard got back to Meaux. On the way she had passed a convoy of coal carts down from Durham.

They had emerged, noisy and massive, from out of the rain-slashed darkness, destined, she guessed, for the Dominicans. But after that there had been no one on the road. She regretted the absence of her hounds after the scare of the masterless gang the day before. There was also the strange sensation of a shadow following her, a phantom, no more, one she knew sprang from her imagination, the result of the malice directed towards her by her assailant on the previous night. She was back soon, however, safe and sound, reluctantly rousing the ostler's lad from his slumbers.

He was bedded down on a bale of hay in one of the stalls but, grunting and dazed, he struggled to his feet as soon as he heard the clip-clop of hooves in the yard. She slid down from the saddle and handed over the reins.

A brief glance showed that the stalls were still empty and she realised with a qualm that the war party had not yet returned from their adventure into the wapentake where William had his stronghold. Full of misgivings, she went to rouse the porter from his lodge. He came out, smiling as usual, when he saw who it was. 'You're out late, sister.' He jangled his keys as he locked the door of his room behind him before escorting her across the great court to the south wing.

'No news of Lord Roger?' she asked.

He shook his head.

The entire abbey lay under a shroud of silence, with the monks asleep in the dorter until the next office at midnight. The only other person out and about was the circulator, gliding noiselessly round the cloisters in fur-lined night shoes. They could see his flickering candle as he passed between the slender columns of the arcade and ascended by the outer stairs. The frail light appeared and disappeared as he went in and out of the cells where the senior monks slept. It blazed briefly as he passed each narrow window in the scriptorium before gliding on like a will o' the wisp to the frater as he made sure all was safe.

Guided by the porter's rush lamp Hildegard was led up a winding stair to a room next to the one Roger had been using in the abbot's lodging. There the porter fixed the light in a wall bracket and asked her whether there was anything further he could do for her. She glanced round the sparsely furnished chamber, little more than a stone cubicle, with a pallet against the wall, shook her head, thanked him and bade him goodnight. The sobriety and careful ordering of events according to the custom of the abbey were reassuring after the alarms and confusions of the last few days and she heaved a sigh of relief as she shook out her cloak and hung it on a peg to dry.

For a long time she sat on the edge of the pallet, her thoughts too busy for sleep. Roger and his men would be lying in some hellish ditch at this very moment, she thought. They could be planning their attack on William's stronghold, or, it was to be hoped, they were recovering from the battle already, with William taken prisoner and Melisen safe under Roger's protection once more. Hildegard wondered what their reunion would be like. Melisen would be astonished, to say the least, at seeing her lord, back from the dead.

Aware that there might be more to her kidnap

than met the eye, Hildegard considered the possibility that Melisen had ordered the yeoman to drug Roger to give her time to make her escape with William. Maybe something had gone wrong. If so, it might explain William's attack on Godric: it was to get rid of the only witness to their plot. Yet there had been no obvious sign that William and Melisen were attracted to each other. Indeed, they had ignored each other as far as Hildegard could remember. During the feast on the eve of St Martin William had eyes only for Ada. Everyone had murmured at that. But what if Melisen and William had merely feigned indifference? Could they have used others to cloak their desire for each other, the squire a mask for Melisen, Ada for William? If they really were conspirators they would have had to take steps to remain unnoticed.

She recalled the way Melisen had flirted with Roger throughout the entire celebrations. It might have been to tease William, to make him jealous. A game of *fine amour* would appeal to her.

William and Melisen. Melisen and William. She couldn't rule them out. They might be the key to everything.

And yet it still didn't make sense. If William believed Roger dead he would not need to kidnap Melisen. He could wait awhile and then approach her openly. He would have to cast off his wife first. No doubt Avice could be bought off. Despite her constant praying it was open to question how devout she really was. But what if the price she demanded was too high?

For William, the rich lands that Melisen as

heiress and widow could bring to him would be an irresistible lure. With Roger apparently dead, only one person stood in his way.

Hildegard got up and paced about the room. She must be wrong.

Outside in the corridor she could hear the shuffle of the circulator's night-shoes as he went by. The light of his candle flamed and vanished beneath the door.

Wondering whether Avice had left for Watton or whether the heavy rain had delayed her, Hildegard continued to pace. At the back of her mind was the separate mystery of the so-called corrodians, as irritating as a stone in the shoe.

She lay down on her pallet, her thoughts and fears running on as sleep claimed her. Soon they began to merge with a dream in which everyone was playing a game of Hangman in the garth. It was night, the figures were cloaked, their faces in shadow but, while she was pursued by the hangman, she found herself trapped in a small windowless cell. She saw, with great clarity, a glittering ruby ring on the finger of the hand that reached out for her. Another shape, in the mask of a cat, with fluttering tippets down one sleeve, lifted a great cloak over her head. A noose slipped round her neck and as it tightened she began to fight for breath.

She woke up with a small cry, fright jerking her bolt upright. Her ears pricked. A sound, no more than a breath, could be heard outside the door. The rush light had been doused but by the moonlight that filtered in through the narrow slit of the window she could make out the dark shape of the door against the whitewashed wall opposite. As she peered into the darkness, she saw the door-ring begin to turn. Her breath stopped. The memory of a rough beard and small, malevolent eyes looking coldly into her own flooded over her. She raised a hand to her throat.

It must have started as a gentle knocking but then a voice, one she recognised, whispered words that mingled incongruously with the remnants of her nightmare. Shaking, she peered across the chamber at a hooded figure standing there. It was her dream again. But she knew this was real.

Lantern light illuminated his features. They were clean shaven. It was the sacristan. His distressed expression sent thoughts of herself flying.

'Quickly, sister, a most terrible calamity has occurred!' As soon as he saw her pull her cloak from its hook he turned and, raising the lantern to light the way, hurried off down the corridor.

Her immediate thought was that something had happened to Avice.

Chapter Seventeen

Aware of the dagger in her belt, Hildegard followed the sacristan down the spiral stairs and out into the garth. On the other side lay the frater, its shape hardly discernible against the black sky, only a splinter of light visible from one of the rooms above indicating its position. Even so the light was too frail to penetrate the gulf of darkness that lay in front of them and they stepped forward like people plunging into a well. To her surprise he did not lead her towards the guest house beyond the court but across towards the building on the other side.

The moon must be behind a bank of cloud, she was thinking as she followed closely on his heels. When she caught up with him, she asked, 'Has Lady Avice set out for Watton yet?' As one of Hubert's obedientiaries he would be fully aware of abbey business.

He shook his head. 'The weather kept her here at Meaux. But, sister,' he lowered his voice in awe, 'this is something unconnected to the Hutton household. I beg you to prepare yourself.'

Without further explanation he led her into the pitch dark, only his flickering lantern, now blown by the wind and shielded by the edge of his sleeve, to serve as guide. He went unerringly to the door of the frater. When he pushed it open they were met by two monks, novices by the look of them. Faces as white as their habits, they gestured for her to follow them to the next floor. She had never been in this part of the abbey before and knew the chamber at the top to be the muniments room where all the abbey charters were kept under lock and seal.

The alarm on the faces of the monks made her hold her tongue until they reached a heavy oak door at the top where the sacristan's shout to open up brought the sub-prior swiftly out. He too was white faced. His hands, she noticed, as they lifted a candle above their heads in order to confirm their identity, were shaking so much they were sending shadows trembling like the flicker of bats' wings across the walls. Such was the fear everyone showed that an alarm ran through her body at what she would find. Hildegard pushed into the room.

The sight that met her gaze brought a cry to her lips. Countless parchments were strewn across the floor. The six iron-bound chests that were the repository for all the deeds, accounts and chronicles, as well as the abbey treasures, had been ransacked. Their lids gaped. Inside, the silver candlesticks, the jewelled chalices, the inlaid crosses of gold, all the gifts from benefactors than were too flamboyant or costly to display in the austere domain of a Cistercian abbey, had been taken out and yet, inexplicably, lay where they were dropped. The only conclusion to be drawn was that the thieves had been disturbed in their task.

The abbot came swiftly towards her but stopped within an arm's distance as if an invisible gate barred the way. His glance rested on her face. Gathering himself, he told her, 'I've sent for the infirmarer but as he's slow of pace you've preceded him. Perhaps you would take a look, although I'm afraid it's too late even for your skill.'

'Infirmarer? But why–?'

He moved to one side and she saw now, among the heaped documents, half hidden behind a chest, what she had assumed was a cloak tossed down with all the other things. But, moving closer, she saw that within its folds was a man. A monk. A young monk, she saw as she bent to look, no more than twenty-one.

He lay on his back, and at first appeared to be sleeping. But then she noticed the gashes on both wrists. Deep grooves, made by a knife. The blood had pumped unstoppably from the main artery that ran from heart to wrist. It was already congealing and had spread stickily across the coarse wool of his habit and soaked into the parchments underneath.

Hubert spoke. 'When he failed to show up for matins the sacristan was worried. Knowing he'd been working in the scriptorium but failing to find him there, he guessed he would come up here to deposit the deeds he was copying.'

'And when did he find him?'

'Just before prime.'

'Recently, then. But not recently enough to save him.' She remembered drifting to sleep as the bell tolled and how it had become part of the confusion of her dreams, like a premonition.

'There is a note.'

She had unconsciously knelt beside the body and the abbot came over. 'It suggests suicide but I know this boy. He understands fully the fate that awaits one who takes his own life.'

'Where is the knife?'

The abbot indicated the sub-prior. Shame-faced, Brother Gilbert stepped forward with a single-edged dagger wrapped in a cloth. 'I picked it up without thinking,' he apologised. 'It was in his hand.'

It was the sort of knife anyone might use at table. Sharp enough to cut a rabbit into strips, sharp enough to gut a man. The hilt was bound in leather. Nothing special to it. The only thing to remark was that it was a similar type to the one they guessed had killed Ada, another single-sided blade.

'The note?' she asked.

'Inscrutable.' Hubert handed her a piece of parchment like that used in the scriptorium. On it in careful letters was written in English: *Fields have their eyes, forests have their ears. None escape notice.* She shivered.

'Was this found in his hand too?' She turned to the sub-prior, who had had the grace to flush at his earlier mistake.

'It was tucked into his belt, sister. I removed it on the assumption it had some import regarding what had taken place.'

She could understand Hubert not wishing to believe that the monk was capable of killing himself and risking hellfire. It would negate the teaching of the order, of the Church itself. The note proved nothing either way. It was, as the abbot had observed, inscrutable. What was more, it appeared to have been deliberately cut from some other parchment. It was covered in blood.

Kneeling beside the young monk, she placed a finger on the side of his neck but there was no sign of a pulse. His flesh was already chilled. His eyes remained open as if staring at something terrifying and she gently pressed his lids down to give him some respite from his ordeal. Around her stood the silent figures of the monks: the abbot, the sub-prior, the sacristan and the two novices. 'Where is the prior?' she asked, noticing his absence.

'Gone to fetch the infirmarer and his man. For what good they can do now. I think it falls to us to ease the passage of our brother's soul to heaven.' It was clear Hubert did not believe in the suicide of the young monk. And yet the wrists were slashed. And there was a message of sorts.

Peering closer, Hildegard noticed a contusion on the side of the young man's head. It might have been caused when he fell. One of the treasure chests was in close proximity to the body. It was not beyond imagining that he had struck his head against its brass-bound edge. Yet what had made him fall? 'You've seen this?' she murmured, indicating the wound.

Hubert crouched beside her. 'Someone cracked him over the head? And, unconscious, he was unable to prevent the attack with the knife?' He sighed with a measure of relief at having his initial assessment of the matter apparently confirmed.

'We shouldn't jump to conclusions,' she reminded him. 'What's your procedure in matters such as this?'

'The coroner in York will have to be recalled.' Hubert gave a grimace. 'My cellarer would normally collate the evidence but it'll be some time before he's able to return from the grange at Tharlesthorp because of the floods. He'd present the evidence to chapter and we would make a collective decision on how best to apprehend the culprit, given, as would be expected, he had fled the abbey lands. All this is assuming we'd reached the conclusion that it wasn't suicide.' He gave her a glance. 'In fairness we need someone to look at the evidence. A person who has no vested interest in the matter. Someone outside our abbatial juris-diction.' He gave her another glance. 'It's most unusual to ask a nun to carry out such a duty, but given your evident knowledge and objectivity I believe chapter would agree to your involvement.' He raised his head and gave his officials a piercing look which would have taken courage to resist.

The sub-prior blew down his nose but nodded in reluctant agreement. 'The prior may have an-other point of view,' he murmured but without conviction.

The sacristan pre-empted any further objec-tions. 'I can offer you the services of a scribe, sister.' When she accepted he beckoned to one of the novices. 'This is Brother Thomas. He has a fair hand and a cool head.'

The abbot suggested that all but Thomas, Hildegard and himself return to prepare for the night office and to give no hint yet about the fate of their brother monk. That could be announced at chapter later that morning when the whole abbey gathered as usual to discuss the issues of the day.

When everyone had left he turned to Thomas. 'You are sworn to secrecy. What I'm about to say was told to me in confidence.' They listened in-tently as he explained that the doomed monk, Brother Nevyl, had come to him in distress shortly before compline the day before after hearing the confession of one of the visitors from Hutton. 'He could not tell me what was said within the privacy of the confessional, of course, but it was sufficient for him to be deeply troubled.'

'But why should that result in his suicide?'

asked Hildegard. 'Did he feel complicit in what he heard?'

'That is not what I intended to suggest.' Hubert frowned. 'Nevyl's distress was on behalf of the person he had confessed. For the enormity of their sin and the hazard of their immortal soul. He believed it might be a matter for the justiciar. What he required from me was advice on the confidentiality of the confessional and whether it was right to break it. I suggested it was a matter between God and his own conscience.'

'And the identity of this person, did he admit that?' asked Hildegard.

'I would divulge the name if I knew it but he hinted only that they belonged to the household of Sir Ralph.'

'Forgive me, but I fail to see the connection between a confession and Brother Nevyl's apparent suicide.'

The abbot sighed. 'So do I. But I have a firm belief there is one. This was never suicide. Nevyl was true of purpose. I offer these facts in nothing more than a spirit of conjecture.'

'You sound as if you think that the person who made the confession regretted the impulse – and decided to silence the only person aware of their guilt,' Hildegard suggested.

Hubert's eyes sharpened. 'It's the obvious inference. I rue the fact that I didn't press him further.'

'You can't blame yourself,' she replied. 'Confession would normally ease a troubled soul, not rouse it to further acts of iniquity.'

'It certainly shouldn't have frightened him into

committing murder. If it did...' He trailed off, uncertainty in his tone.

Thomas, standing silently beside them, made a sudden start. 'If I may be permitted to speak, my lord.'

'What?' Hubert turned abruptly towards his novice, as if having forgotten he was present.

'It so happens, my lord abbot, I saw someone leaving the confessional late yesterday. They were with Brother Nevyl, God rest his soul, for some time. In fact, they were the only ones to come in all afternoon. I was on duty between nones and vespers,' he explained. 'I saw all who came and left.'

'Who was he?' demanded Hubert.

'Not he, she,' said Thomas.

'She?'

When the answer came Hubert uttered a sound of astonishment.

'It was a maidservant of the Lady Sibilla. The one I believe to be the wet-nurse for baby Roger. I was at the lodge when the cortège arrived from Castle Hutton,' he added. 'I saw the entire party debouche from their wagons.'

'That upsets our theory somewhat!' Hildegard exclaimed. 'I can hardly imagine that girl taking a dagger to anyone, least of all her confessor.'

The three of them glanced back at the scattered muniments. 'The two events cannot be connected, then. Maybe it really is a case of common theft that went wrong,' suggested Hubert without conviction. 'And yet, after a cursory inspection, we can find nothing missing. The way the rolls are thrown suggests it was a deliberate attempt to give the impression of a break-in. And the wounds aren't the sort one would expect from a tussle with a burglar. And the note,' he went on. 'Nevyl would never have left a deliberate mystery to confuse and tantalise, whereas a murderer might.'

He gave a sudden grim smile as something else struck him. 'There is something we've missed.' He went over to the body where it lay, waiting for the infirmarer. 'The dagger. I remember how Gilbert unclasped the fingers of Nevyl's right hand to prise it free. In fact,' his tone became more certain, 'the lad is left handed. The dagger was planted. There is no other conclusion.'

Aware that Hubert was keen to prove that his brother monk had not committed a mortal sin, Hildegard was forced to point out that the monk might quite naturally have slashed his right wrist while holding the dagger in his preferred hand, then changed hands to slash his left wrist. 'This would be the natural thing to do,' she reluctantly concluded.

Hubert could not help but agree. He gave a heavy sigh. 'We have to get at the truth. For his soul's sake and for our own peace of mind and to see that justice is done.'

'We need to talk to the wet-nurse,' Hildegard suggested. 'Let's see what she has to say. Perhaps she's awake tending the baby at this hour. It would not be unusual. If you like I'll go to Sibilla's apartment and see what I can find out. At least that will close one avenue of speculation.'

Hubert gave her a warning glance. 'Take Brother Thomas with you. With a murderer on the loose you'd best go accompanied.'

Fields have their eyes, forests their ears. The phrase made Hildegard's flesh creep every time she turned it over in her mind. She felt unseen eyes spying on them as they left the others with the body and returned to ground level down the twisting stairs. It was the sort of phrase the guild men might use in order to maintain control over their apprentices. A warning to anybody against stepping out of line. Whoever the murderers of the five members of the Company of the White Hart were, guildmen or not, they must have had their spies. They would have obtained their intelligence from sources among the manor officials in the fields and from those appointed as wardens of the forests. Had the murderer of Brother Nevyl left the scrap of parchment behind in order to hint at the monk's membership of that same company? Someone had removed the pewter badge of the white hart from the murdered apprentice's tunic. Was it Nevyl himself, or were the two incidents unconnected?

Well used to prowling the abbey in the dead of night, Thomas was a reassuring presence as they made their way across the garth and out on to the other side to the guest house. When they went inside servants were lying around in the corridors, hunched shapes slumbering beneath their cloaks, one or two snores rending the silence. A light burned in a sconce at the foot of the stair leading up to Sibilla's apartment where the baby slept.

'The little mite must be having a peaceful night,' whispered Thomas as they made their way upwards. Treading softly, they reached an upper corridor with doors running its entire length. They looked at each other in confusion. 'The personal servants bed down together in a chamber at the farthest end,' said the novice. 'Maybe in order to preserve the sanctity of their slumbers Sir Ralph and the Lady Sibilla prefer to keep the child at a similar distance?'

'You're probably right.' Hildegard smiled, surprised that a young man, a celibate as he was, should be so knowing. 'Lead on, if you will.'

He glided along the corridor until he came to a door at the farthest end next to a back stair. She guessed it led down towards the privies over the mill race, an artificial sluice constructed by the monks many generations ago. Since then the order had become renowned for the construction of sluices and drains and a canal system had been designed that had already reclaimed tracts of marshland, where they now ran sheep. She waited as Thomas pushed open the door of the servants' chamber and looked inside. A chorus of snores greeted them.

Grasping the shoulder of the nearest man and gently shaking it, Thomas bent down to whisper, 'Quiet now, just tell me where the baby sleeps.'

'Pissing little brat,' mumbled the servant, not knowing or caring who was quizzing him. 'Been put out yonder behind that flimsy door ... don't keep the scratching of a bloody mouse at bay ... me get some sleep now. Bugger off.' Grumbling to himself, he turned over and pulled his cloak around his ears.

Thomas straightened. 'Poor fellow. They work so hard, their sleep is precious to them.' He indicated the next door. 'That must be the one he means.' With a burglar's stealth such that Hildegard wondered about his previous career, he pressed the door ajar. Within all was silent. In fact, it was a silence so complete Hildegard felt her heart turn over with fright.

'The light, if you please, Thomas!'

Standing behind her in the doorway he lifted the lamp so that the small chamber was illuminated in every corner. There was a heap of empty blankets on a pallet on one side and a wooden crib next to it. They hurried over. It too was empty.

'Perhaps the nurse has taken the baby to Sibilla,' Hildegard suggested. 'We must risk waking her. Come.'

Sibilla's quarters were guarded by two sleeping servants huddled on either side of the door. Stepping over them they made their way inside. The room was lit by a solitary night-candle and by its dim glow a bed could be discerned and on it a sleeping figure. Hildegard made her way over and peered down. It was Sibilla. Of the baby, and the nurse, there was no sign. Still praying for some simple explanation for the child's whereabouts, and fearing a certain amount of anger from Sibilla when she woke her, Hildegard braced herself to touch her on the shoulder. 'Sibilla, wake up for a moment, I need to ask you something.'

The woman stirred and at once her eyes blinked open. Thomas moved closer with the rush lamp held before him. Sibilla put one hand over her eyes. 'What? Is that you, Ralph?' She sat up, blinking in the light, and shook her plaits from her shoulders. 'What is it?'

'It's me, Hildegard. Baby Roger isn't in his room. Nor is his nurse. We must speak to her, Sibilla. It's urgent.'

'At this time of night?'

'Where is he, Sibilla?'

'Where is who?'

'Your baby, little Roger.'

'He should be sleeping. Down there–' She pointed vaguely back towards the door.

'The cot's empty. Come and see for yourself.'

With surprising speed Sibilla rose from her bed and, without even putting a robe on over her nightgown, hurried, complaining loudly, down the corridor to the baby's chamber. When she saw the empty crib she gave a loud scream that roused every servant within earshot. They came pouring into the chamber, half dazed with sleep, jostling and complaining, until with a roar one of them stepped forth and told them to hold their noise. It was a servant Hildegard recognised at once.

Shrugging on the jacket with its familiar scarlet tippets, he went over to his mistress. 'My lady?'

Sibilla pointed to the empty cot. 'Where's my child?' she demanded. 'He's gone!'

III

The black-cloaked envoy had taken ship at Damme. The port, situated at the mouth of the River Scheldt, served the city of Bruges where guilds supporting the men of Ghent and their leader Van Artvelde prepared for war. Damme was a convenient port of departure for the envoy as it happened to be the gateway into England via the North Sea and the eastern river estuaries of Thames, Humber and Tyne. The papers he offered before embarking had been accepted without question. Now, comfortably aboard the cog Isabeau, *he was treated with exceptional deference by the captain, who had seen his papers, and with indifference by the crew, who had not. During the thirty hours of the crossing he spoke to no one and no one spoke to him.*

Chapter Eighteen

While Sibilla was raging, her manservant stepped in to take charge. Hildegard took the opportunity to ask one of the maids his name.

'That's Escrick Fitzjohn,' replied the maid. 'He's Sir Ralph's right hand, though if you ask me he does more for the Lady Sibilla, if you know what I mean.' She gave a sniff.

Hildegard was astonished. So he really was one of the inner household, someone trusted, sharing Ralph and Sibilla's private life. She asked, 'Has he been with the family long?'

'Since the age of ten,' the maid answered, 'first as page, then retainer and now, well, as you see–' The maid clearly had no time for Master Escrick.

Just now he was barking orders that should more correctly have been given by Sir Ralph. The knight, it seemed, was still asleep in his chamber and nobody had thought to rouse him.

Escrick Fitzjohn. The man had power beyond the usual for a master of the household and Hildegard asked herself again why he had been meeting William's men in the undercroft.

Now he was packing the servants off to bed, and ordering a maid to attend her mistress. Meanwhile, he'd had a couple of hunting dogs brought in and pushed a kerchief belonging to the wet-nurse under their noses. The brutes whined and began to strain at their chains. With proof that the scent was strong, Master Escrick Fitzjohn announced to all and sundry that he was setting off in pursuit of the kidnapper himself.

Hildegard was struck by his manner. He seemed to take it as a personal slight that one of the servants had absconded. His manner was violent but he dissembled like a courtier whenever Sibilla glanced his way, all smiles and courtesy, but not bothering to disguise his bad temper when she wasn't looking. Hildegard was shocked to see him lash out with his fist at a young page who was slow to jump to a command. She recoiled when he gave a slashing cut of his whip to one of the house dogs which got under his feet. When he strode from the chamber he went with a swagger, chest pushed out, evidently believing he was master of all he surveyed. The maidservant gave Hildegard a knowing glance before bustling back to bed.

Escrick set out with two armed men and the two tracking hounds. With Brother Thomas by her side, Hildegard followed him to the outer gate, even though he gave them black looks. Thomas, however, maintained a benign certainty of purpose, his clever, bony face suffused with an expression that hinted at the abbot he would become in the fullness of time, and there was nothing Escrick Fitzjohn could do against such grace but offer an insolent shoulder and ignore him.

The two henchmen had necks as thick as their jaws, their foreheads concealed under casques with steel nosepieces. They carried bows and clubs as well as short swords and Escrick himself wore a hauberk with a powerful looking broad-sword stuck in his belt. Once outside the gates the hounds circled and checked until they picked up the scent again, then, with a single purpose, they set off after the maid.

Hildegard watched them leave with a worried frown. 'Master Escrick and his men go excessively armed to bring back a poor nursemaid.'

'I expect they fear outlaws, being unsure where the trail will lead them.' Thomas caught her glance. 'But perhaps we might be of assistance, sister, what do you think?' He glanced after the men. 'If she left on foot, as it seems from what the stabler told Master Escrick about his complement of horses, then perhaps we might take a short stroll outside the gates ourselves?'

'I would welcome your company,' said Hildegard, pleased to find he was quick on the uptake. 'First let me get my lymer and my running hound.'

The nurse had last been seen after matins, when the crying of the baby resulted in her being thrown out of the servants' hall. Apparently she had walked up and down the corridor for some time but had then taken the infant out of earshot on to the green. After that nobody knew where she went.

'She must have been standing in the darkness of the garth when Brother Nevyl was found and the sacristan raised the alarm,' Hildegard surmised. 'She would hear all the coming and going and no doubt everything that was said.'

They left the abbey with the hounds and headed off down the road in the direction Escrick and his men had taken. The track led to a wharf on the new canal which ran as far as the next village, where it linked up with the river. It had been built to allow the carters to bring in goods by barge and reload them for the export of staple, corn and honey. On the wharf was a thatched barn for storage, and ahead of them they heard Escrick's men stop for a moment to check inside it before riding on. Two of them began beating the long grass with sticks on both sides of the track as they rode along. By their casual manner it was clear they did not expect to find the runaway hiding so close to the abbey.

Hildegard and Thomas walked noiselessly with matched steps, for Thomas, at nineteen, was as tall as the nun. He possessed a calm and focused physical energy despite hours bent over parchments in the scriptorium and his gruelling year as a novitiate and in his rope-soled sandals he moved as carefully as Hildegard herself. She was glad he was with her.

As they tracked the trackers she whispered, 'The facts of the matter are as follows: the nurse confesses something to poor Brother Nevyl, shortly afterwards he's found dead, and then she runs away. Why?'

'Guilt because she is somehow involved in his murder–?' Thomas looked as doubtful as his namesake. 'Or fear of someone perhaps?' He raised his brows.

'Of someone who did not want her secret to come out, even in the confessional.'

'But what could such a secret be?' wondered Thomas.

Hildegard held her tongue. She had ideas on that score but they seemed too far fetched to mention, even in the otherworldly nature of this night when nightmares themselves seemed to have a life of their own.

They walked on in silence. The horsemen ahead were clearly audible and, having left the abbey, were under no restraint as to their language. Snatches of oaths floated back above the rattle of arms and harness. At one point they clearly heard Escrick call, 'Have a look and see if that bloody festering nun isn't after us, will you?'

One of the men gave a loud guffaw. 'You could soon sort her out, master. You and me, both.'

'Aye, and the lad,' said the third voice. There was raucous laughter but nobody came back to check.

Thomas and Hildegard melted into the trees that lined the towpath as the safety of the landing was left behind. The canal ran on ahead straight into open country. Beside them Hildegard's hounds padded along like fleeting shadows. She and Thomas had thrown dark cloaks over their pale Cistercian habits and this made them almost invisible in the dark of night.

'You must know this region well. Is there any turning off?' whispered Hildegard after they had travelled on half a mile or so.

'There's a chain-ferry further up.' It took workers to the grange on the other side of the canal. But before Thomas could say more they both stopped. Escrick's hounds had started to whine. There was the sound of the horses and hounds milling about on the bank side.

Hildegard put a hand on Thomas's arm. 'There's no sound of a woman's voice.'

After a moment they heard the rattle of a chain.

'They must be hauling the ferry over to their own side of the water,' whispered Thomas. They dropped to the ground to conceal themselves in the tall husked stalks of the rushes that grew along the bank.

'She's makin' for Skella!' one of the men exclaimed. His words floated over the night air quite clearly.

'She won't get far lugging that brat about,' said the other one. The hounds were whining with frustration at losing their quarry. Escrick's voice called out. From the sound, he was still sitting astride his horse. 'Hurry up with that raft then. Put some back into it. We'll soon catch the bitch out in the open on the other side.'

'We are putting our backs into it,' replied one of the men from lower down the bank. 'But nowt's happening.'

'Hey up! What's this?' There was a scuffling as the men seemed to scramble further down the bank. 'God's teeth!' came a shout. 'There's nowt on t' other end. Look here!'

'The crafty mare!' exclaimed the third voice. 'She's gone and cut the rope.'

'She can't have.' They heard a thump as Escrick landed on the path and walked over to the brim of the steep-sided bank. 'Are you sure?' he called down.

'Of course I'm sure. Look!' Evidently the man held up the rope that normally tied the raft to its chain. Escrick had a flare and Thomas and

342

Hildegard saw its sudden blaze as it was lifted up.

'Little cow,' the other man said. 'She cut it. Or got the brat to gnaw through it.'

There were renewed heaves on the chain and a rattling as it was drawn up fully on to the bank. 'Damn her to hell and back,' Escrick said. A discussion ensued with much cursing. Then Escrick's voice was heard again above the others. 'The only way to get across to the other side is to swim and fetch the raft back that way.' They heard him order one of the men into the water and the muttered oath from lower down the bank that followed. Escrick was cursing and stamping about at the top as the unfortunate volunteer stripped off his ironware. They heard him splash into the black water of the canal with another oath and set off for the other side.

'I don't envy him a swim on a night like this,' whispered Thomas.

Edging cautiously through the rushes, they tried to see what progress he was making. A faint ripple reflected his presence. It was the smallest change in the deep nothingness of the canal, but they saw it reach the other side, followed by the blur of the man's arm as he reached for the overhanging grasses in order to pull himself on to the bank. His voice came floating back to them. 'I can't find it!' More splashing followed, then his voice again, aggrieved, hoarse with cold. 'It's not here. She must have set it adrift.'

'She's taken to the water, more like,' called Escrick. 'You,' they heard him say to the man beside him. 'Get along the bank. Keep an eye out. I'm riding on to the lock gates.' Both men moved off, leaving their companion to swim back and haul himself unaided up the muddy bank on to the path. His chattering teeth were audible as he thrust himself back inside his woollen tunic and pulled on his boots. They heard him buckle on his sword and say something rough to his horse, then he was riding away to catch up with his companions.

Thomas and Hildegard got to their feet when the coast was clear.

'We must see this through,' murmured Thomas. 'There's a small boat kept moored somewhere near here. We use it for fishing.' Briskly he led the way back a little way and then, as if by some sixth sense, plunged off into a sea of rushes. There was a splash as he stepped into shallow water covering a half-submerged wooden platform. 'Here, sister. Follow my steps exactly.' Doing so, Hildegard found herself ankle deep in water on a makeshift pontoon, but a hand appeared out of the darkness and with Thomas to guide her she stepped into what she now made out to be a shallow-bottomed craft of withies much like a coracle. It rocked violently until she found her balance.

'I was brought up on the river,' Thomas told her, keeping his voice low. 'I'll scull us up towards the lock. If she's on the water we'll find her more quickly than those louts on the towpath from the height of their horses. Thankfully there's no moon tonight. The darkness may be her salvation.' Indeed, low cloud shrouded the opposite bank and was beginning to swirl across the unreflecting surface of the water.

Using the paddle to push the boat through the

reeds and on out of the inlet, the young novice soon had them floating down the canal. The water ran slow and deep between the high sides of the artificial banks. In only a few minutes he brought the boat level with the broken ferry chain then paddled across to the other side. Checking more thoroughly than Escrick's man, they found no sign of any fresh prints in the frozen mud. It must be as Escrick himself had concluded: the nursemaid had kept to the water.

They moved carefully on down the canal and soon heard the sound of a horse brushing through the grasses at the top of the bank. The novice let the craft drift stealthily under the lee, then he steered them on with single deft strokes, scarcely breaking the surface until they passed unnoticed beneath the place where the horseman was still searching through the long grass.

'Where do you imagine she's heading?' whispered Hildegard when they were safely out of earshot. 'I wonder if she has kin in the locality and is making for them?'

'I have no knowledge on that score,' Thomas replied. 'Would that I had.'

They soon left the horseman behind but their progress was slow. The nursemaid was likely to keep close to the bank and they were determined not to miss her. So far even the baby had not betrayed her presence. 'Maybe she has managed to escape up the other bank after all?' Hildegard suggested.

'It's too steep. I doubt she could manage it, even without the baby. If it was me,' Thomas added, 'I'd stay on the water as far as the lock. I'd get ashore there and seek assistance from the lock-keeper. Master Escrick's probably reached the same conclusion.'

'In that case let's hope she reaches the lock before he does.'

Thomas increased his pace. The mist was beginning to lift. It revealed the ribbon of black silk over which they floated. Hildegard prayed they would find the maid before dawn broke and began to shed its merciless light over the water.

They came upon the second horseman after a short time. He was more thorough, or maybe just in a better temper, than the swimmer. He had dismounted and was laying about the rushes with his club, dredging them with great thoroughness right down to the water's edge. Thomas held the boat under an overhang from where they could wait unseen until he moved further along.

'He must have his sword out to make them snap like that,' said Hildegard. 'The reed-gatherers are going to be upset.' Her light tone belied her fear at the picture of the nursemaid's neck being cropped in similar fashion. There was nothing they could do just now except wait. The mist was thinning and they were able to see that there was no one hiding further along.

'She must have made good time down the waterway. She's bound to reach the lock before Escrick,' said Thomas softly.

'Let's hope so.'

All this time Duchess and Bermonda were moving through the trees beside the path. They

346

would not enter water but were easy about following the riders along its course. Now and then Hildegard gave a low whistle in imitation of a reed warbler to tell them her position. If necessary they could have outstripped any horse and the easy pace of the boat was no hardship for them. Thomas plied the paddle again. Hildegard's attention was fixed so intently on the water she almost missed a slight splash on the opposite bank. It could have been mistaken for a water-fowl at any other time of year. Now it caused her to hiss for Thomas to stay his oar.

'There,' she breathed, aware that the horseman was close. Thomas made no movement but she knew he had seen it too. It was no more than a glimmer in the darkness. They paused with held breath. It seemed as if the presence of living creatures on both sides of the bank filled the air with their being. Each tried to observe the other. The clash of eyes trying to pierce the darkness seemed as if it would bring the men on the bank running with its uproar. Neither side moved. Water continued to gurgle under the keel of the boat, a mere breath of sound, no louder than the ripples over the sedge lying below the waterline.

The horseman urged his mount on to the next bed of reeds. Both sides waited, frozen in place, until he had hacked his way through the brittle winter stalks, found nothing, remounted and moved on. When he was far enough ahead to be out of earshot Thomas turned the bow of their craft towards the opposite bank. There was a more agitated rustling as they approached, for they had obviously been heard if not seen. It was like some animal trying to climb away, frantic but endeavouring to conceal its presence.

Wishing she knew the name of the nursemaid, Hildegard took the risk of whispering a few words of reassurance across the water while Thomas paddled them as quickly as he could to the other side. As they approached she called again.

'Stay! We are two religious from the abbey at Meaux. We intend no harm.' It was not until they bumped unexpectedly against a raft of swaying, waterlogged wood that they realised the pale shape they had discerned was indeed a raft. Hildegard reached out to steady both craft. Under her fingers she grasped a clump of coarse russet and felt a blade against her wrist.

'Don't move.' A woman's voice came out of the darkness.

'You're being followed. Put your knife away.'

The knife didn't shift. 'Who are you? Who sent you?' The voice was hoarse. It trembled but held a note of defiance. The blade pressed more firmly against Hildegard's wrist.

'No one sent us. We came of our own accord,' said Thomas in a voice pitched low enough not to be overheard by anyone on the other side of the canal. 'I'm a novice at the abbey and–'

'What abbey?' interrupted the voice. 'I don't know nowt about any abbey. Why should I? Leave me be. Can't a wife do a little night fishing without being stopped?'

'The river warden might have an opinion,' said Hildegard, 'but we're not concerned with that. Our concern is for the baby and its wet-nurse.'

A brief flurry of movement came from the raft,

tipping them about. The knife was withdrawn, to preserve the balance of the one who wielded it rather than in a spirit of goodwill.

'Shush,' the nun whispered, 'Master Escrick is after you. He knows you took the ferry from its chain.'

'Damn Escrick to hell,' replied the voice. 'And how do you know about the baby?'

'We wanted to talk to you about Brother Nevyl,' said Thomas. 'When we came looking you'd gone and so had the child.'

'Is that poor monk really dead? I'm sorry for him. He was a kind man.' For the first time there was a weakening in the woman's voice. 'But what should I know about it?' Clearly she did not yet trust them, although the knife seemed gone for good.

'We think you may have told Brother Nevyl something that others wanted to keep secret.' Hildegard saw the pale shape on the other craft draw her arms more closely around herself. 'I'm Sister Hildegard from the priory at Swyne,' she continued. 'I think I know you as the Lady Sibilla's wet-nurse.'

There was a sigh that may have been a sob. 'Yes, I do work for the Lady Sibilla, damn her, and you do know me as the wet-nurse–' Her voice faded.

'And?' prompted Hildegard.

'And my name is May. I'm wife to John of Hessle.'

'And the baby?' Hildegard prompted again. Silence. 'I believe the baby is your own,' she said gently.

There was a flurry from the raft.

'You're safe with us. I imagine some strong inducement was offered to make you hand over your own son to them.' She remembered how fiercely May had tended the child, like a mother defending her cub.

May seemed to struggle with some knotted thought of her own but eventually in a low voice she said, 'There's something else.' She paused, then added in a rush, 'The name of my baby is Marianna.'

Hildegard and Thomas took in the meaning of what she said.

'And baby Roger, the son and heir of Sir Ralph and Lady Sibilla?' ventured Thomas just to be sure.

'Baby Roger!' the woman scoffed. 'How long did they expect to get away with that charade, the sot-brained idiots!'

May told them she intended to get as far as the lock then persuade her cousin, the lock-keeper's boy, to help her safely down to Frismersk, where her husband worked. 'We know that marsh and its ways. I'll be as safe as a princess in a stone tower once I get down there.'

'But the baby,' Hildegard pointed out, 'it's too tender to be dragged about the countryside at this time of year.' Her fear was Escrick and his long reach into marsh dragon territory, but she did not wish to alarm the woman more than necessary.

May was adamant. 'I'm not going back to Meaux with Lady Sibilla there. She'll kill me.

And she'll snatch my baby back. I'll let her have her gold, what's left of it. But I'm hanging on to my baby, like it or no.' She would not be budged.

'The priory at Swyne isn't far. You could find sanctuary with the nuns,' Hildegard urged. 'They'll be pleased to take care of you both. At least you'll be safe.' Sensing that May was unconvinced, she added, 'I know Frismersk. It's a wild, desolate place. When the river's in spate you'll be trapped. Some of the sheep-cotes were washed away at the last high tide, weren't they?'

'It's home,' said May, simply.

'Don't you want your baby to be safe?' She could imagine Escrick doggedly hunting the pair across the salt marsh. When he caught them, as he would, there would be no law to prevent him doing whatever he wanted.

May thought swiftly. 'If we go to the lock we can borrow horses. Then I can ride to Swyne. The nuns might send a message to my man? I'll do that if you think the prioress will take us in.'

'It's better than lingering in this ditch with Escrick on the prowl,' urged Thomas.

'Get into our boat, May. There's no time to waste. Your baby's sleeping now but when she wakes Master Escrick will be down like a shot.'

Without further urging May allowed them to help her from the raft into the boat and, though cramped, Thomas managed to scull them quietly into midstream. 'Keep an eye open,' he said, 'and when we get close to the lock be even more careful. Is there any way of getting up the bank before then, May?'

'Not that I know of. I can't say I make a habit

of boating up and down the abbot's ditch.' She laughed. 'It's a good job I'm familiar with rafts and the like. I'd just crossed over and was going to set it adrift when it struck me I could get away on it and leave no trail. I heard them hounds coming out of the abbey, putting the fear of God into me, begging your pardon, sister, then I hit on this way of outwitting them.'

Her spirits seemed restored by her unexpected rescue, and now she settled down to pet the little bundle wrapped inside her cloak. 'As if they could've made out you're a lad!' she murmured.

The baby slept and Hildegard wondered what sort of draught May had given her to make her so peaceful in the middle of the drama.

While Thomas sculled silently towards the lock gates Hildegard asked her why she had allowed her child to be passed off as someone else's. Sibilla had approached her after hearing she was pregnant, May explained, and, giving her a story about the sort of life she would bestow on the child by bringing it up as her own, had offered a dazzlingly large sum of money that could have set May and her husband up for life. The thought of their child living in luxury was too much to refuse. The deal was struck.

'When I was near my time I was brought secretly to Castle Hutton to give birth. They weren't half worried when you sprang from nowhere. Somebody had had the forethought to slip one of Lady Sibilla's rings on my finger but they were in a right flummox, thinking you saw her as she left the birthing chamber by another door.'

'The perfume! So that's what it was. I knew there was something strange but I couldn't put my finger on it.' How our senses reveal the truth, Hildegard thought – and betray us too.

'Everything went according to plan after that. Marianna was born, perfect in every way, except one, according to Lady Sibilla.'

'But then the plot started to unravel?'

May nodded. 'Lord Roger was struck by the pestilence and died. That was the first thing. Then Ada was found with her belly slit open and her mouth laced up in that horrible way. We all knew it was a warning to keep our traps shut. I began to live in mortal fear, I can tell you.' She gave a shudder. 'I didn't know what to do. Sir Ralph was raving, he hadn't reckoned on leaving Castle Hutton so soon, and Lady Sibilla's a very strong-minded woman. Talk about a shouting match! Sir Ralph was all for telling them she was unfit to travel so they should stay there but she wouldn't hear of it. "We need to be seen," she said, "or that bloody brother-in-law of yours will be having himself announced heir in front of everybody." "All the more reason for staying put, here in the castle," said Sir Ralph. "Let him try and take it with us in it." But the Lady Sibilla would not give way. "Tactics, Ralph," she said. "You know all about those." And that was that.'

The horsemen had been left far behind, beating vainly at the empty reed beds, apparently un- aware that their quarry had gone to earth. Soon the lock appeared against the gradually lighten- ing sky. Dawn would soon be upon them. It was lucky, Hildegard was thinking, that they had almost reached their destination before the canal turned into a ribbon of light. She began to breathe a sigh of relief.

But then they heard a grinding sound like a wheel being turned on a wooden spindle. Their boat was now slipping between the artificial banks where the canal had been most heavily engineered on the approaches to the lock.

'There must be a craft of some sort inside,' Hildegard said in alarm as she imagined Escrick pursuing them in a boat he had found.

The sky became lighter by the minute. Then they saw the lock gates ahead of them begin to open. To their horror a man appeared high up on top of the beam above the gate.

It was Escrick Fitzjohn.

He was running towards the second capstan, which opened the upper gates. When he reached it they saw him strain to set it in motion. Behind the gates was a wall of water that would normally empty into the basin thirty feet below where it would be confined by the second gate in order to allow craft to descend to the lower level. With those gates open, a wall of water would surge down the channel in a great wave, carrying everything before it.

'You can see what he's doing! We've got to get off the water!' Thomas exclaimed.

Glancing at the banks on both sides they knew there was no escape that way. Horrified, the three of them watched as Escrick exerted his whole strength against the capstan and it began to grind slowly round until it started the process that would allow the upper gates to open and release the pressure.

The sun was emitting its first rays and in the increasing light they could see a trickle of water begin to seep through the wooden gates as they inched open. Then it began to spout in an increasing spate between the gap.

May clutched her baby to her breast, her eyes widening in horror. 'This is the end! What can we do? O Lord, help us, I beseech you, O Lord, help!'

Chapter Nineteen

Hildegard reacted swiftly. 'Take your child, May. You must climb the bank. We'll help from below.' They might be able to hoist May on to their shoulders so she could get a foothold higher up. Even if she didn't reach the top she and the baby might be safe enough above the worst of the surge.

Thomas gasped. They turned to see a man in yellow running alongside the lock from the direction of the keeper's cottage. The sun, brighter by the moment, began to light the scene in all its detail. When he reached Escrick he grabbed him and tried to drag him away from the capstan. Escrick staggered but did not fall.

'That's the lock-keeper!' exclaimed May.

Thomas dug hard into the water with the paddle and propelled the boat as fast as he could towards the lock itself. 'If we can only reach the gates in time,' he said through gritted teeth, 'we can climb the ladder beside them.'

As they neared the lock Hildegard could just make out the rungs of a rickety wooden ladder fixed to the wall below the keeper's cottage. It must have been there since the gates were first built, she thought. Heart in her mouth, she urged Thomas on as he propelled the craft forward with the strength of desperation.

The lock-keeper was getting the worst of an exchange of blows but then a sudden swing of his club caught Escrick on the side of the head. He gave a roar of rage and fell back, then he snarled something and drew his sword. The lock-keeper dodged past him and ran out on to the wooden beam that formed the top of the lock gate. Having lured Escrick away from the capstan, he jumped the gap through which the water was beginning to spurt, then turned to face him.

It was an uneven contest. Escrick was a trained fighting man. He was armed with steel. He even wore a hauberk. By contrast the lock-keeper was in a loose tunic and woollen breeches and held only a piece of wood.

With a shout of anger Escrick simply took one stride across the gap and ran his sword straight through the keeper's chest. But it was not over. Such was the force of his attack he was unable to withdraw the blade. Although he must have been in agony, the lock-keeper grabbed hold of the blade close to the hilt and, aware that he was already a dead man, deliberately plunged backwards over the gate into the lock basin, twenty feet below, dragging Escrick with him.

There was a long silence as the two men fell. Then they hit the water with a crack and broke through as through a pane of glass.

Tearing their eyes away, the three in the boat switched their attention to saving themselves. Already the partly open gates were bulging with the force of the water behind them. At such an angle, inched partly open, they would not be able to resist the pressure for long. As soon as Thomas brought the boat within reach of the ladder, Hildegard leaned out and grasped hold of the nearest rung. 'Quickly, May, climb up!'

The nursemaid didn't argue. With her baby tucked firmly in her cloak, she began to climb the ladder. Hildegard followed and the novice came scrambling after. When they were high enough to be out of danger they looked back to see Escrick struggling on the surface of the water and the lock-keeper's body in a stain of blood sinking and rising, and sinking again. His hands were still clamped round the sword that had killed him.

There was a shout and a boy's face appeared over the top of the bank. It was as white as a swan's feather. His mouth worked but no sound emerged.

'It's me, Oswin! Give us a help up.' May had recognised her young cousin. With the baby beginning to whimper, she held a hand out for assistance and was dragged on to the path in front of the cottage to safety.

Back in the canal Escrick, weighted by his armour, struggled wildly to stay afloat. He lost his sword when the lock-keeper sank below the surface for the last time. Still clinging to the

357

ladder, Hildegard and Thomas watched in astonishment as he struggled to cast aside his heavy leather belt and, ignoring the threatened deluge, desperately fought his way out of his hauberk. Then they saw him draw in his breath before diving under the water in pursuit of his sword.

At that moment the great wooden gates, that had resisted the pressure of the water on the other side for so long, burst open with a massive splintering of shattered oak. There was a roar as the pent waters surged through the narrow gap. Shards of wood flew in all directions. Hildegard and Thomas scrambled rapidly the rest of the way up the ladder and reached the bank as the wave surfed past. They could do nothing but watch as it continued to smash down in a deadly blaze of white foam on the spot where Escrick had been. Their own small craft was turned to matchwood in an instant and vanished beneath the flood. After a few moments the water began to find its own level and soon all that remained was the swaying and rustling of grasses at the bottom of the bank as the water streamed past.

Oswin, the lock-keeper's boy, was in a state of shock. It was May who seemed the calmer of the two. She took him back inside the cottage and kicked the embers in the fire-pit into a blaze. There was already a pot set there with a mess of day-old pottage in it, and she stirred the contents and told him to sit down and stop his teeth chattering as the sound was getting on her nerves. She said further that there was nothing to be achieved by moaning and he should sup up and do as he was told. A flagon of small beer was thrust into his hands.

'But that was my master,' he kept saying. 'Run through with a sword. Then drowned. My dear master, doing no harm to anybody all his life long.' He began to sob quietly until May put the baby into his arms. 'He saved this one,' she said. 'He didn't die in vain at all.'

Aware that her hounds were loose on the other side of the canal and that there was no easy way of getting over to them, Hildegard gave Thomas a rueful glance. 'Our short walk has turned into quite a journey.'

'And Escrick's men might make it even longer if they find a way over to this side.' He frowned. 'I can't think what Brother Gregory's going to say when he finds me missing from my studies.'

'It might be a good idea to get May and Marianna into safe territory first and then consider the problem of getting you back for your lessons.'

May butted in. 'Oswin will lend me the lock-keeper's old nag. Then he's going to accompany me to this priory you mentioned. There's nothing you could say, sister, that I can't just as well say for myself,' she was quick to point out.

'We'll return to Meaux, then.'

When Oswin had recovered his wits he went out to saddle the mare. Hildegard took the baby on to her lap, while May herself made short work of a bowl of pottage. She was full of vigour despite having given birth so recently and as soon as she had eaten she took the baby to suckle. Now seemed as good a time as any in which to

359

find out more about the plot hatched by Sir Ralph and Lady Sibilla.

'How did they feel about Ada's murder?' Hildegard began. 'When I broke the news to Sibilla she pretended not to know who she was.'

'The liar!' exclaimed May. 'She's been with Lady Sibilla since she was a child. That's why she was chosen to attend the birth. They trusted her. They were forced to let several in on their stupid plan. Escrick because he did all their dirty work, the midwife, naturally, Sibilla's personal maid who attended the birth, for what use she was, dabbing away at me with a little perfumed cloth, and Ada, of course, who at least had some idea what to do.'

'So what went wrong?' asked Hildegard.

'Maybe Ada was less easily bribed than the rest of us.' May looked somewhat shamefaced for a moment, then explained. 'We were happy enough to go along with things, money in our pockets, debts paid, but I think Lady Sibilla grew worried Ada was about to talk. Escrick must have taken things into his own hands as usual. Vicious bastard.'

'What do you mean?'

'You know.' May looked down. 'What I said, him doing what he did.'

'It was Escrick, then, who murdered Ada? Is that what you're saying?' Hildegard felt she must have it unequivocally from the girl's own lips.

May nodded. In a low voice she said, 'I was terrified at what he did to her. Of course, we all heard about the stitching up of her lips. It was clear enough what he was trying to tell us, those

360

of us in the know, that is. The midwife couldn't get out fast enough.'

'And did someone order him to do that?'

'Not when I was around. But I did hear Lady Sibilla say to him: "Have you impressed on Ada the need for secrecy as I asked?" and he said: "I have, my lady." We didn't know till later what he meant. When they heard she was dead Sir Ralph knew straight away what he'd done.'

'It must have been very frightening,' said Hildegard gently.

'It was! But it got worse after I made that confession to the monk.' May gave a shudder. 'I went to confession as soon as we got to Meaux. Even though I've never had much time for the Church I started having visions of hellfire.'

'Guilt is a powerful thing,' said Thomas nodding.

'It was when I was coming out of the church, Escrick just sprang out at me from behind one of them pillars and he says, "You've been in there a long time, mistress." I say, "I've had a lot to get off my chest." I never thought he'd think twice about me telling a monk. But he says, "You seem to have forgotten what happened to Ada and her big gob." Then he gives me a black look and walks off. I'm thinking, I'd better keep my head below the battlements now all right. Then I hear that rumpus in the middle of the night when I'm standing out with Marianna in the garth and there's talk of the monk being killed and I think, oh God, he's going to do me in next, I'd better get out quick. So I gathered my stuff and ran.'

Oswin came in and told them he'd got the cart ready for his cousin and the baby to ride in. Hildegard and Thomas watched them leave with relief. The two men on the other bank would be taken up with the fate that had befallen their master and would have little time to continue the pursuit. All they themselves had to do now was find a way back to the abbey.

As they stooped under the lintel to go out they could hear Escrick's hounds on the other side, whining with disappointment. It was a pitiful sound that came and went, now near, now far, as they coursed up and down through the wet reeds. Of the horsemen there was no sign. Brother Thomas noticed her glance sweep the opposite bank. 'Your own two beasts will be safe. Rest assured.'

'I hope you're right, Thomas. I do fear they'll finish up with arrows in their backs and their heads brought in for bounty. But let's go. The sooner we find a way home the better. If we're quick we may even be back for prime.'

As it was they had no choice in the matter of how to get back. They were forced to take the one path that linked the lock-keeper's cottage with the outside world. In one direction it ran on towards the Humber and the port of Wyke, which the old king had renamed Kingstown, but in the other direction it led all the way back towards the road to Beverley. Thomas reminded her of the pack bridge that spanned the canal a short distance from the gatehouse at Meaux. They would be able to cross back to the other side over that.

It was nearly two miles, walking in the ever-brightening day, until they were level with the outer defences of the abbey grounds. They had seen no sign of Escrick's men on the way. Even his brace of hounds seemed to have run off and joined their cousins in the wilds.

'Just round the next bend we should find the bridge,' Thomas said encouragingly. Even before it came into view, however, they heard the noise of an army of men on the other bank. The clank of chain mail and the jangle of arms came closer with every step. At first alarmed, they realised that it could only be the force belonging to Lord Roger de Hutton. 'Sibilla has not so many men at her command,' Hildegard remarked with some relief.

Even so they halted on the path behind some trees and waited for the men to come into view. There were maybe a dozen or so, some on foot, others on horseback, the casques of the foremost ones gleaming in the misty light as they ranged among the reeds as if searching for something. As they came nearer they saw that they were fully armed and must have come straight from their march against Sir William.

To Hildegard's immense relief she recognised the man at their head. It was Ulf. Lathered in mud from head to foot, his arm in a grubby sling, it could only be him with that wild, sun-bleached hair cascading from beneath his helm. They watched as he led a small posse along the narrow path to another part of the bank. Like Escrick's men, they were beating with the flats of their swords at any tall bulrushes left standing after the flood wave had passed over, thoroughly kicking to pieces every remaining hiding place.

Hildegard stepped from the cover of the trees and shouted across. With an exclamation of joy she saw her own hounds emerge from the trees at the sound of her voice. They pointed their muzzles towards her in silent greeting and, as if echoing her feelings, began to weave patterns of joy around the forelegs of Ulf's steed. The steward lifted his sword as a sign to the men in the vanguard. The whole party came to a halt in a disorderly throng.

'How the blazes did you get over there?' he called. He wore a delighted grin under his mask of mud.

'It's a long story. But I see you're safe and sound. And you have an escort.'

'They came to find me,' he said, gesturing to the hounds. 'I guessed there was something up when they showed their faces without you in attendance. You had me worried. I thought you'd drowned in that wave that's just swept down. Come over the bridge and we'll catch up.'

'We've got a lot to say to each other,' observed Ulf when he greeted her on the bridge. He gave Thomas an assessing glance. 'A challenging part of your novitiate, son, to accompany this particular Cistercian on her daily round?'

Thomas laughed nervously. He seemed overwhelmed by the roughness of the riders as they milled about, battle-stained and ferocious, with their swords rattling in their scabbards. The hearty greetings they gave Hildegard obviously shocked him. Clearly he had only ever met the sort of nun who prayed and embroidered and rarely left the confines of her priory. Giving her a sidelong glance, as if to make sure she was real, he followed the group as far as the gatehouse. 'I ought to attend to my duties, sister,' he told her when they entered the garth. He seemed nervous about missing the daily office as well as his lessons.

'I shall inform the lord abbot at once of every-thing that has happened and of your exemplary protection. God go with you.'

'And with you, sister.'

'I'll tell him he'll need to send men to find the bodies of the two who drowned. Lord Roger's men will no doubt pick up the ones on horse-back. And Thomas—'

He lifted his head.

'Don't forget your duty to me as scribe. You witnessed the confession of the nursemaid. These are facts that will have to be put before the coroner.'

Happy to have played a useful part in the affair, Thomas pulled up his hood and made his way across the great court towards the church to fulfil less physical duties.

The abbot invited them to his chambers after mid-morning mass. Before that Ulf managed a quick word with Hildegard after she had explained what had happened on the canal.

'We had a wasted journey,' he told her. 'God knows where Sir William got to but he wasn't there when we finally waded through his marsh.

How he can live in that swamp God only knows.'

'I'm sure He does,' replied Hildegard, smiling good-humouredly.

'You know what I mean. Anyway, we got all the way to Ravenser, forsaken hole, before finding out he hadn't even been near. Gone to Hutton, says Roger. So we came back here. We're going to press on to Hutton at first light. You should have seen the women's faces when Roger appeared! Philippa was in a real fury once she got over the shock. Sibilla fell into a dead faint. Afterwards she stood there, fanning herself and eventually murmured, "I don't think I can take any more." She went up to her chamber for a lie-down and that's the last I've seen of her.'

'It must have been a shock. First her so-called son and heir goes missing then her brother-in-law returns from the dead. Not to mention her right-hand man being swept away.'

'That wave was felt by some eel-men as far up as Tickton,' Ulf told her. 'The bodies will fetch up somewhere round there, you mark my words.'

He went off to use the fresh water in the monks' lavatorium and find a change of clothes.

Roger, too, had had a chance to wash, she observed when they met. His beard was neatly clipped and he wore it forked. When he saw Hildegard enter the abbot's chamber he smiled foxily and stroked the points with both hands until they were so sharp you could have used them to write with.

As well as Hildegard and Lord Roger the abbot expected the steward, as Roger's main man, to attend as well. Ulf arrived a little late, self-consciously smart, a clean bandage sticking out from beneath his tunic, and his beard trimmed into a neat, straight line, although his sun-bleached hair was as long and unruly as ever.

When they were all present Roger demanded, 'So, what have I missed?' He stretched out his legs towards the fire that was blazing in the abbot's hearth.

Hubert de Courcy spoke first. He told Roger about the murder of Brother Nevyl, the damage done to the abbey parchments, the mess that had had to be left until the coroner could get here and how the body had to be kept in the mortuary surrounded by slabs of ice. Hildegard added that it was almost certain that both murders, those of Ada and the monk, had been committed by Escrick, Sibilla's master of the household, telling them almost word for word what May had had to say.

'Escrick got hold of too much power,' muttered Lord Roger, tasting one of the abbot's best vintages with a grunt of approval. 'Should have been kept in his place from day one.' He glanced briefly at Ulf, who began to study his fingernails.

Hubert inclined his head in acknowledgement, but gave no indication of his own views on the matter. 'The coroner has been informed of the demise of our dear brother and is expected here to conduct his inquest as soon as he can conclude his other business in York.'

'Thomas is writing up the events as recounted to us by May,' added Hildegard. 'We have her version regarding Escrick's involvement and it is

367

hard to doubt, yet I fear the coroner will need something more substantial than the word of a wet-nurse in order to justify his linking of the two crimes.'

'There is something,' said Hubert. He got up from his imposing abbot's chair and went over to his writing table. Picking up a small silver box from among his books he returned and, snapping open the lid, pulled forth what looked at first sight like a fine black thread.

'This is thanks to our ever-vigilant prior with his insatiable eye for detail – not to mention an unswervable ability to wield a fine tooth comb,' he announced with a somewhat ambiguous inflection in his voice.

'But that's similar to something I found in Ada's lacing.' Hildegard fumbled inside the pouch on her belt and brought forth a small container. 'I thought it worth keeping, my lord abbot, perhaps driven by the same penchant for detail as your prior.' She gave him a smile then held something to the light. 'It looks like a hair of some kind.'

'I'll tell you what that is!' exclaimed Roger, leaping up out of his chair and peering at each exhibit in turn. 'It's hair from that damned cat! I'll wager good money on it. How much, Ulf?'

'I'll have to have a closer look first, my lord,' murmured Ulf cautiously. He got up and examined the two exhibits, then turned to Roger. 'I'll not wager against you, my lord. They're very like cat's hairs. And the only cat around here is Master Jacques.'

'Does that confirm–' Roger frowned. 'If I can

get my head around this – does that confirm bloody Ralph has had a hand in all this?' His face had paled with fury.

'Not necessarily,' Hildegard interrupted. 'Escrick was in charge of the cat much of the time.' She gave a sudden laugh. 'And of course, that must have been where he got all those scratches on his face and neck. I've been thinking they must have come about in the struggle with his victims. But they were far too sharp and small. Master Jacques! Is he enough to provide the link?'

'That's for the coroner to decide,' said Hubert. 'Perhaps we can find the cat and match the hairs later.'

No one made a move but they were satisfied with this evidence, slight though it was. A novice was roused to bring more wine.

There was still one question that Hildegard was compelled to broach, despite the soporific effect of the fire and the Guienne. 'It's the question of Godric's poulaines,' she began. 'The prints were clearly there beside Ada's body.'

Ulf interrupted. 'My kitchen lads might provide the missing piece there. If you remember, we were watching them dressing the table and bringing in the salt that day at Hutton? And I said, look at them making a fuss over some salt, and you said, I wonder they don't trip over the points of their poulaines, and I said, I'll have to fine the devils, and you said–'

'Yes, yes, I remember the gist.' Hildegard was impatient.

'Well then. I said to him later, I said, I'm going

to have to fine you, Jack, if you don't do some-thing about them – apparently he sold them to Escrick that very day!'

'So Escrick was wearing them in the grain store?'

'Must have been.'

'And, getting blood on them, I suppose he had to dispose of them as quickly as possible, which in this case meant up the nearest chimney–'

'–which happened to be in Sir Ralph's apart-ment!' Ulf looked pleased as all the loose ends were tied up.

'But why was the red chaperon singed?' Hilde-gard persisted. 'It was hidden – which in itself is significant.

Nobody had an answer.

'There are many mysteries in life,' observed the abbot.

'All that way in pursuit of the midwife for nothing.' Ulf patted Hildegard on the back of the hand. 'Never mind.'

She removed her hand from beneath his and adjusted her coif, aware of Hubert's sharp glance. 'And we still don't know what happened to the midwife,' she said. 'Nor who fired the mill. And,' she added, with the feeling that it should be out in the open at last, 'Nor do we know who that band of riders were we met that night.'

Ulf shook his head and said emphatically, 'No, we don't. They'll be long gone by now.' And his glance slid past hers in a way that made her file it away for later. *The fields have eyes.* He knew something.

'We're really knocking the skittles for six tonight,' pronounced Roger, deeply satisfied. 'I can't wait to get to Hutton tomorrow to bang a few heads together.'

Hubert observed him in silence.

'Well, maybe just William's,' he corrected, aware of the sudden chill. 'Ralph doesn't need his brains rattling. He's unhinged already if he thinks he could have got away with a ruse like that! Passing off a little maid for a page! I ask you. Can you see a maid wielding a sword?' Then he frowned. 'But the biggest mystery of all is: who tried to poison me? Are we any nearer solving that one? I don't think so.'

Later, when the bell for matins had dragged the monks from their beds, Ulf followed Hildegard to the bottom of the spiral stair to her night chamber. Roger was some way behind them, rounding off some yarn to Hubert de Courcy. Ulf put a hand on her arm. 'Before Roger comes, listen. You know and I know that Sir William is the likely culprit in fixing Roger's drink. Melisen must have agreed to do it. Don't ask me how, but she was the only one with any sort of opportunity. And what I'm saying is it's probably best if we let Roger find it out for himself when he gets to Hutton.'

'If William's there.'

'And if it was William,' he added.

They looked at each other.

'We have no proof,' Hildegard said, driven by some perverse desire to keep to the facts.

Ulf tugged at his beard. 'I know that. You know that.'

'Let's call it a night,' she said, seeing how tired he was. 'When are you leaving tomorrow?'

'Almost before my head touches the pillow,' he said. 'Will you come along with Philippa and Sibilla? I think everybody should be there to support Roger.'

Immensely relieved that she could get to sleep without the threat of Escrick hanging over her, Hildegard nevertheless still worried about Roger and what he would do when he discovered that his young wife and his brother-in-law had plotted against him. She offered up a small prayer on his behalf, but was little comforted.

Shortly after dawn, while Hildegard was making her way along the upper ward to the solar in the hope of finding Philippa, Sibilla caught up with her. 'I do hope you'll ride with us to Hutton,' she said. 'It seems Roger wants us all to meet him there.'

'Yes, I know. I'd be honoured to share your wagon. But what about you, how are you feeling now?' The dressing-down Roger had given his brother and sister-in-law had been heard all over the castle.

'I'm still in a daze. It was such a stupid plan and I'm so ashamed.' She lowered her head.

Hildegard wondered whether she would have expressed shame if the plan had worked.

'It's Ralph,' Sibilla continued, 'he can be so persuasive. I just let him lead me on. Not that I want to be disloyal. I'm not putting all the blame on him. But he so hates being dependent on me, having nothing of his own and his brother having so much.'

'And I suppose you'd do anything to help him out of loyalty.'

'He is my husband. But who would have thought that treacherous devil Escrick would go to such lengths?'

Hildegard remembered what the maid had told her about Escrick, and his status within the household. She herself had seen him hand Sibilla down from her silvery mare on the journey through the woods to Castle Hutton on that first day. It had struck her then that there was something familiar if not intimate in the way he held her round the waist. When she slid to the ground with that teasing laugh she had lingered just that moment too long in his arms. Hildegard kept such thoughts to herself and asked, 'Was he in your service long?'

'Years. His father was a bondsman working at our fisheries near Bridlington. He bought his freedom and his son grew up ambitious instead of accepting his place. But when I inherited he was certainly someone to lean on in matters of running the estates. I don't know what I'm going to do without him.' She put a hand over her mouth at the enormity of such a thought. 'What I mean is, he kept the tenants up to scratch. No one ever stepped out of line.'

'Maybe now you know why.'

Sibilla looked chastened.

'I was just going in to look for Philippa,' said the nun. 'Is she coming back with us?'

'She is. You're both riding in the wagon with me.' Sibilla pushed ahead of Hildegard and marched into the solar. They found Philippa standing by the casement, gazing off into the distance. 'We're going as soon as you're ready, sweeting, and we're taking Hildegard with us because she's always calm.'

'*I'm* always calm!' flared Philippa, turning, with fists clenched. 'Don't talk to me about calm. How dare you! I *am* calm! I'm *very* calm! I can't see you being calm if your damned father had just risen from the dead!' She burst into a flood of tears.

Hildegard went over and took her in her arms. She suspected Philippa's distress was not caused by what she had gained by her father coming back to life. It was caused by what she feared she had lost by it. 'Has he sent a messenger to let you know where he is?' she asked gently.

'He was delayed at Rievaulx,' Philippa said, dabbing her eyes. 'A messenger has been sent to ask if he would return to Hutton. We must set off at once.'

She rubbed her face, making it blotchy, and Sibilla said, 'You need some rose-water if you're expecting to assert your allure.' She went over to an aubry and opened it, rummaging around until she found a glass flagon. 'Use this, silly child. I didn't realise it was him you were weeping about. Have you solved the puzzle he set you?'

Philippa dabbed her cheeks with rose-water from the flagon and shook her head.

'Puzzle, did you say?' Hildegard's interest was aroused.

'It's this casket he gave her,' explained Sibilla. 'Some sort of fiendish Italian construction. She can't find a way into it.'

Hildegard went over to have a look. Philippa removed a coverlet to reveal an ornate wooden casket. It had a lion's head carved on the front and the hind legs and tail were carved on the back. There was no key and no visible way of opening it, though it was clear there was a lid, as the line where it might open ran round the lion's body.

'It's a poison casket!' exclaimed Hildegard. Seeing their expressions she added, 'That's the name, but of course they're used for transporting anything precious. The Lombardy men use such things to safeguard their documents and any gold they need to carry with them.' She stared at it in consternation. After leaving the apothecary she had concluded that the poison used against Roger would have been hidden in a casket such as this one. Surely it couldn't mean that Ludovico and Philippa were complicit after all?

Unaware of her alarm, Sibilla said, 'She made such a fuss the other day about losing some ring or other. I told her, at least you've got that.'

'Have you tried to open it?'

Philippa nodded. Sibilla reached out to take it but Philippa snatched it back. 'Ludovico said I must open it myself in private. I believe he sees it as a test of my worthiness to–' She gave a sob. 'But that is all finished now Father is back.' Her tears fell all over the gilded box. 'I shall die an old maid and that's the end of the matter.'

'Don't cry,' said Sibilla. 'I'm the one who should be weeping. Look what's happened to me in the last few days.'

'Bring it with you,' suggested Hildegard, 'we can have a proper look at it on the way over to Hutton, if you like. But we should leave now if we want to arrive soon after the others.'

Philippa rewrapped the casket in its cloth. She treated it as if it was her most precious possession. Hildegard observed her with alarm. Her grief seemed genuine. But was Ludovico to be trusted? Was the poor girl being duped as Ulf had suggested?

As they walked down to where the wagon was waiting she suddenly remembered she had left a small breviary in her room. 'Wait for me. I won't be a moment,' she told them.

The abbey was quiet at this time in the morning. The monks were all in chapel praying for St Martin. Hurriedly Hildegard ran up to her room and went inside. The breviary was where she had left it and, snatching it up, she was about to leave when she noticed something beside the bed.

She bent to pick it up. It was a piece of green weed. She stared at it with slowly mounting horror. It was the sort that grows underwater. It must have stuck to the sole of a shoe and fallen off and...

She held it between shaking fingers. Maybe it had fallen from the sole of one of her own boots, attaching itself when she waded on to the pontoon to climb into Thomas's boat? But no, the planks were smooth, nothing grew on them. Later then, as they climbed the ladder up the side of the canal? But no, there was no weed above the waterline.

She jerked round as if at a sound outside and,

heart thumping, peered into the corridor. It was empty.

This is ridiculous, she thought. He couldn't have survived that wall of water. And even if he had, how could he have insinuated himself back inside the abbey? She recalled the canal path by which Agnetha had forced her way in to put her plea to Hubert over the heriot tax.

This is nonsense, she told herself again. A little piece of weed scarcely bigger than my thumb and I'm sent into a panic?

Heart still beating furiously, she made her way back down the short flight of stairs and out into the garth. From the chapel came the elysian singing of the monks. Everything was neat and clean and pure and looked as harmless as the day. One of the conversi greeted her with a cheerful shout as he hurried past on some errand or other. From the direction of the waiting wagon came the familiar jingle of the horses' bridles as they shook their heads in eagerness to set out. The servants' voices floated pleasantly across the grass as they chatted among themselves. It was all ordinary, a harmless scene where no phantoms risen from the watery depths of a canal could possibly be a threat. Still holding the piece of weed, Hildegard made her way to the wagon and climbed up. It started to move off as soon as she was seated.

As Ralph had taken only a handful of bodyguards with him that morning to escort Avice to Watton, they had a spare man to send as messenger when they passed the end of the lane that led to the priory. By this time the small piece of waterweed had been pushed into a pocket in Hildegard's scrip. Ulf would no doubt put her fears into perspective with some merry quip as soon as he heard her tale, and they would agree that her imagination was running riot.

'Let's see if Ralph got away to Hutton or whether he's been lured into staying with those women there,' said Sibilla with a grim smile, sending one of her men off down the lane with a message for the nuns.

She had been mostly silent once the journey started. Philippa too had been sitting glumly in a corner of the wagon without speaking. The latter was wearing a rather smart green pelisse with a large, straight collar of fur that set off her features prettily. It hung in long, full folds over a surcoat of velvet and had enormous sleeves like those on a scholar's gown, in which small articles might be kept. Despite her finery her expression could have been sculpted in marble.

The messenger caught up with them before they had gone much further. He cantered alongside the wagon and doffed his cap. 'Sir Ralph has not visited the priory this two-year, my lady.'

'Don't talk nonsense, Elfric. He was there last night with Lady Avice.'

'Beggin' your pardon, ma'm, the nuns know nothing of him.'

'What about the lady?'

'Nor of her, neither.' He held his cap defensively flat against his chest, as if to deflect her rage.

'Oh, get away with you!' Sibilla flared, and the

messenger, no doubt pleased to have escaped without being mutilated, rode back up the line of riders until he could mix in without being noticed.

'That's worrying,' said Hildegard. 'Would Ralph change his mind and go elsewhere?'

'He'll have gone straight to Hutton. Though why the devil he'd take Avice with him is anybody's guess.'

They jogged on for the rest of the way in silence. The thick woodland on both sides of the track seemed ever more threatening, and the men-at-arms, wearing Sibilla's triple band argent on a ground vert, rode in close formation alongside the wagon of their lady. Soon they would all be safe within the castle again, where no one could enter without being seen.

Chapter Twenty

With time to mull things over as they jogged along the woodland track to Castle Hutton, Hildegard dreaded what they might discover when they arrived. A picture of Melisen with her throat cut swam before her, but it was really Avice at risk, she reminded herself She's the one who stands in the way of William's ambitions. Melisen is the stepping stone. Even so, she couldn't imagine Melisen being talked into exchanging Roger, for all his faults, for a fiend like William. But then who had tried to poison Roger, if not

Melisen? She must be the key to the mystery.

The day was grey to match her thoughts. Leafless branches arched overhead. A sea roke was fingering inland from the coast, making its way up the narrow dales of the North Riding. They were far from the flat marshlands of Sir William's Holderness domain.

One event had almost been forgotten, the fact that it was now the feast of St Martin. The monks had been at their prayers for the saint right through the night, and along the route they now saw the shrines, candles alight, a priest or other cleric in attendance, the penitents murmuring with bowed heads. Out of respect the wagons slowed to a walk at each stage so that everyone could throw down what alms they had.

As they went deeper into the north they were reminded that it was also the feast of St Willibrod and the beginning of Samhain to boot. The stocks and whipping posts, built by edict of the old king in every place wanting the status of village, were decorated with symbols of the ancient faith, wreaths of ash, rowan and mistletoe, gewgaws and manikins hanging from the branches. Pyres had been erected on every green. To remain unlit until nightfall, they made ominous shapes, effigies in lifelike postures balanced in rough cages on top of the faggots. Some said that human victims were once burned alive to ensure plenty for the next harvest. Hildegard shivered. It was too barbaric to contemplate.

Swarms of villeins, chanting songs in their own dialect, were gathering from all the scattered manors round about. The lanes and thoroughfares were filled with the sound of drumming and the skirl of bagpipes. As the cavalcade of wagons approached with its escort of armed men, silence fell. There was a threat in this sudden lull, as if it would take just one word to unleash a terrible bloodletting. It's as if they're expecting a sign, thought Hildegard, or waiting for a leader to acclaim the white hart. But Wat Tyler, John Ball and their supporters were dead. No one new had appeared.

'They'll be as drunk as judges by nightfall,' remarked Philippa, rousing herself for a moment. She sounded as if, rather than being afraid, she envied them. Perhaps she knows that her father's private allegiance keeps his household safe, Hildegard told herself. Despite this, she could not shake off a feeling of impending dread.

By the time they found themselves rattling and bumping up the lane to the castle it was late afternoon and the day was drawing in. Lord Roger and his men had arrived some time before and were encamped in a meadow facing the south gate. Roger was sitting outside a field tent. He had his men-at-arms round him and Ulf was at his shoulder. It appeared to be a council of war. The stragglers from Meaux climbed down from the wagons and walked over.

'Has anyone arrived from Rievaulx yet?'

'Where's Ralph?'

'Why are you all sitting out here?'

'Stay! I can't answer ten questions at once.' Roger was irascible.

In fact Hildegard's question had been

addressed to Ulf and he shrugged helplessly, nodding towards the castle as if that might give her a clue as to why they were out rather than in.

Roger turned an unctuous smile on Philippa. 'Daughter, my dear daughter, come here.' He still seemed to be smarting from her rejection of him earlier, and now he opened his arms. She, however, maintained a stiff demeanour and, at a distance, repeated her question in clipped tones.

'No one has yet come from Rievaulx, my dear little one, but they will. I know they will. Now, what about some refreshment for you after your tedious journey all this way home?'

'Stop it! I hate you. I'll never forgive you.' Philippa stalked off to the victualling tent and demanded a flask of wine.

'I don't see Ralph,' said Sibilla pointedly. 'Where is he?'

Roger was frosty. 'I thought he'd gone to Watton with Avice?'

'They never arrived.' Sibilla blanched. 'How many guards did he have? What if they were set upon by outlaws? What if–?' Her glance took in Roger's hostile demeanour. One hand went to her throat. 'Oh no! Not your own brother?'

Roger's glance was icy. 'Ralph can take care of himself. He's the best swordsman in the county. After me, that is. Now...' He dismissed her and her unvoiced suspicion and gestured to his men to come closer to look at something he'd drawn.

It was a rough plan of the castle. He had sketched it out with a piece of chalk on the back of somebody's shield. 'I'm locked out of my own home,' he commented when Hildegard bent over with the others to have a look at it. 'Can you credit it? If Master Schockwynde hadn't made such a good job of the new fortifications I'd have been in there as slippy as an eel. But he's contrived such a devilish defence we're stumped as to how to get round it.'

Ulf nudged Hildegard and whispered, 'He's certainly moderated his language since you ladies turned up.'

'Who's inside the castle keeping you out, Roger?'

'Who d'you think? That he-devil with my wife. If he's touched her I'll personally open his guts and wrap them round his ... head,' he finished lamely.

Ulf nudged her. 'That's nothing to what he was going to do before you arrived.'

The men huddled over the plan of the castle and Hildegard looked across the meadow to where the real thing lay. It certainly looked impregnable. Schockwynde had seen fit to model the new defences on a French idea some fellows returning from the wars had told him about. He had explained this to her at some length one very long afternoon at Swyne.

The point of entry was defended by fortified bridge heads at the moat side and as well as the drawbridge leading into the barbican there was a system of not one but two portcullises, the second one, as far as she knew, hardly ever used. Now it was down, as could be plainly seen. Behind it was a strong oak door. On either side of the barbican were turrets, machicolated, the corbelling well forward so that the garrison could pour boiling oil on to the heads of the besiegers through holes in the floor without being exposed to attack themselves. It was fiendishly clever. As far as she knew this had never been put to the test either. The Scots, against whom it was mainly intended as a protection, hadn't been down this way since the pestilence.

'There's simply no way into the damned place.' Roger scratched his head.

'How many men does William have in there?' asked Hildegard, puzzled that he had been able to muster a force so quickly in territory that didn't even belong to him.

'We have no idea. There must be dozens. He'd never have the temerity to try to hold it without a strong force.'

'Have you tried calling him out and talking to him?' asked Hildegard. 'Maybe you can trick him into letting you inside. Once in you can probably rout any of the forces he has in there.' Hildegard couldn't see anybody on the battlements and thought that surely if there was much of a force somebody would at least have been on lookout.

'You expect me to stand outside my own castle shouting up to be let in? I'd rather burn the place to the ground before I did a thing like that.' Roger looked at her as if she were mad.

'Well, that won't get you anywhere,' she said impatiently. 'Can't Ulf go and attract his attention?'

'Willingly.' He was on his way already.

'Tell him he's a dead man!' shouted Roger after his retreating steward.

'That's hardly likely to encourage him to come

out.' Hildegard sighed. 'Does he know it's you down here?' she asked.

'He nearly dropped dead when he clapped eyes on me. Must've thought he was looking at a ghost.' He rocked with laughter. 'I should have played it up. The sot wit!'

They all watched and waited while Ulf strode long-limbed and determined through the short winter grass of the south meadow. When he reached the drawbridge he stopped and, cupping both hands round his mouth, gave a yell. A head appeared on the battlement just above him. Despite the conical helmet the man wore, which was pulled well down, the nose-guard concealing most of his face, there was no mistaking the badge emblazoned on his surcoat when he came fully into view. It was the blue marsh dragon and proclaimed by its gold border that the wearer was Sir William of Holderness himself. And when he lifted his hands encased in their steel gauntlets and roared out an oath of defiance, they knew for sure.

'Where's the blackguard's guards?' muttered Roger.

'Hear this!' Ulf roared back. 'Surrender, or know the worst!'

Hildegard, with another sigh, picked up her skirts and set off at a run down the meadow to where Ulf was waiting for a reply in the attitude of one fully expecting the armed man in the fortified castle to come meekly down to the gates and invite him in. 'Ulf,' she panted when she got within hailing distance, 'Ask him if Melisen is all right. And if he says she is, ask him why he's captured her. Then, when we know what he's after, we can start to talk.'

'He won't think we're soft, will he?'

'What if he does? We know we're not. It might even be good tactics to let him think we're easy meat. Put him off his guard. But for heaven's sake, find out about Melisen.'

Ulf cupped his hands again and bellowed, 'Where is the Lady Melisen?'

'She's here!' came back the reply. William's voice bounced around the moat. When the echoes eventually subsided he added, 'She's my hostage. He can have her back if he gives me what I want.'

'What do you want?' asked Ulf without prompting.

'Not to have to abjure the realm for killing that yeoman. And some drained land.'

'Is that all?' The note of surprise in Ulf's voice was obvious.

'And a share in his wool trade.'

This was obviously an afterthought. Ulf trudged back up the meadow to where Roger was pacing back and forth, wearing a little path in the grass. He gave his steward an eager glance. 'What did the bastard say?'

'Melisen's safe, by the sound of it. She's his hostage, he says. And he says he wants no come-back from killing that yeoman, and some land, drained – oh, and he says he wants a share in your wool deals.'

'With those Lombards? How did he know about that?' Roger frowned but then his expression lightened. 'At least Melisen's safe. Unless he's lying through his back teeth. Will he come down, then, so we can talk?'

'I'll go and ask him.' Ulf trudged back down the meadow.

Hildegard sighed. It was going to be the usual charade. Roger hadn't changed. Seven years had made little difference to his shambolic use of power. He liked nothing better than to frighten people with what he could do if he chose, then surprise them by his magnanimity. The trouble was there was nothing to restrain him. He had no need to take anything seriously – except for the family fortunes, of course – not even, it seemed, his wife's safety. If there was trouble he would buy his way out of it – even buy another wife if this one didn't please.

Looking at him now, smiling in that devilish way and stroking his beard, it was clear that he was enjoying the charade of being kept out of his own castle, knowing that eventually – inevitably – he would get back in. No doubt he would have his minstrels turn it into a topic for a song, and his wiliness would be sung up and down the country in one castle after another, and his fame would increase. She watched him now, playing the part of the injured husband. It was a sure thing that if Melisen proved unfit for the position bestowed on her, then, as Ulf had so succinctly phrased it, she would be out on her ear. And Roger, she was convinced, would shed few tears.

As it was, William's agreement to discuss the finer details was obtained with difficulty. Clearly he was as obstinate as his brother-in-law. The afternoon was already drawing in with mist and

November chill before they achieved anything. Ulf had worn a path between the drawbridge and Roger's encampment, just like the one Roger had worn as he paced between his war cabinet and the victualling tent. But at last William agreed to talk. When the men heard this they began to kick out their campfires and gather up their equipment ready to get back inside their barracks and put their feet up.

'It may be a trap,' warned Ulf. 'We should only enter fully armed.'

'I would never dream of doing anything else.' Roger commanded his attendants to lift his hauberk from its wooden stand on one of the carts. They heaved it over and helped him struggle into it. Then he pulled on his surcoat emblazoned with the de Hutton coat of arms and finally, buckling on his scabbard, he ran his sword up and down inside it, making it rattle, clearly keen to put it to use.

Ulf wore a gambeson and Hildegard inspected that too. 'Is that all you're going to wear? I don't call that "fully armed". It won't be any protection if you get into a skirmish.' She picked at the neck where the quilting that held the wool padding in place was coming loose. 'I could get the point of a small dagger in there. Then where would you be?'

'You can fire an arrow at this, close range, and not break skin,' he protested.

'Don't be ridiculous.'

He grinned. 'You're getting like my mother.' Even so, he went to the cart and dragged his hauberk down. She could understand his reluctance to don chain mail when there was no obvious need. But who could tell how many men were lying in wait within the castle?

Soon everyone was ready but there was no sign that the drawbridge was going to be let down and the portcullis hadn't moved at all. They milled about on the edge of the moat and cast impatient glances to the other side.

Hildegard wondered what kind of game William was playing. Why the delay? His agreement to parley had made it simple. Maybe now he had begun to suspect that once Roger was inside his own castle nothing would make him give an inch. Rumour said that William gloried in bloodshed and maybe that meant he was as simple as barbarous men often were. But now, perhaps, he was having second thoughts about Roger's agreement to his terms. Whatever the case, the defences remained in place.

They made their way down through the meadow and came to an expectant halt beneath the walls. In the hiatus that followed, it suddenly occurred to Hildegard that Ralph was still missing. Sibilla had looked quite shaken as she went through the possible fate that had delayed him. But she had bitten off the words when she had exclaimed that second 'what if–?', as if the thought was too horrible to say out loud. *What if–?* Her expression clearly betrayed what she feared: *what if Roger had ordered his men to ambush his brother in the forest and deal him a traitor's fate?* He had been in a fury when he discovered the trick his brother was trying to pull. Hildegard glanced across at Roger. He was banging his mailed fists together with impatience.

'Command him to open up, and fast,' she heard him growl.

Ulf did as he was asked, but nothing happened.

'If he's harming her,' snarled Roger, 'I'll deal with him personally.' He stepped forward and shouted up, making his voice roll around the high, dank walls like thunder. It brought William's face to one of the loopholes at the top of the barbican.

'I can't get the damned mechanism to work,' he yelled down.

'He's locked himself in,' said one of the men-at-arms. There were guffaws as this comment passed round the men. Roger, of course, couldn't suppress a smile. He stabbed the point of his sword into the ground and looked round for ideas.

'Ask him to let the gatekeeper and his men have a go. It's their job,' suggested Hildegard.

'He's probably killed them all,' somebody suggested. There were a few sniggers of amusement but in a more minor key as this likelihood sank in.

Ulf shouted up to William to release the gate-keeper at once. William disappeared again.

Just then, there was a flurry of activity on the fringes of the crowd and two figures appeared from out of the darkening woods. One of them was sitting side-saddle on a large black horse while the other trailed along on foot leading a disconsolate-looking grey mare. The rider was Lady Avice, the one on foot, Sir Ralph. When he came closer Hildegard could see that his riding boots were worn through, his cloak was flung over the saddle of the mare, as if it were too hot to wear it, his shirt was undone, and his hair awry.

'I'm utterly sick and tired,' he complained as soon as Sibilla rushed up to him. 'She's lamed my horse for me. And I've had to walk nearly all the way.' He threw a bitter glance at Avice.

Sibilla folded him in her arms. 'My poor warrior!' she exclaimed, before giving an embarrassed glance to see whether anybody had overheard. One or two hid smiles behind their mailed fists. Taking Ralph by the elbow, Sibilla walked with him for a couple of paces, and announced in a voice that everyone could hear: 'You'll be shocked and overjoyed to learn that your dear brother Roger is not dead after all.'

Ralph gave a hunted glance right and left but, even if he had wanted to attempt an escape, he would have had less chance than a sprung rabbit. At that point Roger burst magnificently from the midst of his retainers. 'So, brother, greetings!' He extended one magnanimous fist. After he and Ralph had touched gauntlets he hissed, 'Were you serious?'

'Were you?' replied Ralph with commendable spirit. 'You're no more dead than I am.'

'You reprobate,' Roger said. 'I'll deal with you later. Meanwhile, there's another problem to be solved.' He gestured towards the battlements. 'William has locked himself in my castle with my wife and we can't prise him out. I've tried every blessed trick I can think of.'

'I can prise him out.' It was Lady Avice. She

beckoned to a couple of men to help her down from Ralph's charger. She shook out her skirts as soon as her feet touched the ground and came over to them all. 'I'll go in and have words with him.' There was no way of guessing whether this was a threat or a promise. Her expression was neutral. She shaded her eyes and gazed up at the castle as if able to see through its walls.

On her finger a ring flashed and her cross, larger and more costly than any Hildegard would consider wearing, swung between her breasts as she turned. Roger's glance was caught by it and he shrugged and growled, 'He's your man. Go ahead. Bring him to heel.'

'What can she do?' murmured Philippa. Hildegard was staring hard at the ring.

'I don't know but I fear what William might do to her,' she replied.

Just then there was a sudden yell from one of the men. They all turned to see the portcullis beginning to inch open. The men cheered. It took a good time for the defences to be opened, first portcullis number one, then the drawbridge, then portcullis number two, and finally the porter's small gate set within the great oak doors, although these last remained as firmly closed as before.

The men drew their swords and arranged themselves in formation. Then, with Lord Roger at their head, followed by Ulf and Sir Ralph jostling for second place, they tramped across the wooden bridge. When they were massed on the other side William's voice rang out.

'Stop right there! I'm not going to parley with a

host. Send a deputation. But not you, Roger. You're too slippery. Just stay out of it. You can send your steward instead.'

'Oh, thanks very much,' muttered Ulf.

'Of course I'm damn well coming in. It's my wife we're discussing here,' Roger roared back.

'Take it or leave it.'

'Let me go in.' Avice, who had crossed over with the women, pushed her way from the back. 'William! I'm here! Parley with me.'

'I'm coming with you.' Hildegard forced a path through the ranks of men. Avice gave her a glance when she reached her side but, when she saw the determination on the nun's face, she gave a thin smile.

'Suit yourself, sister. I won't waste time offering advice to the contrary as I know it won't be taken.'

The porter's gate was opened. Only wide enough for one person at a time to enter, anyone of normal height had to bend double. When Hildegard squeezed through after Avice she turned when she felt someone right behind her. 'I'm in this as well,' said Ulf.

'That's enough of you!' shouted William. He didn't sound at all cowed. 'I'm not holding a leet court in here.' But Ralph had slipped through before the one guard standing there could stop him. It was one of Roger's trusties on the gate and, with his hands bound with kitchen twine, he gave a shrug as if to say it was literally out of his hands.

Immediately within was the gatehouse and this

was defended in much the same way as the barbican. There was a cunning staircase inside, with very narrow and easily defended doors, so that if Roger and his men had managed to penetrate so far the defenders could retreat to the upper floors and shoot at them through the murder-holes in the vault. Then, even though they might get as far as the inner court, they could still be shot at from all sides.

William was nowhere to be seen. Nor was there any sign of a squad of men to defend him. Edging forward, eyes darting from one side of the battlements to the other, they moved further in until they were standing in the middle of the bailey. Hildegard knew they were vulnerable in such an open space, aware that at any moment William and his men could come pouring out to hack them to death. She kept an eye on Avice, praying for her safety, should her suspicions about William prove true.

Ulf, as Roger's steward, elected himself spokes-man. 'Bring forth the Lady Melisen!' he demanded to the echoing walls.

A sound of steel from somewhere high up made them lift their heads. From a window in the solar on the first floor William leaned out. He seemed to have spent most of the afternoon running from one aperture to the next. 'She's here but I want proof that Roger will accept my demands.'

'You should have let him come in with us, then,' replied Ulf. 'You could have had his promise from his own lips.'

'I'd sooner trust a friar.'

'Your choice. Just show us she's alive then we

can discuss what guarantees you want. Then I'll go and tell him.'

William was just launching into an argument when Avice broke free of the group and ran like a hare across the bailey towards the stairs that led up to the private apartments.

'Wait, Avice!' shouted Hildegard. 'He desires your death!' She kilted her skirt and began to run after her. She could hear Ulf pounding along in her wake and possibly Ralph too but she didn't pause to check. She simply had to get to William before Avice did. The woman would not understand the danger she was in.

The first floor was reached by a circular staircase in one of the towers. Avice disappeared inside and her footsteps could be heard in a dwindling echo as she ascended. Hildegard followed, taking the stairs two at a time and reaching the top just as Avice pushed the door ahead and ran on into the solar. Hildegard's blood went cold when she heard her shriek one word, 'William!' and a deathly silence follow.

Breathing hard, she threw herself through the door then came to a skidding halt. Instead of plunging a knife into his wife's heart, William was simply staring at her as if she were an apparition. Avice, meanwhile, had thrown her arms round his neck and was looking up at him as adoringly as a young maid in the first flush of love, her fingers lacing though his beard as she whispered endearments to him.

Astounded, Hildegard could only stand and stare. Her suspicions about William's ill-intentions were wrong after all. He looked confused, not murderous. She stepped forward. 'Sir William,' she began in a conciliatory tone, 'are you now willing to release Lady Melisen from captivity?'

William lifted his dark head and gave her a startled glance. 'Never!' he roared with something of his usual vigour, thrusting Avice to one side.

Avice was unperturbed. 'But where are you hiding her, my sweeting?' she purred, trying to take him in her arms again.

'Melisen is locked in the upper solar and that's where she's going to stay until Roger accepts my demands!' he snarled.

Before either Avice or Hildegard could remonstrate with him there was a commotion in the doorway. Ulf and Sir Ralph appeared. Ralph drew his sword with an ominous hiss of steel. His face was deathly pale.

'This is your day of reckoning, William. I've had enough of you trying to oust me from my position. If Roger is going to bestow lands on anybody it's going to be me!' He advanced like a dancer, sword outstretched.

William gave a vengeful laugh and unsheathed his own massive weapon. 'So be it, brother-in-law! Your wish is my command! To the death!'

Then there was the clash of steel on steel as the two men engaged.

Out of the corner of her eye Hildegard noticed Avice slip from the chamber. With the sound of battle ringing in her ears, Hildegard followed. She was in time to catch sight of the hem of Avice's grey gown as she turned a corner and when she chased in pursuit she saw her hurrying along the corridor towards the stair that led up to the next floor. The grey shape vanished round the first spiral but by then Hildegard was close behind. She reached the top in time to see Avice turn a key and fling herself through the door into the room beyond.

By the time she reached the door herself, Avice was walking towards Melisen with her arms outstretched. Hildegard was puzzled. Then she noticed her fingers and on one of them the ring. It was large, with a jewelled boss that would open and close. Suddenly she remembered where she had seen such a ring before. It was like one that had belonged to Philippa, the one that had gone missing. And at the same moment she recalled what the apothecary had told her about the pope's poison. One touch, he had said, that's all it takes.

These thoughts passed in a flash through her mind. Even so, Avice was almost within reach of Melisen. The girl had been sitting on the sill looking down through the loophole at the little stream that wound round the castle far below and flowed off down the dale. Bedraggled, tear-stained, and half dead through lack of sleep, though still beautiful of course, she now lifted her head. She could have had no idea that an army of men had been encamped in the meadow on the other side of the castle. She must have believed until this very moment that she was quite alone with William.

She rose to her feet. 'Avice? You?' Her glance flew in confusion to Hildegard. 'Sister?'

Hildegard slipped her knife from inside her sleeve. 'Don't take another step, Avice!' Her hand shook.

Avice jerked to a stop at once and turned her head. 'It's you, is it, nun? I should have guessed you'd follow. Too late now, though!' She turned back to Melisen. 'My poor, dear child. What has that brute been doing to you? Come to me!'

'Don't go near her!' shouted Hildegard, flinging herself after Avice. Melisen looked startled and drew back. Catching Avice by the shoulders, Hildegard pulled her to a stop and the two women grappled for a moment until Hildegard was able to twist Avice's arm behind her back and hold her still. 'I know your game, Avice,' she said. 'Don't move or you'll regret it!' The knife gleamed in her right hand.

Melisen gathered her wits with alacrity and ran over. 'Will someone explain?'

Tightening her hold on her struggling captive and panting a little with the exertion, Hildegard said, 'When William abducted you, Avice feared he had transferred his affections, so she decided to get rid of you. The ring she wears she stole from Philippa. The boss is hollow. It contains a deadly poison. One touch and you'll breathe your last.'

'Heaven forfend!' exclaimed Melisen. Then, thinking quickly, she said, 'I'll get the ring, Hildegard, and then I'll bind her wrists.' So saying, she produced a kerchief, prised the ring from Avice's grasp without touching it, and let it drop into the cloth. Then she took a long braid of plaited yellow silk from inside one of her sleeves. Deftly, she tied Avice's wrists together.

Avice struggled in a fury but there was nothing she could do against the two of them. 'You think you've won! But you won't get away with this!' she hissed into Hildegard's face. Her own was contorted with rage at being foiled.

From the lower floor came the continuing clash of steel. Hildegard pushed Avice down on to the window seat where Melisen had been sitting. 'We'd better hurry or William and Ralph will kill each other—' she urged, turning to the girl.

Without waiting for further explanations, Melisen took the key from the lock and when they were in the corridor she turned it on their prisoner despite her shouts of protest. Then she led the way rapidly along the maze of corridors towards the gallery overlooking the hall. She knew the route like the back of her hand. When they arrived they peered over the parapet.

Ralph had fought William into a corner. His swordsmanship was stylish and swift, a blur of flashing steel. He was, as Roger had observed, well able to take care of himself. Ulf was standing on the sidelines, in rapt admiration.

William, however, was the bigger man. He was wily too. And he was determined not to be beaten. His lands, his life and his honour – such as it was – depended upon winning. They heard him give a great roar of rage and watched as he threw himself bodily at Ralph, who, taken aback by his brutal technique, faltered, allowing William time to snatch something off a nearby chest. He waved what looked like a fur tippet above his head. 'Hold!' he commanded.

Ralph gaped and lowered his blade. 'That's Master Jacques! How the devil did he get in?'

William pointed the tip of his sword at the animal and gave Ralph a baleful glance. 'Well? Are you going to yield and save your cat? Or do you want him dead?'

Apparently unconcerned by his imminent fate, Jacques yawned, revealing tiny predatory teeth, then he stretched his legs in a token attempt to wriggle free. William tightened his grasp.

Ralph looked on helplessly. 'Let him go, you brute!'

'Put up your sword, then,' replied William. He waved the cat above his head. Master Jacques seemed quite content to make the best of things, especially when William wedged him in the crook of one arm the better to wield his sword.

'Master Jacques...' Ralph whispered.

At the sound of his name Jacques was transformed. In the twinkling of an eye he became a raging beast, all fangs and snarls, and, leaping upwards, he landed with four barbed paws on William's face. William dropped his sword in astonishment. Ralph at once sprang forward and pushed the steel tip against his brother-in-law's throat. 'Now will you yield? Or will you die?'

With his weapon clattering under his feet as he stumbled blindly about with the cat nailed to his face, William had no choice in the matter. 'Get this thing off me!' he roared. Blood was beginning to course down his cheeks. 'My eyes! Help! I'm being blinded! Get it off!'

'Let me hear the words,' said the implacable Ralph, slicing his sword through William's sleeve so that it flapped as he struggled.

'I yield, Sir Ralph.'

Ralph put up his sword. 'Jacques! That's enough.'

The cat tried to disentangle his claws from his prey but William's beard, left too long, was coarse and curly.

'Somebody's going to have to help him,' said Ralph, with a nonchalant shrug. He took out a cloth and ran it deftly over his blade with the air of a man who has done a good job and doesn't mind who knows it. Ulf went over and shook him heartily by the hand.

While everyone's attention was engaged a rabble of armed men wearing the de Hutton blazon appeared in the doorway. Sizing up the situation, they grabbed William by both arms. One of them picked up his sword and hefted it admiringly before Ulf took charge of it. Master Jacques was persuaded to disentangle his paws and was restored, at arm's length, to his owner.

From the gallery came the sound of applause. Melisen turned to Hildegard. 'That was excellent!' Tears filled her eyes. 'If only Roger were alive to see it.'

Hildegard took the girl by the hand. 'Melisen, there is something you should know.'

Just then there was a commotion from outside. With a great shout of jubilation Roger himself came storming through the door into the hall. 'I missed it, damn it! What a fight! The men are going wild!' Indeed the windows on to the bailey were thick with faces.

A cry from the gallery made him lift his head.

Melisen was leaning over the parapet. As her eyes met her husband's, she gave another cry and dropped down in a dead faint at Hildegard's feet. The nun knelt beside her. The girl's face was as white as snow.

Chapter Twenty-one

Hildegard placed a tincture of chervil on Melisen's forehead where there was the beginning of a bruise. Carried, unconscious, into a private chamber and laid gently on the bed by Roger himself, she was just beginning to come round. Her eyes were still shut, however. Fumbling to find the nun's hand, she grasped it and began to speak in a wispy voice.

'I had the most angelic vision, sister. It was like a dream of paradise. I thought I saw, entering the Great Hall, my dearly beloved lord, as hale and merry as ever.' Melisen's lashes fluttered like black butterflies on her rose-pale cheeks, and with an effort she opened her lustrous eyes and gave a little groan in acknowledgement of her throbbing head.

Hildegard slid out of the way as Roger pushed past the gawping onlookers and heaved to his knees beside the bed. He smothered his wife's hands with kisses. 'No dream, my precious martlet, for here I am, in the flesh.'

Hildegard, fingering her wooden cross, found herself drifting back against the far wall. Ulf came to stand beside her. 'Look at them,' he whispered. 'They're like two turtle doves.'

Hildegard kept her thoughts to herself, merely saying, 'I expect they'll want to be left alone after all that.'

While Ulf cleared everyone from the chamber, leaving Roger and Melisen to bill and coo in private, Hildegard made her way down the stairs to the Great Hall. The kitchen staff had already been released from their imprisonment in the buttery, where they had been happily playing dice all afternoon, and the rest of the servants were quickly freed from their bonds and invited into the hall for refreshment. William's audacity in trying to take the castle with no more than a handful of men to help him was the subject of much merriment. There was some admiration too, and his showing against Ralph was praised for its optimism. Thrust by thrust the sword fight was gone over and over. First one version was given, then another, but the ultimate judgement was always the same – Sir Ralph, despite his gossamer looks, was a swordsman without equal.

Roger briefly came down from the solar to tell Ulf that he would be holding an inquest into the whole matter later that evening. Meanwhile he would be busy, he told him, obscurely, and he'd better get everybody victualled without delay.

'How am I going to sort this lot out?' grumbled Ulf when he rejoined Hildegard in the hall. Everybody was in holiday mood. The wine was already flowing, ale too, and the kitchen staff, though swearing and panicking as usual, were working with a will to provide enough roast ox to go round.

'It is St Willibrod's Day, don't forget. They're due for a holiday. And I must say they've rallied round Lord Roger with remarkable loyalty.' She gave him a level glance.

In reply he led her to a bench on one side of the main concourse. 'Loyalty, eh?'

She watched him as he gathered his thoughts.

'Of course I have spies,' he began at last. 'We don't want to be murdered in our beds, do we? And things have been unsettled since that trouble down in London.'

'And?' she prompted.

'Remember I mentioned old Lord de Melsa out by the coast and the trouble that followed when he had nobody to succeed him? Well, Roger thought it a good opportunity to extend his own domain, as you guessed. It was purely in the interests of public order, you understand. That burning of the mill near Driffield was one of several incidents that have taken place recently. Those horsemen you met had already approached me to do a deal. They wanted Roger to lay off de Melsa's lands and in return they'd sell their produce to him. To show they meant business they fired the mill, making sure the miller and his household got out first. Of course, I didn't know that was their game when I let you and Egbert go out after the midwife. I'd never have put you in such danger.'

'Yes, there was a definite chill in the air when they saw my habit.'

'In fact,' he continued, 'it turned out quite well, because what you told me when you got back showed just what sort of villeins I was dealing with.'

'White Hart villeins?' she suggested.

'That's fizzled out,' he said emphatically.

'And now?' she asked, quickly moving on.

'It's not right that folks over there should have to pay through the nose to have their own corn ground, so I've persuaded Roger to rebuild the mill. In return they'll bring in their wheat and we'll grind it at a fair price. Everybody happy. They'll also bring in their other produce from the masterless manors so Roger can sell on the surplus to a contact in York.'

'That all seems very fair.' Then she widened her eyes. 'Did you say masterless manors?'

'Yes, why?'

'You mean, ones with no one to run them?'

'At the present moment, yes.'

'I don't suppose there's a modest grange going, where a few women might live and work?'

Ulf gave a slow smile. 'I do believe there could be one such. Perhaps you'll ride out with me tomorrow and take a look?'

William was in the doghouse. This was a small prison next to the barracks. When the feasting was under way he was brought out, still man-acled, and asked to account for himself. Avice, her hands also bound, stood beside him. The ring she had stolen from Philippa and filled full of what was rumoured to be pope's poison from Avignon had been scrubbed clean and the poisoned run-off disposed of by burning. It had given off a weird purple flame that had fascinated the spit boy who was given the task of throwing it into the brazier. Philippa replaced the ring somewhat gingerly on one of her fingers.

Now the two miscreants stood before Roger and his hastily appointed court.

'I could have you hung by your neck, William,' he began. 'You as well, Avice. You're my sister, for heaven's sake. What do you mean by trying to poison me?'

'That's a lie,' she answered with a sullen look.

'You tried to poison Melisen. We've just had a look at the evidence.'

'I admit that. But I didn't *in fact* poison her and probably at the last minute I would have thought better of it.'

'Probably!' exclaimed Melisen with a derisory laugh. 'Well, thank you, lady!'

Roger gave a bellow and gestured to one of his men, but Hildegard leaned forward with a hand on his sleeve. 'What does she mean, she didn't try to poison you?'

'Yes, what do you mean?' demanded Roger.

'I mean I didn't poison you. It wasn't me!'

'I can probably vouch for her and tell you who did it,' called a voice from the back of the hall. With a lot of pushing and shoving the priest forced his way to the front.

'You did it?' asked Roger, furrowing his brow.

'Not me, no, heaven forfend! But I know who did. He confessed it to me. It was an accident. He was utterly contrite. Now he's dead the confidentiality of the confessional is null and void.'

'Dead?'

'William killed him.'

'Explain,' demanded Roger.

Everyone leaned forward.

'What I know is poor Godric came to me asking for absolution for accidentally killing his liege lord as he believed,' the priest began.

'How the devil did he do it?' Roger demanded.

'He didn't go into detail. It was something to do with salt and a touch of henbane. Don't ask me. I don't have to make sense of what they tell me, I just have to listen.'

'I know what he means. It's falling into place at last. The salt. Of course.' Hildegard stepped forward.

'Don't talk in riddles, Hildegard!' Roger said tetchily.

'It's like this. You've been complaining lately about an insatiable thirst. Everybody's heard you. The cause? Not some creeping disease as I thought. No. It was simply the fact that salt was being added too liberally to your food. It makes sense.'

'It makes no sense to us. Say more.'

'I was puzzled by what it was you could have drunk in your wine to send you into a coma. Various herbs could have had that effect, some easily available in the meadows and ditches, others bought from an apothecary. Like the one in Beverley I went to consult,' she added.

Melisen gave a little cough and hastily picked up her goblet and hid her face in it.

Hildegard chose her words with care. 'He told me not only that the pope in France had a poison that could kill whomsoever touched it,' she glanced at Avice, 'but also that someone fitting the description of your yeoman Godric paid regular visits in order to purchase cures for a wide range of everyday ailments. Quite innocent ones,' she added, being careful to avoid looking in Melisen's direction. 'He bought potions for sleep and the like. He'd also been asking questions about the dangers of lead piping and the overuse of salt, among other things, and what harm they might do to a man. And that must be what he decided to do! He was salting your food, Roger, out of his great anger with you. Not to kill you but to cause discomfort.'

'Why should the devil be angry with *me?*'

'Well, you were rather mocking of him. Making him bow and walk backwards and so forth for the amusement of your guests.'

'It was only a little joke.'

'He was a very proud fellow.'

'I see.' Roger looked abashed.

'Anyway, it seems he wanted to cause you some physical discomfort to get his own back. At the same time he knew you might be taking other remedies–'

'Did he?' He glanced at his wife but she was still inspecting the contents of her goblet.

'And that evening he must have decided to add a little extra to your wine. Just his little joke, of course. But what he didn't know was that it turned out to be not a little but a lot when added to all the other things you were imbibing. It was his undoing. With such a melange of potions on top of the wine, you collapsed. You could have died. But luckily the electuary I had with me brought you round–'

'And rendered me sick as a dog. Yes.'

The priest was nodding at all this. 'It fits in exactly with what he told me,' he said when Hildegard finished speaking. 'He really believed he'd poisoned you, my lord. I had to talk him out of putting an end to himself.'

'Well, I'll be damned.' Roger seemed relieved. 'But what about William? Did he discover the truth and then kill the fellow?'

At this, William perked up, as if scenting a way out.

But for truth's sake Hildegard had to disappoint him. 'Unfortunately, no. It wasn't like that. William couldn't have known any of this. He stabbed Godric in a fit of rage because he'd heard the rumour that he'd murdered Ada. Somehow it got out that the prints of Godric's poulaines had been found beside her body.'

'I don't see why that should make him kill the man.'

There was a pause.

Melisen put a hand on Roger's sleeve. 'Think about it, my sweeting.'

Avice turned on William with blazing eyes. 'I knew there was some stinking slut in the picture.'

Before she could start a tirade of abuse, she was dragged to a safe distance and had a gag tied over her mouth.

Roger stared anew at William. After a long moment's consideration he said, 'You sad devil. A serving wench? You did that for a–? Even so, you deserve to be punished.'

'He's going to make him abjure the realm,' muttered Ulf.

Roger overheard him. 'I think not, my fine steward. I have a better punishment in mind. One from which he might learn something.' He gave his old roguish smile. 'I'm going to send you on a very, very long pilgrimage,' he announced to William. 'And I'm going to send you with your wife. Both of you. Together. Go to Jerusalem!'

William looked desperate. 'I'll willingly go to Jerusalem. Anywhere. To the Russias. To uttermost Thule. To the land of the Saracens. But alone, walking, walking barefoot even, as befits a knight, in abject humility. But not with–'

'Your wife?' asked Roger ingenuously. 'But I thought I was being lenient?'

The audience in the body of the hall began to laugh. If ever a man's face expressed dismay it was William's, and Avice saw it too. Thoroughly humiliated, they were both dragged out to the stables to the mocking cheers of the guests. There they were given a horse each, a pack-bag of kitchen leftovers and orders to leave the domain of Roger de Hutton, high lord of the northern lands, before the hour of twelve was struck.

'In fact,' proclaimed Roger, 'go now!'

To make sure they obeyed, three armed men were to escort them as far as the port of Ravenser where they would take ship for Flanders.

Everybody poured out of the gatehouse to watch them leave. Cheers followed them and the four turncoats did an impromptu jig. William had not been popular with his men.

Soon the pilgrims and their escort were small figures at the edge of the forest.

As everybody began to turn back inside to

continue the feast in honour of St Willibrod and the Triumph of Fair Play, something stopped them. Burthred, who had been standing on the fringes with Hildegard's two hounds, had noticed something. His excited shout made everyone turn.

Spread out across the south meadow and on up the hill beyond for as far as the eye could see was a panorama of flickering lights. On closer inspection it seemed to be an encampment of some sort. And then it was seen that the lights were flares placed between an army of tents.

When everyone fell silent the sound of many horses apparently hobbled for the night could be heard out of the darkness. There was the distant rattle of mail and a barked order that could only come from the mouth of a serjeant.

Roger had reached the drawbridge but when he saw what could only be an army arranged for battle in one of his own meadows, he stared with the same astonishment as everybody else.

Chapter Twenty-two

By now the village was getting into its stride for a final night of celebration. Thick smoke from burning tar barrels drifted across the dale. It almost obliterated the south meadow and the army encamped in it and for one startling moment made it look like a scene from hell.

Roger recovered his wits before anyone else.

411

'What the devil–? Who are they? Are they Scots? I didn't know they were on the rampage again. Why the hell wasn't I warned?'

He turned furiously on Ulf but he had already gone. They watched as he strode down the path to the nearest sentry. He said something to the man and a short discussion ensued. The sentry kept pointing with his pike to the top of the meadow, where a pavilion, larger than all the rest, was pitched. By the light from the flares they could see it was dancing with pennants. There was a flag, too, and Roger nearly exploded when somebody with keener sight than all the rest said it looked very like Roger's own ensign flying there.

'Don't be a sot-wit,' he growled.

Then Ulf came panting back. He was terse. 'It's Sir Edwin, your son.'

'What? What the bloody hell's he thinking? Attacking *me!* Are his brains in his arse?'

'He believes you dead, sire, and is intent on ousting the one he thinks has usurped your castle.'

Roger's rage turned to laughter. When he could eventually bring himself to speak he said, 'Go and tell his herald that the usurper challenges Sir Edwin to a man-to-man combat within the bailey. Now we'll see what the milksop's made of!' He turned on his heel then swivelled back. 'On second thoughts, tell him to meet me in the jousting yard at midnight. That'll give him something to think about!'

They all watched as the challenge was carried back along the line up to the top of the meadow until it reached the commander. There was a brief pause. Then they saw the reply carried back by a runner with a flaming torch. He had a word with the sentry who turned, paused for a moment, then put two fingers up at the Hutton crowd. Everybody gasped.

Ulf returned the salute with a jubilant, 'We're on!'

Hildegard was appalled. 'You can't do this, Roger. What if you kill your own son?'

'What if Edwin kills his father?' cried Melisen.

Hildegard caught Ulf by the hilt of his sword. 'You must stop them, Ulf. It's madness.'

'If it starts to look nasty I'll get some of the men to break it up.'

She was still doubtful. She knew what they were like, these men, once they started to fight.

There is nothing more sure to arouse the pain of remembered grief than the yearning wail of rebecs and the deep surge of shawms and gitterns. Hildegard tried to fortify herself against the sudden surfeit of memories their music aroused. Uppermost was an image of Hugh and how they had walked together that last night before he left for the wars in France. She found the chamberlain. He was wearing his long black fur again but looked pinched with cold despite the roaring heat in the hall.

'Would you mind asking the minstrels to play something less melancholy, chamberlain? This isn't a wake.'

He gazed at her as if she were a figure in the distance. 'Oh well,' he replied at last with a deep

413

sigh, 'I like the old tunes. I requested this one myself.' But, noticing her steely expression, he rapped on the floor with his staff and, when he had silence, ordered the musicians to play a dance.

In a moment or two the floor was thick with people from the highest to the lowest linking hands in a branle. Hildegard smiled as she watched the dancers move round the circle in step, looking as graceful as you could wish. As the music speeded up it became more and more frenetic until finally, amid great guffaws of delight, it finished up like the brawl of its name.

Loosening his jerkin, Ulf flopped down on a bench beside her when it was over. He wiped his glistening brow. 'That was good! Don't they allow you to take to the floor?' he asked.

'I suppose not. The question never arises.'

He nudged her arm and murmured, 'Ah, Hildegard, Hildegard,' in an unexpectedly gruff voice that suddenly suggested the opening of new worlds.

Picking up on the way his thoughts were wending, she said, 'I shall have much to tell my confessor about the trials I am put through in this world of men when I eventually get back to Swyne.'

'You tell him everything?'

'I have to.'

'As for what I said about you being like my mother,' he went on in the same tone, and apparently heedless of her warning. 'For one thing she's five foot flat and as wide as a flour barrel. Whereas you–' He stopped and put both hands

414

over his eyes and gave them a rub as if to blot out his sight.

In an attempt to divert the conversation on to safer ground she said, 'I'm still rather puzzled by the singe on the red chaperon. How would you explain it?'

'As your lord abbot said the other day: the world is full of mysteries.' He turned to look at her. She noticed, not for the first time, how disturbingly blue his eyes were.

'I suppose the yeoman must have been standing too close to the fire behind the screen,' she continued, hurriedly. 'His clothes would get scorched and, being prone to the sin of vanity, he must have decided to get rid of the chaperon at the same time as the shoes.' Ulf's eyes were fixed on her lips as she said all this. The intensity of his gaze made her voice waver. 'Imagine how he must have felt, standing there for hours, trying to bring himself to slip some henbane or whatever it was into Roger's wine while everybody else laughed and danced the night away. His mind must have been in turmoil. And then to believe he had actually killed Roger when all he wanted to do was teach him a lesson.'

Ulf's glance remained on her lips and he murmured, 'I do believe you feel sorrow for the blackguard.'

'I'm sad that he should have felt driven to such extremity,' she agreed, trying to release her gaze.

Just then one of the serving women came laughing towards them, her arms outstretched, but Ulf, curt, refused her invitation to dance.

Hildegard looked at him sidelong. 'I'm surprised you haven't married by now, steward. You must be very well set up. Have you never found anybody to take your fancy?'

After a pause he said, 'There was somebody–' He gave a quick grimace. 'I suppose I'm still in mourning for what's been lost.'

'I didn't know. Nobody breathed a word.'

'I'll tell you the full story one of these days. Meanwhile, sister, life goes on. But come, let's follow the crowd to the tilt yard.'

She looked up and realised that people were beginning to drift outside. She had wanted to tell him about the river weed found in her chamber at Meaux and her subsequent fears, but now the opportunity had gone. Besides, in the safety of the castle, it seemed overwrought and nonsensical. Gathering her skirts and with a deft adjustment to her coif, she accompanied Ulf to the trial of arms between Lord Roger and his son.

The yard was situated beyond the kitchen court near the stables. It was about fifty yards long with a tough oak fence down the middle to stop the horses running into each other and strengthened at intervals by posts set in the ground to prevent it collapsing if a horse fell on to it. A small stand was placed at one end with an awning under which the members of the family and any guests favoured by Roger could sit and watch.

One of the ushers handed Hildegard to a seat beside Melisen, Philippa and Sibilla. They were watching the preparations with varying degrees of anxiety. Some officials of the household sat behind them, among them a surprisingly animated chamberlain, but Ralph was standing down in the yard with one of his pages.

Hildegard thought he looked worried. Roger had still not meted out a punishment and he must be in terror at what awaited him. He would realise that his deception over the baby and the dreadful events that followed could not be excused. Unless, she thought, his swordsmanship and his resulting popularity among the men has made Roger think twice.

Because it was night-time, braziers burned at both ends of the yard and their light was supplemented by flaming rush lights strung at intervals beside the track. At opposite ends the two chargers snorted and tossed their heads with a brace of grooms apiece clinging to their halters. Both horses were richly caparisoned but under all the silk and show they wore body armour as protection against an accidental thrust of a lance. Their saddles gleamed in the light from the flares. Even their hooves were polished, flashing like mirrors as they pawed the ground in their eagerness for battle.

The contenders had already entered on foot to the chamade of nakers and the piercing squeal of clarion. Now both men stood at opposite ends, adjusting their armour. There was a palpable air of excitement in the yard. Lord Roger made the most of it, now and then raising his sword high in the air to draw roars of approval from those behind the wooden fence. He was wearing a breastplate over his gambeson, with a hauberk of mail over that, and, as were his opponent's, his legs were encased in jambeaux made from cuirbouilli. They made him walk straddle-legged but there was no doubting his physical power. He wore his visor down to conceal his identity, and to aid the deception his surcoat bore a simple cross of St George. As a veteran of the battle of Navarette he had a right to it.

His opponent, visor up, looked disarmingly young. As he waited for his page to make some minor adjustment to his gear he surveyed the gathering crowd with a handsome scowl. He was heard to refer to them as disloyal dogs who needed a good whipping. He evidently believed they had simply transferred their allegiance to the usurper without a backward glance.

Ulf was in his element and kept explaining the finer points to Hildegard, as if she hadn't once been married to a knight herself. 'He's fallen for his old man's ploy and hasn't guessed who he's pitted against,' he observed. 'But what a contest, eh? Son against sire, youth versus age, raw energy against the cunning of the seasoned fighter.'

Roger was hoisted into the saddle by a couple of brawny grooms to a roar of applause. He shortened his reins and his horse danced on the spot, eager to be off.

His supporters were going wild. The pretence that he was some usurper from elsewhere was being maintained by a lot of ham acting from his household staff which, if Edwin had been more watchful, might have given the game away. But it was night. He was angry. And he was, as Hildegard had to keep reminding herself, in mourning, when his judgement might be expected to be impaired.

Apart from the scowl aimed at the crowd, he looked surprisingly cheerful for one who has just lost a beloved father. He strode up and down, swapping banter with his men, chaffing his opponent's supporters and flexing his biceps to the delight of the women, then he strolled over to have another look at his lance, a twelve-foot pole of lovingly planed cypress which he caressed most sensually.

At last the herald trotted out on a little pony and put a horn to his lips. The crowd hushed itself. Edwin was hoisted swiftly into the saddle. The banner was raised, the horn sounded, the herald's pony skittered off to the side, the banner was dropped. From both ends of the yard came the sudden hammer-beat of hooves as the two massive horses careered full tilt towards each other.

The crowd couldn't help itself. It roared like a single beast. Then there was a sigh as the riders passed each other with no more than a slithering crack of their lances which didn't even make a dint in the round shields both men carried.

They turned at the end of the lists and, when the sign came, set off again. It was the best of three. This time they made contact. Edwin's lance was sliced down to the hilt but Roger fared no better. He had taken a blow full in the chest and was visibly shaken. He looked as if he was about to fall but somehow managed to regain his balance. Hildegard shot a glance at Ulf but he was totally absorbed in the contest.

The third tilt was different. Edwin seemed to have got the measure of his opponent and this time gave him such a crack he almost lifted him out of the saddle. Melisen stifled a gasp. Somehow Roger managed to hold on until, as if by design, he was able to collapse to the ground when he reached home and let his grooms take his mount's bridle. Attempting to conceal a wince or two, he strode over to where the women were watching and reached for the cup Melisen held out. He lifted his visor enough to down the contents in one gulp then turned, ready to embark on the second set.

But now there was a surprised buzzing from the crowd. Sir Edwin, still mounted, had taken his helmet off and, crooking it under one arm, was trotting back down the tilt yard to where his opponent stood. When he got close enough he saluted then slid down from his horse. There was a surprised muttering from the crowd. Looking as fresh as when he started, he walked over and threw himself at Roger's feet.

There was a gasp as they all heard him say, 'I beg leave to submit!' then, before pandemonium could break out, added for everyone to hear, 'I submit only to you, my lord and *father!*'

The onlookers went wild.

When they had quietened down it was Roger's turn. He yanked his helmet off. 'How the devil did you know it was me?'

Edwin still knelt at his sire's feet. But he looked up, smiling. 'Only one man would try that feint with his lance then come in under the shield. You taught me how to counter it when I was eight and still tilting at the quintaine.'

Roger looked proud. 'You nearly unseated me

with it, you tricky little beggar.'

'And I shall do yet if you don't accept my submission.'

'Of all the cocky devils! I've a mind to try you!'

'Oh, Roger, sweetness, please. Won't you stop now? Accept his submission. We ladies are ready for bed.'

Roger's face flushed with more than the heat of battle at Melisen's words. But he turned back to his son and prodded him with the point of his sword until he forced him to his feet. 'So what the hell are you doing showing your face round here? I thought I threw you out?'

'And I thought you might be having second thoughts, for surely now you don't believe those rumours about the Lady Melisen and me?' Jaws dropped. Ignoring the effect he was having Edwin said, 'She's enough to pierce any man's heart but, alas, I'm betrothed to another.'

Roger rumbled deep in his chest and gripped his sword. 'Not following in your uncle's footsteps and tupping some serving wench, are you, you young dog?'

There was the rasp of a sword being drawn swiftly from its sheath and a man, walking with a familiar military swagger, pushed himself forward. 'Take that back, sir, or by God I'll make you rue it!'

'What's it to you?' asked Roger with a bland smile, well aware of the proximity of his men-at-arms, not to say his swordsman of a brother.

'The lady he refers to is my sister, sir. She is Lady Eleanor of Teesdale.'

'And my son's betrothed to her? By St George!

But she's the daughter of one of my oldest enemies!'

'Not any longer, father. The breach is healed by our betrothal.'

'Why, you canny devil.' After that Roger seemed lost for words.

Melisen rose to her feet. 'Come now, my lord, let's within. This has ended most happily. Welcome home, Edwin, and welcome also to your friend. We are all well met.' With the grace of a duchess she allowed her maid to fling a fur-lined cape around her shoulders, then she stepped down from the stand and led the party firmly back towards the Great Hall. Without argument everyone followed.

Too astonished to say much at first, the onlookers pressing against the rails gradually spread the news to those at the back. When it was clear who was who and what was what the whole crowd started to clap and cheer. Caps were thrown into the air. Lord Roger was alive. His son and heir had returned.

Then somebody started an impromptu farandole. Soon everybody was linking hands, groom with page, cook with scullion, ale-master with priest, and even the chamberlain picked up the hem of his cloak and joined hands with two servants. Laughing and singing, they followed the leader back inside, where, moving faster and in ever more complicated patterns, he led the human chain snaking round the Great Hall. Hildegard followed them in. It was clear that the celebrations would continue throughout the night.

Time to make myself scarce, she thought with a twinge of regret for all that her vows denied her. Ulf noticed her leave and followed her out.

'That was a turn-up and no mistake! I knew he'd welcome him back into the fold before long. And it was all over nothing... I suppose you're going back to your chamber now?'

'I am, yes.'

'Don't forget tomorrow. I meant what I said. I'll clear it with Roger afterwards. Once you get your grange and some land the novices will come pouring in.'

'Just six will do, nuns or novices both.'

'I thought you wanted seven?'

'I found one, a dairy-woman called Agnetha living down in Beverley.'

Ulf skimmed the edge of her coif with the backs of his fingers. The smile he gave her was a sad one, full of regret at what might have been. Then he left to join the dance.

During the night something woke Hildegard up. It was more than the continued sounds of celebration coming distantly from outside. It was like the rumble of the drawbridge being let down, followed by the clatter of several horsemen entering the gatehouse. Guessing the Lombards had just ridden down from the north, she smiled and turned over. But sleep would not come now she was awake. She lay for some time, ticking off the minutes, listening to the faint sounds of merriment from below, then to an owl that hooted out in the bailey, and after that to the sound of the timbers creaking as the wind got up.

She had almost managed to trick herself back to sleep when a different sound brought her awake again. It was its stealthy nature which alerted her. Her ears pricked. It was like the sound of a door being pressed open along the passage and then a moment later and just as quietly being pressed shut. She held her breath the better to listen.

Footsteps dragged along the creaking boards outside. They came to another stop. She waited. There was no sound, not even the husk of someone's breath. Convinced that she was mistaken, she was just about to pull the blanket over her head when it came again.

This time it was nearer. She heard the door to the neighbouring chamber open. Again a pause. Again the door closed. The footsteps were closer now and she held her breath when they halted outside her own door.

Stealthily she sat up. The hair on her scalp prickled. There was someone standing outside. She was sure of it. She waited for the door to open. When nothing happened, she was about to ask who was there when some instinct made her reach for the knife on her belt instead.

The door creaked as it opened. On the threshold stood a hooded figure. She could hear him breathing as if it was a difficult thing to do. There was a pause then out of the darkness a hoarse voice whispered, 'So I've found you at last, sister. And without those hounds to protect you.'

She realised she must be visible in the strip of moonlight that lay across the room but she could only peer through the darkness in a vain attempt to see who was looking in at her. Full of dread, she managed to croak, 'Who are you?'

'Never you mind. You'll know me soon enough.' He gave a suggestive snigger. 'I think you're going to regret not joining the dance.'

Her voice shook. 'What do you want?'

'I want redress, since you ask.'

'What do you mean?'

'I made a vow. But you thwarted me. And I want redress for that. So now I'm going to thwart you in one of your vows. That's only fair, isn't it?'

Trying to steady her voice, she said, 'I don't know what you mean. What vow of yours have I thwarted?'

'Don't you remember? I'm sure you do. I vowed to teach you a lesson.'

'What lesson?'

'No bitch does what you did to me.'

She drew in her breath. 'It's not possible–'

The hooded figure grunted. 'Anything's possible where I'm concerned.'

Hildegard gripped her knife beneath the blanket and whispered through trembling lips, 'I know your name. You're Master Escrick Fitz-john.'

'And what if I am? What's in a name?' He took a heavy step over the threshold. She could see the gleam of his leather jerkin and something silver, long-bladed, in one hand, as he stepped into the light of the moon.

'And now, my lady, the time of reckoning is come. I've certainly had a long wait.' He pushed back his hood to reveal his face. It was distorted by a grimace. She could see a fresh wound running from brow to chin. But it was Escrick all right. He was breathing savagely, like an animal. Wounded, he was more full of hatred than ever.

Her fingers tightened on the handle of her knife.

He said harshly, 'I nearly drowned because of you. Took a bucket of water in my lungs. All but did for me. And it was your fault. I'd have got away scot-free but for you and your meddling.' He took another step forward. 'But you're going to pay, my lady, and I'm going to make you pay, and there's not a blind thing you can do to stop me.' He took another step and began to laugh. His pleasure at her helplessness curdled her blood. He said, 'I'd start praying now, if I were you.'

Before she could reply there was a commotion at the end of the passage and she heard Ulf's voice as plain as day saying, 'This way, sire, follow me. I trust you'll find your quarters comfortable after such a long ride?'

This was followed by hearty shouts of assent and the noise of several people wearing spurs marching in a crowd along the passage.

Quick as a snake, Escrick moved to the door. 'Don't think I've finished with you, nun. I'll be watching, waiting, following. You'll never get away. The fields have eyes.' The black shape vanished. One moment there, the next gone.

Hildegard was out of bed and across the floor in a trice and was just in time to see his hooded figure melt into the darkness at the far end of the passage before Ulf and the Lombardy men approached from the other end. She flung herself into their path.

'Ulf! Quick!' She gestured down the passage. 'It's Escrick Fitzjohn! Back from the dead!'

Ulf placed both hands calmly on her shoulders. 'He's dead, you saw him drown. I must have woken you from a dream.'

'No! Listen to me! He came into my chamber and he... Go after him!' When she saw he did not believe her, she said, 'Then I'll go! He must not escape!'

Convinced by the desperation in her voice, Ulf drew his sword. 'Show me! Where is this phantom? If he's made of flesh and blood I'll run him through! Come on, Ludovico!'

The prince and his men needed no second bidding. They made off down the passage with a drawing of weapons and she heard them go clattering down the outer stairs into the yard before she even had time to draw breath. When she caught up with them at the bottom of the steps they were milling about in confusion. The bailey was crowded with people of every degree, singing and dancing with abandon. One of Ludovico's men held a stiletto to the throat of a protesting servant.

'Let him go.' Not looking back, Ulf came over. 'If it was truly Escrick Fitzjohn, he's concealed himself in the best of all places. We'll never find him in this throng. By the time we've hauled them before us one by one he'll have made good his escape.' He took her by the arm and whispered, 'Are you sure about this, Hildegard?'

'I am. Every malign threat he uttered is written on my mind for all time.'

IV

The Isabeau *was sailing to the lee and making good time up the east coast. The wind raking her decks buffeted the villages nestling in the wolds and further inland tore savagely at the massive defences of the city of York. At the mouth of the Humber the cog changed direction in a turbulence of sail and met the overfalls with a final pitching that brought the traveller out on deck. Leaning on the rail in his billowing cloak, he watched for the tantalising spit of land in whose inner curve lay the port of Ravenser. He might have been longing for a first glimpse of home. Or he might have been searching the coast with the avid glance of a glutton at the prospect of the feast that would shortly be laid before him. His glance never strayed as the ochre waters of the estuary diminished moment by moment bringing closer the pencil-line of his destination.*

Chapter Twenty-three

Hildegard entered the garden at Meaux to find the abbot standing alone among his sunlit plants. He was inspecting some straggling herb beds and turned when he heard the gate.

He looks tired, she observed, as she walked down the path towards him. Hubert's eyes were ringed with shadow but, with his cowl thrown back to catch the last of the sun's rays, it struck her again how fine he was, especially now when he must have just had the monthly shave his Order allowed and his features were revealed with such clarity.

Unaware of her appraisal he came towards her. 'Sister, greetings.' The austerity of his glance softened and a good-humoured gleam entered his eyes. 'They tell me extraordinary things have been going on at Castle Hutton.'

'Things you will find hard to believe.' She returned his smile. And some you will never know, she thought.

'Come. You must tell me everything.'

He led the way to a stone bench set against the east wall from where they had a view of the westering sun. It was an unseasonably warm evening. A solitary bee was humming languidly among the last of the roses. A blackbird swooped in a graceful arc across the lavender beds. Distantly, from within the echoing vault of the abbey, came the frail sound of the choir. Hilde-gard gave an involuntary sigh. It had turned into one of those days when summer reaches back to offer a final gift to winter and seems to hold the season on a single thread. At such times the opening of the heart in response brings an unexpected languor. The abbot, too, seemed part of this voluptuous embrace of nature and she became vitally aware of his presence beside her. Instead of spilling out the whole story at once as she intended, she let the deep perfection of the moment speak instead.

Eventually, returning to his question, she began to bring him up to date with what had gone on since they last met, reserving only personal events which could not interest him. He was amused, alarmed and sorrowful in turn at what she told him.

'But Master Jacques!' he exclaimed when she came to the fight inside the castle. 'Who would imagine Sir William would use him to try to get the better of Sir Ralph! And what about Lady Avice? That was an evil thing. Where did she get such a poison?'

'The apothecary might have given us a clue when he happened to mention the French pope.'

'Ah,' said Hubert. His jaw tightened. Her pur-pose was to assess his allegiance but apart from that involuntary movement he gave nothing else away.

As if oblivious to the dangers of the ground she trod, she continued swiftly with her story. 'I was a dolt not to guess the identity of those two corrodians at Hutton. Not until the joust, when

Edwin's friend the Earl of Teesdale's son drew his sword and swaggered forth, did I realise who they were. They had laid bets that they could enter the castle in defiance of Roger and spend a night there undetected. When his father died, as it seemed, and left the succession in jeopardy, Edwin hurried north to rouse forces in order to regain his inheritance.'

'A lad of spirit. Glory or trouble lie ahead, I'd guess. And his stepsister? I believe you have a soft spot for her.'

Hildegard nodded. 'Dear Philippa, she eventually got over her rage with her father. It was due to fear as much as anything. She thought he'd try to hold her to an unwanted betrothal. Her Lombardy prince turned up with his men in the middle of the night, having ridden like furies all the way from Rievaulx Abbey at the first opportunity. By then she had solved the puzzle and opened the casket. Having seen one of these devices before, I suggested she twist the lion's tail,' said Hildegard in an aside.

'And within–?'

'Not the remainder of the poison as I briefly feared but a ring. A plain and simple gold band with her own name and Ludovico's inscribed on it. So she is now betrothed again, but this time to someone she loves with all her heart and who, we hope, loves her.'

'And Roger is no doubt delighted with the profitable alliance he has made.'

'Quite so. But I must tell you something to make you smile. Lady Melisen, who, by the way, had a small though innocent part to play in

Roger's collapse through her overzealous use of a certain herb useful in matrimonial matters,' they exchanged knowing glances, 'saw Roger reading some document the Lombard put before him. Astonished, she exclaimed, "But my lord, can you read?" "Just a bit," said Roger with unusual modesty. And Melisen said, "My father the earl says why bother when you can buy a clerk to do it for you?"'

Hubert began to chuckle.

'But that's not all. Roger's eyes sharpened to needle points when he heard this and he said: "You mean your father has to rely on the honesty of his clerk to know what he's signing up for?" And that, Hubert, is a situation that may be watched with interest in the coming months, don't you think?'

It was the first time she had called him Hubert. The name was out before she could stop it and she watched in alarm to see how he reacted. He let it pass.

'We must watch our own dealings with Lord Roger too.' His glance found hers and held it. When he continued his words seemed charged with meaning. 'He is one of those people with a disarming manner.' He looked deeply into her eyes. 'It's the sort of thing that could lead a more sanguine man than myself to forfeit some of the abbey's interests without even realising it.' He paused, as if dealing with a difficult thought, then, in a sudden change of mood, said, 'I was astonished at the folly of Sir Ralph and Lady Sibilla in trying to pass off a servant's child as their own. Although,' he added, 'it's a trick that has been tried before with some success. But how did you guess the truth about the baby?'

'I was very slow and should have accepted the promptings of my intuition sooner. But it seemed too outrageous an idea to be taken seriously, beginning with nothing more than a hand.' She explained. 'It was Sibilla's ring, or rather the rough hand of her maid and the fact that the ring did not fit her properly, that puzzled me. Apparently they pushed it on to her finger to allay suspicion should anyone not in the conspiracy enter the birthing chamber. May's hand was rough, a hand used to hard work, not that of someone who never lifts a finger except to run it over silks and velvets or slip inside the soft leather of a hawking glove. It looked odd but I didn't realise the significance until other discrepancies mounted up.'

'Such as?'

'A fading scent of jasmine, Sibilla's perfume and other things as slight.'

'Ah, the feminine power,' he said with a thoughtful expression. 'But what penalty did Roger devise to punish such deceit?'

'Nothing so far. He plays a long game. I suppose he thinks, let the hoodman hang himself! All he said was that when Sibilla has a child of her own he will make it his ward in court.'

'Is it likely she'll conceive?'

Hildegard shook her head. 'Who knows?'

'Mysterious are the ways indeed.' He sighed. 'And what about the midwife who was so helpful to them? What happened to her, poor soul?'

'Not so poor. Gone into retirement on the

proceeds of her work. She's now living with her aged father in York where she'll have plenty of employment with the daughters of the burgesses, if she wants it. I'm told she was attending one of the miller's daughters in secret and that's why her pony was tethered out of sight. Then the mill was set on fire and she saw the outlaws drive away the inhabitants. Before she could make her escape, we arrived, stole her pony, as she saw it, and she was left to return to her father's assart on foot.'

'And, finally, to crown all, I'm told the murderer got his just desserts. Master Escrick Fitzjohn, a devil incarnate to be sure. What was his motive in such a killing spree?'

Hildegard hesitated before she spoke. After consultation with Roger, she had come to the conclusion that it would be best to play along with the belief that Escrick had drowned in the canal. The idea was that it would be easier to flush him out if he imagined everyone but Hildegard thought him dead. He would become careless. The net, claimed Roger, would be drawn in secret until they had him well and truly in its folds.

Now she said, 'I fear it was loyalty to Lady Sibilla and maybe a kind of thwarted love that drove him to try to prove himself in that extreme fashion. But again, I have only hints to lead me to that belief. I remember certain looks that passed between them. An air of complicity. And I can well imagine her own attraction to a man so unlike her husband.'

She felt Hubert give a start, but then he bent to pick up a pebble from the path and she could not see his expression, only his fingers repeatedly turning the piece of coloured stone as if it held the solution to some problem he was trying to solve. The moment stretched while she tried in vain to understand. Such was the nervous labour of his fingers that all she knew was that there was a mystery here.

'Sibilla herself mentioned Escrick's ambition,' she continued, confusion making the words sound forced. 'She seemed to admire the way he rose from a lowly position as son of a bondsman to one of considerable power, entirely by the singleness of his purpose. I myself saw how he strove to make himself indispensable to her. Nothing she asked was too much trouble.'

'The truth is he risked hell for her.' Hubert's voice roughened. He threw the stone into the grass.

Hildegard turned to look at him. His face was like alabaster. After a pause she said, 'Yes, I suppose he did.'

'And his body has not been recovered?'

'That is the story.'

He gave her a piercing glance. 'Have a care, sister.' From his tone she could not tell whether he meant for her soul or for her corporeal self. Without explaining he said, 'As the body of the valiant lock-keeper fetched up close to the pack bridge, still impaled on the sword, we had him interred here and sang a mass for him. It's to be hoped the body of Master Escrick will turn up in the reed beds one of these days. Then we'll all sleep safely.' He gave her another sharp glance.

'And do you have any news about the youth I

found in the woods?' she asked, hurriedly changing the subject.

'My man went to York as instructed and managed to search out the fellow's kin. He was one of six apprentices who left York with the intention of gaining support from their brethren in Beverley.'

'Support?'

Hubert looked thoughtful. 'I believe it was you who mentioned the Company of the White Hart?'

'Your man–' she faltered, suspecting he referred to his spy, a fact the prioress would find interesting. 'Did he find proof that the youth was a member of that particular company?'

'He has little doubt. The story he heard was that they were pursued by a gang got together in York by another guild. They were followed to the gates of Beverley itself. There have been killings within both towns. These five were caught and executed in the brutal manner you saw, the sixth cut down while trying to escape with the relic you found in his hand.' His expression was sombre. 'It's a great sadness when they try to solve their differences by resorting to violence. It can only breed more violence.'

Despite his obvious regret for the boy's death, Hildegard could not help but understand his words as a warning. He was telling her he knew as much as anybody else about plans for insurrection in the Riding.

After this they sat quietly for a moment or two, busy with their own thoughts. The sun slid its shafts between the branches of the trees and as it sank below the horizon its dying light dappled them in colours of scarlet and gold. Time itself seemed to hold its breath. For a moment all the strife of mortal men yielded to a deeper truth. A sense of eternal peace had dominion over all things.

Reluctant to break the spell, Hildegard eventually forced herself back to other matters. 'For some days my hounds have been in the safe-keeping of a little kitchen carl from Hutton called Burthred. His future is on my mind.'

'Be content. Their little warden has prospects. The lad made himself so agreeable here, if Roger will release him one of my grange managers is willing to take him on. The lad has a way with animals. He also expressed a wish to serve with our conversi when he's old enough.' Hubert was referring to the lay brothers employed to work the land and deal with the livestock. This would suit Burthred down to the ground. Animals were what he lived for. 'The conversi are the backbone of our community,' the abbot observed. 'Without them we would be poor indeed.'

'But without your business sense and ability to handle the affairs of a great estate the conversi would be poor too.'

'You make it sound like a marriage made in heaven,' he murmured. His ivory features acquired a sudden tint of colour that came and went in the blinking of an eye.

'Something troubles you, Hubert?' she blurted in surprise.

There was a pause while he appeared to choose his words from a vast and complex store.

'Many things trouble me, sister,' he said at last. He gave a wan smile. 'My confessor has much work to do these days, poor fellow.' His tone changed and became businesslike. 'One thing I can freely confess, something trivial in itself, but an irritation to me.' He cast a glance at the garden with its tumbled weeds. 'I had hoped that when I was appointed Abbot of Meaux I could make a garden for rare herbs, ones with medicinal properties beyond the everyday cures already known. But you see, I've failed badly.' He looked unexpectedly helpless. 'It's a mess, isn't it?'

'What's happened to make it look so ... well, unkempt?'

'Poor Brother Selso has always run the gardens but now he's too crippled with rheumatics to deal with it. To preserve his feeling of usefulness in his old age I can't appoint anybody else to take over just yet. I wonder, you wouldn't put Selso's nose out of joint if you–'

'Offered a little help now and then?'

'My very hope.' His face broke into a smile and he lifted one hand as if about to take one of hers but then let it drop. Hildegard was mystified when he fumbled for his cloak and rearranged it rather unnecessarily.

When he suggested a look round the rest of the garden she rose to her feet with relief. As she did so the abbot broke off one of the rosebuds that grew around the arbour then stood with it in his hand as if not sure how he came to be holding it. Hildegard watched to see what he would do next. He came to himself and, using it to gesture towards the path, suggested, 'Let me be your guide.'

His words reminded her of the phrase at the beginning of Dante's long poem. 'Take my hand and let me guide you...' And together, so it went, they ascended to the gates of paradise. She felt her cheeks burn.

Inhabitants of the real world with the ever-present threat of damnation in the next, they strolled together under the stippled shadows of the pear-tree walk. Aware that they were bound by the strict Rule of their Order and the wisdom of having a care for the perils of the times, their conversation skirted any issue that might lead to controversy. Instead, in the fading light, they touched on abstract matters of mutual interest: the difference between belief and superstition, the ethics of the mendicants, the value of contrition, until, eventually, Hildegard raised the subject of the grange she had been to see the previous day.

It brought a frown to Hubert's face. 'Did someone escort you? I expect it was that rough Saxon fellow, was it?'

'If you mean Lord Roger's steward, yes.'

His frown deepened. 'So this grange he recommends, I suppose it's up near Castle Hutton?'

'No, not really.'

'Far from here, though?'

'Not very.'

When she explained that it was no more than ten miles away his mood seemed to lighten. 'It sounds quite suitable. If your heart's set on it I trust your prioress will say the same.'

She was astonished at such words after his hostility when she had first approached him.

Then even distant Yedingham had seemed too close. Now her feelings were mixed. It looked as if the prioress was going to get her way. Meaux was about to be squeezed.

But it was what she wanted too: permission to inspect the buildings more thoroughly and if she still deemed them suitable to take the necessary steps to procure the lease from Roger. And then the real work could begin.

They reached the bounds of the garden and stood looking out across the now placid waters of the canal to the trees on the other side. Night creatures were beginning to call to each other in the echoing shadows. The sky behind the branches turned to pearl.

Hubert gazed into the darkening woodland. 'Hildegard–' he began. It was the first time he had used her name. But then inexplicably his voice fell away to silence.

Next morning she made her way to the stables carrying her leather travelling bag, a wedge of wastel and a flask of wine. Already mounted and waiting was a small group of pilgrims, merchants from the north. They were visiting several shrines on a leisurely journey to London and had invited her to ride with them as far as Swyne. In the continuing dry weather they could expect to reach the priory shortly after noon.

The sharp scent of manure and horseflesh met her as she stepped inside the stable to take her mount. One of the lads, his sleeves rolled, was wiping down a steaming grey that looked as if it had just that moment been brought in. He glanced up when he heard her at the door. 'I'll be with you in a trice, sister. Just got this poor brute to see to.'

She stepped closer. Gouts of blood stood out where spurs had raked the horse's flanks. The animal quivered and steamed. 'Surely one of the monks hasn't been riding her so hard?' she demanded, outraged at such treatment.

'No. It was some foreign gentleman. Thrashed her all the way from Ravenser. Spoke not a word when he got in except *"prenai"* or some such. Then threw the reins at me and dived in to see the abbot.'

Shaking his head, he finished his task quickly and saddled up a horse for her. In the freshness of the morning, she set out safely with the group of pilgrims for home.

Epilogue

The prioress was in the chapel when Hildegard arrived. She was standing in a blaze of light that came flooding through the south window. Her strong-boned face seemed lit from within. She glowed with purity and strength. 'Don't waste time telling me about Roger de Hutton. I've heard all about it!' She smiled. 'I want to know about that other matter, sister. What news there?'

'He plays a close hand, Mother.'

'And forswears outward splendour. Yes, I know.'

'He wore the silk stole you sent him.'

The prioress looked gratified.

'He has a spy whom he sent to York.'

'He has?'

'An elderly Yorkshireman wearing the habit of a Cistercian. He was sitting in the abbot's chamber with the rest of them when I went in one day.'

'That's news to me. Find out more when you go back. What else?'

'The abbot cares greatly for the poor and has several schemes for helping them. He's making a garden where he can grow medicinal cures and has asked for my help.'

'Cures for fighting men, that's what that's about. Don't be fooled. I hope you said "yes". Easier to keep an eye on things if you have a bona fide function.' She gave her an appraising glance that took Hildegard by surprise. 'Let me tell you about the letter you delivered to the archbishop.' She beckoned Hildegard to follow her into a small cell attached to the chapel. The prioress's table, chair and cabinet of books were all it contained. There was a wooden stool in a niche and she told her to sit.

'That was a missive from the papal spies in Burgundy. As we suspected this Philip they call the Bold is heading an invasion against us, instigated by their anti-pope Clement down in Avignon. Pope Urban's people have been aware of this ambition for some time. Now they have proof. As Duke of Burgundy, Philip controls the government of France. Taxes are being raised to extortionate levels. Why? To finance their invasion of England. This little sideshow in Flanders is only a beginning, though it won't

446

seem like that to the Flemings. I'm told he's intending to pay over a thousand foot soldiers six months in advance. That's how seriously he's taking it. But we'll soon see how bold he is when he comes face to face with our men forewarned and forearmed.'

'And the archbishop?'

'He is firm for Richard. But what about the other one in Canterbury? I wouldn't trust Milord Courtney further than I could throw him. Of course, if they decide to come in over the Channel again it'll be up to Kent and Essex to show their mettle. They'll not be bought by Courtney. But there is another way into the kingdom. Through the back door.'

'The back door?' Hildegard was stunned. 'Do I understand...? Do you mean...? Surely not? Through Ravenser?' Suddenly it began to make sense. 'So this is why Avignon have put one of their own men into Meaux?' It was startling. Terrifying. 'If he uses the abbeys as he might, being Cistercian with allegiance to the French pope, they would have a string of safe houses for their spies all the way up to Scotland!'

'Not only safe houses. They would have un-limited supplies from the rich granges of the abbeys to feed their entire army. Six months would be as nothing. They could support a war indefinitely. After that they could become centres of repression and hold the country in a strangle-hold for generations.'

Hildegard shivered in a confusion of emotions. 'And you believe Hubert is aware of all this?'

'Hubert, is it?' The prioress gave her a piercing

glance. 'He preaches well, so I hear?'

Remembering the excited crowd of women when she first arrived at Meaux, she nodded. 'Whether his words are taken as he intends is somewhat doubtful.'

The prioress gave a grim smile. 'Don't forget he was sent by Avignon. He is their chosen man. He was put in as abbot for a purpose. He can have no affection for us English. His father was a diplomat sent over to discuss terms with King Edward in the fifties. His pleasure happened to be one of the queen's ladies-in-waiting. They were married. But when the mission eventually came to an end he returned to France, leaving his wife and son behind.'

'Maybe Hubert rather feels for his English mother in that case?'

'We cannot know. One thing we can know, however, is how to turn him to our view and against that of the anti-pope he now serves.' She gave Hildegard a compassionate glance. 'Never forget, sister, it is more than heart and head at stake. It's a question of life itself, of everything we know. It's a question of who we are and who we wish to remain. Our Church, our king, our people. These are the stakes we play for. The feelings of one man or one woman and their earthly desires aren't worth a bale of straw.'

'I believe he is unaware of the strategic importance of Meaux.' An image of Hubert holding the rose stem in his hand, his kind glance, the compassion in his eyes when he spoke of the poor ... and his linen undershirt that time she had walked in on him and the way his expression had

448

softened when he wished her God speed and–

She received a harsh glance, as if her thoughts could be heard. Her superior said, 'You came across the bodies of those lads from the Company of the White Hart. This is the reality that faces us: murder, anarchy, another violent blood-letting. Many in high places are aware that the supporters of Tyler are plotting to continue the rebellion. Next time they won't confine themselves to London and the South-East. They'll seek support for their cause in every part of the country.' The prioress's face was full of sorrow. 'They've shown themselves to be stout lads, they've been treated badly, they deserve justice. But those deaths are nothing compared to the slaughter that could follow an invasion.'

She gave Hildegard a piercing glance.

'What we must never forget is that the real enemy is Avignon, the Duke of Burgundy, this young king they've got in Paris, and the conniving of all three with the Scots. They know as well as we do: if the North is taken the rest of England falls.'

Hildegard remembered the arrival of the foreign horseman from the port of Ravenser before she left the abbey that very morning. Now it had a darker significance. She told the prioress about it.

Her strong face hardened. 'So, the enemy is within the gates. It begins here.'

The interview seemed to be at an end and Hildegard got up to leave, but when she reached the door the prioress stopped her. 'I believe you have something for me?' she asked.

449

It took a moment before she realised what she meant. Fumbling in her sleeve, she brought out the glass phial, the relic with a fragment of the bloodied banner in it.

The prioress held it between reverential fingers. 'When the twelve fragments are brought together it will be a sign. The humble will be raised up. The people of this nation will achieve their destiny. All else will come to nothing.'

Hildegard left the holy cell with a thoughtful frown. How had the prioress known about the relic? Someone must have told her. But no one else knew about it except Hubert, and it was unthinkable that he would pass on the inform-ation, especially in view of his suspected allegiance to Avignon.

It could mean only one thing: her bag had been searched either at Meaux or at Hutton. But who would do a thing like that? She remembered the strip of water weed, evidence enough of a prowler in her private chamber, but it couldn't have been Escrick either because she had been carrying her bag with her when she discovered that token of his visit.

The fields have eyes. None escape notice.

She shuddered. There were spies on all sides. It had been safer in her hermitage than living out here in the wild world. Now she was out she would have to brush the cobwebs from her eyes and let nothing slip past unobserved. If, as her prioress believed, the invasion had already begun by stealth, it would not continue that way for long. Soon it would be out in the open. Choices would have to be made, oaths of fealty sworn, traitors called to account. And blood would flow.

She summoned an image of Hubert standing in the calm beauty of his private chapel where she had left him that morning. The memory made her think about earthly desires. They were a small thing when set against the great affairs of nations and yet a great thing within the solitude of the human heart. Whatever might happen, and whatever stood between them, all fear fell away in the certainty that they would meet again.

V

The envoy from Avignon was sitting in Hubert de Courcy's inner sanctum. The documents he had carried all the way through France in such haste and secrecy were spread out on the table under the window. He spoke French to the abbot who understood it as well as the spy himself. At his ease after his recent hard ride from Ravenser, he raised his cup of wine in a toast, quoting the motto of his master, the Duke of Burgundy. 'Il me tarde – *I long for victory!*' *Hubert remembered the rest of the phrase differently:* il me tarde ... tant que tu reviennes. *Translating it into English, he thought: I long for your return. And he too raised his cup.*

Acknowledgements

My starting point for writing the Abbess of Meaux series is the chronicle written by its abbot in the 1390s. Although *Hangman Blind* is fiction, the abbey, with its wealth and power based on the wool trade and the business acumen of its abbots, really did exist. Abbot William describes the day-to-day concerns of the monks and even mentions a predecessor, who, like Hubert, had a liking for beauty and precious artefacts and, to the disapproval of his order, greatly augmented the abbey's collection of gold chalices and jewel-studded crosses. The Talking Crucifix existed too, and was a big draw to pilgrims at this time. Like the abbey itself, it has disappeared without trace. The abbot also mentions a priory at Swyne – a place usually given a different spelling that fails to reflect the charm and tranquillity of the building as it is today, nestling among tall trees in a landscape that has long been drained by more than the abbot's ditch. A certain prioress held sway in the fourteenth century. A redoubtable woman, she was caught up in an incessant round of litigation with the monks at Meaux but fought back splendidly, being excommunicated by the pope no less than three times for her temerity in standing up for herself and her nuns – an early example of the feminist spirit coupled with Anglo-Saxon bloody-mindedness. If you go to the East Riding you can still see the choir built in her time. As for Roger's stronghold at Hutton, it exists only as an amalgam of several once-grim castles built to subdue the natives in that turbulent period after the Conquest.

Hildegard, Hubert de Courcy, Ulf, Lord Roger de Hutton and the others exist in fiction but some of the minor characters have had walk-on parts in history as revealed in manorial rolls and town records. Sueno de Schockwynde is one of these, although whether he ever worked as master mason on either Beverley Minister or St Mary's is unknown. Records show him working in the Midlands but then, masons were mobile and went where the work dictated and he may easily have had a part in building the magnificent minster at the shrine of St John in Beverley. Of course that great Yorkshireman, John Wyclif, existed. Even though he doesn't appear in the series, he defines the thoughts of those who do just as his influence shines down the years and shaped the Reformation to which we owe so much. I see him as a rallying point for the dispossessed and can still grieve for the ruthless way in which Gaunt and his fellow barons exterminated the opponents of their rule and nearly succeeded in erasing Wyclif himself from the records.

My view on the period is my own but a valuable resource has been Dr William's Library in London. My gratitude to the librarians there is unbounded. They have the happy knack of being able to summon long unread texts from the archive as if by magic. Still in the thanking vein, I must mention the Institute of Historical Research and the Society of the Medieval Studies in the University of London with their excellent seminars on the period; also Dr Ian Mortimer for a long and interesting conversation about Gaunt, his son Bolingbroke and King Richard, for although we sit on opposite sides of the fence, his defence of the usurper in his book *The Fears of Henry IV* has helped consolidate my understanding of the ambitions that informed Bolingbroke's actions and fuelled a lifelong animosity that would eventually lead to the death of Richard and the long and bloody conflict between the houses of York and Lancaster.

Other sources I found helpful are: *Yorkshire Monasteries* by Bernard Jennings, *The Evolution of British Justice* by Anthony Musson, *The Hound and the Hawk* by John Cummins, *Medieval Costume and Fashion* by Herbert Norris, *Shoes and Pattens* by Grew & de Neergaard, *Medieval Women* by H. Leyser, *Wyclif and Huss* by J. Broome, *Wyclif and the Beginnings of Nonconformism* by K.B. McFarlane, *Richard II* by Nigel Saul, *The English Rising of 1381* edited by Hilton and Aston, and *The Peasants' Revolt of 1381* ed. R.B. Dobson. Many conversations with the custodians of churches and museums on diverse topics relevant to the period are too numerous to mention individually, but have my gratitude nevertheless.

Finally I would like to thank the people of Rosa Mundi in North Yorkshire for their detailed practical knowledge of daily life in medieval times and their generosity in sharing this with me. One wet Sunday afternoon learning to dance the farandole will stay pleasantly in my memory for some time. Others generously winkling out sometimes obscure facts which have played an essential part in building the story of *Hangman Blind* are Larry Bruce at the Middlesbrough reference library, Mike and Trevor Silkstone, Silvester Mazzarella, the nuns of Ladywell, and finally Liz and Bill Hinchley for their Anglo-Saxon belief in the value of good cheer. Ge be!

The publishers hope that this book has given you enjoyable reading. Large Print Books are especially designed to be as easy to see and hold as possible. If you wish a complete list of our books please ask at your local library or write directly to:

Magna Large Print Books
Magna House, Long Preston,
Skipton, North Yorkshire.
BD23 4ND

This Large Print Book for the partially sighted, who cannot read normal print, is published under the auspices of

THE ULVERSCROFT FOUNDATION